Jake Arnott

Jake Arnott was born in 1961, and lives in London. His debut novel, *The Long Firm*, was published by Sceptre in 1999 to huge public and critical acclaim. *He Kills Coppers*, *Truecrime*, *Johnny Come Home* and *The Devil's Paintbrush* have followed to equal acclaim. Both *The Long Firm* and *He Kills Coppers* have been made into widely praised TV dramas.

Praise for The House of Rumour

'The world of intelligence, the world of creativity, the world of
the occult – all these dance round each other flirtatiously. We
never quite know for sure who is using and who is being used...
Arnott is not just a cynical games player fascinated by the
possibilities of structure and thought experiments. He has the
capacity to make us care about humanity, even of a monster
like Hess. Whatever he touches on feels right'
Ros Kaveney, *Independent*

'It isn't a book, it's a revelation.' *Geek Syndicate*

'A story that delights in unexpected connections between
literary figures and historical events...A conspiracy thriller
filled with bewildering connections, dark conjecture and arcane
information, *The House of Rumour* perhaps most resembles
The Da Vinci Code, rewritten by an author with the gifts of
characterisation, wit and literacy.'
Mark Lawson, *Guardian*

'A potent mix of fact and fiction that takes on 20th-century
history but remains a page-turner' *Elle*

'The ironies sparked as Arnott rubs fantasy and reality together
could easily ignite a flashy, but meaningless narrative bonfire.
Adept at parody and allusion, *The House of Rumour* is acutely
self-conscious. Yet, the sheer verve of his storytelling, and the
depth of his characterisation, puts flesh on the bones of his
ideas...a brilliant achievement that invites repeated readings.'
James Kidd, *Independent on Sunday*

the house of rumour
jake arnott

S

SCEPTRE

First published in Great Britain in 2012 by Sceptre
An imprint of Hodder & Stoughton
An Hachette UK company

First published in paperback in 2013

1

A CIP catalogue record for this title is available from the British Library

Paperback ISBN 9780340922736
Ebook ISBN 9781848945067

Printed and bound by Clays Ltd, St Ives plc

Hodder & Stoughton policy is to use papers that are natural, renewable
and recyclable products and made from wood grown in sustainable
forests. The logging and manufacturing processes are expected to
conform to the environmental regulations of the country of origin.

Hodder & Stoughton Ltd
338 Euston Road
London NW1 3BH

www.sceptrebooks.com

At the middle of the world, between earth, sea and sky, a point where all three regions of the universe join, there is a place from which all that exists can be seen, no matter how distant, and every voice heard by listening ears. Here Rumour lives, in a high tower she has chosen for herself, with innumerable avenues and thousands of entrances that are never closed. Open night and day, her house is built of sounding bronze that hums and echoes, repeating all it hears. There is no rest within, no silence in any room, but no clamour neither, only the murmur of voices, like the sea's waves heard from afar, or the last tremors of thunder after Jupiter has clashed storm-dark clouds together.

Crowds occupy the hallways, a fickle throng that come and go with myriad rumours, circulating confused words, fiction mixed with truth. Some fill idle ears with gossip, others pass on stories, each consecutive narrator adding some new detail to the telling. This is the haunt of Credulity, rash Error, empty Joy and unreasoning Fear, impulsive Sedition and Whisperings of Doubtful Origin. Rumour herself spies everything that passes through the heavens, every occurrence on earth and at sea, her scrutiny ranges the universe.

OVID, *METAMORPHOSES*, BOOK XII: 39-63

O

the fool

I still look up to the stars for some sort of meaning. As a kid I thought I was seeing the future. Space, this was where we were headed, I was sure of it. Now I know that it was always the distant past I gazed at. With the light pollution over LA at night it's sometimes hard even to trace a constellation.

As a science fiction writer I dreamt of other worlds and other possibilities. We saw such changes it seemed that fantasy itself had conjured them into being. Now the space shuttle has just been cancelled and for the first time in fifty years America no longer has a working manned space programme. It's become old-fashioned, that foolish optimism we had about reaching faraway stars and planets.

Yet I look up at the heavens with some sort of hope. I think of the Voyager probe, still travelling over thirty years into its mission, still responding to its ground control and sending data back from the far reaches of our solar system. It's on its way out into the galaxy. So we did launch a starship, after all. Unmanned, of course, but maybe hope is unmanned.

As above, so below.

The past becomes more uncertain than the future. I am of the generation that filled pulp magazines with cheap prophecy. Now the events in my own lifetime seem more fantastic still.

For example, an obituary has just appeared in a British newspaper:

'*The Times*, Tuesday, 24 September 2011. Sir Marius Trevelyan GCB, CMG, diplomat and intelligence officer, died on 30 December, aged 91. He was born on 12 February, 1920. Marius Trevelyan's long and distinguished career in the art of deception was characterised by his taciturn nature and an essential modesty. An acknowledged genius in counter-intelligence and disinformation, he was one of the last of the cold warriors for whom discretion was not merely the better part of valour but the very name of the game. A testament to this is his brief entry in *Who's Who*, in which his career is simply given as "HM Diplomatic Service" long after MI6 and its departmental chiefs had been officially identified.'

Five paragraphs giving discreet details of his career in the Intelligence Service follow, then an intriguing conclusion:

'In November 1987, Trevelyan was questioned by Scotland Yard detectives over a brief sexual encounter he had had with a male transvestite prostitute who was later found dead in suspicious circumstances. Official concern over this affair stemmed from a series of allegations by the prostitute, known as Vita Lampada, including a claim that he had acquired a document containing official secrets from Trevelyan. In the event, Ministry of Defence officials satisfied themselves that this episode had constituted no threat to national security.'

What does this curious fragment of history have to do with me? Well, the 'document' mentioned is almost certainly the one in my possession. A manuscript that carries a fascinating narrative; an artefact with a provenance that is quite a story in its own right. Passed and palmed like a marked card in a shuffled deck, it somehow ended up in my hands. I became the custodian of a mystery, even though mystery was never really my genre. I'll leave it to others to give you the whole story, but here are the facts surrounding the matter.

Marius Trevelyan first worked for British Intelligence during the Second World War, serving with the Political Warfare Executive, an organisation specialising in counter-intelligence and disinformation. He was part of black propaganda operations around the time of the curious episode involving Rudolf Hess: the Deputy Führer who flew to Scotland in the spring of 1941, a crucial point in the war. In 1987, Trevelyan was brought out of retirement by the Service to compile a report on the suicide of Hess in Spandau prison that year.

Enter Vita Lampada, a transsexual hustler who picked up the retired spy in Mayfair. They went back to Trevelyan's flat. There's a good reason why prostitutes call it 'turning a trick'. Vita was something of an unstable element; he or she was a wild card, a joker in the pack. Vita stole Trevelyan's briefcase with the afore-mentioned document. Now this wasn't the official report on Hess, but some sort of personal account of the case.

Vita had convictions for fraud, had fed stories to the gossip columns and was even known to have indulged in blackmail on occasion, but she was way out of her depth here. She played a game with the press as she had done in the past and for a while they were interested, until they realised how much trouble it might bring them. When she was found dead from a drug overdose in her flat a few weeks later some people suspected foul play, though most figured it was suicide. Vita, whose real name was David Fenwick, had a history of mental illness and had been seeing a psychiatrist as part of her gender reassignment process. An inquest delivered an open verdict.

What she stole from Sir Marius Trevelyan was never recovered by the authorities. Vita had given it to a friend of hers, a perform-ance artist who went by the name of Pirate Jenny. Jenny herself went missing soon afterwards and is still officially a missing person. Whatever happened to her is the real mystery. But I know that the document was passed on to Danny Osiris, a British singer living in LA, because ten years later he gave it to me.

Those are the facts, but even here we're dealing with uncer-tainties, improbabilities. Looking back, I find all kinds of other obscure data that connect me with Marius Trevelyan's story: no clear linear narrative, merely quanta of information, free particles that fire off each other. Wonderful stuff, with cults and charismatic rocket scientists, and an unlikely conspiracy known as Operation Mistletoe. It's like something out of *Amazing Stories* magazine, with tales that split and converge. A whole arcana of speculation, playing cards that can be used for games of chance or sleight of hand, even for divination.

Yes, those of a psychic inclination are liable to look for what they call a 'reading', but you have to be careful when you look for mean-ings. I've tried to keep a clear head when it comes to theories and conspiracies, because I saw my first wife go crazy with them. I've tried to accept that my life, like any other, has no special face value, that it could be played high or low. And that I was less of a joker, more of a fool, stepping out into the abyss. Come to think of it this is a useful image to start with. This is what the world was like when all this began in 1941. As I've said, it was a crucial point in the war and perhaps this moment in history is the one thing that connects everything. Time and space, seventy years ago, when the whole world was on the edge.

Yet when I think of southern California back in the early spring of that year, I see it as a kind of paradise. The land around the coast was so empty then. We would drive out to the point at Palo Verdes, park above the cliffs and climb down to deserted beaches. An uninhabited planet we could colonise with our dreams. I remember the thump and hiss of the breaking surf, the sun going down over the Pacific, as we gathered driftwood to build huge bonfires that would snap and crackle and spit great sparks up into the night.

I tend to idealise this part of my life and think of it as a time when I was still innocent. But innocent is such a big solemn word. Dumb would be more to the point. I knew nothing about the world. In fact for most of the time I was looking away from it, gazing out into the universe with a naive sense of wonder. I was a shy and awkward young man who still lived with his mother, struggling to become some sort of writer. A self-confessed fantasist. Oh, I was a fool all right. And my memories of that time become fractured, unstable. Yes, it was a time of uncertainty. Nuclear fission had just been discovered. But there was also a cataclysmic split in the unsteady matter of my self. It was, after all, the year I first had my heart broken.

I'd had a bad case of mumps as a child and all through my teenage years I'd had trouble with my sense of balance. At first I was diagnosed with labyrinthitis, an inflammation of the inner ear. It seemed that there was a dysfunction in the vestibular system, the bony maze of passages that regulate and guide our sense of motion. But when no physical evidence of this could be detected, it was suggested that my problem might be psychological. In extreme stress I could experience panic attacks and heart palpitations. These could be symptoms of labyrinthitis, or perhaps the manifestation of an emotional trauma that was the true cause of my sense of imbalance. So I had been seeing an analyst called Dr Furedi who had a practice in Beverly Hills.

It was a golden age of sorts. It's now generally thought of as the start of the 'Golden Age of Science Fiction'. And I had just sold my first full-length story, a twenty-eight-thousand-word novelette. *Lords of the Black Sun* was set in 2150 with the Third Reich of the future, having conquered earth, embarking on an interstellar *blitzkrieg*. *Fabulous Tales* ran it as a three-issue serial and it was featured on the cover for the first part with a four-colour illustration of a fearsome-looking spaceship with swastika markings. *Fabulous* paid a cent a word, which was the going rate back then. I was nineteen years old and $280 seemed a king's ransom.

I'd had some early success with a short piece called 'The Tower' that had run in *Amazing Stories*, but for a long time I had felt blocked. It was my analyst's suggestion that I write something based on my long-absent father and I think that gave me some sort of breakthrough. So Graaf Thule, the intergalactic Nazi warlord, was born.

The Los Angeles Science Fiction Society met at Clifton's Cafeteria in downtown LA. The place served free limeade, which suited a good deal of our membership who had scarcely a nickel or dime to spend. And yet I felt a bit gauche when I first attended the Thursday-night meetings, more nervous fan than serious writer. The decor of Clifton's was absurdly kitsch. A waterfall cascaded through an artificial glade with plastic foliage and plaster rocks. A forest mural covered one wall. A gallery above held a tiny chapel with piped organ music and a neon cross. I always felt unduly sickened by this bizarre interior, which seemed to exacerbate my labyrinthitis. Dr Furedi explained this feeling as an 'externalisation of inner anxiety' and suggested that I obviously feared not being good enough to be part of this group. But once I had really achieved something, I felt a bit more confident.

The only person I really wanted to impress, though, was Mary-Lou Gunderson. She had sold as few stories as I had but she had a fierce presence. She seemed as self-possessed and outspoken as any who attended the weekly meetings of LASFS. Tall, blonde and athletic, she always made me feel ludicrously tongue-tied whenever she was near. I liked her stuff too. *Thrilling Wonder* ran her story 'Atom Priestess' in the summer of 1940. Set in a future that had descended into barbarism, it was about a religious sect that unknowingly worships long-lost theories of particle physics. And she had just started to write the series 'Zodiac Empire' for *Superlative Stories*. Mary-Lou was proud but she never bragged about her work; in fact she was meticulously self-deprecating. I think it allowed her to feel a little aloof about the strange trade that we had found ourselves in. She wanted to go beyond the ray guns and bug-eyed monsters. And secretly I did too.

'Well, if it isn't Larry Zagorski,' she called across the table at Clifton's. 'The man who put the goddamn Nazis in space. What did you want to go and do that for?'

'Er, um, well, Mary-Lou,' I stuttered. '*Lords of the Black Sun* is, you know, speculative.'

'Well, of course it's *speculative*,' she boomed. 'But what, you want them to win?'

'Of course not, no. It's like, you know, a warning.'

'A warning?'

'Yeah,' I said with a sudden certainty. 'A warning from the future.'

'Hmm,' she pondered. 'A warning from the future. I like that.'

Many years later a 'serious' science-fiction critic cited *Lords of the Black Sun* as an influence on Philip K. Dick's *The Man in the High Castle*, Norman Spinrad's *The Iron Dream* and countless other novels that dwelt on what might have happened if the Axis powers had gained world domination. But I certainly wasn't the first to come up with what has now become almost a sub-genre of literature. I got the idea from a strange English novel titled *Swastika Night* by Murray Constantine, though I did have something like an original twist to the idea and I wanted to share that with Mary-Lou.

'I got this idea from Jack Parsons. You remember, that rocket scientist at Caltech who sometimes comes to the meetings?'

'I'll say,' she drawled. 'He's cute.'

I gave an embarrassed cough.

'That's as may be,' I went on. 'What I remember was that he said German rocketry is already far in advance of anyone else's. And that got me thinking. What if the Nazis conquer space?'

'Yeah, terrifying thought,' she muttered. 'They say he's into black magic, you know.'

'What?'

'Jack Parsons.'

Parsons was something of a legend even then: tall, dark, strikingly handsome, a brilliant scientist who dabbled in the occult, like some fully formed figure from fantasy fiction. I was hardly surprised that he intrigued Mary-Lou, but I had no idea then that her flippant comments were my own warning from the future.

And looking back now I can see something else I didn't know at the time: Parsons was an acolyte of a notorious English occultist who became linked with the Hess case.

I felt just about bold enough to offer Mary-Lou a lift home to her boarding house in West Hollywood. She invited me up to her room for a nightcap where she produced the remains of a bottle of kosher slivovitz. As we sipped plum brandy she asked me about quantum mechanics.

'Cause and effect start to get weird on an atomic level,' I tried to explain, wrestling with ideas I didn't really understand. 'You know, with Newtonian physics it's like pool. The cue ball hits a colour, that hits the eight-ball and so on. In quantum theory one particle can influence another without the need for intermediate agents joining the two objects in space.'

She frowned and I struggled on, speaking of wave and particle duality, geodesics and the Uncertainty Principle.

'It hardly makes any sense to me,' she complained.

'Well, that's okay, Mary-Lou. They say that anyone who isn't confused by quantum mechanics doesn't understand it.'

'Oh, Zagorski, I just knew you'd come out with something like that!'

'Why?'

She smiled and poured me another slug of liquor.

'Because it's just the sort of dumb thing you would say.'

'Gee, Mary-Lou, I really don't understand it. Most of what I learnt about it I got from Jack Williamson's *The Legion of Time*. That was the first time I'd heard that time and space can be warped. You remember the story? *Astounding* ran it a couple of years ago. There are two possible futures: one like an ideal society, the other a horrific dictatorship. The hero is contacted by each of them because his actions will determine which one comes to pass.'

'Oh yeah, I read it. He's visited by a winsome girl from utopia, and an evil vamp from dystopia.'

'That's right.'

'Hmm, that figures. Don't they choose him because his actions will determine whether some kid becomes a scientist or not?'

'John Barr, yes; his ideas will go to create the perfect city of Jonbar. But only if he picks up the right object one day when he's a child. If he chooses a magnet, he becomes interested in science and goes on to discover new theories that make this bright future possible. If he picks up the stone next to it for his slingshot, we're headed for this totalitarian nightmare.'

'What's this got to do with quantum mechanics?'

'Well, it's as much to do with the Uncertainty Principle. By observing something you can change it, so the measurement of the position of a particle alters its trajectory.'

'But it's a political conundrum too, isn't it?'

'Is it?'

'Of course it is. Like you said, a warning from the future. That's what we should be writing, don't you think?'

'Er, yeah.'

Along with everything else, I was politically naive at that point in my life. I had worked out that Mary-Lou was left wing and that somehow this did not necessarily mean she was pro-Soviet Russia, but beyond that I was liable to get confused. I wanted to show willing because of the way I felt about her but I was never sure I was doing the right thing. *Lords of the Black Sun* was meant to be anti-fascist but the illustrator had made the Nazi spaceship look so impressive that the cover issue became a favourite with the German–American Bund.

'We've got to fight for the future, Mary-Lou!' I declared, emboldened by the second glass of slivovitz.

'That's right, Larry. And it's finely balanced. Just like in *The Legion of Time*, it could go either way. In Europe, in Africa, in Asia. In the whole world!'

We were staring into each other's eyes and it seemed to me like a portentous moment of epiphany, as though we shared the destiny of planet earth and the vast dominions of space beyond. I made a silent promise that I would learn more about politics and philosophy, that I would try to understand science properly so that I could share this precious wisdom with Mary-Lou Gunderson. Her eyes appeared to blaze with all the hope of some great utopian future. Then she yawned.

'Sorry, Zagorski,' she sighed. 'I'm beat. And I need to sleep. Got to work tomorrow.'

She had a part-time job reading scripts for one of the studios. She saw me to the door.

'Thanks for trying to explain all that long-hair stuff,' she murmured.

'I'll see if I can't find out some more,' I offered.

'Thing is, Larry, I'm just too impatient. I want to know it all. And right now.'

'Yeah, well—'

'I do,' she cut in, as if the idea had come to her at that moment. 'I want to know everything! Goodnight, Larry.'

She quickly kissed me on the cheek and hustled me out of the door. I staggered into the clear cold LA night. I was light-headed but, for once, steady on my feet. My mind fuzzed with ideologies, theoretical physics and plum brandy. My soul reeled in speculative fantasy. I was in love.

I was also a virgin. Perhaps my attraction to writing about the future was that it was only there that I had any worldly experience. I was as keen to rid myself of my childlike imagination and wonder as I was to use them to generate stories. Dr Furedi had encouraged my writing as a cathartic process, though he was concerned that my obsession with fantasy and science fiction reflected my neurotic condition. He pointed out that many of the problems I'd had with it were symptomatic of an unconscious resistance within myself. Now I'd had a small breakthrough with my fiction and, I felt, had made real progress towards the possibility of a relationship.

I was finding it hard to get on with my next story, though. 'Lightship 7 from Andromeda' now seemed a banal space adventure. I obsessed about my feelings for Mary-Lou and easily lost concentration when I sat down at my typewriter or would wander about in an unco-ordinated daze. At bookstores or news-stands it had long been my habit to scan the racks of the pulp magazines, for inspiration as well as just to see what was out there. The gaudy covers would often carry a female form: amazon warrior in sleek and curvaceous armour, or bound and barely clothed captives. But what had once been cheap titillation had now become a nagging reminder of an infatuation I had no idea what to do with.

We went to the cinema together: *Dr Cyclops* was playing in a double feature with *The Monster and the Girl*. Afterwards, over a soda, we agreed that both films were absolute trash and the sort of thing that gave science fiction a bad name, but it was hardly a romantic evening. We did meet to talk about work, though. Mary-Lou had none of the problems I was encountering with output. She seemed unsatisfied with 'Zodiac Empire' but she could produce copy at a phenomenal rate. She dismissed it as her 'space-opera' (some fanzine had just come up with the term) but she did have a strong idea that she wanted to pursue: that the different planets of the solar system had specific characteristics and influences – an astrology for the future, she called it.

Meanwhile I was trying to give myself a political education. Fascism was evil: that seemed clear enough. Capitalism was wrong, not just because it was unfair but also because it was unscientific. But Soviet communism wasn't the answer. What was needed was some kind of socialism that wasn't totalitarian. The pact the Russians had made with the Nazis had done a lot to discredit the USSR, but America wasn't in the war either. Haunted by distant cataclysm, we all felt a peculiar sense of detached speculation. The world seemed as awkwardly balanced as I was.

One afternoon on passing a news-stand Mary-Lou pointed to all the catastrophic headlines – LONDON BLITZED, THE ATLANTIC WAR CONTINUES, TANK BATTLES IN NORTH AFRICA – then to a little man who had picked up a magazine.

'After all that,' she remarked darkly, 'he still wants *Action Stories*. What are we *doing*, writing for the pulps?'

'Maybe we're finding a solution. You see the news? What's real now? Submarines, flying machines: that was the science fiction of a hundred years ago. What we are imagining now: that might be next century's news.'

'Jesus, Zagorski, think of the horrors we might come up with then.'

'That's why it's important how we use our imaginations,' I said, instinctively reaching for the latest issue of *Astounding*.

'In dreams begins responsibility,' said Mary-Lou.

'Huh?' I grunted, already absorbed by the glossy binding.

'Don't worry, Larry. Just quoting W.B. Yeats at you.'

'Magic City' was the cover story with a ruined Statue of Liberty rising out of a post-apocalyptic wilderness, a lithe huntress in furs standing in the foreground and a long-haired caveman crouching before her.

'At least *Astounding* runs interesting stuff,' I said, holding it up.

'Yeah,' Mary-Lou agreed. 'That's who we should be writing for.'

It was clear to both of us that *Astounding Science Fiction* was by far the best and most ground-breaking of any of the pulp magazines of the time. Its new editor, John W. Campbell, had completely transformed the field, nurturing a group of exciting new writers: Isaac Asimov, A.E. van Vogt, Theodore Sturgeon and especially Robert

Heinlein, who lived in LA and was said to run some kind of literary circle. This was the world that we wanted to be part of.

Mary-Lou had grown tired of the LASFS Thursday meetings and would sometimes disparagingly refer to that crowd as the 'limeade brigade'. I still attended. I had sold 'Lightship 7 from Andromeda' to *Fantastic Tales* and it looked as if I was becoming something of a regular writer for them, so I now was shown quite a lot of respect at Clifton's Cafeteria. Mary-Lou never said as much but I got the feeling she thought it was playing safe, mixing with them, that we should really be taking more risks with our writing rather than churning out the usual stuff. And maybe thinking of her made me bold because when Robert Heinlein walked in one night I wasted little time in making a beeline for him.

Heinlein had a presence that was more than a little intimidating. Gaunt and saturnine, with swept-back hair and a pencil moustache, he looked very much like a gloomy Douglas Fairbanks Jnr. And he had seemed to come from nowhere. Having published his first story only a couple of years before, he was by then one of the brightest stars in the genre. There were all sorts of rumours about him: that he was a radical, that he had made his fortune silver prospecting, that he was into free love. I praised his latest story, '– And He Built a Crooked House –' that had been in the issue of *Astounding* I'd picked up at the news-stand with Mary-Lou. It was about an architect who designs a four-dimensional house, a hypercube in the form of a tesseract that collapses in on itself after an earthquake into what appears to be a single cube. Those trapped inside can still pass through the original eight rooms, all of which appear to occupy the same space, with the stairs now forming a closed loop so that on reaching what they think is the top storey, the people find themselves back on the ground floor. At one point they look down a hallway to observe their own backs. I seem to remember that I said it was like a prose version of an M.C. Escher woodcut and that Heinlein smiled and nodded. What I am certain of is that, as his attention began to drift and he started to turn away, I boldly thrust out my hand and announced:

'I'm Larry Zagorski, sir. I wrote *Lords of the Black Sun*.'

Heinlein laughed and clasped my palm in a firm grip. He frowned at me.

'Yeah?' He shook my hand the way a dog shakes a rabbit. 'I saw the story. In *Fabulous*, wasn't it? Made the fascists seem a bit glamorous, didn't you?'

'That was the illustrator's fault,' I protested.

He laughed again.

'Only kidding with you. I liked it. But we got to be careful sometimes, haven't we? You know, being of the devil's party without knowing it.'

He tapped his nose. I nodded sagely but I had no idea what he meant.

'Look, kid,' he went on. 'We have a little soirée every now and then at my place. Call it the Mañana Literary Society. Why don't you come along?'

'Can I bring someone?'

'Your girl?'

'Yes,' I blurted, then thought better of it. 'I mean, no, I mean, well . . . she's another writer. A good one.'

Heinlein laughed once more and wrote out his address for me. He lived with his wife Leslyn in Laurel Canyon, on Lookout Mountain Avenue, a side road that twists up into the Hollywood Hills. And when I took Mary-Lou with me to our first meeting with the Mañana Literary Society, I felt that a whole new bright world was opening up for the both of us. It was the closest thing to a salon that science fiction had at that time and we were a part of it. Most of all I hoped it would mean that Mary-Lou would take me seriously and that I would be able to find the courage finally to say how I really felt about her. Oh yes, I felt really pleased with myself at the start of that evening. I thought I was so clever. But I was a fool, a complete fool.

I

the magician

1 / CASINO ESTORIL

Fleming watched Popov walk through the lobby of the Hotel Palacio with a sense of possession, that odd feeling of intimacy he derived from having seen a man's file. It was a curiously inert experience, presenting an advantage while revealing a weakness of his own. Each person is a dossier, he mused. A bundle of half-known facts, misleading reports, document extracts, fragments. Dossier, from the old French for back, a loose binding, bracing the chaos of information into some sort of recognisable posture. Like the book with its spine holding up an unlikely story. Fleming had concluded long ago that real lives exist only in secret. But it had become his job to form impressions, to summarise. He had acquired a talent for the brief appraisal.

So he noted the awkward line on the buttoned front of Popov's dinner jacket and took a moment to consider what might explain the square bulge below the breast pocket. The outline of an automatic pistol, perhaps? Fleming smiled, aware that he had become known for the brash style of his memoranda. But no, he decided, it wasn't a gun that gave the extra weight to this man's left-hand side. No, he thought, his smile becoming a grin. It was a big, fat slab of money, the eighty thousand dollars that rightly belonged to British Intelligence.

The ornamental gardens that surrounded the Palacio were veined with narrow gravel pathways that forked here and there, making a discreet pursuit almost impossible. Fleming was acting not so much on initiative as on compulsion, since shadowing Popov had nothing to do with his mission in Portugal. That had already been completed earlier that day with the meeting at the Café Chiado in Lisbon. Operation Mistletoe: an audacious operation to catch a top Nazi. This hastily improvised tail-job was a mere sideshow, but he found the prospect of it just as exciting as the astonishing information he had received that afternoon. For some it was the game, but for Fleming it was always the story. And here was a good one, he felt sure of it. Inspiration, yes, that's what drove him to follow this man. Something he might use one day.

The archives of Room 39 had furnished the sparse details of the individual he now studied at close hand: Dusko Popov, Yugoslav émigré, code-named 'Tricycle', posing as a spy for the Nazi Abwehr while working for the British. A lethal double act. The man was a light-footed adventurer; the one who watched him was forever weighed down by ideas. Popov was all that Fleming aspired to and sometimes pretended to be: handsome, charming, something of a playboy, whose designation Tricycle was said to refer to his fondness for the *ménage à trois*. Fleming stalked him in jealous fascination.

He knew that the eighty thousand dollars were funds from the Abwehr to pay for an entirely fake spy network that Popov was running in London. He was due to hand it over to an MI6 agent the following day and had obviously decided it was better kept on his person than in the hotel safe. Unless Popov had had a better idea, such as a taxi into Lisbon and then a flight somewhere the next day. The Pan American flying boat was departing for Rio de Janeiro from Cabo Ruiva dock tomorrow morning. Popov would have enough money to disappear and live his cherished high life without any of the risks. Was that the story? A capricious choice that could change a whole lifetime. The dry tracks in the grounds of the Palacio fanned out, each path a possibility.

Popov made a play of doubling back at a corner junction, passing by Fleming without looking at him but with a half-smile on his lips. Fleming stopped. He could hardly change direction now without giving the game away. Yes, it was definitely the game for Popov. And Fleming would be hard pressed to beat him at it. Paperwork, not fieldcraft, was his forte, he concluded gloomily. But cold analysis had its uses. He might have lost his quarry for now, but he had a very good notion of where he was headed.

Where else but the House of Games? The Estoril Casino, its grey, melancholy walls skulking amid more serene surroundings, looking like an office building or a workshop. Which indeed it was: the bureaucracy of bad luck, the sweatshop of short odds. The perfect setting, thought Fleming, as he passed through the *vestiaire* into the gaming rooms. He entered a theatre of calm excitement, filled with the repetition of muted sounds and stifled gestures. A static impersonal space, where anxiety and relaxation could be enjoyed in equal measure. A collective trance: where all are actors, all are audience to both shared and private dramas.

The Estoril Casino was the very hub of an enclave of neutrality where all sides in the war rubbed shoulders. It was peopled by many exotic species, which Fleming divided into flora and fauna. The flora were the refugees, various types from many nations. Some were wealthy beyond measure and squandered their money as if there was no tomorrow (as, indeed, there might not be). Others were so poor that they would gamble what little they had and sell anything, which usually meant themselves. The rest came to move unnoticed among them. What the flora had in common was that they were all waiting. Waiting for transport elsewhere, anywhere away from occupied Europe, and where better to wait than in the Casino.

Then there were the fauna: those who preyed on the flora. Businessmen, international officials, racketeers. And spies, of course. Agents and informers of all hues and natures. This was Popov's world, where he so often operated. Fleming looked for him at the roulette table, knowing that it was here that Popov would go to get directions for a meeting with his German handlers. A female Abwehr agent would, at a prearranged moment, play the table three times, the numbers indicating consecutively the date, hour and minute of the rendezvous. She would then bet on either zero or thirty-six, the former directing him to a safe-house in Estoril, the latter to one in Lisbon. An expensive code, one that appealed to Fleming's imagination. But Popov was not there. The *chef de partie* of the roulette table kept a tally of the numbers that had come up since the start of play that afternoon. Fleming studied it for a moment, wondering if any sense could be made of this list of arbitrary figures. Luck is a code without a key. As he looked up from it he spotted the Yugoslav making his way to the baccarat table.

Fleming had always preferred the familiarity of playing cards to the impersonal turn of the wheel. They offered some sort of meaning beyond mere chance. A sense of order: the Devil's Bible with fifty-two pages (fifty-four if you included the jokers). He approached the crescent of players and spectators that surrounded the dealer. Bloch, a short, pug-faced Lithuanian, held the bank, which gave him the power to determine the stakes for the next play. Obscenely wealthy and arrogant, Bloch liked to dominate the card tables and was known haughtily to declare, '*Banque ouverte*,' indicating that there was no upper limit and that the players could bet whatever they wished. It was suspected that the Lithuanian was a Nazi sympathiser who channelled illicit funds to bankroll Abwehr operations. Popov had taken a vacant seat at the table. Fleming stood behind him at his left shoulder.

'*Banque ouverte*,' Bloch announced.

'*Les messieurs debout peuvent jouer*,' called the croupier.

Popov reached into his jacket pocket and as he did so turned his head so that Fleming could see his sharp profile. It was as if he was acknowledging his shadow. The Yugoslav then swiftly pulled out his thick sheaf of banknotes.

'Fifty thousand dollars,' he said calmly and began to count out a pile of notes on the table.

The baccarat table at once became the focus of the whole casino, a hush sucking in sound from all corners of the room. Soon there was silence but for the clatter of the roulette ball and the whispered oaths of countless languages. Everyone watched as Popov slowly laid out his stake in one-thousand- and five-hundred-dollar notes. Fleming felt a slight swoon in his stomach, a brief euphoria at this dramatic moment, this *coup de théâtre*. Then nausea at the prospect of reporting how Agent Tricycle had lost a small fortune of government money at a gaming table. Bloch squirmed in his seat, clearly outbid and humiliated. Popov turned to the croupier.

'I suppose that the Casino will back this man's bet, since you didn't object to his "*banque ouverte*".'

'The Casino never backs any player's stake, sir.'

Popov huffed audibly and with a show of irritation swept his money off the table and stuffed it back into his inside jacket pocket. Fleming sighed. It was a joke. A game. Popov scraped back his chair and stood up.

'I trust you'll call this to the attention of the management,' he said, addressing the croupier while all the time glaring down at Bloch. 'And that in future such irresponsible play will be prohibited. It's an insult to serious players.'

As he turned to leave he looked at Fleming briefly and smiled. Then he was gone. Bloch scraped together his stake money and scurried away in disgrace. Fleming found himself slipping into the vacant chair left by Popov, bemused that the Yugoslav's outrageous performance had been partly for his benefit. He reached into his own pocket. He had fifty pounds sterling. It was all he had brought with him on this brief mission to Portugal. But the stakes on the table had now reverted to a reasonable rate, and were within his scope, at least for a while. Only a couple of players remained seated. The crowd of onlookers was drifting away, eager for some new spectacle now that the climax of the baccarat seemed over. The croupier looked bored as he snapped out the cards from the shoe, but Fleming's mind buzzed with details and atmosphere, with ideas. All at once a germ of a story came to him. He became his other self, the empty hero who sleepwalked through his daydreams. A British agent pitted against the paymaster of a foreign power in a game of cards. Imagine if one could bankrupt the entire Abwehr in Portugal in one night? He gazed across at his opponents – mediocre men in creased dinner jackets – and imagined them as the enemy in a greater game. He felt an absurd thrill as he fingered his meagre winnings.

He ordered a whisky and lit a cigarette. He found that smoking incessantly seemed to enhance his prowess. He held the bank for a while and built up a sizeable stake. Then he lost it all when he should have passed. Bridge was more his game, where there was at least some sort of narrative. Baccarat was simply harsh numerology: Fleming tended to read the cards when he should be counting them. And it disturbed him that the court cards, the only discernible characters in the deck, had no face value in this game. He attempted a resigned grin at his fellow players when he once more lost a round. It was not acknowledged. He realised that the dull men who concentrated on an essentially banal strategy with such sombre diligence would consider him an amateur. It took him some time to lose all his money, but the point soon came where the tension lay merely in how long he might delay his annihilation. It was almost three in the morning when he was finally cleaned out. Yes, he thought, as he rose from the table, this was part of it too. Part of the story. The anxiety and nervous exhaustion, the tension of fear and greed, the very smell of failure.

2 / A MEETING WITH M

M was standing by his office window when his private secretary entered, and seemed to be sternly surveying the grey Thames below. To the west a dismal mist crept around the bend in the river at Chelsea Reach. She could tell by his imperious frown that he had spotted something human. He gave her a brief nod of acknowledgement as she approached, then pointed the stem of his pipe at his quarry below.

'See?' he demanded.

She followed the trajectory of his gaze. A young man in a cheap raincoat was walking slowly along the Embankment with little attempt to conceal the apparent aimlessness of his movements. M sighed and shook his head.

'It's the utter lack of discretion that galls one,' the spymaster commented bitterly to his assistant.

She said nothing, knowing that it was best not to provoke him when he was in this kind of mood.

'Well, what is it?' he asked her finally.

'It's 17F here to see you, sir.'

M broke from his gloomy reverie and turned to her with a smile. 'Excellent. Send him in.'

When she went through into the adjoining reception room she found 17F sitting on the edge of her desk. The handsome commander attached to Naval Intelligence stood up and smiled as he saw her. They had met twice before and had developed a sort of competitive flirtatiousness. He was pleasingly tall and slim, if a little too narcissistic for her taste. A broken nose softened his aquiline features. He flicked at the stray comma of hair above his right eyebrow.

'Miss Miller,' he murmured playfully.

'Commander Fleming,' she replied, with an edge to her voice.

She felt determined to see him as her equal, her sense of self-regard reflecting his. She was proud of her good looks, charisma and ambition. Besides, they held similar positions. They were both personal assistants: Fleming to the head of Naval Intelligence and herself to Maxwell Knight, known to everyone in the Service as M, the boss of B5(b), a clandestine subsection of Counter-Espionage. But his being a man meant that he held a military rank while she remained a drab civilian.

'You can come through now, Commander,' she told him.

'I was just asking Bill,' Fleming nodded towards M's Chief of Staff, whose desk was opposite hers, 'if this is really a good moment to catch the old man.'

Only the merest of smiles played upon her lips as her bright eyes held him in cold appraisal.

'Oh, he'll be pleased enough to see you,' she said, perhaps a little too knowingly.

M was sitting at his desk, refilling his pipe, when Fleming entered.

'May I, sir?' Fleming asked, taking out his cigarette case.

'Certainly. How was Lisbon?'

'Very busy, sir.'

'Quite. I'm led to believe by your report that we may have hooked ourselves a bigger fish.'

Fleming tapped a cigarette out on the flat silver lid. A letter had been intercepted from an academic working for German Foreign Intelligence addressed to a British aristocrat, suggesting some sort of clandestine peace meeting. A reply had been forged in the manner of a lure. Now it seemed a member of the Nazi inner circle was ready to put his head in the noose.

'Perhaps.' Fleming lit his cigarette. 'A couple of factors need to be in place before Operation Mistletoe can proceed.'

'A couple of factors?'

'Well, yes. The first involves persuading the other side to believe that the Link is still active.'

'Surely it's not hard to give the enemy the impression that there remains a strong pro-peace element in the country? Good Lord, the way the war's been going half the Cabinet seem ready to make terms.'

'Yes, sir, but to convince them there is still this Link organisation, that's pro-German, even pro-Nazi – there needs to be some evidence.'

'Well, the idea was that we put it out that it had gone to ground since the round-ups last year. Can't someone from the Double-Cross Committee file a bogus report or something?'

'I'm afraid it has to be something stronger than that, sir.'

'What then?' M demanded impatiently.

'Something, well, demonstrative, sir.'

'Demonstrative?'

'Yes, sir. Some significant act that would make it seem that there is an effective Fifth Column in operation in the country.'

'Hmm, well, I could put my assistant on to it.'

'Miss Miller?'

'Oh yes. A very effective field officer. She uncovered a whole nest of them last year.'

'Of course. I read the Special Branch report. But won't she be vulnerable if there are any real quislings left?'

'Hmm, well, let me deal with that. What was the other thing?'

'I'm sorry, sir?'

'The other factor you mentioned.'

Fleming shrugged as if slightly embarrassed.

'The, er, paranormal aspect of the operation, sir.'

M laughed out loud.

'Goodness me, Fleming, there's no need to be sheepish about it. It might all seem a bit far-fetched but isn't that the whole point of counter-intelligence?'

'The whole point, sir?'

'A story should sound improbable. If it is too logical it's liable to appear contrived. And, of course, there are powers that we do not completely understand. Greater forms of disinformation, if you like.'

'You mean, you give credence to some of this stuff, sir?'

It was known that M held some obscure beliefs and Fleming himself had begun to notice strange coincidences ever since he had been involved in Operation Mistletoe.

'That's neither here nor there,' M replied. 'We have to understand what the enemy is using. Goebbels had some of the prophecies of Nostradamus printed in a leaflet and dropped during the invasion of France. There are all sorts of rumours that Hitler takes astrological advice. The important thing now is that the subject of Operation Mistletoe actually believes in it. I like to keep an open mind. Haven't you ever experienced an event that has been foretold?'

Yes, he had, Fleming thought. He just didn't know how he might explain it to M.

'Well, something has been bothering me about the whole plan, sir. Something I read in a book.'

'Not that silly comedy your brother wrote.'

A Flying Visit by Peter Fleming had been published the previous spring, before the fall of France. It was an imagined story of Hitler flying to England, a playful satire with cartoons by Low, that now in the heat of the Blitz seemed woefully outdated, even in poor taste.

'No, not that,' Fleming replied. 'Something else, sir.'

'What?'

Fleming was about to speak then stopped. He would have to think it through first.

'Oh, it's nothing, sir.'

'Look, Fleming, you're right about the paranormal stuff. What we need is a real expert. You know, the man I told you about. The Magician. He's ideal for our purposes. Have a look at his file when you get back to Naval Intelligence. He worked for your bunch in the last show. Did a lot of what the Political Warfare Executive are call- ing "black propaganda". Go and see him and I'll sort out that other business with the Link.'

'Yes, sir.'

'And remember, this is a cross-departmental operation, but it goes without saying that the fewer people who know about it the better. I'm briefing someone from Political to run liaison. It's far- fetched, yes, but it could be our biggest coup of the war. Read up on the Magician and make contact with him.'

'Yes, sir.'

As Fleming got up to leave, Joan Miller was called back into the office. M stood up and went to the window, once more turning his back to her.

'He's still there,' M muttered. 'Dirty little creep.'

He beckoned her over. She hesitated. It was as if he was trying to provoke her in some way.

'Did you want something else, sir?'

'The Political Warfare Executive are going to reactivate the Link. They need you to go back out into the field for a spell.'

'But, sir, I can hardly do that.'

'Come here! Look. He's got one.'

She joined M at his vantage point and saw another figure approach the man in the shabby raincoat.

'I mean,' Miller went on, 'I've been compromised with the Link and the Right Club, sir. I gave evidence in court for goodness' sake.'

'Wait.'

M held up his hand for her to be quiet and they both watched the little vignette below. As the two men drew close, the one in the raincoat produced a cigarette and placed it in his mouth with a flourish, allowing his other hand to rest on one hip with a slight twist of his torso. The other produced a match and cupped the sulphur flame. With the briefest exchange of words, the smoker passed on, then his companion, flicking away the match and glancing furtively around for a moment, followed.

'Yes,' M hissed. 'The dirty buggers.'

M had pointed out this little dance between men to Joan Miller before. She had been his assistant for nearly a year now and had spent weekends with him at the safe-house he had set up in Camberley. He had declared his love for her and she had supposed that he had wanted her as his mistress. Except nothing had happened beyond the diligent choreography of romance. They would always sleep in separate rooms. At first she had thought that this was somehow her fault. But the war had brought an end to all innocence. He turned to her.

'Political are being rather insistent on this one, I'm afraid,' he told her.

'I see.'

'But I wouldn't want to order you on a job like this, Joan,' he said.

There was an odd expression on his face. She couldn't tell if he was smiling or baring his teeth.

'M—'

'You will volunteer, won't you?'

There seemed a soft threat in his words, as if he was implicating her in something unknown. She had come to know all his little prejudices. He had toned down his anti-semitism, at least for the duration, but he often voiced his vehement dislike of homosexuals. It seemed part of his brutal and ruthless side, which included a strange insistence that she conspire in his own self-loathing. He seemed to be goading her, testing her to discover whether she knew the truth or not. He stared at her.

'Well?' he demanded.

She knew now that he feared blackmail, disgrace. It would be unendurable for such an arrogant man to be in another's power. He would do anything to protect himself.

'Of course, M,' she said. 'Just concerned about security, that's all.'

'Good,' he rejoined, with a cold smile.

There had been the odd business with the chauffeur who had been hastily dismissed. That time she had spotted him hanging around a cinema tea room. And, of course, the young bus driver from Leicester who had come up to Camberley to help fix M's motorbike. He had once pointed out with disdain the particular demeanour of male prostitutes in Piccadilly, yet as Joan had been shocked to observe when she spied M from the bedroom window, he had walked towards the garage, and the bus driver, in precisely the same manner. From then on many things about her boss had become clear to her.

3 / ROOM 39

Room 39 was a vast office on the ground floor of the Admiralty, crammed with desks and filing cabinets, resounding with telephone bells and the constant clatter of typewriters. Fleming sat at the far end of it, next to the glass door that led to the inner sanctum of Naval Intelligence. He had called up NID's file on the Magician and was shuffling through the pile of papers in front of him. He glanced at an old memorandum of his that had finally been returned to him. 'Operation Ruthless' had been a plan of his to seize one of the new high-speed German launches that patrolled the Channel, to overpower its crew and steal its code devices.

> I suggest we obtain the loot by the following means:
> 1 Obtain from Air Ministry an airworthy German bomber.
> 2 Pick a tough crew of five, including a pilot, W/T operator and word-perfect German speaker. Dress them in German air force uniforms, add blood and bandages to suit.
> 3 Crash plane in the Channel after making SOS to rescue service in plain language.

4 Once aboard rescue boat, shoot German crew, dump overboard, bring boat back to English port.

He had even volunteered to lead the operation personally. Anything to get out of Room 39, to prove himself more than a mere staff officer. And there was, after all, a desperate need to crack the enemy's codes. The Government Code and Cypher School was building a mechanical brain somewhere in the Home Counties. His project had eventually been rejected.

Fleming had begun to see himself as merely a component in a vast thinking machine. So much of intelligence seemed to be about generating obscure ideas and intellectual exercises. Departmental subsections and research units were springing up everywhere. Operation Mistletoe had emerged from this arcane world of speculation and second-guessing.

The Magician's file made for fascinating reading. The subject had worked for Naval Intelligence in New York during the last war, posing as an Irish Nationalist and a German sympathiser, disseminating scurrilous and extreme propaganda that was aimed at discrediting both these professed causes. This was, as M said, what was now being called 'black propaganda'. The Magician also had significant contacts with German occult organisations and individuals. He was just what they needed at this point in the operation. Fleming had heard of him, of course, from bohemian gossip circles and newspaper exposés. Intrigued, he arranged to visit him the next day at his rooms in Jermyn Street.

The mournful wail of the air-raid siren was giving its nightly call to prayers as he got back to his own house in Ebury Street, a converted chapel with a book-lined gallery – a special library containing his dearest possessions, which, despite all his years in the City, were also his wisest investment. He had started his collection over five years before but instead of merely buying first editions of literary novels, he sought out works of social and scientific significance that the rare-book dealers often overlooked. He had one of the few remaining copies of Madame Curie's doctoral thesis of 1903; Koch's paper on the tubercle bacillus;

first editions of Freud's *On the Interpretation of Dreams* and Nils Bohr's *Quantum Theory*. But the strangest volume he possessed was splayed out on the dining table where he had left it the night before.

The book's red dust jacket was stamped with the provocative motto: LEFT BOOK CLUB EDITION. NOT FOR SALE TO THE PUBLIC. Not an imprint he would usually subscribe to; indeed, he was outspokenly conservative (though in private far more liberal than he seemed). It was titled *Swastika Night* by Murray Constantine and it contained a premonition of the plan that he was forming, shaped by the meetings he had had with M, the rumours that had come to light from a German anti-fascist underground organisation known as the Red Orchestra, and his rendezvous at the Café Chiado in Lisbon. It was a faint glimpse of the scheme that had been unfolding over the past few weeks, which might turn the course of the entire war.

The setting of the book was peculiar enough: a dystopian tale, though quite unlike the playful satire of Huxley, it presented a dark, horrible vision of what might lie ahead. A stark warning from a possible future, in which the Nazis had won, the Jews had been exterminated and the Christians were then being rounded up. Women were considered subhuman and kept in camps for the purposes of breeding. But amid this scenario of doom was a storyline far more disturbing to Fleming, involving a high-ranking Nazi called Hess who leaves the inner circle and travels far to the north, to Scotland. Somehow the author seemed to have predicted Operation Mistletoe. He would have to find out who this Murray Constantine was. Someone in the Political Warfare Executive might know. They had more contact with left-wing circles than any other department.

4 / THE RUSSIAN TEA ROOMS

They had met in the Russian Tea Rooms in Kensington. Joan Miller had got there first and was glad to find the place crowded. With its polished wooden furniture, panelled walls and open fireplace, it was the sort of café a woman could visit unescorted without drawing attention, or raising questions about her reputation. But Joan had felt awkward and uncomfortable as she waited for her contact from Political. Shifting in her seat, she pondered what seemed a foolish plan: to revisit the haunts of the fascist network she had helped to expose last summer.

It had been easy to spot Marius Trevelyan when he arrived. A bookish type in a tweed jacket, with a mop of straw-coloured hair and heavy horn-rimmed spectacles. In his early twenties, Joan had estimated, though he could almost pass as a schoolboy. There was something not quite fully formed about him.

He had ordered vodka and potato piroshki in flawless Russian. He had studied modern languages at Cambridge, he explained.

When the bill arrived he turned it over and discreetly showed her the address that had been scribbled on the back. The Tea Rooms were run by White Russian émigrés, known to have connections with fascist sympathisers.

'That's where the party's being held,' he said with an awkward wink.

He paid up and they left together, making their way along Harrington Gardens.

'Look, Trevelyan.' Joan came to the point now that they could talk openly. 'I'm not quite sure what I'm supposed to be doing here.'

'Didn't M brief you?'

'He just said that Political wanted me along.'

'Oh no. It was his idea that you become part of this operation.'

'Really?'

'Oh yes. He was quite insistent.'

'But—'

She thought better of what she had been about to say.

'Did he tell you why?' she asked instead.

'Not really. You know M. Likes to play things his own way. Said you made a plausible fascist.' Trevelyan laughed. 'Think he meant that as a compliment.'

'But you know I was at the trial last year. Someone might recognise me.'

'Don't worry. We've got them under control.'

'Control?'

'Oh yes. Political's been running a little group. Saving them up for a rainy day. Look, we're nearly there. We should get into character.'

He told her that they would be pretending to be a Mr and Mrs Fairburn from Tufnell Park, with Blackshirt connections, who had been members of the Anglo-German Fellowship in 1938.

'I expect you can remember the patter you learnt last June,' he added. 'Oh, and you'd better take one of these.'

He took two silver buttons from his jacket pocket and handed her one.

'Got them from Special Branch evidence store.'

It was a badge depicting an eagle swooping on a viper, with the letters PJ embossed below.

'Under the lapel, I suppose,' said Trevelyan. 'By the way, what does the PJ stand for?'

'It means "Perish Judah",' she replied.

'Oh, I say.'

The meeting was in the basement of a terraced house in Earl's Court. Twelve people, Joan counted, crowded into a candlelit room. A short man in a three-piece suit and watch-chain stood before them. He raised his hand and began to speak.

'I want to talk to you tonight about peace,' he announced.

The flickering light gave a mesmeric ambience to the assembly. The speaker's voice began in a soft drone like an incantation. Peace was coming, he assured them solemnly. He had heard it from the highest authorities. So many well-placed people in the Establishment were now determined that this futile and unnecessary war must end. If it continues we will lose the Empire, we will lose everything. We will become a pauper nation forever in debt to the Americans. The people do not want this war. They know in their hearts that as Anglo-Saxons we share so much with our German brothers. Soon it will come, he went on. The white races will unite against the true barbarism that inhabits this earth. We will rise up against the traitors in our midst. Soon it will come, he promised. Peace.

For a moment the word sounded soothing and plausible. Joan suddenly realised how tired she felt. How exhausted everybody was by the endless bombings and privations. Then the man's voice began to rise to a higher pitch.

Churchill will be deposed. Yes, he insisted, this is certain. People that I know of in government are ready and waiting. People like us who share our feelings are waiting in the wings. Germany is willing to make terms, we know that. An honourable peace that will leave us our Empire while they bring order to the Continent. Only one group of people want this war, and we know who they are, don't we?

There were murmurs of agreement and a shiver of agitation in the room. She felt someone prod her in the back and she shuffled forward. The speaker started an extended harangue against the Jews. They will be made to pay for all of this, he promised. The audience gleefully hissed its agreement. A woman called out: hang them from the lamp-posts! Joan felt a quickening within her as the anger began to rise in the basement. The suburban voices that found such relish in hatred and horror were familiar and English.

Later, as she and Trevelyan walked back from the meeting, she still felt shocked that these ordinary-seeming people could be so virulent. She remembered that this was what had disturbed her so much when she had spied on the Right Club for M the previous summer.

'Recognise anyone?' Trevelyan asked her.

'No,' she replied.

'And what did you think of our speaker tonight?'

'A thoroughly ghastly little man.'

'Convincing, wasn't he?'

'You mean—'

'Yes. One of ours.'

'Good God.'

'Yes. It's been quite a project for Political. I trust you'll give a glowing report to M. Come to think of it, I'm having a drink with Commander Fleming at the Dorchester later. Maybe you should come along. I sure he'd be interested in your impressions of our little nest of vipers. Would it be terribly churlish to leave you here? If I'm lucky I can get a bus back to my digs from around the corner.'

'Don't worry about me. I can walk to my flat.'

They shook hands clumsily and Trevelyan wandered off. Joan started to walk home through the blackout. The streets looked empty but she had the uneasy feeling that she was being watched. Everything seemed confused in her mind. All the double games that were being played. The evil little rabble-rouser was an agent provocateur, on their side. Yet he had talked so persuasively of peace. The word now appeared as a taunt to her. Soon the sirens would come, and a sleepless night lay ahead. M had given her some pills but they didn't do much good.

All at once, the only certainty she felt was that someone was indeed following her. Even from her cursory training in fieldcraft she knew that it wasn't a very professional tail-job. Perhaps it was someone trying to pick her up. If nothing else the blackout had increased the sense of sexual opportunism, as M had pointed out with those two men the other day. She had once been pursued by a man who, it turned out, she vaguely knew from the War Office, who had told her: 'When I saw you in the street I told myself that if you were a tart I'd take you to bed, and if you were a lady I'd take you to dinner. Will you come?' he had added with a playful chuckle. 'I mean to dinner, of course.' It was a remark that would have been almost unthinkable from someone of her class before the war. The constant danger of the Blitz had made people more relaxed: as death became casual, so did life. Tonight, though, Joan was in no mood for fun and games. She stopped and turned, waiting for her follower to catch up so that she could confront him.

She peered along the pavement. The footsteps behind had ceased but she could not make anybody out through the gloom. She started walking again, at first determined to go slowly. But she found her pace picking up. She tried to stay calm but she could not. By the time she had reached her doorstep she was quite out of breath. As she went to close the door behind her, she took a moment to look out into the night. No one was there, she decided. She had imagined it. But as she hung up her coat she noticed that someone had marked a cross in chalk on her back.

5 / THE MAGICIAN

An old man with a childlike gait, thought Fleming, as the Magician shuffled through the hallway to greet him. Two tufts of hair sprouted on either side of an otherwise bald head like impish horns, and a mischievous smile lit up haggard features. The eyes were sharp and vigilant, though. The whites showed all around the irises, giving him an alert and forceful gaze.

Shown through to the study, Fleming found himself drawn to a picture resting on an easel at the far end of the room. A brightly painted panel of about ten by twelve inches depicted an androgynous figure in a green robe decorated with bees and serpents, flanked by a white lion and a red eagle. Encircling this tableau was an inscription in red on a golden arc.

'Visita Interiora Terrae Rectificando Invenies Occultum Lapidem.' Fleming read the words out loud. The Magician smiled.

'How's your cryptology?' he asked.

'Well, my Latin's a bit shaky. Let me see.' He studied the motto once more. 'Visit the interior of the earth, rectifying or by rectification . . . um . . . you find, no, you *will* find. You will find *occultum lapidem*. The hidden stone. Is that the philosopher's stone?'

'Yes!' replied the Magician with a delighted clap. Fleming noted that his hands were quite yellow and curiously small.

'An alchemical formula?'

'It is indeed. But I'm afraid you haven't quite cracked it.'

'I'm afraid code-breaking's not my department, Mr Crowley.'

'My dear boy,' his host retorted, 'I can assure you that this one is not beyond your obvious talents. Go on, have another go.'

For a second Fleming bristled at being so obviously teased. Then he smiled. He looked across the room at this extraordinary man whose playful eyes danced in a wizened skull. He had not known what to expect from the Magician after all the incredible stories that had been told about him, the strange details in his dossier. He had expected to find him disagreeable, yet he found that he liked the man almost at once. He was not quite sure why. Perhaps it was the perverse candour that he displayed, in his speech, in his very appearance. Crowley was in his sixties, his lined and jaundiced flesh bearing witness to the countless sufferings of pleasure. But there was a corporeal honesty about him. His own body had been his greatest luxury, Fleming thought with an odd sense of admiration. The Magician had not squandered his life by trying to conserve it. He had used up his time. Fleming turned back to the picture and swiftly considered the simplest cypher that came to mind.

'V,' he began, counting off the first letter of each word. 'V, I, T, R, I, O, L. Vitriol. That's sulphuric acid, isn't it?'

'Yes indeed. The solution, if you like. The universal solvent. Vitriol here actually refers to the principal alchemical elements of sulphur, salt and mercury. A magical interpretation that only initiates of the ninth degree can comprehend. Anyway,' he pointed at the picture, 'it's the fourteenth trump card of the Tarot. I'm redesigning the whole pack. It's the Book of Thoth, you know.'

'Thoth?'

'The Egyptian god of language. Lady Frieda Harris is doing the artwork for this new set and I am writing the commentary. Her husband is Liberal Member of Parliament for Market Harborough. Rather a dull politician, I'm afraid. Known as the "Housemaid" due to his ability to empty the Chamber whenever he makes a speech. His wife has quite a talent, though, wouldn't you say?'

'Certainly.'

'Well, this one's been causing her a lot of bother. It's commonly known as Temperance. "Temperance is a kettle of fish," she told me in a note. I've decided to rename it. I'm calling it Art. What do you think?'

'I wouldn't know. Haven't had much luck with cards myself recently.'

Crowley laughed.

'My dear boy, the Major Arcana is not some game of chance. The twenty-two trump cards compose a complete system of hiero-glyphics representing the total energies of the universe.'

'Quite,' Fleming rejoined with an arch smile.

'Now I see that I'm boring you. That will never do. Come.' He indicated two armchairs by a table in the middle of the study. 'Let's sit down. I've been waiting for Naval Intelligence to make contact. I take it you've seen my file?'

Fleming nodded as he walked over. The Magician sighed and lowered himself slowly into his seat. A chessboard was set out on the table between them.

'Yes,' Crowley went on. 'I've done the state some service. You know that there's a long tradition of those with occult powers being employed in espionage. Doctor Dee, Queen Elizabeth's court magi-cian, was also one of her best spies, you know. She called them her "eyes", with two circles indicating this and then a number. Dee was the seventh of her "eyes", so his code sign was double-O-seven.'

'Is that so?'

'Yes. I suppose I'm secret agent 666.'

'Actually your code name in the department is the Magician.'

'Quite,' said Crowley, slightly out of breath. He began to wheeze and pulled out a Benzedrine inhaler from his pocket, taking a sharp snort in each nostril. A tear lingered in the corner of one eye. 'Sorry, it's my wretched asthma,' he explained. 'Now look, my dear boy, since you've had a good look at my file you know that what I did for your department in the last war cost me dearly. Disinformation and all that, I know. Disseminating absurd German propaganda to discredit the enemy. Worked a treat. But rather cast me as the villain. Don't think I can go through all that again.'

'Don't worry on that account. We've other plans for you.'

'Good. All the scandal, my great notoriety, it's ruined me. It's not easy being the wickedest man in the world, you know.'

'I don't suppose it is.'

'I'm an undischarged bankrupt. Like our own great realm, I'm now dependent on American support for my survival. Oh yes, my own Lend-Lease scheme. The Agape Lodge in California is providing some funds. Just had a charming letter from a new member in Pasadena. A very promising young rocket scientist, would you believe. Rather dashing, too, it seems. You see, my Order is already grooming my successor. I don't have much time, I know that. The mind's still sharp but the body, well.' He made a plaintive gesture to the picture on the easel. 'I want to finish this. Sorry if I sound pompous about it but it really could be my magnum opus.'

'A pack of cards?'

'Yes. A fitting epitaph some would say. To my sinful life.'

He bared his discoloured teeth in a rueful grin. There was sadness in his expression, but little remorse. Holding Fleming's gaze with an unfocused stare, he started to address him in a direct and intimate manner, his voice soft and hypnotic.

'You know, of course, that there was an eighth deadly sin, don't you? Oh yes, the worst of the lot. The early Christians called it *acci-die,* the sorrow of the world, a deadly lethargy and torpor of the spirit that was known to engulf whole villages in the Middle Ages. The most frightful devil of all is this noonday demon of melancholy. Boredom, my dear boy, a terrible vice, and the only one I have been truly determined to resist.'

Fleming suddenly felt as if the Magician was peering into his own soul, that he saw how disappointed he felt in life. All of its empty pleasures and futile plans of action had left him cold. He might be flippant and withdraw into a pose of detached superiority but he was endlessly taunted by the noonday demon, a sinful weariness of the heart. It was this that forced him to seek refuge in a solitary world where he plotted out his secret stories. That other life of obscure substance: the autobiography of his daydreams.

As he began to outline Crowley's designated role in Operation Mistletoe, he found himself becoming far more expansive in his briefing than was usual. He had hitherto developed a method in the handling of agents where they would be carefully kept in the dark as to the overall nature of their assignment and fed information only when it was strictly required. But with the Magician he felt that he could tell him everything. All the details of this fantastical project that had been conjured out of unofficial and increasingly bewildering interdepartmental strategies of disinformation, counter-intelligence and black propaganda. It struck him that this supremely arcane intellect alone could truly comprehend the complex absurdity of such a scheme. And no one would believe him if he ever told the tale. Crowley was himself a cypher, a hidden stone, a key to all the foolish mysteries and rumours in the world.

As Fleming spoke he watched Crowley closely, instinctively gathering intelligence for his own internal memorandum. Another brief appraisal: a version of the man's character that he could use. Crowley no longer wanted to be cast as the villain in real life, but in fiction, yes, he would make the perfect malefactor. An extravagant counterpoint to the empty hero of Fleming's private narrative.

'My dear boy,' the Magician announced when the briefing had finished. 'This is marvellous stuff! Preposterous!' He broke into a laugh that soon turned into a gasping huff. He took another double hit of his inhaler and caught his breath. 'It's . . .' he panted. 'It's completely implausible. That's the genius of it.'

'Yes,' agreed Fleming, knowing then that he was right to tell Crowley all of it. 'But you will be able to make contact with certain elements within enemy territory? Your, um, Order, it began as a German mystical society, didn't it?'

'The Ordo Templi Orientis, yes, a banned organisation in the Reich, I'm afraid. As you might know, the Nazis have been clumsily imposing their own monopoly on the dark arts. But I still have something of a network out there. Heh heh, my own Secret Service if you like.'

'And might you be able to get a man close to our subject?'

'A man, yes.' Crowley pondered. 'Or maybe a woman.'

'A woman?'

'Yes.' Crowley looked up wistfully. 'Astrid. It's been a long time but she might be just the person for this job.'

'One of your many protégées?' asked Fleming.

'Oh no,' Crowley replied with a smile. '*She* initiated *me*.'

6 / THE BOMBPROOF HOTEL

The downstairs Grill Room at the Dorchester was already crowded when Joan Miller arrived. Cabinet ministers escorting nervously respectable wives or casually disreputable mistresses, steel-grey brigadiers with hatchet-jawed adjutants, off-duty airmen and on-duty tarts, cinema producers and motor-car salesmen, American war correspondents, playboys, actresses, writers: all the high and the low who could afford it seemed to have found sanctuary from the Blitz in the supposed safety of the hotel's modernist steel and reinforced-concrete womb.

Miller struggled to assume a calm air, to attune herself to the forced gaiety that surrounded her. She had come straight from her flat to this fashionable 'bombproof' hotel with a sickening sense of anxiety and fear. Someone must have recognised her at the meeting and had marked her out as a target. An intangible danger waited for her in the blackout beyond and she was no longer quite sure whom she could trust. She spotted Fleming in conversation with Cyril Connolly and an elderly colonel, and staggered over to join them.

'Now look,' Fleming was declaiming loudly at the old soldier while gesticulating dismissively towards the short and tubby Connolly. 'This is Connolly, who publishes a perfectly ghastly magazine full of subversive nonsense by a lot of long-haired drivelling conchies who will all be put away for their own good for seven years under Section 18b. So perhaps you'd better subscribe to the thing, now you've got the chance, just to see what sort of outrageous stuff they can get away with in a country like this during wartime.'

'I see.' The colonel nodded with a vacant sagacity. 'Very interesting.'

'Got you another subscription there, Connolly,' Fleming whispered, patting the stout man on the back.

'Don't take any notice of Fleming, Colonel,' Connolly countered. 'He's become all high and mighty since he's been at the Admiralty but you know what they call him there? The Chocolate Sailor.'

Miller noticed Fleming wince slightly at this sting, then steel himself with a very deliberate grin.

'*Touché*, Cyril,' he muttered, then looked up and saw Joan. 'Must go. Oh, by the way, you don't happen to know a writer by the name of Murray Constantine, do you?'

'Constantine? Hmm, doesn't ring a bell. What's he written?'

'A queer novel called *Swastika Night*. Published by the Left Book Club.'

'Hardly your sort of thing, Ian.'

'I know, but I want to meet the author.'

'Well, I could have a word with Victor Gollancz if you like.'

'Could you?'

Connolly nodded and began to scuttle away. Fleming turned to face Joan.

'Ah, Miller,' he said. 'Glad you could make it.'

'Fleming, I need to talk to you,' she blurted out.

'Of course.' He frowned at her. 'But we'd better find Trevelyan.'

'Yes, of course,' she rejoined breathlessly.

'Is everything all right?'

'I'm fine,' she replied. 'Where's Trevelyan?'

Fleming turned and craned his neck, his jagged profile scanning the room like some massive wading bird.

'There.' He cocked his head, his broken nose pointing obliquely. 'He's with Teddy Thursby. Tory Member for Hartwell-juxta-Mare. Was a junior minister in the Department of Health until he had to resign. A Select Committee is investigating some matter of undisclosed Czech assets. He's not a very happy man. Trevelyan thinks he might have his uses.'

Miller followed Fleming's gaze to the bar where she saw Marius Trevelyan listening intently to a middle-aged man in a bow tie and double-breasted suit, with a drink-maddened face. As they shuffled their way through the throng, Fleming touched her gently on the arm and stooped slightly to whisper in her ear.

'You said you needed to talk.'

'Yes.'

'To me? Or to me and Trevelyan?'

'Well, if we could have a word in private later.'

'Certainly.'

As they came close to Trevelyan and Thursby, it seemed clear to Miller that the younger man was drawing out his drinking companion in some way. There was an unctuous passivity in the way that he indulged Thursby's hurt indignation, quietly urging him on in his anger. They caught the end of the politician's tirade.

'Winston's been a complete shit over the whole wretched business!'

'Steady on, Teddy!' Fleming announced his presence.

'Ah, Fleming.' Thursby looked up with a slightly chided expression. 'Well, I was just explaining to this young man here, you know, loyalty, it goes both ways. I stuck by the old bastard for all those years, and now?'

'I know,' Fleming replied in a consoling tone. 'Terrible show, I'm sure.'

'It's not as if I've had my hand caught in the till or anything. Just a speech here or there, a couple of questions in the House. Not declaring an interest, they call it. It's a bloody disgrace!'

'Quite,' Trevelyan interjected softly.

'You know what the worst thing there is to be these days? One of Winston's old friends. He's stabbing us all in the back now he's in power. All in the name of National Government.'

'Stabbing you in the front, it seems,' Fleming retorted.

'Exactly. Yes.' He puffed through his lips as if he had run out of steam. There was something comical in his deflated anger. Miller suddenly thought how apt his first name was. Thursby looked like a furious teddy bear. 'Well,' he went on with a sigh, 'I need another bloody drink.'

'Fleming, Miller.' Trevelyan hailed them as Thursby wandered off to the bar. 'Shall we find somewhere quiet to debrief?'

'Not yet. That.' Fleming pointed at Thursby's back and waited for the MP to get out of earshot. 'You need to keep working on that. Persuade him to say something – no, even better, *write* something just a little bit indiscreet. Maybe place an article somewhere, you know, subtly critical and full of hints about an alternative. We need to keep this anti-Churchill thing alive. Especially now.'

'Yes, good, but what shall I tell him?'

'I don't know. It's supposed to be your speciality at Political. Keep him drunk, that's the main thing. Meanwhile Miller can tell me all about this evening's lecture. I'm keen to hear an objective assessment.'

Trevelyan glanced at them both with a slight frown. He nodded and went to join Thursby at the bar. Fleming and Miller found a quiet table in the corner.

'Looks like you could do with a drink,' he said.

'Yes.' She sighed.

'I know just the thing. A martini.' He beckoned to a passing waiter.

As he ordered for them, it seemed to Miller that he was going through some sort of rehearsed performance, a precise litany of pleasure.

'Two martinis, very dry, with vodka if you have it.' He turned to her briefly. 'Gin has the taste of melancholy, I always find,' then back to the waiter: 'Three measures of spirit to one of vermouth, shake them well so that they're ice-cold. And a long thin slice of lemon peel in each. Got it?'

He watched the man nod and then tapped out a cigarette. He offered her one. She shook her head. He sparked up an elegant Ronson lighter and drew in a lungful of smoke with a satisfied hiss.

'Now then, tell me all about this witches' Sabbath,' he entreated.

'Tell me what you know first,' she countered.

He grinned but his grey-blue eyes remained impassive.

'Not my part of the operation, I'm afraid. Some barmy group of Fifth Columnists that Political is running, that's all I know. M told me you had some experience in this area. Said you're an excellent field officer too. But it's all under control, isn't it? I mean, otherwise . . .' Fleming frowned.

'Otherwise, what?'

'Otherwise M wouldn't have sent you in, would he?'

Miller couldn't be sure of Fleming but she decided that she would trust him enough to tell him what had happened. His was a cold charm but it carried some sense of integrity. Their drinks arrived. She took a sip of the chilled spirit and felt her senses relax and sharpen at the same time. She quickly recounted the events of the early evening in the manner of a succinct report, giving all the details swiftly and precisely, so as not to dwell upon the embarrassing fear she had felt at the time. He had drained his martini by the time she was finished.

'Good Lord,' he murmured, casually gesturing to the waiter once more. 'So it's not safe.'

'No,' she agreed. 'No, it isn't.'

'Right then. We'll have another drink and I'll tell you what we're going to do.'

7 / VITRIOL

It was still dark at the all-clear and they were lucky to find a taxi in the gloom of Park Lane. Fleming ordered the driver to take them to his house in Ebury Street first. There was something that he had to pick up, he told her.

She waited in the cab as he went inside. In his bedroom he took off his jacket, opened a drawer of his dresser and removed a light chamois-leather holster. He pulled its straps over his left shoulder so that it rested a hand's width below his armpit. He then reached into the drawer once more and carefully took hold of the small, flat Baby Browning .25 automatic that had been given to him when he had joined Naval Intelligence. This weapon had not been issued so much for his own use but rather for the protection of his boss, Admiral Godfrey, on such occasions that might be deemed necessary.

He slid out the clip, removed the single round in the chamber and then worked the action a couple of times. He squeezed the trigger and it made an empty click. As he began to reload the deadly little machine, he caught sight of his reflection in the looking-glass. A saturnine smile curled on the lips of his other psyche, the hollow man of his imagination. This was the persona of a dream, not one of slumber but of half-sleep, the other self that he would dwell upon at night as he waited for oblivion. He slipped the pistol into the slim purse of the shoulder-holster, giving it a gentle, reassuring pat. He put his jacket back on and went downstairs to the waiting taxi.

As he got in the car he wondered for a moment if Miller would detect any change in his demeanour. With a glance he noticed that she too wore the dull mask of those who anticipate danger or action. They made the taxi stop a street away from her flat. Fleming let Miller lead the way and show him exactly how she had gone home that evening. He followed closely, noting every detail of the route. There was a red glow in the sky from fires far to the east of the city. They stalked along the street to where she lived but there was no one about, nor could they find a clear vantage point from which her premises could be kept under surveillance.

'We'd better go in,' he said.

Her flat was on the first floor of a Georgian terrace. Fleming took the key from her and turned it slowly in the lock. He let the door swing open and took out his gun. They crept through into the living room. Miller switched on the light to reveal the figure of a man slumped in an armchair who rose swiftly to his feet, grabbing at something in his jacket pocket. Fleming raised the pistol and clicked off its safety catch.

'Now look here,' Fleming snapped in a patrician tone. 'Don't . . . Just don't do anything clever. I'm licensed to use this thing, you know.'

He winced inwardly. Not only was his statement incorrect, it was an appallingly crass line. The man faced him in a simian squat, one hand still holding something hidden in his jacket. Fleming had to stop himself from laughing at this absurd tableau. He should shoot, he mused, and the other self would have done so. The other self would have killed by now. But he hesitated, realising that the prospect of actual violence repelled him. It was not so much that he lacked courage, but that he just had far too much imagination. He made a clumsy show of pointing the gun once more.

'Come on,' he went on, struggling to find something to say that didn't sound like an awful cliché. 'Put your hands . . . um, let me see what you've got there.'

His opponent's face was contorted in a peculiar smile. A rictus of hate or fear, maybe both. The man remained still but for the hand he slowly drew from his jacket pocket. It was holding a little bottle.

'Drop it on the floor,' Fleming ordered.

As the man did so, Miller went to pick it up. It was ridged on one side and on the other was a white label. OIL OF VITRIOL, it read. She gasped and nearly dropped the thing.

'What is it?' asked Fleming.

'Acid,' she replied.

'You bastard,' Fleming spat.

'I was only going to scare her, mister. That was the plan. Just scare her.'

'Dirty little Nazi. I ought to shoot you.'

'I ain't a Nazi,' the man protested.

Fleming told him to sit down and watched him as Joan went to the bedroom to phone Special Branch. Luckily the duty officer was someone she knew and he agreed to send a couple of officers straight away. As she put the phone down she noticed a tremor in her right hand. Fleming was attempting to interrogate the intruder as she came back into the living room.

'Our little friend here actually denies he's a fascist,' Fleming told her. 'But then he would, wouldn't he?'

'Oh, I don't know,' replied Joan. 'They're usually terribly proud of it, you know, triumphant. Calling out that the invasion's coming and we'll all be on the list the Gestapo's drawn up.'

'So,' Fleming turned to the seated man. 'If you're not a quisling, what were you doing at the meeting yesterday?'

'Meeting?' The man scowled. 'What meeting?'

'Oh well,' Fleming sighed. 'Better let Special Branch give him the third degree.'

Miller frowned, trying to remember if she had actually seen the man in the basement the day before.

It was dawn by the time two plainclothes policemen came to take him away. With just the two of them in Joan's flat, all at once the mood became strangely formal. While they had kept vigil over the intruder or dealt with the official rituals of Special Branch, the atmosphere of external tension had somehow allowed for a covert intimacy. A shared smile or a reassuring glance, a fleeting moment of intense eye contact that needed no explanation. But now they were alone together, they were possessed by a peculiar awkwardness, a kind of static charge.

'I really should stay for a bit, you know,' Fleming offered hesitantly. 'You've had quite a shock.'

'Oh, I'll be all right.'

'I'd like to,' he said softly.

'What?'

'Stay.'

An attempt at a nonchalant grin smarted on his face. As she held his gaze he noted that her eyes were deep blue. Cool, direct, quizzical.

'Stay then,' she said with a shrug.

He frowned. Women are such difficult characters, he reasoned. His inner text demanded that they should be an illusion, nothing more than a thorough but simple physical description. Miller's appearance certainly fitted his ideal. She was undeniably attractive.

Wide-set eyes and high cheekbones; an elegant curve to the jaw framed by a mane of raven hair cut square to the nape of her neck; a bow-lipped mouth, full and sensual. Fleming found it easy to draw up an account with the banal symmetries of detail. But now there was too much depth to his impression of her, and he felt that he already knew her far too well. And it annoyed him that she seemed more at ease than he was.

Miller laughed.

'What is it?' he demanded.

'You look like a lost little boy.'

He suddenly felt horribly inert. He tried to empty his mind, to assume a seductive charm, but it eluded him. He was full of desire but knew that if he was unable to focus on the possibility of simple animal pleasure this urge would quickly vanish.

'Come here,' she said.

He went to her but the moment was already lost. Now she had the initiative, and this would never do. She kissed him lightly on the mouth. His lips were cold and he couldn't help but flinch slightly as she gently stroked his face with her fingers. They pulled away from each other.

'Look,' he began, not knowing what to say.

'I suppose we're both a bit on edge,' she offered. 'Aren't we?'

'Yes. I suppose.'

He offered her a cigarette and for a while they stood smoking in her living room. All at once they reverted to the casual tone of procedure, going over their report of the night's events and their implications.

'Marius Trevelyan's cover is now blown too, of course,' Fleming remarked. 'Though maybe this incident could be used to provide what Political wants. You know, a demonstration that the Link is still active.'

'Yes, but—' Miller stubbed out her cigarette, grinding it into the ashtray as an odd thought throbbed. 'What if—' She shook her head, at once unsure where her thoughts were leading, and broke into a yawn.

'I'd better let you get some sleep,' said Fleming.

'There's hardly much time for that,' Miller murmured.

For a moment there was something strikingly vague in her expression, a marvellous vacancy in her eyes. But no, Fleming realised bitterly, she was thinking about something. He suddenly felt the strong urge to be on his own.

'I'd better be off,' he told her.

'Very well then.'

She walked with him to the door.

'Thank you,' she said.

'What for?'

'For tonight. For dealing with that awful man.'

Fleming walked home through streets strewn with rubble and debris. Piles of bricks here and there, heaps of broken glass swept into the gutters. Scraps of paper fluttered through the smoke-scented air; the morning birdsong trilled harsh and neurotic. He passed a ruined house that was not much more than a scorched shell, yet it revealed part of one wall still intact, with wallpaper, fireplace and a framed print still tacked above the mantelpiece. The city turned upside down, all of its secrets rudely shaken out.

Visita Interiora Terrae Rectificando Invenies Occultum Lapidem. The rhythm of his stride tapped out its maddening aubade. His mind was hungry for dreams. Reality was always far too complicated. He felt a quiet fury at how action had once more been frustrated by doubts of conscience and official procedure. The hesitation when he'd pointed the gun, all the bother of waiting for the Special Branch to turn up, the banal chatter with Miller. Why couldn't he have just killed the man and made love to the woman? Already he was returning to his mental refuge, the simple narrative of fantasy. Soon he would be trapped in the martial bureaucracy of Room 39, or sulking in his study where his rare books would taunt him from their shelves. But for now he had a storehouse of ideas, of characters and settings, and he would save them up. For the day when he came to write it all down.

*   *   *

Miller washed her face and walked into the bedroom. As she pulled back the heavy blackout curtain, a column of light slowly stretched across the floor. Her eyes watered slightly as she blinked against the brightness. She looked at herself in the mirror, a trace of a smile on her pale lips. Fleming's diffidence had made her bold. She had enjoyed playing with him. She might even have slept with him if he'd been brave enough to stay. She picked up a lipstick and held it to her mouth. Her hand trembled. What had she been thinking earlier? About the Political Warfare Executive, that was it, the strange notion she had had that maybe they had set up the whole incident. An outlandish idea but there were some things that just didn't seem to make sense. She finished applying the deep red to her lips and then pouted at her image in the looking-glass. As she put the lipstick down she noticed a trace of white on the dresser. At first she thought that she must have spilt some powder there. As she looked again she saw that it was the letter M lightly chalked on the polished woodwork.

8 / DEBRIEFING

M made a show of casually filling his pipe when she entered but he was looking up at her all the time. She knew that he would be carefully gauging her expression, noting her reactions to any comment or gesture. He had often said that he could read her mind. It had been something of an endearing joke between them. He certainly believed in the faculty of extrasensory perception. It had now become the instinct of a bitter intimacy. And yet the most shocking thing about the whole affair was that she still felt a lingering affection for him. His very duplicity gifted him with an indestructible charm. Perhaps it was this quality that had attracted her to him in the first place. It had certainly made him a formidable spymaster. He intrigued and exasperated her and yet she felt a protective anxiety about him. She knew that deep down he was more scared than she could ever be.

'I've had a good look through the Special Branch report,' M declared, tapping the cardboard dossier on his desk. 'Anything you'd like to add?'

She had prepared herself thoroughly for this strangest of debriefings. She knew that it would be a coded match, that to say anything explicit would be dangerous. She tried to judge what signals to give.

'Well, I did voice my concerns about my suitability for field work in this area, M.'

'And you were absolutely right, Joan. I mean, you could find yourself in danger again, couldn't you?'

She tried to react as calmly as possible to this tacit threat. She knew now that he had set the whole thing up as a message to her. A warning shot. Despite the implied brutality, she felt sure that he did not mean her any real harm. It was merely a petulant reminder of his power over her. Now they were caught up in a self-generating algebra of distrust. A farcical algorithm: that she knew that he knew that she knew that he knew and so on. She had to find a way out of that, to let him know that she could keep a secret.

'There's been a security risk,' she offered. 'And we'll have to proceed with extreme caution.'

'My thoughts exactly,' M rejoined.

'The important thing is that proper cover is maintained, for everyone in the department. For this operation and any other.'

'Yes,' M agreed with a thoughtful nod. 'Proper cover must be maintained.'

Of course she had been his cover for that long double game of his life. She loathed the deception that he had practised on her but could not help but respect the way that he had carried it out. This capacity for deceit and utter ruthlessness had become necessary for the times they lived in.

'It's been a wretched business, Joan,' M said with a thin smile. 'But you've acted with initiative and, might I say, with extreme discretion. I'd like to put you out of harm's way for a while. You're due a bit of leave. Take a couple of days off.'

'That's hardly necessary, M.'

'Please,' he insisted. 'It'll be for the best.'

'Very well then. Thank you.'

It would give her time to think, she reasoned. She could not go on being his cover for much longer but to ask for a transfer now would never do. She would have to find someone to replace her first. She took a good look at Maxwell Knight. The epitome of the English gentleman of a certain class, the finest dissembler on the face of the earth. He could lie from the depths of his soul. His flair for espionage was at one with his odd occult beliefs and clandestine sexuality. But it suddenly struck her that this perfidious world could one day be tricked by its own guile. That this theatre of treachery, of disinformation and counter-intelligence would inevitably deceive itself. M put his pipe to his mouth, clenched his teeth around it and lit a match.

'Now,' he puffed, drawing in the flame, his gaunt visage wreathed in smoke, '17F should be here by now. Can you show him in?'

Joan stood up and walked to the door. She was light-headed from lack of sleep. Her nerves were shot but she knew that she had to keep calm and carry on. Like everybody else. A minor character in the drama, playing out the simple surface rituals. Going out into the ante-room to engage in a silly flirtation with the handsome commander from Naval Intelligence.

2

the female pope

When Anna asks you about your sister, you know it's serious.

And this is your chance to make your confession. To tell the story of Jenny.

The sister you got rid of all those years ago.

Jenny was the creative one in the family, you say. We grew up in the suburbs, a nice upbringing but, you know, boring. Jenny always made things seem more exciting than they really were. She was a punk before anybody else we knew. She went to Slough Art School and then dropped out in the second term. She left home and moved to London.

You stop for a moment and glance across the table at her. Anna Guttridge. A harsh name for someone so pretty. You met her at Andy Begg's party. You flirted with her and she seemed interested. You talked about the 1980s: it's some sort of project of hers. You meet for a drink and it turns out that she's a writer, researching a book on the New Romantic scene or something. And she knows about your sister. Usually Jenny gets written out of that story. Maybe because she never played the game with the press. And it's her voice in your head, saying: Johnny, she's a journalist, of course she seems interested in you, but she's only interested in the story. You want to reply that you can't help yourself, that you have to take every chance you can get. It's not easy, you know. Jenny never foresaw how hard it would be for you. To get close to people.

And in order to get close to anyone you'll eventually have to tell them what happened to your sister. What you did to her. And you hope, well, maybe this time they'll understand. At least Anna seems interested in Jenny in the first place. And despite everything you do want to keep her memory alive. You owe her that much. You continue: in 1978, 1979, Jenny was moving around. She ended up squatting in this big terraced house in Islington. She was singing in a few short-lived punk bands.

Where did she get the name Pirate Jenny? Anna asks. You tell her that it came from this Bertolt Brecht/Kurt Weill song about a servant girl in a port town who dreams the pirates are going to come and kill all her masters. Jenny used to say that our only honest sense of utopia is dreaming of a dystopia for our enemies, that we want vengeance as much as we want redemption. Anyway, she'd got hold of this buccaneer outfit that had been hired from Berman's and Nathan's in Shaftesbury Avenue and never taken back. This was a good two years before Vivienne Westwood had a runway show of her first pirate collection and well before Adam Ant started his swashbuckling act. Sartorially, Jenny was way ahead of the game. And in other ways, too.

How? Anna asks, and you watch the quizzical curl of her top lip, the blue-green eyes that seem slightly out of focus, a smatter of tiny freckles around her nose. You marvel at the beautiful curiosity of her face.

Well, you know, right after punk no one was sure what was going to happen. Jenny had plenty of ideas. Then Anna asks: and where were you around this time?

And there's that voice again. The voice in your head telling you to be careful. Jenny's voice. She's still looking out for you, despite what you did to her. You've got to be careful how you tell her story. You don't want to scare Anna off. You got away with it after all these years but you still remember those questioning looks you used to get when you first started going out after she disappeared. The looks you still get sometimes.

Oh, I was still living at home, you say. I used to go up and stay with Jenny some weekends. When she got the band together, you know, Black Freighter, I used to roadie for them.

This is not quite the truth but not exactly a lie either.

Black Freighter, right. Danny Osiris's first band.

Oh no, you correct her. It was always Jenny's band.

Sorry, it's just—

I know. Danny's such a big star now. But back then he was still Danny Ogungbe. It was odd because when they met they were living in the same street. Almost next door to each other. With a Nigerian father and a Polish mother, Danny was a working-class soul boy who still lived with his parents in a two-room flat with no bath and an outside toilet. That part of Islington was pretty squalid back then. That's why there were so many squats in the area, you know, a lot of empty houses declared substandard by the council. Anyway, Danny was a bright kid and very good-looking – the combination of African features with pale skin and fair hair made him appear quite other-wordly. He'd grown up on the wrong side of the Essex Road but he was full of dreams. He'd done acting classes at the Anna Scher school and had taught himself to play jazz-funk on a battered old Fender copy. And he had this fantastic soul voice. He started going around to Jenny's squat to practise. They both knew other musicians so a band began to take shape. It was Jenny's idea at first, it was her project. The Black Freighter was a ship of fools come to liberate the world from reason. She'd got hold of a Minimoog, one of those early analogue synthesisers that played only one note at a time, which was actually ideal for Jenny. She was never that musi-cal, you see. But she was full of ideas and she wrote fantastic lyrics. The idea was to be adventurous without being self-indulgent. They were plugged into that post-punk, year-zero feel.

But Black Freighter didn't last very long, did it?

No. Jenny always wanted to be experimental. Danny, well, he had his eye on the main chance. Who can blame him?

So was it musical differences that split the band up?

That old cliché. No, it wasn't that. Jenny and Danny carried on writing together even after the band fell apart. That bit always worked, you know, his music, her lyrics. No, it was in the attitude that they parted company.

The attitude? Anna asks. She has thick, dark eyebrows that inter-sect in this fantastic frown. And you wonder about her attitude. She's intrigued by you, you can feel it. But maybe she suspects something.

Yeah, the attitude, you repeat. Jenny was more into a sort of performance art aesthetic. She became part of the gender-bender scene, except she took it one step further. Boy George and Marilyn had this simple gestalt, you know, boy looks like girl. Jenny liked to dress so that no one could tell if she was a boyish girl or a girlish boy. She wanted to keep them guessing. The pirate has no boundaries, she used to say.

That's cool.

You look straight into her turquoise eyes and watch the inky pupils dilate. You search for some sort of signal from her. Like a lovelorn teenager. But then you are a late starter. You've had a sort of second adolescence in your thirties. At an age when most people are ready for a mid-life crisis, you're still stuck in puberty.

Tell me about that time, she says, holding your stare.

Why are you interested in this stuff?

Well, it's fascinating, I guess.

And it strikes you that maybe she thinks you're gay. It's a common enough mistake: people see the goatee, check the slightly fey demeanour. Maybe her interest in you is just a faghag thing.

Yeah, well, Jenny could get extreme about gender politics but she was an idealist really. She dreamt of a world where none of it would matter. She spent a lot of time in the clubs, you know, Billy's and the Blitz. The beginning of that New Romantic thing was fabulous.

And that's when she ended up in the David Bowie video?

You laugh out loud.

What? she demands.

And you love the way she can smile and frown at the same time. And you want to tell her everything.

Look, Anna, you say. About gender politics.

You stop. You feel that you're about to make a complete fool of yourself. You know you've got to be careful. If she finds out too early it could blow everything. You stand up.

What is it?

You want to say, but you're not ready yet.

I've got to go, you tell her.

Johnny, whatever's the matter?

You start walking and she follows you out of the bar. Outside on the street you turn to her.

Look, this is really stupid. I know you're only really interested in Jenny but—

But what?

I'm interested in you, Anna.

She smiles.

Well, the feeling's mutual.

Yeah? You can hardly believe it.

Yeah.

And she kisses you gently on the lips. You get all excited but you know you've got to take your time over this.

Then meet me here tomorrow night, you tell her. And I'll tell you the story about the David Bowie video.

The next night you pick up where you'd left off.

It was a complete disaster, you say.

What happened?

Bowie had come down to Blitz one night, unannounced. Can you imagine? There was an uproar. Every single person in that club would have had his poster on their bedroom wall as a kid. He'd been sneaked in around the back and was upstairs in a private room. Everyone wanted to go up and see him. Especially when word got round that he was looking for people to appear in his next video. Jenny was in with Steve Strange, you know, who ran Blitz. He'd already been picked, so she managed to blag her way in. It had been decided that the costumes should be space-age ecclesiastical: dark flowing robes and gothic headgear. Jenny got into a conversation about Gnosticism with Bowie. She told him how she knew that his song 'Station to Station' was about the Kabbalah, and mentioned some other occult influences in his work, the Crowley references and so on. He was impressed, if a little wary. She got chosen to be in the video.

The pick-up was for six o'clock the following morning outside the Park Lane Hilton. The club didn't close till two-thirty so Jenny just took a bit more speed and kept going until dawn. So, she was a bit wired when the coach turned up to take them to the location, which was on a beach in Southend. Bowie was in a pierrot costume, walking along the shoreline, followed by Steve Strange, Jenny, and two other girls in their robes with a bulldozer coming up in the rear. It was a simple enough set-up but it needed to be precise so people had to concentrate and follow their marks. Jenny was very talkative, from the excitement, the lack of sleep, the amphetamines, and, well, she was going a little bit mad. At first she was charming, you know, raising the energy of the shoot. Clever, too, she talked about the costumes and their meanings. She started to bang on about archetypes, saying Bowie was the Fool in his jester's motley and she was the Female Pope in her ceremonial gown.

She soon began to get tiresome. In between takes she insisted on engaging Bowie in an intense conversation that he clearly wasn't keen on. Jenny had no idea how annoying her behaviour was becoming. The final straw was talking to Bowie about the notorious incident at Victoria Station in 1976, when it was alleged that he had made a Nazi salute. Well, he certainly didn't want to be reminded of that. But in some mad way Jenny thought she was reassuring him, like she was doing him a favour by bringing it up. She announced rather grandly to him that she knew that it hadn't been a fascist gesture he was making, that it was the sign of Baphomet.

The sign of Baphomet?

Yeah, it's some hermetic thing. You raise your hand towards heaven, then you lower it to point to the earth. It's supposed to connect the two. It means: as above, so below, or something like that. From Kether to Malkuth, she kept chanting. There she was, manically demonstrating this sacred *sieg heil* to David Bowie on a beach in Southend. Well, that was it. She was hustled off the set and paid off with the fifty-pound fee. She never actually appeared in the video, though her memory distorts on that one. She was convinced it was her up there, and when 'Ashes to Ashes' came out, she even told everyone she had helped with the choreography. There's this bit where Steve Strange lifts his arm and makes this bowing movement. But it isn't the sign of Baphomet. He's moving the hem of his robe so it doesn't get caught in the shovel of the bulldozer.

She smiles. You check out how she looks at you. That flicker in her eyes. You're sure now that she really does find you attractive. You do look good, after all. Pretty more than handsome, but that's probably what she's into. It's just your confidence that's the problem.

After that Jenny started acting really weird, you say.

What happened? she asks.

She started wandering around in a trance in her high-priestess drag. Taking too much speed, not sleeping, making scenes.

And it all catches up with you for a second.

It was, you give a little shrug as if trying to shake something off. Embarrassing.

You notice that Anna Guttridge has this look of concern on her face. You know, you can play this for sympathy but you can't help but feel a kind of guilt. Which is stupid.

I tried to talk to her, you say. I tried to get her to calm down, but she wouldn't listen to me, not back then.

And the voice in your head adds: oh, but she listened to you in the end, didn't she, Johnny boy?

She told people that she'd been consecrated in a Gnostic Mass, performed by the Holy Fool before a juggernaut god. She declared that she was the Female Pope, come to save humanity.

What's with this Female Pope?

Well, you know, there was supposed to be a woman pope. Sometime in the eleventh century. Pope Joan.

Wow.

Yeah. And you can imagine how Jenny loved that idea. She came up with this mad belief system of her own. She called it matriarchy. It was all about the reversal of power. The Female Pope was like a direct assault on patriarchy, attacking it at its highest point. The world had to be turned upside down, she insisted, then we'd have utopia.

Sounds interesting.

And suddenly you feel angry. At Jenny. At yourself.

Oh, yes, it was interesting. There is a catch in your voice. It was interesting when she was picked up babbling incoherently to the ducks in Regent's Park at four o'clock in the morning. It was interesting when I found her in a pool of her own vomit after she'd OD'ed in the squat.

Another pause.

It must have been hard for you.

Yeah.

And you realise now how much grief you still feel about Jenny. It was so clear at the time. Rational. You want to explain to Anna how it all made perfect sense. That after Jenny's last suicide attempt failed she asked for your help. And you promised that you would help her do it properly. But you can't tell Anna that. Not yet.

You were close to her? she asks you.

Yeah, you say with a smile, trying to make sense of the idea. But she was far away from me.

How do you mean?

I was always somewhere in the background. Her shadow, if you like.

And what is it like now?

What?

Now that she's, you know—

Officially missing?

Yeah.

Well, Jenny never did anything completely officially. Not even her disappearing act.

Were you jealous of her?

Oh no. If anything it was the other way round.

You hope that Anna will be able to understand what happened. You need a bit of time to unravel it all for her. To unroll the scroll. You decide to tell her about Danny. Everybody wants to know about Danny Osiris.

It was Danny who helped her through the worst of those bad times, you say. He'd got himself a manager and a solo record contract. All that street credibility and bohemian chaos had never really appealed to him. He'd seen enough squalor as a kid. He wanted real success. And he knew that he needed Jenny to help him get there. They spent the first winter of the new decade writing what would become the *Up Above, Down Below* album. Musically, Danny knew exactly what he was doing; I mean, the album sounds pretty middle of the road now but it was so, I don't know, calculated. It's the lyrics that make it special. They have a deep romantic melancholia that was way beyond him. And there's a tone and vibration in his voice that he got from her. Before that it was all technique. She taught him how to sing like a man, the real sadness of that sound. He got something else as well. It's hard to explain in any terms other than the metaphysical. This will sound slightly ridiculous.

Try me.

Danny needed someone to sell his soul to. See? I told you. When I say this, people think that I mean selling out, but that never bothered him. Danny was clever enough to know that there was going to be two types of eighties – you know, the squats, the riots, the warehouse parties, and then the yuppies, the big bang and selling off the family silver. And he was sharp enough to know it was going to be a one-horse race. He knew all about compromise, but this was more than that. It was an energy he needed. A magical energy.

He believed in magic?

Oh, they both did. Jenny always said she merely respected the Western esoteric tradition but there was plenty of ritual and hocus-pocus with those two. I mean, pop music is so tricky, so seemingly insubstantial. A good recording session is always a bit like a seance, you're channelling something. And when it works it's like casting a spell. Danny definitely needed Jenny's energy. I mean, he was having his own problems with identity.

Really?

I suppose you want to know all about that.

No. Not really.

Oh, come on. The enigmatic Danny Osiris. The press are always speculating, you know: is he or isn't he?

I'm not really interested in that, honestly.

Well, most people are. Of course Danny knew, when he became

a big star, especially when he moved to LA, that the important thing was to keep a sense of mystique. America is essentially a puritan nation. Besides, the great artist who's a little bit repressed, that's always going to be more interesting than someone who's completely open about themselves. It's all about dreams, isn't it? Hidden desires. Jenny always wanted more than that.

And what did happen to Jenny?

Oh, well, that is a mystery. But anyway, most people want to know about Danny. He's the one that became the superstar, after all.

I'm more interested in Jenny.

Well, they parted company, her and Danny. Sometime in the mid-1980s. On Tottenham Court Road, as it happened. They were both walking past that Church of Scientology place, you know, where those disciples hustle outside and try to get you to go in for a free personality test. Well, they both went in. Just a laugh. Or so Jenny thought. Turns out Danny took their bullshit seriously. Signed up on the spot.

That was the end of it. Jenny thought it was all just too ridiculous, while Danny didn't need Pirate Jenny any more. He didn't need the Female Pope. He'd found a more established religion. Always had an instinct for the main chance, Danny, even when it came to the paranormal. And it turned out to be very useful for him in the long run. Especially when he got to LA. Fantastic for contacts in the business, and especially when he started getting acting work. And now with these rumours about Danny's sexuality, Scientology's been a kind of protective network. Anyway, back in 1987, Danny goes off to the States, and Jenny disappears somewhere else.

You really don't know where she is?

Nope. That's enough of Jenny for now. Let's talk about Johnny. And Anna.

She smiles. And you have this happy feeling of anticipation. You can get to know her better. Then you'll be able to tell her the whole story.

There is just one thing, though, she says.

What?

There's someone else Jenny knew then that I'm really interested in.

Oh yeah? You feel a sudden stab of dread from somewhere. Who?

Vita Lampada.

Oh.

You try to keep calm, not to react, but she's bound to see the panic in your eyes.

Vita, yeah, you mumble. Well, Jenny knew her, yes.

And you think: oh Christ, she already knows. So she knows all about what happened to Jenny. For all this time she's been playing some sort of game with you. You force a laugh and try to make light of it all.

What do you want to know about that old tranny?

You try to smile but you know. She's on to you.

She died in suspicious circumstances, says Anna.

So they say.

And Jenny was close to her near the end.

I don't know about that.

Don't you?

Anna's curiosity has narrowed into an inquisitive squint.

I don't understand, you protest.

She smiles and her face opens up once more.

Look, Johnny, she says with a sigh. I should have told you before. I'm doing a story on Vita Lampada.

I thought this was about the New Romantics.

That's a part of it, of course. But it's Vita's story I'm interested in.

So you know what happened to Jenny.

No, I—

Come on, you knew all along. And I actually thought you were interested in me.

What?

I thought you wanted to get to know me. Instead you've just used me for your own purposes.

No. I really like you, Johnny.

I'm just part of your research, you mean. I suppose this has been a lot of fun, hasn't it? Digging up the past. My past. But I do exist now, you know.

What?

She's looking all wide-eyed and innocent but you don't buy it.

Whatever you might think, you tell her, Johnny is a real person.

Of course he is, I mean, you are.

Do you have any idea how difficult it is just to be me?

Johnny—

You get up from the table and stare down at her.

A lot of people say that Pope Joan didn't exist, you tell her. You know, modern scholars, they dismiss the whole Female Pope story as a medieval legend. A crazy idea dreamt up to ridicule the papacy. Or maybe a feminist rewriting of history. Wishful thinking. And what's wrong with that? The fact is that there is no record of a Pope John the twentieth. The succession goes straight from the nineteenth to the twenty-first. So there is a gap there. There's always a gap in history. And that's where some of us live.

Anna Guttridge gazes up at you, bewildered. Like she has no idea what you're talking about. You don't care. You turn around and walk out with the sincere hope that you'll never see her again.

You get back to your flat and you're still full of anger and self-doubt. What really hurts is that you've been made to feel false, even though it is you who have been deceived. You've been made to feel guilty and that's unforgivable. There's a message on the answerphone from Anna, asking you to call her. You ignore it. You're like some stupid kid. Jenny would never have fallen for this sort of bullshit. She would have seen right through that scheming bitch, you tell yourself. But you? You sigh. You remind yourself that you're a late starter. And you've got a lot of catching up to do.

You pick up the phone and call Danny Osiris in Los Angeles. It's three in the afternoon there, and Danny sounds terrible, scarcely articulate. You ask him whether he still has the document that Vita stole from Marius Trevelyan. He says yes and you tell him to find a safe place for it.

Then you try to relax. You remember what your therapist said: that for somebody to love the person inside of you, you have to have a clear and centred sense of yourself that doesn't depend on anybody else. You have to be strong there, to know who you are. And you can allow yourself to miss Jenny. You know, getting rid of the body, that was easy. Burying the rest of her, now that was the hard part. You cry a little and it makes you feel better. You manage to get some sleep.

You wake up feeling stronger. You realise that it doesn't matter what Anna knows about you. Or what anybody else knows or suspects. You can deal with it. There's another message from Anna. This time you call her back.

You arrange to go around to her place in the evening. You dress casually, but carefully. T-shirt and loose-fit jeans, leather boots, leather jacket, tough-guy stuff. Butch drag, as Jenny would have called it. But you mean to mean business. And you're packing something special. A little surprise for Anna.

And you take around a bottle of red wine. You know you'll need a drink. Anna shows you into her little one-bedroom flat; you open the wine. You both get a little drunk. There's this tension in the air. A buzz of potential charging up.

I don't appreciate the way that I've been used, you say. It's humiliating.

I said I'm sorry.

The way you flirted with me. What was that? A journalist's trick to get information?

No. Well, not entirely.

Still playing games.

Why can't you believe that I might actually like you?

Oh, please. I mean, you know, don't you? About me.

About you?

About Jenny and me. This ridiculous brother and sister act I've been playing.

I have no idea what you're talking about.

I find that hard to believe. Anyway, you wanted to know about Vita Lampada.

Only if you want to talk about it.

Yeah, well. That poor queen got involved in some serious stuff. Vita was a strange one. She was part of the New Romantic scene but always looked out of place. She was like an old-school tranny in the middle of all these fashionable gender benders. She used to get a lot of stick. Jenny liked her, respected her. They had a fellow feeling, you know? They both felt that they didn't really belong. Jenny always said that she was stateless, and that's what made her a pirate. But Vita and her were travelling together. Just in opposite directions. They met halfway. Vita had had an interesting life. A bit of a con artist, but clever with it. She had a great imagination. She was a fantasist really. I mean, she loved the form, you know, fantasy, science fiction, anything other-worldly. It was where she felt at home, I guess.

Is that why she liked the New Romantics?

The funny thing was she said near the end that she knew what Spandau Ballet meant. Robert Elms, the writer, he'd come up with the name of the band after seeing some graffiti on a wall in Germany. But Vita reckoned she knew what it meant. It was something she'd learnt from that Secret Service guy she picked up.

Marius Trevelyan?

Yeah. Silly cow tricked up this old punter in Shepherd Market and stole his briefcase. Turns out he's high up in British Intelligence. Well, she was really in trouble after that. Anyway, she had heard him say something about Spandau. It was that prison in Berlin where they put all the big Nazis that they didn't hang. Trevelyan told her that it was like a dance.

What did he mean?

Cold War stuff, I suppose. Spandau was the last institution governed by the Four-Power Authority – you know, the system that the different occupying forces used in Germany after the war. Control of the prison would rotate. That was the ballet, apparently. It made the place an important point of contact between East and West. But look, Vita might have been making all this up. Her imagination could be very vivid. She had this document that had been in the briefcase, some sort of manuscript. She gave it to Jenny to look after.

What happened to it?

Well, after Vita committed suicide, or was killed or whatever, Jenny got scared. She knew she had to get rid of this thing. So she sent it to Danny. He was in the States by then and he had the resources to put it somewhere safe.

And then Jenny disappeared.

Yeah.

Don't you think that's suspicious?

Oh come on, Anna, you know what happened to Jenny.

No, Johnny, I don't.

You look her in the eyes and you know she's telling the truth. And you laugh out loud.

Christ, you're not much of an investigative journalist, are you?

She doesn't know what to say. Her face opens up with that beautiful curiosity once more. At last you've got the upper hand and you know what you have to do.

Do you want to know? you ask her.

She nods. Looks kind of scared. Maybe it's the expression on your face. You must be looking a bit wild about the eyes.

Come here, you tell her.

You're standing close together in the room, both of you feeling this intense nervous energy. But you're in control now and she's staring at you, bewildered. Fear in her eyes. And desire, you're sure of it.

You kiss her. She lets out a little gasp as you pull back to look her in the eyes once more. Her hand comes up and strokes your chest gently. You take hold of it. Press it flat against your heart.

You see, you murmur, almost to yourself. I am real.

You kiss her again and let go of her hand. It snakes around to hold your back. You feel her breasts push against you, her hips shifting slightly, rubbing softly against yours.

Wait, you say, and push her away from you.

You pull your T-shirt over your head.

Look, you say, baring your chest to her, showing her the horizontal scars along the lower edge of your pectorals.

You see, Jenny got tired of trying to change the world. So she changed herself.

You unbuckle your belt and pull your jeans and boxer shorts down.

And she became the person she had always been. Me. Here, you say, taking hold of your penis. It's beautiful, isn't it? I mean, aesthetically.

She's glaring at it, eyes wide.

I'm very proud of it. It's my favourite one. Custom built, you know. I had three fittings at this place in Amsterdam. Here, have a closer look.

And you gently detach it. It fits so neatly and you can hardly notice the extra-lightweight transparent harness that lightly girdles your hips.

Cyberskin, you tell her. A blend of five different silicone materials with a flexible rod at its core. Its even got an internal urinary tube so I can piss with it standing up if I want to. I didn't want genital reconstruction surgery, well, not until they can come up with something you can fuck with properly. This, you say, holding it up, well, it's an improvement on nature. It's real enough. Like the rest of me.

I was Jenny, you say. Now I'm Johnny. Now love me for what I am.

3

the empress

There is an art to forgetting. History soon becomes dementia, a babble of voices clamouring to be heard. One has to have a selective memory to make any sense of the past. To forget is a cautious act of the will, more the gaining of a faculty than the loss of one. And through all the long days of his confinement, he had made it his study, his device. A trick. Revenge on the clever ones that had tricked him. Over the years there had been so many occasions when he had methodically assumed a state of amnesia that even he was unsure whether it was faked or not. And then he would have to work his way back to the beginning.

Memory: this is how we travel in time. Backwards and forwards, trying to escape the prison of present consciousness. Forgetfulness was his liberation. His retreat. His place of refuge. This secret world with no official record.

Half his life had seemed a preparation for senility. Now he truly felt as old as Methuselah, sitting in the summerhouse, waiting for the end. He had long wondered if old age might grant him its promised release from recollection. A true oblivion after all his long days of pretence. But time had its own trick to play on him. His mind was almost as sharp as the night on which he had made his flight nearly fifty years earlier. Now he was ready to fly once more, he decided. He could go right back. It was all as bright and vivid as ever.

A childhood in Egypt. Alexandria. The nights in Ibrahimieh, in a garden by the desert with its rich evening scent of violet, anemone and narcissus. He would walk out with his mother beneath the vast celestial canopy. She was the empress then, the queen of his universe. She would trace the shapes of constellations that wheeled above and pick out the brighter stars, naming them for him in a magical incantation: Vega, Cassiopeia, Aldebaran. Pointing to the wandering planets, she would tell him that the heavenly bodies had fixed courses, which mapped each lifetime that passed below. You will be a bright star one day, Rudi, she promised.

The days brought a harsher light to their quiet suburb of Alexandria, the fierce sun with its burning-glass focus. The chamsin wind conjured sandstorms and a salt breath to the air as it foamed the waves of the sea beyond. He would hide from the sunlight as it threatened to darken the olive skin he had inherited from his Greek mother. His father recounted the country of his golden ancestors. 'We have our place in the sun, Rudi,' he was told, an echo of something that had recently been said by the Emperor, 'but remember you have a homeland. Your fatherland.'

One afternoon he noticed a thin Greek man in the street outside their house, standing absolutely motionless at a slight angle to the universe. Remembering his manners, he asked the man if he might help him. The Greek gave him an absurdly beatific smile.

'I walked here by chance,' the man told him and pointed up at a balcony across the street. 'I used to visit here when I was young. Now this one and the next one are rented as commercial offices. Ah! The room, the Turkish rug, the shelf with two yellow vases.'

Rudi pointed to the villa of his family. 'We live there,' he said.

'Yes, yes,' the Greek replied absently, shielding his eyes with a hand as he looked up at the window opposite.

'Soon we will be leaving.'

The man turned to look down at him.

'Leaving?'

'For Europe.'

The Greek laughed.

'Perhaps it's Alexandria that's leaving.'

'That's silly.'

'Yes it is, isn't it?' The man sighed and began to wander away, gazing up one last time to study the wall of the house beyond, the balcony, the window. 'But when you go, bid farewell to the Alexandria you are losing.'

The heat had become unforgiving and he imagined, as he often did, a cold land far to the north. A mythical island set in a frozen sea. He dreamt of a black sun, an opening in the sky, a cool tunnel that he might fly through to the pure Arctic wastes. Even from the beginning he had longed for flight.

He was twelve when they left Egypt. They took a steamer from the port and he stood on deck with his father who pointed out the column of Pompeius and the lighthouse built by Alexander the Great. 'Take a long look at that land,' he told Rudi. 'You won't see it for many years to come.' He thought of the Greek man in the straw hat as he watched the coastline slowly recede from sight.

This was his first attempt at the art of forgetting: that the home of his childhood could become an immemorial dream. An ancient myth. At boarding school in Germany he was awkward and conscious of his Levantine looks, his delicate manner. His classmates mocked his oily black hair and beetle brows, calling him 'The Egyptian'. He grew determined to prove his bond with his father's land, adopting a strict sense of patriotism. He learnt the Fleet Calendar by heart and could recite the statistics of all the principal imperial battleships. He developed a passion for astronomy, to understand the stars he had observed with his mother, though it was made clear that he was expected to follow his father in the family export business.

Then the Great War came and liberated him from the tedious trade of commerce. 'Rejoice with me,' he wrote to his family when he had enlisted in the 1st Bavarian Foot, 'I am an infantryman.' Through pitch-black nights he crouched in the sunken mud-filled trenches, watching the old fighters squat among the milk-white faces of lads who, a few days before, garlanded with flowers and singing, had marched away through the streets of home. In the glaring lights of rockets and star shells, the youngsters gazed bemused at their fellows lying so still through the bombardment. Despite the dreadful noise, the awful scent of putrefaction mingled with the acrid clouds of gas and high explosive, comrades would huddle together and find a bitter comfort, each man gently leaning on a friend, seeking out a respite from the terror.

One cold morning, gazing up over the rim of the trench, he spied a formation of aeroplanes glinting in the dawn light. Like watching heavenly angels from an open grave, he mused with a smile. He knew then where hope belonged: in the sky.

At Verdun he took a shrapnel wound and was sent to a hospital at Bad Homburg. On convalescent leave he applied for a transfer to the Flying Corps. He was turned down and posted to a reserve regiment on the Eastern Front. Here he was injured once more: a Romanian bullet went right through him, missing his heart and his spine by a finger's breadth. It was after he recovered from this, in the very last year of the war, that he was accepted into the imperial air force.

Flight! Yes, it came so naturally to him. His calling, his mission in the world. The sky was his element. Mankind's future would be determined in the air, he decided, just as its destiny was written in the stars beyond. A war in heaven would end all arguments. He flew reconnaissance sorties for the final offensive on the Western Front.

And then came the terrible betrayal. Armistice and surrender. The shameful peace in the Hall of Mirrors. So it had all been in vain, he wept, all the sacrifices and privations just for a band of criminals to get their filthy hands on the country. No more Empire. No more Emperor. Revolt and starvation: mutiny in the ports, bread riots in the capital. All reason would now be forgotten. The only hope was to cherish hatred and nurture revenge.

He arrived in Munich the following spring at the height of the Bavarian Soviet. A degenerate utopia had been instituted, a comic opera of anarchists and café intellectuals who staged peace festivals and composed revolutionary hymns. A self-appointed Commissar of Public Instruction ordered an end to the study of history – 'that enemy of civilisation'; a Governor of Finance declared himself in favour of the abolition of money; the new Foreign Minister had only recently been discharged from a mental institution and tested even the extreme radicalism of his colleagues by declaring war on Switzerland and Württemberg.

But there were meetings of a secret club in private rooms of the Four Seasons Hotel: a mystical society that called for a new dawn of blood and honour. Members had to prove that they had no Jewish ancestry for at least three generations. He was deeply anxious that his appearance might not pass muster: there was open criticism of exotic features, suspicion of dark complexions, even of excessive hairiness. But when he cautiously explained that he was half Greek he was admitted warmly into the fold. It was explained to him that the name of this cultural order, the Thule Society, referred to a Greek name for the ancient Arctic homeland of the Aryans, a Hyperborean Atlantis of godlike men. This was the meaning of his childhood dream! The wondrous infantile prophecy of the cold land of the North, with a holy symbol of a black sun. That he had been born in Alexandria no longer caused him embarrassment. Egypt, declared one of the speakers, had been the home of sacred wisdom, a true religion of hermetic magic that had been corrupted by Judaism. 'The Jews are the slave-race who stole the ancient knowledge,' the man insisted contemptuously. 'The Jews are the excrement of Egypt!'

Other candidates for membership were not granted such hospitality. A young count had his application to the Thule Society rejected when it was discovered that his mother was of Jewish descent. In a rage of disappointment he took a pistol and assassinated the head of the Munich Soviet on the Promenadestrasse. Terrible reprisals followed. Leading figures in the Thule Society were rounded up and executed. Rudi only just avoided being caught himself. He slipped away in the night to join the Freikorps.

These were the men who refused to be demobbed. A generation of angry losers bred by a dishonourable peace. War had taken hold of them and would never let them go. They had forgotten the civilisation that had betrayed them, their minds having been wiped clean with a pure nihilism. 'Kaput!' declared one of them, pointing a finger to the side of his head. 'In November 1918 I blew out my brains. We have already died for our nation. Now we are dead men on leave.' They had found a comradely love amid the filth and stench of the trenches. With no stomach for the soft life any more, many would never go home. A battle-hardened trooper told Rudi he could find sleep only on a camp bed with rough blankets. 'I can no longer abide sheets,' he explained. 'They remind me of the flag of truce.' Yet this old soldier was found in a disgraceful attitude of surrender in a hotel room years later on the Night of the Long Knives.

Rudi had learnt to control the temptations of intimacy. The love of men was not to be squandered on base desires. Some of the Freikorps had become so used to action without conscience that they had lost their moral sense. He sought a greater will, a belief in something pure. It was a deep love that he felt, which soared up to the heavens. He found a girlfriend to share the healthy outdoor pursuits that would clear his head. They would go on hikes together through the mountains, to breathe the clean air of the Fatherland.

He found his professor too: Dr Haushofer, a retired general who lectured in geopolitics at Munich University and tutored him in new ideas for a mystical future. The struggle for survival was the struggle for space, the professor declared; space is what the German people needed. It lay to the east, to be conquered as it had been before by the Teutonic crusaders. Rudi dreamt of a space beyond the horizon, reaching upward to the stars. He learnt a new and mournful word: *Weltanschauung*, the world-view, the destiny of nations. He spent days of study in the lecture theatre, nights of struggle in the beer-halls. He was waiting for the man who would lead them forward.

When he first saw him in a back-room meeting of a minor nationalist party, the man looked unremarkable. He held himself stiffly, with that tense and uncertain authority that one associated with the non-commissioned. His hands were clasped flat against the front of his shabby grey overcoat. But when his turn came to speak, a strange and shocking animus was unleashed. A howl of pain pierced the muttering gloom. His was the song of their suffering, the melody of their anger. He had a rhythm, too, that stirred them, a cadence and gesture that seemed to channel their sad rage. To them this was no mere rhetoric. They had long grown weary of that. No, this was shrill delight, the sweet aria of their fury.

'I am just a drummer,' this man said when it became clear that their promised leader had been found. Rudi called him the Tribune and followed him faithfully ever after: even into Landsberg prison after the failed putsch.

This was his time of joyful confinement, as amanuensis to the Tribune while they worked on his great book together. Professor Haushofer helped them forge ideas of sacred geography and political mysticism. Rudi held the memory of this time close to him, even when he would feign forgetfulness of everything else. In all the other places where he had been incarcerated after his flight – the Tower, the country house where he was first held for interrogation, the hospital in Wales, his cell at Nuremberg and now here, in the summerhouse of Speer's garden at Spandau – Landsberg had been his one prison of happiness.

He remembered the moment when one night the Tribune read to him a passage he had written, describing the life and death of his comrades in the Great War. The Tribune read slowly and haltingly, his face drawn and weary as he struggled to articulate his seemingly boundless concepts. The pauses grew longer and more frequent until he suddenly dropped his head into his hands and sobbed out loud. Then, he rose majestically from this posture of despondence and burst out: 'Oh, I shall exact a pitiless and terrible revenge on the very first day that I can! I shall take revenge in the name of all whom I shall see then before my eyes!' It was then that Rudi knew that he would always be beholden to his Tribune. That he loved him.

And it was Rudi who would always remain the closest to him. While others in the party nursed their own petty ambitions, his fulfilled wish was simply to be the Deputy, the Tribune's loyal second. At rallies it was his duty to introduce him to the crowd and to lead the cheers at the end. At functions he would act as attentive escort. The seeming passivity of his ceremonial role inspired many arch and facile comments. The spiteful murmur of gossip dubbed him 'Fräulein', 'First Lady', even 'Black Paula'. Yet he felt aloof from these stupid remarks. Only those who could truly grasp the purity of his devotion had any power to judge his character. Such as his own loving wife, who always understood that the Tribune came first.

There was a truth, though, behind the absurdity of these nicknames. Rudi held a latent power, always ready to be used. When they had conquered half of Europe and there was much celebration of the Tribune's imperial status, it was reported to him that a middle-ranking party official had been heard to say: 'Well, if Hitler is the Emperor, then Hess is his Empress.' He had seen to it that the man had been punished for such sedition, but was secretly glad that such a blasphemous name had been given to a destined role that even within himself he had found hard to acknowledge. A feminine potency, one that could surpass all others. Yes, this was the meaning of his flight. His one great act of love for the Tribune. Like in a chess game when the queen suddenly leaps from her consort's side across the board to break the stalemate.

Now all the pieces on his side were gone. They were all dead except him. He had been the first and the last. He waited in the summerhouse in Speer's garden. He was ready. Ready to fly once more.

4

the emperor

I know too much. My thoughts are dangerous to others. I read somewhere once that radio waves are never lost but fly up from the world and travel forever through space. Maybe thoughts do this too. Maybe these dangerous thoughts will somehow transmit themselves and you will receive them, whoever you are. So I call upon you, witness from some other time and place: my name is Hans Brauer, remember me. I offer you this precious information for your safe keeping. Do not let it fall into the wrong hands.

Where to begin? There is so little time. The whole story of how I first became involved with the Circle would take too long. I will start from the morning of 28 April 1941. Three days ago.

White blossom was falling from the trees in the park as I walked to the university. I recall a sense of indignation that spring would dare show its face in this godforsaken country. And a feeling of dread. Even nature has its propaganda, its scattered leaflets of lies and deceit. I knew the truth then: that white flowers are flowers for the dead.

I met Kurt in the atrium and we discussed our essays set by Professor Dietrich on the great romantic Heinrich von Kleist. I, like most of the class, had concentrated on his epic play *Die Hermannsschlact* with its depiction of the Battle of the Teutoburg Forest, the glorious historical victory of our German race. I had written an appallingly crass tract on national destiny and the sacrifice of the individual in the service of the Volk. But then I needed to appear to be a good student and a diligent National Socialist. Kurt, on the other hand, always seemed determined to be reckless.

He had instead chosen an obscure work for his critique and one not on the official reading list. 'On the Marionette Theatre', Kurt explained to me as we made our way to class, was a curious philosophical treatise by Kleist in the form of an ironic dialogue. In it one of the interlocutors asserts the astonishing notion that grace appears in a purely bodily form only in a being that either has no consciousness at all or an infinite one: that is to say, either in a puppet or a god.

In class, after a brief and sombre discussion on the romantic tradition, Kurt began loudly to argue Kleist's strange observations on the excellent quality of 'lifeless, pure pendulums governed only by the laws of gravity'. Mankind's fall from grace, he went on, was in its consciousness, and the effect of eating from the tree of knowledge has made us clumsy and full of self-doubt. I felt sorry for Professor Dietrich as he attempted to steer the debate into more orthodox waters. He has already been denounced for allowing 'degenerate' ideas to be discussed in his department and it seemed obvious to me that Kurt was using this obscure work as a satire on the vain ideals of classicism. But most of the class appeared merely confused by his arguments.

They imagined him as a harmless fool but I knew Kurt to be fiercely intelligent (though he always tended to get carried away with wild imaginings). He had become my closest companion since my brother Ernst was taken from us.

'Behold our puppet utopia, Hans,' he said to me afterwards as we watched a squad of the National Socialist Students Association march out to the playing fields.

'You should be more careful, Kurt,' I chided him. 'Talk like that can get you into trouble.'

'Only a god can be equal to inanimate matter,' he told me. 'That's what Kleist was really getting at, that we need to go all the way. We've left the Garden and the door is barred behind us, but if we make the journey all the way around the world maybe we will find an entrance at the back of Paradise. We must go on to absolute understanding.'

'You mean that we must eat again from the tree of knowledge to regain our innocence?'

'Certainly,' he replied. 'Kleist says that when that happens it will be the final chapter in the history of the world. And "On the Marionette Theatre" was his last work. A year later he shot himself and his lover on the banks of the Wannsee.'

'Kurt.' I lowered my voice and with a nod beckoned to my friend to bring his face close to mine. 'Do you really believe that we live in a puppet's utopia?'

He grinned, as if relishing a sense of intimacy and intrigue.

'Oh yes!' he whispered, his eyes darting to and fro.

'And what if there were people secretly working against it?'

Kurt giggled.

'Not you, Hans, surely?'

'What if I was?'

His face froze into a solemn mask.

'Hans,' he muttered, 'I hate this wretched state of life. I wish I could find the back door to Paradise.'

'Then join us.'

'What?'

'I'll explain tomorrow. I'll come to your apartment.'

I left Kurt and made my way to the Mühlbergers for my violin lesson. I brooded on Heinrich von Kleist's suicide pact. I think I mused on how sweet it would be to find someone whom one loved so much that one could die with them. I certainly feel that now. With somebody else to go with, death might not be such a cold and lonely business.

Heinz Mühlberger was a teacher and an amateur-theatre director, his wife Elsa a musician. It was my brother Ernst who first got to know them before the war, when he was in their drama group. Ernst served in Poland and came back on leave with terrible stories that he could not tell our parents as they simply would not believe him. So he discussed what he had seen with the Mühlbergers and, as he confided to them his growing sense of anger and disaffection, it soon became clear that the couple were part of a clandestine network of resistance known as the Circle.

'Imagine a pebble dropped in a pond,' Elsa told him. 'It might make only a ripple but its circle expands and communicates with others.'

Ernst joined them and soon recruited me. He arranged violin lessons for me with Elsa Mühlberger as a cover so I could be used as a courier, with a false compartment in my violin case to carry messages, even anti-government leaflets. Ernst was killed in action in France last spring.

When I arrived at the Mühlbergers they were preparing a surprise for their son Melchior's sixth birthday the next day. In a corner of the living room they were arranging a collection of tiny painted wooden animals. With green felt they had fashioned fields dotted with little trees of coloured paper. A hand mirror served as a pond for a family of miniature ducks, above which hung a mobile of the moon and stars attached to the ceiling.

The Circle had been in crisis since last summer. Every new German victory proved us wrong. All of our secret protestations against fascism seemed useless as it marched on in its unending parade of success. We had all but given up producing anti-government leaflets and instead concentrated on developing communications within our own group and with other anti-fascist networks that were supposed to exist. We were also gathering intelligence that we might pass on. Heinz Mühlberger made contact with a man connected to the Russian embassy with the code name Nebula. There were even rumours of approaches to the Circle from the British Secret Service. But the possibility of involvement in espionage only accelerated the sense of fear and desperation among us.

The Mühlbergers argued in whispers as Heinz painstakingly herded model pigs into a cardboard farmyard. How can we trust the Soviets since Stalin made his devil's pact with Hitler? What if the British are secretly negotiating a peace with Germany? Heinz looked up at me.

'Hans, we need you to run an errand.'

'We shouldn't involve him in this,' Elsa protested. 'He should be trying to organise the students. They're the future.'

'I think I'm about to recruit one of my fellows,' I told her.

'That's good.'

'But I'm not scared of carrying out actions for the Circle.'

'Elsa, you know we can't go ourselves.'

'But—'

'What is this errand, anyway?' I asked.

Heinz beckoned me closer and told me of a woman with a message from British Intelligence, who wanted to work with the Circle and its contacts. She had information to prove that this proposition was genuine.

'It's too dangerous,' Elsa murmured as she carefully placed in position a farmhouse fashioned from a box that had once contained sugar lumps.

'Her name is Astrid Nagengast.' Heinz gave me an address to memorise for the following evening. 'Be careful.' He smiled. 'She's a fortune-teller.'

When I got home my stupid parents were huddled around the wireless, the cheap little 'people's radio' with its dial restricted to approved stations and its big round speaker that every household secretly knows as the 'Goebbels-snout'. Fanfares preceded the announcement of the German army's march into Athens. As I crept past, my father stood up and grabbed my arm.

'Hear that?' he declared, a fat tear rolling down his face. 'England is finished! We'll soon have vengeance for our Ernst.'

Next day when I told Kurt that I had to postpone our meeting until later that evening he became suspicious and provocative.

'Are you on a secret mission?'

'Please, Kurt, don't make foolish jokes.'

'Maybe you just don't want to see me.'

'Of course I do. We'll talk later.'

Astrid Nagengast had a sharp face and bright eyes, with a mass of silver ringlets scattered across a high, proud forehead. It was hard to tell how old she was. Fifty? Sixty, even? What was certain was the striking elegance and vitality in her looks and demeanour. Age is life, the only real proof of it. Youth always seems closer to death, I thought, recalling the fallen blossom of the day before.

'Do you know what you've come to collect?' she asked me as she showed me into a small study cluttered with books and peculiar objects.

'No.'

'Don't worry. It's a simple thing, foolproof. It shouldn't put you in any danger.'

There was an African mask on one wall, a chart of the zodiac on another. Above a desk littered with papers and curios hung an etching of some alchemical diagram. I looked around, wide-eyed.

'Esoteric knowledge,' she said with a smile. 'Nothing to be afraid of.'

'Are you really a fortune-teller?'

'Well, one has to be careful. There's been something of a clampdown in the past few years. It's completely illegal in Berlin. I'm a voice teacher mostly. And a breath therapist, but I still have plenty of psychic consultations. If anything, there's been a rise in demand.'

'What?'

'For astrologers, clairvoyants. The future has become a serious business lately. For example, so many people wanted to know when the time was right, you know, to leave.'

'You mean Jews?'

'Jews, yes, and others. Most of us left it too late.' She sighed. 'And there are the others who believe in it. I've had army officers as clients, worried about upcoming campaigns. It's been amazing how many secrets they've let slip. Plenty of the higher-ups are superstitious too. We can use that against them. And they've had fortune on their side for so long, they're scared that their luck is about to change. Well, it is.'

She opened a drawer in her desk, took something out and handed it to me. It was some strange kind of playing card. I looked at it. In profile a crowned and bethroned man held a sceptre and at his side was a golden shield emblazoned with an imperial eagle. The face of the figure was slightly smudged. At the top of the card was the number IV, at the bottom the legend: L'EMPEREUR.

'That's the message you're to take to the Circle. It proves we're acting in good faith.'

'It's a code?'

'Yes. And if your friends are able to understand it, then it will in turn give us proof of the Circle's operational status. In itself it's a harmless token. If you get stopped and asked about it just say you found it in the street. Tell your friends that we need to pass something on to a contact in the Deputy Führer's office.'

'Another card?'

'You're a clever boy. There'll be something else, too. But the cards are a good basic cypher. They're a memory system. You'd better go now, you know far too much already.'

I called at Kurt's flat on my way home. He lived in a fifth-storey apartment with a small balcony. Here we could converse freely, away from the anxious family table, far above the fear-haunted streets.

I talked about what had happened with my brother Ernst: how he had realised that the war was wrong, that everything the party said was a lie. I told him how Ernst had joined the Circle through the Mühlbergers and how I had become involved. Kurt shuddered when I told him about the atrocities Ernst had witnessed in Poland.

'With so much of hell in the world,' said Kurt, 'there must be a heaven somewhere.'

'We have to work for it,' I told him. 'For peace. For justice. There's a group of us. Will you work with us?'

'I don't know,' he said. 'I can hardly believe it, Hans. Is this real?'

'Of course.'

'But this evening, for example. You said you had to go somewhere, some secret mission or other. How do I know that it's not all some sort of made-up story?'

'Why would I do that?'

'I don't know. It could be a trick. Or a trap.'

'Kurt, really.'

'Look, Hans, this is treason you're asking me to get involved in.'

'I know that.'

'Then trust me. Show me something so that I know this isn't just a game.'

I took out the playing card from my violin case and held it up. I explained to him that it contained a message.

'How marvellous,' said Kurt. 'A code. Have you worked out what it means?'

'Of course not. I'm simply meant to pass it on.'

'Let me see it.'

He took it from me.

'It's some sort of trump card,' he said.

'It's a memory system.'

'Yes,' Kurt squinted at it. 'Number four, *L'Empereur*. The clue could be in the number and the arrangement of letters. Or in the image itself. The Holy Roman Emperor.'

'Kurt, I don't think we should be doing this. I'm just the messenger.'

'See? The face has been marked. There's a blot of red ink. Maybe that's been deliberately added. It's around the chin. The emperor with the bloodstained mouth. The bloodthirsty emperor?'

'I'd better put it back.'

'Of course!' he suddenly exclaimed. 'It's the beard. See? The beard was white but it's been coloured in. The emperor with the red beard. It's Barbarossa!'

Of course we knew of Barbarossa, Emperor Frederick I who reigned in the second half of the twelfth century. We had often been told by our history teachers that it was Barbarossa who first established the German people as the true heirs of Roman imperial power. And there were many legends about him.

'Yes,' I said. 'Is it true that he sleeps with his knights beneath Mount Kyffhausen?'

'How can he be there when he drowned in a river in Asia Minor on his way to the Third Crusade?' Kurt retorted. 'But it's said that it was not just a crusade that took him east. He was looking for the land of Prester John.'

'Prester John?'

'Yes, you know, the mythical Christian ruler of a lost kingdom beyond the infidels. There had long been rumours of him, but then Emperor Barbarossa actually received a letter from this Prester John, telling of his enchanted land with many wonders and strange creatures in it. Dog-headed men, boar-tusked women, giants and griffins. A wondrous fantasy world, beyond known space and time!'

Kurt was becoming quite animated, waving his hands around as if conjuring up a vision.

'It was like a report from another planet. Full of monsters and miraculous devices. Most wonderful of all was the promise that beyond the realm of Prester John lay an earthly paradise. That Eden yet exists as a Garden of Earthly Delights. One legend of Barbarossa has it that Emperor Frederick did not die but found his lost paradise and lived on for many years in a luxurious palace surrounded by beautiful gardens. As in Kleist's essay, he went around the world and found a way back to Eden.'

'To utopia.'

'Yes!' His eyes were wide and bright. 'Wouldn't that be precious? Oh! What could be better than imagining strange new lands, to forget the dreadful one we live in?'

'Oh Kurt, you're such a dreamer.'

'So? Isn't this Circle of yours supposed to be fighting for a dream?'

'Yes, but not a fantasy.'

'Why not?'

I took the card from him.

'I'd better be getting back.'

'You think I'm silly, don't you, Hans?'

'No. Why do you say that?'

'Oh, everybody does. And I can see it in your face, too. I'm sorry if you think that I'm silly. I want to be serious. I want to get involved.'

'That's good. But, you know, we mustn't draw attention to ourselves.'

'I know. I wish it was just our secret, Hans.'

'That wouldn't be much good.'

'Our own private conspiracy. We could become blood brothers. We could do it now. I'll get a knife and we can swear an oath to each other.'

'That's enough, Kurt!'

I snapped my violin case shut and stood up.

'Please don't be angry with me, Hans.'

'I'm not,' I protested, even though I was. 'It's just that what we are doing is so dangerous. If any of us get caught it means the People's Court. The guillotine.'

I noted the look of fear in Kurt's eyes at this, and at that moment I was glad. I felt then he needed to be shocked into reality. I wish I hadn't done that now.

I left his apartment and made my way back home. As I crept upstairs the radio howled in the living room. A broadcast of a party rally, waves of applause like the drone of a swarm. I felt that I really didn't understand people at all. I felt a lonely desire to get away, to be on my own on some wide and desolate plain.

The following day I looked for Kurt at the university but I couldn't find him. I wanted to talk with him, to apologise for losing my temper. Elsa Mühlberger was right: it was essential to find a way of making contact with more students willing to be part of a resistance network. I was thinking of the future, though I had grim forebodings about it.

When I arrived at the Mühlbergers' to deliver the message, I knew something was wrong. Their front door was open and I could hear strange voices coming from their apartment. I turned on my heel and headed back to the staircase but a man in a leather coat blocked my path.

'Not so fast, son,' he told me as he grabbed me by the arm. 'I think you'd better come with me.'

He pulled me along into the Mühlbergers'. Their flat was being ransacked, books pulled off the shelves, papers scattered every-where. A tall, sad-eyed man stood in the corner watching. I was dragged over to him.

'What do we have here, Krebs?' the man asked in a soft voice.

'Found him outside, sir.'

'Inspector Glockner, *Geheime Staatspolizei*,' he announced, showing his identity badge with a flourish. 'Let me see your papers, young man.'

I handed them to him.

'And what is your relationship to Heinz and Elsa Mühlberger?'

I explained about the violin lessons, holding up my case for him to see.

'Open it. Ah, yes! What a beautiful instrument. Frau Mühlberger taught you, yes? You know that the Mühlbergers have been taken into protective custody? Hmm, why not play us something?'

'What?'

'A little demonstration. Something you've been learning.'

I took the violin out and put it under my chin. I tightened the bow, tuned the strings. I felt sick.

'Please,' Inspector Glockner entreated with a smile.

I played 'Song of the Morning Star' from *Tannhaüser*, an appropriate piece that I had up my sleeve for such an eventuality. I scraped the first notes badly. Then I tried to relax, remembering what Elsa Mühlberger had told me about not exerting too much control, of letting go of the bow action. As if any of it mattered. But fear had this strange effect, giving me just the right balance between concentration and surrender. I was in a trance, as the words of the aria whispered in my ear: like a portent of death, twilight shrouds the earth. The soul, which yearns for those heights, dreads to take its dark and awful flight. A star points the way out from the valley.

'Wonderful,' said Glockner, when I finished. 'Don't you think that was wonderful, Krebs?'

His henchman grunted. Glockner had gone to stand in the corner where the Mühlbergers had made the model farm for little Melchior. He beckoned me over.

'Rather pretty, isn't it?' he said, picking up a model cow and holding it up to a mournful eye.

The Gestapo had by now turned the Mühlbergers' place upside down. Order remained only in the toyland they had lovingly constructed for their son. Perhaps they had made it for themselves, too. Knowing that they were doomed, they had regained a moment's paradise, a tiny world hidden in the vast and cruel universe.

'Did you know that the Mühlbergers were communists?' Inspector Glockner demanded, his voice at once harsh and official.

'No.'

'Traitors, subversives, enemy spies. And are you one of them?'

'No. No, sir.'

'What do you think, Krebs?' He shot a glance at his man.

Krebs shrugged. Glockner smiled.

'I think we should let him go,' the inspector went on. 'For now. On your way, young man.'

He handed me back my papers. I went down to the street, breathless, my heart fluttering like a trapped bird in my ribcage. Thoughts came quickly, stacking up in my mind. The Mühlbergers interrogated, tortured. Names named. How long before mine came up? Did they already know? I kept looking over my shoulder, feeling the shadow of something behind me. Now I was imagining that I was being followed. I was going mad. I looked back again. But yes, there really was somebody after me. That was the game. Cat and mouse. The Gestapo would let me go and have me tailed to see who I'd lead them to. I'd already thought of Kurt, that I should warn him. Poor Kurt, caught up in all this, scarcely knowing what he was getting into. Yet I was the only one who could implicate him. How much could I bear before I betrayed him? I tried to clear my head, to stop thinking these horrible thoughts. I would go home. Home, yes. A moment of calm. Home. But what then? What would happen when they came for me there? What would my parents think? Their own son a traitor. It would kill my mother.

Footsteps were close behind. I picked up my pace.

'Wait,' came a voice and a hand clawed at my elbow.

I tried to shake him off. I'd had quite enough of being manhandled. But he clung on to me tightly.

'Wait, you little fool,' came the voice again, a harsh whisper at the back of my neck. 'In here.'

He pulled me into an alleyway. He seemed terrifically strong and agile, though in the shadows I saw that he was shorter and thinner than I was. He looked me up and down as if trying to decide something.

'Do you know who squealed on your friends?' he asked me.

I shook my head.

'Maybe they gave themselves away,' he went on. 'Bloody amateurs. You'd better come with me.'

'Who are you?' I asked him.

'You can call me Nebula.'

We took a tram to a shabby district of warehouses and run-down tenements. I followed him into a boarding house that smelt of carbolic and boiled cabbage. We came to a door on the first floor and he rapped a swift tattoo on it with his knuckles. It opened an inch or two. I thought I spotted a pair of eyes surveying us from the gloom. Nebula murmured something and all at once the portal opened wide to swallow us up.

'Who's this?' the man demanded as he slammed the door behind us.

'One of the Circle,' Nebula replied.

The blinds were drawn and it took me a while to adjust my vision to the half-darkness. The occupant of the room was thickset with a pudgy face. He made a derisive sniff in my direction, pouting his lips.

'Christ, a schoolkid,' he muttered.

'This is Starshine,' Nebula told me. 'He's a comrade.'

'Are you part of the Circle?'

Starshine laughed.

'No, kid, we're with the band.'

'The band?'

'The Orchestra. That's what Fatherland calls us. The Red Orchestra. Speaking of which, what's in here?' Starshine took my violin case from me. 'Let me guess, you use this to carry messages, right?'

'You work for the Soviets?' I asked them.

'Well, since Motherland made this cosy little pact with Fatherland we've been on short time,' said Nebula.

'Watch what you say in front of the kid,' said Starshine.

He had put my case on the bed and taken the violin out of it. He pulled out the bow, checked the little compartment for the chin-pad and rosin.

'Here.' I took it from him and pressed the bottom lining until it came away, revealing a small space with the playing card in it.

'Nice,' said Nebula, taking out the card. 'What's this?'

'Is that a message from the fortune-teller?' Starshine asked me. I nodded.

'See?' Nebula held it up for his comrade to squint at it in the gloom. Starshine studied the card for a moment.

'They know the code word then,' he said.

'That's proof that British Intelligence know about Directive 21.'

'What are they telling us for?'

'They've cracked Fatherland's codes and want to pass on information to Motherland through our channels.'

'Yeah, but why would they want to do that?'

'So that Fatherland won't know that the British have broken their cyphers. They'll think that Motherland got this information from its own sources.'

'Yeah, but maybe it's not information at all. Maybe it's disinformation.'

'Oh for fuck's sake! Enough of this. Everybody knows what's going to happen. There's been one intelligence report after another, all with the same conclusions; now this, and still the bastard won't believe it!'

'Careful what you say, comrade.'

'I bet even this little fucker knows.' Nebula turned to me and held up the Emperor card. 'You. What does this mean?'

I shrugged. 'Er, Barbarossa?'

'See? Even this amateur resistance cell knows.'

'Yeah but they're rife with bourgeois tendencies, they can't be trusted.'

'All hell is about to break loose in the East and Stalin does nothing.'

'Whatever happens, the Red Army will hold.'

'Hold what? Its bollocks? Its entire officer corps has been purged out of existence. And, not content with that, he's dismantled what was left of our intelligence network. Just to keep Fatherland happy.'

'I'm telling you, all this talk of invasion could be British counter-intelligence,' Starshine insisted. 'They want to drag us into their imperialist war. There was something else that was to come with this message, wasn't there?'

He turned and grabbed hold of my collar.

'What?' I protested. I was having trouble keeping up with what they were saying. It seemed some strange game and yet I somehow knew that it was all concerned with something cataclysmic.

'What else did the fortune-teller say?' Starshine demanded, giving me a little shake.

'I don't know. Something about a contact in the Deputy Führer's office.'

He pushed me away. 'Well, we know what that means.'

'Do we?' asked Nebula.

'Peace feelers. They're everywhere. In Lisbon, in Madrid. In Switzerland. There are Abwehr reports that the British government is on the verge of collapse and is ready to make terms in secret.'

'Well, *that's* more likely to be the work of British counter-intelligence, isn't it? To persuade Fatherland that the war in the West is nearly won and that it can turn its attention elsewhere.'

'Perhaps.' Starshine nodded. 'Perhaps. But what if the British really do want to make peace?'

Nebula sighed.

'Then we're fucked.'

'Well, we're finished here,' said Starshine. 'Looks like this Circle is being wiped up. What do we do with this one?'

He made a terse nod in my direction.

'I don't know,' Nebula mumbled, as if to himself.

'We can't leave him behind. He knows too much.'

The two men exchanged a glance of some shared and dark meaning. In the gloom I saw it as a combination of a grimace and a tilt of the head. Starshine touched his throat gently.

'No,' said Nebula.

'It's a security matter.'

'Fuck that.'

'Remember your training.'

'My training?' Nebula retorted scathingly. 'Listen, comrade, I've been working underground for nearly twenty years. My school has been the life of a militant. Organising in Poland in the twenties. Fighting the colonialists in Palestine. Setting up fronts for the party all over Europe. That's been my *konspiratsia*, chum. Experiences worth more than all of the espionage courses in the world. Solidarity: it's what the struggle's all about. I say we take this one with us.'

'No.'

'Yes. The Corridor can take one more. Who knows, he might come in useful.'

'Then he's your responsibility. You organise it.'

'Fine.'

Starshine lit a cigarette and lay on the bed blowing smoke at the ceiling. Nebula explained to me that they were going to take me over the Swiss border with them.

'How?'

'Let me worry about that.'

He walked over to a dresser by the bed, pulled out a drawer, took something out and put it in his pocket.

'I'll go and see Schmidt,' he told Starshine, who grunted in acknowledgement. 'You stay here,' he said to me.

I found a chair and sat down. Starshine stubbed out his cigarette and rolled over on to his side. All the light slowly bled out of the room. I took off my jacket and rolled it up for a pillow. Curling up on the floor I tried to sleep.

I was prodded awake by Nebula's foot sometime around dawn. A pale light leaked around the edges of the blinds. Starshine was sitting on the edge of the bed, smoking.

'We're moving this afternoon,' said Nebula.

I yawned and rubbed my face.

'What about . . .'

'Your family?' Nebula read the thought. 'You can't go back. Even to say goodbye. Your name might have come up by now.'

'I could see a friend.'

'Someone in the Circle? Forget it. It's too dangerous.'

'No. He's not even connected.'

I was thinking of Kurt, that I should warn him. When I explained to Nebula he sighed.

'Be quick about it, then. And make sure nobody else sees you.'

It was still early so I decided that the best thing to do was to lie in wait for Kurt as he left his apartment to go to the university. There was a wild look about his eyes when he saw that it was me coming after him.

'Hans!'

I put a finger to my mouth.

'Keep quiet, Kurt. Please.'

'I didn't know what happened to you,' he whispered.

'Quick. We need to find a place to talk.'

'Then come back to my place. Mother and Father have already left for work.'

I sat on the couch in the living room as Kurt brewed tea and made toast in the kitchen. I tried to relax, but my whole body seemed twisted up from my night on the floor. I stood up and stretched. I caught my reflection in a gilt-framed looking-glass over the mantelpiece. My face was ashen, one side of my hair flattened into an absurd crest. Kurt entered and, laying the breakfast things down, came to stand next to me in front of the mirror.

'Dear Hans,' he said, putting an arm around me. 'Try not to look so gloomy.'

'I came to warn you, Kurt.'

I told him about the Mühlbergers and that I was leaving the country. I didn't say where I was going.

'Yes. You take action bravely. But what does your other self do?'

He pointed to the image in the glass.

'There is a magic mirror in Prester John's enchanted kingdom, in which distant objects and events appear. Other realities, too, so we see what might have happened. Here we all are, after all. The four of us together. You and me and me and you.'

Kurt let out a peculiar giggle. Dizzy with fatigue and hunger, I turned to look at him. There was an absent quality in his gaze; his eyes seemed to focus on something beyond.

'Whatever we do as one person, it is as though all of us have done it. Do you think that paradise can really exist on earth, like the communists say?'

'I don't know, Kurt. You must be careful how you talk about things.'

I sat down and took a sip of tea. I began to devour the toast. I was ravenous.

'I know now what the Emperor card meant, Hans. It was a sign.'

'You really must forget about all that now,' I mumbled through a mouthful of bread.

'It is the token of earthly power,' he went on. 'We must render unto Caesar what is Caesar's. In this life.'

I had soon finished off my little breakfast. I fell back against the softness of the couch and let out a long yawn.

'In our other life,' Kurt continued, 'we render to God what is God's.'

I rested my head and closed my eyes. I just needed a short nap. Then I'd be ready. As I drifted off Kurt came over and gently stroked my brow.

'Yes,' he said softly. 'Rest. Sleep. Sleep and have your dreams.'

I was in the court of Barbarossa, paying homage to the great Emperor. A scribe was reading out a list from Prester John's letter, a bestiary of exotic species: hippopotami, crocodiles, methagall-innari, camethernis, thinsiretae, panthers, aurochs, white and red lions, silent cicadas, wild men, horned men, fauns, satyrs, pigmies, giants whose height is forty cubits, one-eyed men, a bird that is called the phoenix, and almost all kinds of animals that are under heaven. Barbarossa pointed down at me, demanding to know what kind of creature I was. 'He is with the Red Orchestra, sire,' it was announced. The Emperor stroked his crimson beard thoughtfully. Then he looked at his hand in horror. It was covered in blood.

I came to with a start, that sensation of a sudden fall. I knew at once that something was wrong. Footfalls in the hallway, muffled voices. Kurt was saying something hushed and urgent. As I stood up he came into the room. Behind him was Inspector Glockner, the Gestapo officer I had met at the Mühlbergers'.

I called out Kurt's name.

'I'm sorry, Hans. But you did warn me.'

'What?'

'When you talked of the People's Court, the guillotine. I couldn't let that happen to us. They said they wouldn't punish me, Hans. If I told them all I knew. It'll be the same for you. They promised.'

'It's true, young man,' said Glockner. 'Work for us like he has. It's the only way.'

I looked at Kurt.

'You informed on the Mühlbergers?'

'At first I was just scared out of my wits. Then I realised that by betraying them here I would be setting them free in the other world. I'm just a puppet after all, Hans. But we have to go all the way. Through the whole world and all its secrets. Know everything. Tell everything. Absolute understanding. Maybe the way to heaven is through hell. And there we'll find the back entrance to paradise.'

I let Kurt approach me. As he came close I grabbed him by the front of his shirt and pushed him hard. He fell back against Glockner and in a tangle they toppled to the floor. I turned and made for the French windows that led out onto the balcony.

So these are my last thoughts. I'm on the ledge. Glockner approaches, a look of professional concern on his face. For a moment I imagine that I see something more: true compassion in those sad eyes of his. I remember the words of the song that I played for him.

'Be sensible,' he implores me. 'Please. You're a young soul, led astray by degenerates. Listen to your friend and save yourself.'

But I know too much. My thoughts are dangerous to others. I entrust them to you, witness from the future. Take care of my memory.

Five storeys up, I conjure thoughts of escape, of being lifted up somehow. An aria. The soul, which yearns for those heights, dreads to take its dark and awful flight. The evening star might point the way. But I think of the fallen blossom in the park. A brief shoot of life, of youth, of death. That is enough, surely. In a moment it will all be over.

5

the hierophant

The Mañana Literary Society. There was an impressive group of writers at the Heinleins' house in Laurel Canyon on that fateful night when Mary-Lou and I attended. Jack Williamson, my great idol, shy and diffident in person; Leigh Brackett, one of the few women writing SF back then and a great inspiration for Mary-Lou; Cleve Cartmill, a newspaperman crippled with polio who had just started writing for *Astounding*; Anthony Boucher, who was more of a mystery writer; and L. Ron Hubbard, a prodigious all-rounder of the pulps who, it was said, could write two thousand words an hour without revisions. Looking back, I'm liable to put aside the sense of how star-struck I was in the presence of all this talent. I even tend conveniently to forget the miserable way (for me at least) the evening eventually concluded. Now I'm inclined to remember it as the first time I ever met Nemesio Carvajal.

He was a young and very earnest Latin-American science fiction writer who had just come from Mexico. He had contacts with the radical circle that Heinlein was still part of in those days. Tony Boucher was fluent in Spanish and able to translate for us but I recall Nemesio Carvajal as having pretty good working English even then.

'Nemesio?' L. Ron Hubbard asked when they were introduced. 'That's a hell of a name, kid. But then you Latinos have a bit of a flair when it comes to baptism, don't you? You know the joke? If Jesus is Jewish, how come he's got a Mexican name?'

'Well, you're one to talk,' Heinlein interjected. 'Isn't your first name Lafayette?'

'Yeah.' Hubbard sighed. 'That's why I use Ron.'

Glasses were poured of cheap white sherry, which I soon discovered was the propulsion fuel for those evenings. A toast was proposed.

'To all the stories that will be written tomorrow.'

'Then this is the Tomorrow Literary Society?' asked Nemesio.

'No, kid,' Hubbard told him. 'Mañana, no translation needed. As you know, the word has another meaning. A lot of these hacks aren't as good as me at meeting deadlines.'

Nemesio frowned. Boucher tried to explain that English speakers used the word more to mean procrastination.

'It's a bit of a gringo thing, Ron,' he added. 'You know, this easy-going Latin, always putting off today what he can do tomorrow.'

'Well, excuse me,' Hubbard retorted. 'You know, I once tried to explain "mañana", in my own gringo way as *you* have it, to an Irishman. He told me that there was nothing in the Gaelic that conveyed the urgency of such a term!'

Hubbard paused for some sporadic laughter and then tried to continue to hold the room by launching into an improbable story of a recent expedition of his to Alaska. It was clear that he liked to dominate any assembly and to portray himself as an adventurer, a fearless explorer. He had written so much outlandish pulp fiction that he was already finding it hard to distinguish it from fact.

But he wasn't allowed to get away with it for long. The imaginative competition was far too much for him. The conversation turned to the concept of parallel worlds and alternate futures, the notion of time being non-linear, the possibilities of precognition. The world was ripe for the speculative genre with all the uncertainties of war, the bewildering potential of new discoveries in science and technology. But amid all these great events I couldn't help thinking that my personal life was on the brink of something, that this was a crucial night in my own history.

Heinlein began to hold forth on the curvature of space–time, of world-lines and points of divergence. Nemesio Carvajal intervened to speak of an Argentine writer who had just published a collection of stories. In one a character is described as attempting a novel that would describe a world where all possible outcomes of an event occur simultaneously with each one leading to further proliferation.

'It is titled "El Jardín de senderos que se bifurcan" ,' he explained.

'The garden of paths that bisect?' Boucher offered a swift translation.

'Yes. You see, in the story there is a novel and a labyrinth. It turns out that the novel is the labyrinth and the labyrinth is the novel.'

'Sounds interesting,' Boucher continued. 'What's this writer called?'

'Borges,' Nemesio replied. It was the first time any of us had heard that name.

'So what's his genre?' Hubbard demanded. 'Mystery or fantasy, or what?'

'Those things, yes,' said Nemesio with a smile. 'And more. He is also an important poet.'

Hubbard huffed indignantly.

'We're definitely at a place where the paths are diverging,' said Cleve Cartmill.

'But surely,' Leigh Brackett interjected, 'in the world, in *our* world, whatever that is, there will be one reality if totalitarianism goes on unchecked and another if it is defeated.'

'Not necessarily,' Heinlein argued. 'It could be that different worlds can co-exist. In the past as well as the future. That's why this kid's story is so important,' he nodded over at me. '*Lords of the Black Sun* shows us the worst that will happen. By imagining it perhaps we can avoid it in our own reality.'

Feeling foolishly pleased with myself, I caught Mary-Lou's eyes across the room. She smiled at me and in that moment I imagined our future together. Then Jack Parsons walked in.

There are many images that can attest to the dark and passionate features of the glamorous rocket scientist. Jack Parsons was undeniably photogenic so one can still appreciate those deep-set eyes, that quizzical mouth, the thick curls swept up into a crowning mane. But none of these portraits can ever do justice to his charisma, that delicately soulful presence one felt when he entered a room.

His voice was soft and slow, his manner hesitant. His gaze was open, searching. He looked romantically dishevelled in a fine flannel suit that needed pressing and an open-necked shirt naped with grime. There was a light sheen of sweat on his brow. With scant introduction and a gentle insistence, he joined in the conversation.

'We're certainly approaching a crucial moment,' he said.

'In your rocket experiments?' asked Heinlein.

'In that, yes,' Parsons replied. 'But in the Greater Work too.'

'You mean this mystical stuff?' Jack Williamson demanded.

'Look, I know you think it's all a bit far-fetched, but didn't you say once that science is magic made real?'

'I did, yes,' Williamson conceded.

'There must be any number of ways to break through the space–time continuum. We should experiment with them all. Soon there will be a chance to test some of this unseen wisdom. The Hierophant has ordered a special Mass that might just help change the course of the war.'

'Wow,' Mary-Lou murmured, her eyes wide and bright.

I realise now, of course, that he was talking about Aleister Crowley and that perhaps Jack had some knowledge of Operation Mistletoe. All I noticed then was the way Mary-Lou looked at him.

'What's a hierophant?' asked Leigh Brackett.

'It's a fancy name for a high priest,' Hubbard explained.

'So, you've finally joined this Order,' said Heinlein. 'I hope you haven't given up on the science.'

'Oh no,' Parsons replied with a smile. 'I'm following both paths now.'

The fact that Jack Parsons was actually quite shy and nervous only seemed to add to his charm. He appeared to be channelling an enchantment from another dimension. And there was a reticence in how he described his experiments that was intriguing for all us fantasists. He had to be discreet, he explained. The US Military had become interested in missiles and jet propulsion, and was now funding the California Institute of Technology's rocket group, which was testing secret prototypes out in the desert. He gave a vague account of the group's activities that conjured visions of mystics raising fire demons in the wilderness. The desert as an empty stage beneath a theatre of stars, a limitless temple of research. He was equally obscure about this occult sect of his, the Ordo Templi Orientis. He was living a strange double life, one of wild asceticism and divine exhaustion, toiling beneath the harsh sun by day, enacting sacramental rites at the Agape Lodge of the OTO by night. He embodied a weird fusion of modern science and ancient wisdom, part hip technocrat, part Renaissance wizard.

He certainly cast some sort of spell over the room that night. It was an energy that seemed to split the discussion into waves and particles. No one voice could hold all the attention after that point. The party began to fracture and oscillate. Hubbard was in one corner detailing an improbable jungle adventure to Cleve Cartmill. Anthony Boucher was exchanging rapid Spanish with Nemesio. Heinlein and Williamson were circulating. Leslyn went into the kitchen for olives and more sherry. I had already noticed a buzz of attraction between Jack Parsons and Mary-Lou. I watched with dread as she slowly, inexorably, began to gravitate towards him.

They were in deep discussion about astronomy and astrology when Heinlein pulled me into his orbit. He announced that he was going up to his study to show Jack Willamson his 'Timeline of Future History' and insisted I join them. We went upstairs. Heinlein had on his wall a chart that mapped out a chronology of all the futuristic stories he had written and was planning to write. I stared at it blankly as Williamson made enthusiastic comments. When I think of it now I see the strange comment *The Crazy Years – mass psychosis in the sixth decade* next to the 1960s, but perhaps that's because it was the one prediction Heinlein really did get right. At the time I'm sure I simply looked dumbfounded by the imagined course of the next two centuries as if searching for some clue as to what was going to happen that evening.

I excused myself and went back downstairs. I was beginning to feel the effects of the sherry. I took a wrong turning and found myself in a utility room. I felt as if I was trapped in the labyrinthine tesseract of Heinlein's story. I eventually found my way back to the lounge and looked around like a lost child. Hubbard caught my eye.

'She's outside, kid,' he drawled with a cruel smile.

I went to the door and spied Mary-Lou by the front porch

standing close to Jack Parsons. He was pointing up at the sky, tracing a constellation as he talked in a low, intense drone. I felt as if I was losing my footing and I held onto the door for support. I went back inside, walking in an absurd crouching posture. Leslyn Heinlein frowned as she handed me another glass of sherry and asked Nemesio about Mexico. He said that he was actually from Cuba. I tried hard to concentrate as he told me his story. Like many young men he insisted on a pattern to his as yet unformed life. He was always late, he concluded. He had planned to go to Spain to fight with an anarchist militia. Two days before he was due to embark from Havana, Franco marched into Madrid. He then went to Mexico to study, with the intention of meeting Leon Trotsky. He finally obtained a letter of introduction only to arrive at Coyoacán four days after Trotsky was assassinated by Ramón Mercader.

'I think this is why I started writing about the future, so as not to be late,' he explained with a grin. 'But I am also interested in tech-nological utopianism.'

He had come to LA, making contact with a disparate group of American radicals: Trotskyists, members of the Technocracy Movement and libertarians like Heinlein, who had been involved in Upton Sinclair's End Poverty in California campaign back in the 1930s.

The party was beginning to break up. Mary-Lou came back into the lounge.

'Larry,' she said, somewhat breathlessly, 'I'm getting a ride with Jack.'

'But, but, Mary-Lou,' I slurred. 'I thought I was driving you home.'

'It's okay, Larry. You'll want to talk some more.' I remember the way her eyes sparkled as she said: 'Hasn't it been a wonderful evening?'

Then she was gone. My recollection of the evening after that begins to jump around. Leaps in time and space. I was in the kitchen helping myself to another drink. Joining in with a dirty limerick recitation (*There once was a fellow McSweeney/Who spilt some gin on his weenie/Just to be couth/He added vermouth/And slipped his girlfriend the martini*). Throwing up in a plant pot. Collapsing onto the couch in the lounge.

The following morning's hangover was ghastly, augmented by wretched feelings of guilt and humiliation. I apologised to the Heinleins for my behaviour. Leslyn was certainly annoyed with me but Robert just laughed it off and plied me with strong black coffee. Nemesio had also stayed over, sleeping in the spare room in a more planned and civilised fashion. I gave him a ride downtown to where he was lodging with an elderly couple who worked for the League for Industrial Democracy.

When I confided to him about Mary-Lou he gave a long sigh.

'*Siempre,*' he declared. 'With love it is always hard.'

Nemesio always seemed older than his years. He was actually a few months younger than me but from the start he assumed a sense of seniority in our friendship. I never minded this. He was, after all, far more mature than me in so many ways. He gave me a political awareness and something of a sentimental education. We had experiences in common that acted as a kind of emotional bond: we had both grown up without fathers. We agreed that we would see each other at the next LASFS meeting.

After dropping him off I went home and spent the rest of the day trying to ease a blinding headache and to placate my mother who, having waited up for me in vain, had spent the previous night phoning hospitals and police stations, certain that I had become the victim of some gruesome incident.

For the next few days I stayed indoors, struggling to write but mostly brooding about Mary-Lou and Jack Parsons. I found myself rereading an article on his rocket experiments that had appeared in *Popular Mechanics* the previous fall. His handsome face taunted me as it stared out of photographs between illustrations of test sites and diagrams of launch trajectories. Thursday came around and I went along to Clifton's. I tried to clear my mind of it all but before long I was talking about Jack Parsons.

And there was plenty of gossip about him. It was said that he was married, though he and his wife took other lovers; that he was actively recruiting for the Ordo Templi Orientis, hosting discussion groups on literature and mysticism at his home in Pasadena. There were stories too of parties at the OTO Lodge, tales of spiked punch, near orgies and invitations for all to join in the Gnostic Mass in the attic temple.

Luckily Nemesio turned up and managed to distract me from my wild imaginings. He had already acquired the nickname 'Nemo' from the LASFS crowd, which would become his name from then on.

'It's a good one,' I told him. 'Like Verne's submariner in *20,000 Leagues Under the Sea.*'

'It also means "no one",' he replied with a shrug.

He then went on to recount his theory of how Verne had based his Captain Nemo on the nineteenth-century submarine inventor from Barcelona, Narcís Monturiol.

'Narcís?' I retorted. 'Hubbard's right, you know, what is it with these Spanish names?'

'Well, he was Catalan, actually. But, you know, Narcís Monturiol was a visionary, a true exponent of liberational technology. He had written many pamphlets on socialism, pacificism, feminism even. He supported the setting up of utopian communes in the New World. When that failed he became interested in science and technology. His was the first fully functional submarine.'

'Well, a lot of guys on the Atlantic convoys won't thank him for that.'

'Yes, but his was a craft for exploration.' Nemesio began to sketch the design of an underwater craft on a napkin. 'A pilot ship for mankind's journey into the unknown. And his ideas then were still in advance of what the Nazis have now. He developed an independent underwater propulsion system, with a chemical fuel that could generate enough energy to power the vessel and produce oxygen as a side product. It was truly remarkable.'

Nemo showed me his drawing. It was of a fish-shaped craft with a row of portholes along its side.

'It looks like a spaceship,' I remarked.

'Yes,' Nemo agreed. 'Maybe that's what it was. Maybe that is the answer. If you can't change the world, build a spaceship.'

When I walked out of Clifton's that night Mary-Lou was waiting for me. She was wearing slacks and a windcheater with the collar turned up. She looked like a fugitive.

'Hi, Larry,' she said. 'Can we talk?'

We found a bar on South Broadway. We ordered beer and I went to the payphone to call Mother.

'She gets worried if I'm late home,' I explained.

'You're such a good boy, Larry,' she said.

I know now that this was meant tenderly but at the time it was like a jab in the gut. I made my call and then we found a quiet booth. Mary-Lou looked different, her face pale and ethereal, her eyes intense. All at once she began telling me of the strange new things she had learnt, about the Ordo Templi Orientis and its peculiar English Hierophant, Aleister Crowley. She spoke of the power of the will and the gaining of universal knowledge through symbolic ritual.

'Remember that night when I said that I wanted to know everything?' she said, her eyes burning beneath the neon light. 'Well, now I think I can.'

'But that's crazy, Mary-Lou.'

'You see, every man and every woman is a star. Everyone has to find their own destiny. The law of the strong is our law and the joy of the world.'

'The law?'

'Love is the law.'

'Love? Is that how you feel about Jack Parsons?'

She sighed.

'Oh, Larry—'

'But he's married, Mary-Lou.'

'That's just a superficial institution, Larry. We're living in a new age. Monogamy is redundant. If we get rid of jealousy we can really set ourselves free. I mean, look at you.'

'Me?'

'Yes, you. You're so goddamn buttoned-up and neurotic. You should come to the Lodge, you know. It would be so good for you.'

'Er, I don't think so, Mary-Lou.'

'Well,' she said with a curious smile. 'Think about it.'

And then the conversation turned to more or less small talk. We asked each other about our writing, of course. She told me that she had outlined the whole of her space-opera 'Zodiac Empire' for *Superlative Stories*. She was working through the planets towards a final instalment that would centre on the sun. Nemo had told her about a Renaissance heretic and revolutionary called Tommaso Campanella who had written a utopian book titled *The City of the Sun* and she planned to base it on that. We finished our drinks and I dropped her off on my way home.

I hadn't exactly been looking forward to my next appointment with Dr Furedi but even I could not have foreseen such a difficult session. I tried to explain what had happened in the previous week but such was my agitated state, I must have appeared manic and obsessive. And the details, well, I suppose that they did seem a little too much like the demented fantasy of someone who read too many pulp magazines. It soon became clear that my analyst was treating it all as the delusional ravings of some paranoid condition. The good-looking, diabolical scientist was, of course, merely a symptom of my hysteria. Dr Furedi became particularly interested in my reference to 'rockets', obviously interpreting them as the phallic objects of my repressed imagination. I left his consulting room a gibbering wreck.

And the worst thing was that there was an element of truth in his distorted perception of my problem. I was irrationally obsessed with Parsons. And though I was jealous of him for having taken away the presumed object of my affections, I was also jealous of Mary-Lou, in that she had become the focus of his attentions. I was pretty sure that this was not sexual jealousy but with scant practical experience of these matters I felt in serious danger of having some kind of breakdown. It was with a sense of desperation that I decided to face my anxieties head-on.

The Agape Lodge of the Ordo Templi Orientis was in a large wooden house on Winona Boulevard. I persuaded Nemo to come along to an open meeting with me. I was a little scared, to tell you the truth, but I wanted to find out what all this was about. The first part of the meeting was very informal. We were shown into an upstairs lounge buzzing with a bohemian crowd, a mix of young and old, some flamboyantly dressed, others theatrically solemn. I spotted an ancient silent-movie actress chatting to a man whose catlike face was dusted with powder and rouge. We were offered punch. I'd already decided that if this stuff was drugged, well, it would all be part of the experiment. I took a tentative sip. It tasted dark and sweet with a liquorice aftertaste. Suddenly Mary-Lou was next to me.

'Glad you could come, Larry. Go easy with that stuff,' she said, nodding at the cup in my hand. 'It's got a kick to it.'

I stared at her for a second and then drained the rest of the punch in one.

'I'm feeling adventurous.'

She laughed.

'That's good. Because if you come up to the Mass, you've got to take communion. That's the rule.'

A gong sounded and the party began to make its way up a wooden staircase through a trapdoor. As Mary-Lou went on ahead she turned back to me.

'See you later, Larry. Stick around. We're going on to Pasadena later. There's going to be a special party.'

The attic temple was small and gloomy. Wooden benches faced a raised dais where two obelisks flanked a tiered altar lined with candles. There was a hushing of voices as the congregation settled. A trill of soft laughter ran along the pews and a sharp scent of incense filled the air. There came a low drone of a harmonium playing the slow chords of a prelude, though I'm sure I heard in counterpoint the melody of 'Barnacle Bill the Sailor'. At the time I thought this was my febrile imagination but I later found out that the organist liked to improvise around a jaunty tune slowed to a funereal pace.

The Priest and the Priestess entered and the ceremony began. It was not what I had expected. I had imagined some brooding satanic ritual but this seemed almost light-hearted. There was certainly nothing demonic about it. The ceremony had much medieval symbolism: swords parting veils, lances and chalices – Freud knows what Dr Furedi would have made of it all. My mind began to spin very slowly. The drug was taking hold. It was not an unpleasant feeling. The Mass became a long monotonous chant punctuated by sudden moments of exuberant gesture or astonishing verse. Images of burning incense beneath the night stars of the desert, of the serpent flames of rocket launches. Alien dialogue in some far-flung adventure. And I was somehow part of it. I felt relief flood through my usually anxious self. I figure now that it was probably mescaline that had spiced up the punch.

At times I found myself enthralled by the drama in the temple and at others almost oblivious to the proceedings. The Priest and the Priestess appeared to show real passion for each other as they enacted a strange sensual fertility rite. The woman spoke urgently of pleasure, pale or purple, veiled or voluptuous, of a song of rapture to arouse the coiled splendour within and for a moment I was utterly enchanted. Then the Priest began to chant an unintelligible dirge and my thoughts diffused. I drifted into a trancelike state and before I knew it the Mass was at an end and we were all summoned to a communion of wine and rust-coloured wafers. As we filed out the organ played a recessional of ominous chords with a slow ditty over it that sounded much like 'Yes, We Have No Bananas'.

Back in the lounge I was talking with Nemo. The conversation seemed urgently heightened and languidly casual at the same time. There were moments when we seemed to be having the same thoughts simultaneously. We felt sophisticated, wildly intellectual. Our eyes locked and I noticed that his pupils were as sharp as pencil leads. We both agreed that this Mass would not seem out of place in a pulp fantasy, that so many of the stories we had been exposed to appeared to hark back to a warped idea of the Middle Ages, with knights, maidens, quests and supernatural revelation. Nemo spoke of how so much space-opera seemed to be a rendition of some interstellar Holy Roman Empire. We had begun to speculate on what kind of religion a science-fiction writer would come up with when Mary-Lou came over to join us.

'You took the host then,' she said to me. 'You know they're prepared with animal blood.'

I shrugged, not knowing what to say but determined not to be shocked as she thought I would be. I noticed Jack Parsons at the far end of the room, holding court amid a small circle of people. The Priest and Priestess stood near him, touching each other with a casual intimacy.

'The Priestess seems to be in love with the Priest,' I said to Mary-Lou.

'Oh, that's Helen Parsons,' she retorted. 'Jack's wife.'

'You mean . . . ?'

'I told you, Larry. We have to reject hypocritical social standards.'

I felt my face flush at the thought of it. I let out a peculiar giggle.

'Larry?' said Mary-Lou.

'Mary-Lou,' I replied.

I wanted to say that I loved her. Love! To call it out just as the celebrants had done in the Gnostic Mass.

'You're coming out to Pasadena with us?' she asked.

I nodded and my teeth clenched in a manic grin. My head raced with curiosity and delirious expectation.

The May evening was warm when we reached the Arroyo Seco, the dry ravine that cuts through the San Gabriel Mountains. The scrubland at the edge of Pasadena was then a suburban wilderness, a homely arcadia thick with chaparral, sycamore and tangled thickets of wild grape. The Caltech rocket group had the lease on three acres that had been cleared as a launch site. There was a group of corrugated-sheet metal huts, a sandbag bunker and an arcane assembly of test apparatus. These were the beginnings of the famous Jet Propulsion Laboratory.

Some kind of party had already begun. There was wine and beer and a sense of pagan revelry. I was passed a thin, hand-rolled cigarette. Marijuana, I thought with an exuberant sense of sinfulness. I took a puff and broke into a spluttering spasm. Nemo took it from me and inhaled the drug with casual expertise. He had tried it in Mexico, he confided to me. Mary-Lou explained to us that tonight was a ritual to influence the space–time continuum. This was the special Mass that Jack Parsons had spoken of that night at the Heinleins', the one ordered by the Hierophant to change the course of the war.

Parsons arrived in white robes, clutching a spray of mistletoe in one hand, a sickle in the other. The party started to form itself into a circle around him. It was then that I saw the rocket on its stand. Taller than he was, it seemed to tower above us, a totem, a faceless idol. On the ground around it were scorch marks and what looked like runic markings. Parsons began an ululating invocation to the god Pan. Drunk and drugged, my mind reeled but my body assumed its tranquillised equilibrium. I felt a wonderful balance: my weight in the earth, my head in the sky. I turned to Nemo and he nodded to me, wide-eyed and smiling.

'Yeah,' he said. 'We're going to make contact, man.'

I nodded back. I had no idea what he meant but at that moment it all seemed to make sense. The sky darkened and Parsons motioned for the circle to widen. At nightfall the rocket was launched. There was an explosion of thrust, an exultant rush of energy into the heavens. The crowd gasped as one.

'Yes,' Nemo hissed as the vehicle reached its zenith.

The rocket released its payload, a parachute flare that floated like an angel of grace over the Arroyo Seco. As it descended, Nemesio pointed to something beyond it high up in the firmament.

'See?' he implored. 'They're here, man!'

I couldn't tell what he was gesturing at. All I could see were some dim stars that were just making themselves visible.

'Come on,' he said and began to make his way towards the San Gabriel Mountains. 'They're coming in to land!'

I went after him for a while but he moved like a man possessed, following a track up into the canyon. I called after him as he began to climb the hillside. Then he was gone.

I went back to the party. A bonfire had been lit and shadow figures danced in the convulsive firelight. My once-benign mood of narcosis began to fade and the evening's saturnalia now seemed harsh and sinister. My anxiety returned, unwelcome but familiar. I wandered about, trying to find Mary-Lou. I thought I caught a glimpse of a wild goat gambolling in a darkened glade. I followed and found myself in a clearing. There was a trickle of laughter and by the flickering light I could make out bodies cavorting in this sacramental grove. Yellow flames licked at the pitched gloom and here and there naked flesh glowed amber or albescent. A bright flare from the pyre lit up a face, which turned and caught my gaze. It was Mary-Lou. She smiled as she saw me, her eyes brimstone, her mouth a lewd grimace.

'Come on, Larry,' she implored in a harsh whisper. 'Join us!'

I froze. My whole body clenched into an apoplectic spasm, but for a heart that hammered away in a wild palpitation. I felt a terrible sadness. The image of the twisted bodies was already seared on my memory, my timid desire overwhelmed by a dreadful sense of loss. This was the death of love, I suddenly thought.

Perhaps Mary-Lou caught my look of dismay, I don't know. Her face went blank for a second and then she turned away from me, into the embrace of Jack Parsons and two or three others.

I stumbled away unsteadily and out of joint, coldly sober but reeling about like a drunken fool. I lay down in the dust and felt the world spin against my back. Looking down at the starry depths, I felt the lonely vertigo of the universe. My own sorry little space-opera stretched out into infinity. Eventually I regained enough balance to pick myself up and walk to my car. I clambered onto the back seat and fell into a troubled sleep.

I woke to Nemo gently shaking my shoulder. I got out of the car and adjusted my eyes to the powdery haze of morning.

'What happened to you?' I asked him.

He shrugged and stared back at me with dead eyes. He looked as if he had been dragged through a forest.

'It's hard to explain, Larry,' he said. 'I saw something.'

I never got the whole story of what he witnessed that night. Over the years he would refer to the time when he had seen 'something from another world' but he always seemed reluctant to elaborate further. For a while I thought he worried that I might think he was crazy. But maybe he just wanted to keep it to himself. To save it for his fiction. And the influence of this experience can certainly be found in his work, in stories such as 'Interstellar Epiphany' and 'The Uninvited Guest'. At the time neither of us really wanted to talk about the previous night so we drove back to LA mostly in silence.

Mother was predictably upset when I turned up at the house looking wild-eyed and dishevelled and I was unnecessarily blunt with her when she asked after my whereabouts, loudly declaring that I had been at an orgy.

'Larry!' she chided me.

'Oh, don't worry, Mother,' I called out as I went up to my room, 'your precious son is still a virgin.'

I came down later to find her in the kitchen. Her face was red and puffy; she had obviously been crying. I said I was sorry and then all her pitiful guilt came out. She declared that she had not been a good mother, that she had driven away my father who had left us when I was three. That useless slob of a husband whom she still loved with a pathetic insistence. Poor Mother, I thought for the millionth time. But it was then I knew that I had to get away from her somehow.

Mary-Lou phoned me the next day, saying that she wanted to meet up and talk. Part of me wished that I had the strength to say no but I didn't. So the following Tuesday I walked into Clifton's to find her sitting at a corner table reading the *LA Times*.

'See what we did, Larry,' she declared, holding up the headline for me to read:

BERLIN DENIES KNOWLEDGE OF LANDING OF REICH LEADER IN SCOTLAND.

It hardly registered at the time. Recently I've got to thinking that the 'special Mass' Jack Parsons had officiated at that night was part of Operation Mistletoe. There are stories that Crowley organised similar rituals in a forest in Sussex at about the same time. Whether or not they actually had any effect is another matter. Were they part of some obscure propaganda campaign? At that moment I was so wrapped up in my own private drama that I didn't pay much attention to the news story. I just sat down opposite Mary-Lou and gave a nervous little shrug. She smiled at me but there was a mournful look in her eyes.

'Look, the other night,' she said, trying to break through the awkwardness of the moment. 'I know you don't approve but—'

'It's not that,' I broke in.

'Well—'

'I love you, Mary-Lou.'

'What?' She frowned at me.

'I'm sorry. I just had to let you know.'

She gave a weary sigh.

'Well, I kind of guessed,' she said.

'And it's a simple, conventional, boring kind of love. I just want you and nobody else.'

'Poor Larry.'

'Please, Mary-Lou, don't.'

'I know how you feel.'

'No you don't.'

'Yes I do. I want Jack. But Jack is in love with Betty.'

'Betty? Who's Betty?'

'Helen's sister. Remember Helen? Jack's wife.'

'Who's having an affair with the High Priest of the Agape Lodge.'

'Yeah.'

'And now Jack's taken up with his sister-in-law?'

'Uh-huh. You know, being a script reader, you think you know all the plots. I missed that one.'

'What will you do?'

'Oh, carry on loving Jack. All these personal relationships can get melodramatic, but there is a higher love. I'll stay true to that.'

'How very wild and unconventional of you,' I muttered bitterly.

'Oh, Larry.'

'I'm sorry, it's just—'

'Can we still be friends?'

'I don't know, Mary-Lou,' I said. 'I really don't know.'

As I stood she looked up at me, her sad and plaintive smile like a stab in the heart. I know now that amid all her emotional confusion what she really needed was a friend. She already looked exhausted by the madly idealistic world she had been drawn into.

Soon after that, all the symptoms of my labyrinthitis seemed to diminish, then disappear. I felt somehow cured and at first was unsure what had restored the equilibrium in that delicate maze of the senses. Had it been the effect of the mescaline or the marijuana, or even some strange influence of ritual magic? All my problems with balance or vertigo began to recede and my anxiety resolved itself into a calm melancholia. Perhaps it was the heartbreak that gave some bifurcated stability to my inner life. Finally I had felt something real in my life, even if was just emotional pain.

I gave up going to see Dr Furedi and put all my energy into my work. I spent a lot of time with Nemo that summer. We would both snatch a bit of time off from writing and drive out to the coast. On one occasion Nemo arranged a double date for us that predictably didn't work out for me. Another time we organised a full-scale beach party for the LASFS. But usually it was just me and him walking along the shore, clearing our heads and talking our ideas into life. Then back to the clatter of the typewriter, chasing tight deadlines and new stories. Nemo could take inspiration from almost anywhere and so swiftly transform it into prose. One afternoon he got the spark of an idea from observing the eccentric street hustlers on Hollywood Boulevard and by the next morning he had turned it into 'The Hermit', which he sold to *Incredible Stories*.

I could talk to Nemo about my feelings, about Mary-Lou and the problems at home with my mother. Dr Furedi had always insisted that most of my emotional hang-ups were somehow connected to being deserted by my father. But Nemo had been through that, too, so I no longer felt strange or weird about it.

And he eventually got me to understand something of the

complicated politics on the left. He even took me along to a few meetings. He was certain that Trotskyism was the last hope for utopian socialism.

'It can't exist in just one country,' he insisted to me one night as we sat on the beach and watched the sun go down. 'It's got to be international.'

'Maybe it's got to be more than that, even,' I countered.

He turned and squinted at me.

'What?' he demanded.

'Well,' I replied, unable to stop myself breaking into a smile, 'maybe we can't have socialism on one planet alone. Maybe it's got to be interstellar!'

Nemo let out a brief spatter of laughter. Then he sighed and gazed wistfully at the darkening horizon.

'Who knows?' he murmured.

Nemo felt proud that he could retain the idealism that had been compromised by orthodox communism. Then Germany invaded the Soviet Union and theoretical discourse became overwhelmed by the practical horrors in that massive clash of ideologies. I think that he felt helpless and guilty as he was once more a mere spectator to the grinding wheel of history. Party members now became indignant and self-righteous; ordinary citizens seemed relieved that these great behemoths were now slugging it out so bloodily on the Eastern Front. The West seemed safe, at least for the time being.

I went up in front of a Draft Board in August and remarkably I was designated 1A – available for unrestricted military service. A lot of my contemporaries were looking around for ways of avoiding being called up. Mother offered to put me through college in the fall, which would keep me out of it for a while, but I refused. I was happy enough to have become a healthy specimen at last.

And for the most part I could get on with my life and not dwell on Mary-Lou or Jack Parsons. But I couldn't quite shake them off in the fictional world that I sought refuge in. 'Greek Fire', which I sold to *Fabulous Tales*, features a rocket scientist unsure of whether to use solid or liquid fuel, who travels back in time to the Byzantine Empire to investigate the dual properties of the ancient incendiary weapon of the title. I saw it as a cathartic exercise, especially the final scene with its huge laboratory explosion. And though I managed to avoid running into Mary-Lou in person, I found it impossible not to read her work. Her 'Zodiac Empire' series became more and more mystical and obscure, an epic of conflicting planet colonies in the solar system set against alien influences from distant constellations. Mary-Lou had told me that it was to culminate in its transcendent conclusion, 'The City of the Sun', but that instalment never appeared.

It had been a year of quantum leaps, of diverging time-lines, alternate futures and crucial moments where things could go either way: 'jonbar points' as SF writers had already started to call them after the title of Jack Williamson's seminal story. So when I heard the news of the attack on Pearl Harbor, which shocked the whole nation, I felt hardly surprised by it. In fact, a strange calm descended upon me as for the first time in my life I knew exactly what to do.

On 8 December I joined the USAAF. I didn't want to wait for the call-up and I had some insane idea that I wanted to fly. It wasn't so much out of patriotic duty, or a sense of political commitment. It was more a lonely impulse, simply to take action and to be ruled by fate. And I could break free, leave home without any sense of guilt or responsibility. I hadn't an inkling of what this supposed independence would cost me and Mother was out of her wits with worry. But now we both had something bigger to blame.

I had a drink with Nemo the night before I shipped out. After we had said our farewells I had the sudden urge to say goodbye to Mary-Lou. I think I had this drunken notion of making some sort of noble exit, full of stoicism and fake nonchalance. But when I called by she wasn't in. The next morning I was on a bus to the West Coast Air Corps Training Center in Santa Ana and I didn't see her again for four years.

6

the lovers

'Bloomsbury's blown to bits,' K blurted out as our train pulled into Paddington. We had been talking of our last sortie to London, at first in a flippant & almost jolly manner, but by the time we had reached the suburbs of the besieged city the mood darkened considerably. K seemed gripped with a dread of arrival and recalled the horrors we had witnessed last September – all the wrecked buildings in West Central & fires everywhere from the incendiaries. But I remember that it had been the time bomb in Mecklenburgh Square that had disturbed K the most. She had fancifully imagined that the Germans had come up with a secret weapon that had some means of exploding time itself. Of course, given the way that she has played with that dimension in her own work, it was hardly surprising that she might conjure up such a curious conceit. I first thought that she was making a joke, but she was genuinely disturbed by the notion & I had to try to explain that it was merely the business of a delayed fuse. The whole area had to be roped off, which was a disaster for the ~~Woolfs~~ Wolves (!) who had only recently set up a new office for the Hogarth Press in the square. Then a month later their house in Tavistock Square took a direct hit. Trust K to come up with a grim formula that trips so lightly: 'Bloomsbury's blown to bits.'

It seems odd now but once powered flight had seemed to bring such hope. Like the aeroplane writing in the sky in *Mrs Dalloway*; the great women pilots Amelia Earhart and Amy Johnson. Well, Earhart and Johnson are dead and all around us is the devastation brought by the air raids. Of course it became a symbol of failure with Chamberlain ('If at first you don't concede, fly, fly, fly again'). And in K's novel the Sacred Aeroplane of Munich becomes a holy relic of Hitlerism.

K took a long time to leave the carriage & as we walked along the platform she again declared that she ought never to have let

Victor republish the novel, that she knew it would mean trouble, etc. There was a crowd huddling around the barrier & we stood for a while waiting until all the other passengers had gone through. I grabbed her hand & held it tightly &, checking that nobody was looking in our direction, sneaked a kiss on her cheek. She smiled & pulled me along, turning to point at the poster that said: IS YOUR JOURNEY REALLY NECESSARY? & we both broke out into a short salvo of much-needed laughter.

Arrived at the Gollancz offices in Henrietta St at about 3 p.m. The place was almost deserted, just a secretary who served us tea with condensed milk. Victor's moved most of his operation out to his country house in Brimpton. He seemed in an ebullient mood though, saying the Left Book Club edition of *Swastika Night* had sold over seventeen thousand copies & how this was impressive for sales in wartime etc., but K was impatient to get to the heart of the matter – the nature of Victor's strange summons. It appears that there has been a request via the War Office for an interview with 'Murray Constantine' by an intelligence officer. This rattled K & she once again made clear her reasons for continued anonymity. He tried to reassure us but we know the drastic measures that many of us have considered if the worst was to happen. Victor himself has boasted that he's got hold of a 'poison pill' & is ready to take it if we lose the war. There is this Gestapo list everyone talks of – it's the reason that K used a pen name in the first place. He doesn't even know what exactly the matter with the WO might be. K tried to insist that her confidentiality be maintained though Victor pointed out that this might be difficult if it was a 'matter of security'. An ominous phrase. Agreed for Victor to arrange a meeting on Monday.

On the way to our hotel K appeared distracted & vague. That queer manner she adopts, as if possessed, when she is about to compose something. I tried to lighten the mood & joked that she looked as if she had 'a book coming on' & she suddenly snapped out of it. Something was stirring her imagination, she told me. Not an idea for a story, though. 'What then?' I asked & her face creased in self-astonishment. 'An awful premonition,' she said.

Thursday, 27 March 1941

To Margaret Goldsmith's who seems v. keen to work with K again on another book. But now K seems adamant that she has given up writing 'for the duration' & will instead engage in war work (though quite what she has in mind escapes me). Can't help thinking that this business with the WO has thrown her. Margaret went on to recount a particularly gruesome Blitz tale – the Café de Paris in Leicester Square caught a direct hit a fortnight ago (it had been thought safe because it was in the basement of a cinema). A note of hubris in the story – the rich in the West End enjoying themselves while the East End bears the brunt etc. A sense of Grand Guignol too, scores of bright young things killed, the bandleader decapitated, looters robbing the dead & dying etc. And oh the irony of it all – the dance hall had been modelled on the ballroom of the *Titanic*! There's a certain relish in the way the liberal left dwell on such examples of punished decadence.

With careful diplomacy we asked after Frederick Voigt & she told us that he is now employed in a research unit in some secret location involved in propaganda & is rather appalled at the level of lying and duplicity. Thought for a moment that Frederick might be useful in advising us on this possible 'security' matter & that it was a shame that he & Margaret are now divorced. Didn't articulate the latter sentiment, needless to say, or that we are to visit Vita Sackville-West tomorrow – knowing how awkwardly Margaret's affair with her turned out.

Quiet night & no air raid.

Friday, 28 March 1941

Arrived at Sissinghurst late morning. Glorious day & Vita led us around the grounds. She has had a wretched time of it this week – one of her Alsatians killed another dog & had to be put down & her budgerigars are all dying (she can no longer get the correct food for them or something). Yet despite (or maybe because of) this she seemed deliberately effusive & gay. She showed us where she planned to plant her great 'White Garden', gesturing at imagined white clematis, white lavender, white agapanthus, white double primroses, anemones, lilies & a pale peach pulverulenta. A rather wondrous scheme – though she has neither the resources nor the labour to carry it out at present. 'Let us plant & be merry,' Vita declared, 'though it all might be destroyed in an instant.' K spoke of gardens as utopias. 'A small patch of Earthly Paradise.'

'Yes,' Vita replied, 'amid the sorrow of war, small pleasures must correct great tragedies.'

'*Il faut cultiver notre jardin*,' I chipped in clumsily.

Vita: 'Oh yes, darling, we've got to dig for victory & that doesn't just mean beans & potatoes.' But soon a bleakness caught up with us. 'I've asked Hadji how on earth we are going to win this war,' Vita said (using her pet name for Harold Nicolson), 'and he's hard pressed to give me a straight answer.'

There's a general feeling that recent events in the Med. & N. Africa have turned very badly against us. Once again desperate measures are mentioned. Vita & Harold too have their suicide pills – the 'bare bodkin' they call it (after a line in *Hamlet*). K complained of a migraine & went indoors to lie down. She is so affected by this gloomy talk of suicide and I feel that she really doesn't approve of it.

Vita spoke warmly of K, and of how much she admires her writing. 'I've been inspired to write my own cautionary tale. Another meditation on what might happen if we lose this wretched war. I hope she won't mind.' Mentioned that we had seen Margaret G. in town & Vita's smile seemed at once knowing & wistful. She breaks hearts & yet feels sorry for it – maybe out of guilt, but more likely because she hates it when anyone she has loved withdraws their affection. 'I never like to completely drop anyone,' she confided. 'Instead, well, they keep part of myself. Emotional alimony, Margaret used to call it.'

'I hope you don't think that you owe me emotional alimony,' I retorted with mock indignation (while all the time remembering old wounds).

'Heavens, no,' she replied. 'You'd hardly need it anyhow. I've scarcely seen two people so deeply in love' (meaning me & K). 'The desire & the pursuit of the whole, that's what Plato called it,' she went on.

'Called what?'

'Love. With me it's complex. It's Hadji, of course. And the garden. And all my foolish affairs. And—' She let out a deep sigh & confessed to me that Violet Trefusis wanted her back. 'I love her perennially but I can't trust her or allow myself to . . .' Vita trailed off then burst out suddenly: 'She's like an unexploded bomb! And I don't want her to explode. I don't want her to disrupt my life again.'

K slept through the afternoon & woke up dazed, her eyes wide & filmy. 'I had a drowning dream,' she told me drowsily. 'Or a dreaming drown.'

Saturday, 29 March 1941

Harold arrived from London at lunchtime. Much talk about Vanessa Bell's daughter Angelica now living with Bunny Garnett. Given that Bunny once had an affair with Angelica's father, the situation seems rather complicated. Inevitably the conversation moved to Virginia W. Vanessa had apparently mentioned on her last visit to Sissinghurst that she feared her sister was becoming ill again & on the verge of a nervous breakdown. 'But she was fine when I last saw her,' Vita said. 'And I had a jolly letter from her only last week.'

Harold has spent all week at the Min. of Information, keeping quiet about British & Commonwealth troops landing in Greece. He is confident of the long term but only if we can hang on. His worst fear is that we might get so worn down by foreign campaigns that we keep losing & will be so starved out by the bombers & U-boats at home that we might be forced to accept terms. K vehement that we must carry on the war. Funny, she used to be such a committed pacifist. All those years we spent being for peace & now so determinedly in favour of fighting.

We talked of this paradox on the train back to town. It was the twisted minds of men that got us into this mess, the cult of the male that made fascism possible. And yet we now have to watch our men fight with no power of our own. How do we fight? With our minds, of course, with our imagination that might realise an alternative in the future. K declared that she was tired of this mental struggle, tired of writing. She wants to do something practical, until the war is over at least. She is v. sensitive to any collective feelings of despair, the allusions to suicide & madness. 'I can imagine giving up for good,' she told me with a sad smile, 'letting the current pull one under, the water closing above.'

Sunday, 30 March 1941

An air raid this evening (the first one we've witnessed this time in London). Talk has been that the Luftwaffe have been busy pounding the provinces & the capital has been quiet for the past week – well, they're back again. Made our way to a public shelter. V. gloomy with frightful stench of humanity & carbolic. We heard a strange groaning from a darkened corner & at first thought someone had been taken ill. Soon realised that it was a couple having sexual relations. Strange how plaintive & mournful the act sounds when overheard. All-clear sounded at 4 a.m.

Monday, 31 March 1941

To Gollancz for this meeting with the intelligence officer, a certain Commander Fleming. K insisted that I be present so we both waited in a room that Victor had made ready. Both v. nervous but from the outset this interview had all the makings of a delightful farce with themes of mistaken identity & gender transformation that could have come straight from K's fiction. Commander Fleming entered, expecting presumably to meet a male author, only to be confronted by not one but two women. He quickly realised something was afoot & for a moment was clearly flustered. Then when he finally asked which one of us was Murray Constantine, I was tempted to add another twist to the deception & confess to being him myself but K spoke out first. 'Surely you must be used to cover names in your line of work,' I said after K had identified herself.

'Of course,' agreed Fleming then turned to K & asked: 'But why a man's name?'

K replied that at first she reasoned that male authors are always taken more seriously than female ones & added that she always felt that 'the writer is essentially androgynous'. The commander looked mildly shocked at this. K went on to explain that also, since the Spanish war & all the events since, it seemed wise to continue to use a pseudonym.

'Well, you certainly offer a harsh critique of fascism,' he concurred & then went on to talk about *Swastika Night*, calling it 'astonishing' & praising K for her grasp of 'ideology & geopolitics'. I mentioned our past friendship with Frederick Voigt, who had been diplomatic correspondent to Germany for the *Manchester Guardian* when Hitler came to power, & also pointing out that he was now working for some intelligence dept. Fleming made a note of this but now seemed concerned with specific details in K's book. He asked about the use of the name Hess for one of the characters – the 'Knight' in the story & a reference to this man being a descendant of Rudolf Hess, the Deputy Führer.

'It's set in the future,' K explained.

'Yes, but was there any reason why you chose Hess out of the entire Nazi inner circle to provide the ancestor for your character?'

'I call him von Hess, actually.'

'Well, this Hess, or von Hess of the future, suddenly leaves the inner circle of the Nazi Party and flees to Scotland. What inspired you to write that?' K shrugged & Fleming went on: 'All I want to know is, did you get the idea from anybody else?'

'No. I mean, all of my stories come from somewhere else. I'm not sure where. They visit me.'

'Like a premonition?' the man asked.

'Perhaps. Though the word premonition always seems a little hopeless. I mean, we can never know what we predict until it happens.'

'Indeed,' Fleming agreed, looking rather intense and intrigued.

I added that K's creativity was much like tuning in to some radio wave, that the writer in her was like an alien being. He then asked about the process of writing. 'Why are you interested?' K retorted.

'Are you working on something yourself?' At which the man looked rather sheepish.

'Do you discuss it, with your, um—' He nodded at me, clearly unsure of our relationship.

I fully expected K to describe me as her 'companion' but instead she reached out, took my hand & declared: 'With my lover, you mean? Oh dear, that does rather put us on the Gestapo list, doesn't it?'

The commander was completely taken aback by this & he struggled to regain his composure, forcing a smile & nervously flicking at a stray curl of hair at his brow. One noticed for the first time how handsome he was. Men can be quite charming when they drop their guard. He brought the interview to a close & assured us that everything said in the interview was in strict confidence & implored us not to talk of it to anyone else. And that was that. After he had left we said our goodbyes to Victor & got a taxi to Paddington.

We found a corner seat in a packed carriage on the train home. 'Back to our lives as eccentric country gentlewomen,' K joked. I told her that I was glad she had said what she did. 'About being lovers?' she rejoined. 'Well, I don't suppose we should shout it from the rooftops too often.'

Thursday, 3 April 1941

Short report in *The Times* this morning: 'We announce with regret that it now must be presumed that Mrs Leonard Woolf (Virginia Woolf, the novelist and essayist), who has been missing since last Friday, has been drowned in the Sussex Ouse at Rodmell, near Lewes.' It seems clear that she took her own life. Terrible sense of shock & grief. Well, Bloomsbury really is blown to bits now. And after all the past week's talk of suicide there's an irrational feeling of complicity. K feels certain that Virginia was in some sense a victim of a collective despair and says that she felt some kind of premonition. She points out that it might well have happened that afternoon at Sissinghurst when she had her 'drowning dream'.

7

the chariot

'I have been reading today of the deaths of the Soviet cosmonauts,' Hess remembered telling the American commandant in the garden at Spandau in the summer of 1971. 'As I have been studying space travel now with the help of NASA for so many months, I do have some ideas on this.'

He had been an enthusiastic observer of the space race from its beginnings in the late 1950s right through to the lunar landings. After the moon it had been the space stations. There had been an accident on Soyuz II when it had been undocking from Salyut I, the first operational orbital base.

There he had sat, on a warm afternoon in Speer's garden, a sharp sun lighting up the architect's folly. That miniature province that the former Minister of Armaments and War Production had built in the prison courtyard. In the fifth year of his confinement Speer had drawn up plans and landscaped the enclosed area. Pathways fanned out from a central axis flanked with elaborate arrangements of topiary and sculpted herbaceous borders. Then he set to work on the monumental rock gardens: squared blocks of stacked brick that formed raised beds in an infantile proportion to his lost triumphalism. Lying on the grass beside them, Speer would gaze up and see the walls and towers of a great city. A miniature vision of the *Welthauptstadt*, the world capital Germania, his last and unfinished project now realised as an ornamental parterre.

Yet once it had been completed, Speer seldom spent much time within his botanical domain. At exercise time he would walk around it, keeping to the perimeter track, avoiding the forking paths of the enclosure. Like a degenerate angel or forgetful Titan he would absently wander at the edge of his creation. Then he began to imagine journeys and measure their distance as he trod around the yard for hours on end. He first walked to Heidelberg, then on through Europe, eastward in a clockwise loop. Given his nature, it was inevitable that he would conceive a plan to walk the earth. This would be the conquest that could redress the failure of the architect's most notorious client. To circumnavigate a schematic world with four corners, an oblong Mappa Mundi with its holy subdivisions, its monstrous memories, its hidden Earthly Paradise. He moved through continents at a rate of forty-nine kilometres a week, using guidebooks and friendly guards to provide the details of his journey. By the time of his release in 1966 he had reached Mexico.

Speer's great rock garden had seen something of a decline, that was for sure: weeded and overgrown, with some of its tiered masonry displaced. But the architect would approve, Hess mused. Speer, with a pompous aesthetic that yearned to make glorious ruins, had imagined himself as Europe's last classicist. Hess sighed and his mind muttered: a taste for grandeur was always our weakness.

'These cosmonauts have been in orbit for twenty-four days,' he had told the American commandant. 'No one has remained in zero gravity for that long.'

And yet he had been weightless for decades. Ever since his flight. He had never quite landed, never quite made it back to terra firma. His had been a long, slow orbit, a continuous fall. And just as Speer bestrode the earth, he had continued to look to the heavens. Each person has his journey through life; his was across the sky. And so he had developed this hobby, an obsession with the space race. He had corresponded with NASA and they had even sent him some star charts, maps and photographs of the moon. Of course many of their top scientists were old colleagues really, party members some of them. Oh yes, it was the Germans who had conquered space.

He had seen the beginnings of it as he had planned his flight, at the Messerschmitt works in Augsburg. After practice sorties he would relax in the canteen with the test pilots, discussing technical points and modifications he might require for his mission. He enjoyed their company, the sense of a shared temperament. He remembered that extraordinary woman flyer, Hannah Reitsch, who had tested dive-bombers, helicopters, the massive transport gliders, even a missile with a cockpit. Yes, it was she who had told him of the rocket launches at Peenemünde.

Hess had endeavoured to keep up with all the astonishing innovations by scientists working for the Reich. He had set up the Department for Matters of Special Technical Importance. And Willi Messerschmitt, that great inventor, was sympathetic to Hess's aspirations. Goering had refused to give him a plane but Willi was happy to provide him with one. He showed him the new prototypes at his factory where he had lovingly built sublime vehicles of martial beauty, like the earlier master craftsmen of Augsburg who made the elegantly fluted steel armour for Emperor Maximilian in the imperial workshops there. Willi's aircraft looked aquiline, fearsome. Hess knew then that he was staring at the future. Such sleek vessels, with turbojets and curious exhaust nozzles, strange fins and gills. Mythical beasts of prey made to soar and swoop. The Me 163 rocket plane with swept-back wings, seeming more like a spacecraft than an aeroplane. The Me 262 jet fighter with its huge turbine engines, its shark-like aspect of rounded nose with flat underside, built for minimum drag and maximum speed. How could they lose with such power?

And this is what he would tell them on his mission of peace: that their aircraft production was unbeatable. It was this that could give them air supremacy but they were aiming for the stars. They could bring an end to the war in the heavens. Once there was peace in the West the true crusade could begin. And he was nearly ready. There were promising reports from secret meetings in Madrid and Lisbon. There were other portents to consider also. The astrological aspect had to be precise. He was waiting for the correct prediction from a new advisor, a woman named Astrid. In the meantime he had received a single card reading from the Tarot: the Chariot. It indicated the desire to progress but also impetuousness, impulsiveness, anxiety. The problem with any single card is that it can have two separate, and often opposite, readings. The Chariot could mean success, recognised merits, great ambitions, the ability to lead; but it could also mean failure, incorrect judgement, the sudden loss of a sure result.

He had to make a decision soon. His aircraft was ready. A twin-engined Me 110 fitted with drop tanks for a long-distance flight. A newly assembled machine that had been approved by the inspectorate and issued with a work number and a radio code. Instead of being delivered to an appropriate operational unit, it was at his disposal. It was freshly painted with a grey-green mackereling on its upper surface, pale-blue sky camouflage on its underside. It looked beautiful. He realised then the significance of the Tarot card. This was his Chariot. He sat in the pilot's seat and checked the controls. He shifted his position to find a comfortable posture for such a long journey.

'Of course, re-entry can be the most dangerous stage in a space mission.' Hess stood up and began to walk. The American commandant followed him along the central path of the garden. 'And with long periods of weightlessness the body tends to atrophy, the heart works with less energy, blood does not flow properly. Perhaps it was the sudden changes of pressure and gravity as they came back into the atmosphere that proved fatal. Maybe they needed to adjust much as a deep-sea diver does before he can come to the surface. Or perhaps this zero-gravity degeneration needs to be corrected by artificial means.'

The American commandant watched the gaunt figure of the solitary prisoner become animated, gesturing with his bony hands as he described his plans for a revolving platform for the interior of a space station.

'Anyway,' said Hess, folding his hands behind his back and striding forward, 'why not send into space fanatical scientists who are prepared to give their lives to research? Or people who are ill with cancer who could volunteer what is left of their lives to science and the clarification of what period a man can stay weightless in space? The programme must go on of course. It is absolutely necessary to explore space.'

Hess nodded up towards Tower No. 3, where a Russian guard had been watching them both.

'After all,' he went on, 'the Soviets are ahead of you with this space station. Is it only for scientific purposes? It could be a launch platform for atomic weapons.'

He stopped and turned to the commandant.

'They'll never let me go, will they? Like they did with Speer and the others. Tell me the truth, Commandant. I know you had dinner last night with one of their generals. What did he say?'

'He told me that we Americans treat war like a game of cowboys and Indians,' he replied. 'He said that his country had lost over twenty million people in the war. He says that you flew to Scotland to make peace with Britain so that you could attack the Soviet Union on a single front.'

Hess shrugged.

'Well,' he sighed, 'that's as may be. But it is you who must conquer space. Not those barbarians. You are the future. This Russian general, he is right in one respect. Americans have a wonderful naivety, this simple and marvellously misguided conception of culture. You somehow imagine it to be concerned with growth rather than decay, which is what we Europeans are condemned to understand.'

He wandered back through Speer's garden up to the main cell block.

'This is surely the reason that you should not only inherit the world, but colonise new planets also.' Hess turned and gave the American commandant a mischievous smile. 'We have given you the means, after all.'

Back in his cell he lay on his bunk and scanned the eight square yards of his room. This was his chariot now. His cockpit, his space capsule, with its vaulted white ceiling, its green and cream walls. *O God, I could be bounded in a nutshell and count myself a king of infinite space* – he had once learnt this line of Shakespeare – *were it not that I have bad dreams.*

Above the bed were the maps and photographs from NASA tacked to the wall. The moon, yes, that had been his that night. A sign from heaven, full and bright as a searchlight. But it had been a lure to trick him. He had been obsessed by the moon, his own space race. Hitler was right to hate it so. It was inconstant, deceitful. Insane. Yes, thought Hess, the moon. That had been the cause of his madness.

8

adjustment

ROCKET SCENTIST KILLED IN PASADENA EXPLOSION. The front-page headline in the *Los Angeles Times* was stark and strange, like comic book arcana, past prophecies of pulp magazines and science fiction B-movies. Cosmically terse, like a one-line horoscope. I knew at once that it was about Jack. But the real shock was that there was no shock. I'd somehow always known that this was going to happen. I had long since given up on the supernatural but in that instant I knew that I had always had a prescient sense of Jack's end. And I couldn't bring myself to read the news. I had to adjust to this moment. So I kept my gaze up and scanned the masthead: *Late News, 9 a.m. Final, 18 June 1952*: the exact point in time that I was finally free of Jack Parsons.

I remembered something he had told me about rocket science. When they brought the captured German V2 missiles back to America, they took them apart to see how they worked. They call it 'reverse engineering'. And I knew that that was what I would have to do. I'd have to take it all apart and put it back together again.

A photo of Jack by the headline. A blurred headshot: a pattern of dots tracing the perfect curve of his cheekbones, his soul-deep eyes. Even in inky pointillism he looked absurdly handsome. My dark angel. My bright demon. The most beautiful man I ever knew, cursed with a mercurial genius and a sublime gift for enchantment. No one could blame me for falling in love with Jack, for making a fool of myself over him. And no one could blame me for betraying him in the end. Sometimes you have to kill love or it will destroy you.

When we began our strange affair I thought that I could deal with the fact that he was with somebody else. Jack had so many lovers, it was ludicrous to hope he would be faithful only to me. And for a while I imagined that I was above all the petty jealousies of life. I was on a mystical path, after all, on my way to a higher order of enlightenment, which he had become master of. Sexual freedom was to be a sacrament to this greater love. But I soon learnt that it wasn't enough. That it wasn't freedom, rather some kind of enslavement. I felt lost. Life had seemed a series of adjustments I had never been able to keep pace with. But the real problems started in 1945. The war had changed everything. The whole world was readjusting itself. I only really started to notice how different things had become when Larry Zagorski came back from Europe.

Larry was on terminal leave from the USAAF when he came to visit at 1003 Orange Grove Avenue in Pasadena in the late summer of 1945.

'Wow,' he murmured as I showed him through the grand hall with its sweeping mahogany staircase. 'So this is the famous commune.'

Jack Parsons had leased the mansion in 1942 as a new headquarters for the Agape Lodge of the Ordo Templi Orientis, and I moved in along with other serious members of the Order. It was to be a 'Profess House', a utopian mission where we could live according to the ideals of our new religion, the Church of Thelema. An ideal community where we would realise the dreams of our Hierophant, Aleister Crowley, whose vigilant likeness watched over us from above the stairway. It didn't quite work out like that. Despite the resolute optimism of our little spiritual collective, so much of our actual communion was taken up with emotional tension and nagging quarrels over practicalities. And there had been endless splits and schisms in the Lodge. Many of the original members left and new people moved in who were not necessarily part of the Order. We even gave up holding a Gnostic Mass on a regular basis. Number 1003 (as the house came to be known) became more of a pragmatic refuge, a boarding-house sanctuary for the weird and wonderful.

'We've tried to make it work here,' I said to Larry as I led him into the kitchen. 'It hasn't always been easy.'

'I guess not, Mary-Lou.'

He still had that goofy grin but his baby-blue eyes now gazed hard and distant. That off-kilter stoop of his had been replaced with a neurotic swagger.

'So, how are you?' I said.

'Well, I'm back. At least I think I am.'

I asked about his experiences but you could tell that he didn't want to talk about them. He had seen far beyond anything purely rational. He had flown as a radio operator in B-24s over Germany and occupied Europe, and was full of grim tales he had no urge to relive. So he made light of it all. And suspecting that I missed the shy kid full of amazement at the heavens, he picked out the fantastic from the dread horrors he must have witnessed.

'We saw some weird things flying around out there, Mary-Lou. Strange-shaped things that came from nowhere, then – whoosh! They'd shoot off. Lights in the sky, balls of fire that seemed to follow you around.'

'What were they?'

'I don't know. We called them the "foo fighters". There were these things that we could never seem to make sense of. Some of them were these new German aircraft. Stuff from the future. Rocket planes and jet fighters. Experimental weapons, prototypes. But there were times when it seemed like . . .' Larry shrugged.

'Maybe they were spaceships.'

'Yeah.' He grinned. 'Wouldn't that be great? But you know, what with altitude sickness, lack of sleep and so on . . . Remember that labyrinthitis I used to have? It used to give me vertigo and problems with my balance.'

'I remember that.'

'Well, I was clear of it in the air force. Fifty-two missions, never a problem. But maybe it was just that the symptoms changed.'

Larry had regained his physical sense of balance, but psychologically he still seemed at a slight angle to the world. When I asked him about his writing he made this queer little shrug, like he had an itch on his back that he couldn't reach.

'Gee, Mary-Lou, I'm finding it hard to write that outer-space stuff these days. I mean, don't you find it difficult?'

I told him that I was busier than ever with my job as script girl at the studio and that it was difficult selling stories to magazines because of the paper shortage but I knew this was an excuse. I had hardly written anything for months.

'Whatever happened to "The City of the Sun"?' he asked.

'*Superlative Stories* went out of business.'

'But you never finished the story?'

'No.'

'You should. It was a good idea.'

'Thanks. Maybe I will.'

'But I don't know, Mary-Lou,' he went on, 'sometimes it feels like all our great futures are already behind us.'

I knew what he meant. There was a distinct feeling that the age of wonder was over. A lot of science fiction writers came by number 1003 that summer. Nemo Carvajal would often stay over – he lived close by in Burbank where he had a job at the Lockheed factory. Robert Heinlein was back from doing war work out east for the navy and he came to visit. As did Jack Williamson and Edmond Hamilton, all of them possessed with a more sombre attitude to the future.

Tony Boucher had written a mystery novel set in the SF and fantasy scene of the time, a *roman-à-clef*, featuring thinly disguised fictional versions of members of the Mañana Literary Society. Jack had appeared in the book as CalTech scientist Hugo Chantrelle. It had conjured much of the wistful optimism of the pre-war science-fiction world. But it was called *Rocket to the Morgue*, and I remember even then how ominous that sounded to me. Now, of course, I see how accurate a prediction it was of Jack's death, even of the headline in the *LA Times*. But then the mid-forties would be the last time that science fiction really had the edge of prophecy. Cleve Cartmill wrote a story for *Astounding* in 1944 that so accurately described a Uranium 235 atom bomb that he was investigated by the FBI.

And though the summer of 1945 began as a summer of hope – peace in Europe, imminent victory in the Pacific, people coming home – it ended with Hiroshima and Nagasaki. We had foreseen it, we had made it possible. So it was hard for us, as science fiction writers, to find any detachment from the horror of these weapons, or to share the numbing sense of disbelief that stunned the average citizen. We were to blame, in our imaginations anyway. And we had to adjust to the reality of the worst of our fantasies. It was a cold world that Larry had come back to.

He was living with his mother once more and supporting them both thanks to the Serviceman's Readjustment Act – the GI Bill that guaranteed him one year of self-employed income. As a free-lance writer he could claim twenty dollars a week for any time he wasn't earning. But as he admitted to me this well-meaning subsidy acted as a disincentive at a time when he was already so unsure about his work. He went into stasis, overwhelmed with ideas that he could not transmit. Larry and Nemo spent long hours together talking, drinking beer and smoking marijuana. Nemo was very taken by Larry's tales of the strange objects seen in the skies over the Rhineland. But Larry was genuinely troubled by the 'foo fight-ers' and speculation as to what he might or might not have seen became the basis of much of his later work.

'Maybe they were just hallucinations,' he once said to me. 'But *real* hallucinations.'

'I don't understand,' I told him.

He tried to explain to me that he had found out there was another possible symptom of his labyrinthitis that could be mani-festing itself. It was known as 'derealisation', an alteration in the perception of the external world that could be caused by a chronic disorder in the inner ear.

'I mean, if everything seems unreal,' he said, 'how do I know if I'm seeing things or not? How do you know I'm really seeing you?'

I felt an edge to that last comment, a new sharpness in his tone. Whatever problems Larry had with reality, he was certainly more knowing than he had been before the war. I missed that awkward inno-cence of his. He had grown up the hard way, adjusting to the obvious horrors of war and then to the more subtle terrors of peacetime. But despite any mental anguish he might have been suffering, he seemed more confident physically and emotionally. I gently ribbed him about the many girlfriends he must have had as a glamorous airman, expecting him to go all coy on me. Instead he spoke softly of a dispatch rider called Joyce who he had dated when he was stationed in England and I found myself nursing a pang of jealousy that I had no right to bear. We went to the movies one night and he casually snaked an arm around my shoulder during the second feature. I snuggled up to him, unsure of what this careless intimacy might mean but happy enough for the comfort of it. He drove me back to number 1003 that evening and we dallied on the porch in a moment of charm and uncertainty. I went to kiss him but he drew back and fixed me with a pair of steel-blue eyes.

'You're still in love with Jack, aren't you?' he asked.

'Larry—'

'Mary-Lou, look, I don't want to give you a hard time. I care about you. But if you really do love him—' he shrugged.

'What?'

'You can't just hang around hoping it's all going to work out somehow. You've got to do something about it.'

Larry was right. I knew that things couldn't carry on as they were. The Lodge, indeed the whole Order, had encouraged the rejection of possessiveness in relationships but the house at number 1003 had become an exhausted burlesque of anxiety and confusion. Individuals were dogged by expectation and disappointment; partnerships were strained by instability and suspicion. Jealousy became all the more potent an enemy because we were supposed to have become immune to its poison. And I was the worst of the lot. I wanted Jack Parsons all to myself.

And I knew I had long felt that this was meant to be. I had become bonded to him: emotionally, intellectually, spiritually and sexually. A casual relationship was not enough. The problem was that Jack had more or less settled down with Betty, his own sister-in-law (his wife Helen had gone off with Wilfred Smith, the former High Priest of the Lodge). Adultery with a hint of incest gave the thrill of trespass to what was essentially a domestic arrangement. Petite and blonde, Betty played this little-girl act that I found nauseating, though it sure as hell worked on most of the male occupants of number 1003. Jack was fixated on her and she knew just how to manipulate him. She was supposed to be taking writing classes at UCLA, but she always seemed to find a reason to skip them. Instead she liked to run the household, collecting rent money and food stamps. But she was so busy ruling the roost she didn't notice how unhappy Jack had become.

The world had caught up with him. The war had taken all his idealistic dreams of rocketry and burnt them up in its grim purpose. Ballistics became respectable and developed an orthodoxy. The Jet Propulsion Laboratory that he had helped set up had become a fully funded military enterprise more concerned with missiles and weaponry than the exploration of space. There was no room now for the eccentric pioneer whose ideas bordered on the subversive. He became sidelined: never fully accepted at CalTech (he was not a conventionally trained scientist; he didn't even have a degree) and persuaded to sell his shares in Aerojet, the aeronautical company he had co-founded.

'Besides, they've got a whole bunch of captured Nazi scientists out in New Mexico,' he explained to me. 'They've got all that German rocket technology. They sure as hell don't need me any more.'

With time on his hands, Jack became morose and indolent. He started drinking quite heavily, his drug use now habitual as much as ritual. He retained a taste for reckless experimentation: denied outer space, he was determined to journey inward to test himself with the dangers of his own psyche. He looked for the extremes in magic. The Order had always warned against this; indeed, Crowley himself had written to Jack, urging caution against rituals that risked invoking evil or causing harm. But Jack liked high odds and he loved the forbidden. And I encouraged him. I felt a connection with his darker energies. It was what had attracted me to him in the first place.

I tried to muster my own occult forces. I had got to know a new arrival at number 1003, Astrid Nagengast, who had just come over from Germany. She was a formidable woman, a senior member of the OTO. A friend of Aleister Crowley, she had even known Theodor Reuss, the founder of the Order. She worked as a fortune-teller and as some sort of voice coach. I studied the Tarot with her and we talked about other forms of clairvoyance and ways of channelling the unseen. She insisted that the most important thing was the power of the will: the principle of Thelema, a central tenet of the Order. Astrid had been through hard times: she had been part of a resistance movement during the war. She was convinced that supernatural powers had helped her survive under the Nazis. Though I wasn't sure how much I believed this, there was something very inspiring about Astrid and I realised, as Larry had so bluntly pointed out, that I had to do something about my feelings for Jack.

One night we met at the pergola in the grounds of number 1003 that was sometimes used for ceremonies and the Gnostic Mass. Betty had gone to bed; the sky was heavy with stars. We talked of the new Tarot pack that Crowley had been creating with a woman artist in London. The Strength card was now designated as Lust. The image of a female form wrestling with a lion.

'The Scarlet Woman,' said Jack, 'who rides the Beast.'

I pulled his face towards mine by his thick mane of hair.

'Strength is vigour,' I whispered. 'The rapture of vigour.'

He kissed me, his breath scented with smoke and liquor. Sweet tokay and reefer. His locks slipped through my fingers, chrismed with brilliantine.

'Knowledge and delight,' he murmured. 'And bright glory. Wine and strange drugs, divine drunkenness and ecstasy.'

Soon we were naked. He bade me kneel and then crouched behind, his hot mouth against my neck, murmuring obscene incantations. As he covered me I bowed down on the tiled floor in supplication. I arched my back as he pushed against me. There was pain, my whole body rising up against his onslaught. Then the siege was broken and a sudden rush of pleasure overwhelmed me. We rutted with a bestial frenzy, consummating the love of Baphomet, the eleventh degree of sex magic that Betty had denied him. I felt a sense of sinful transcendence, convinced that this manner of ritual sacrifice would give me power over him.

Afterwards we lay on our backs, looking down on the heavens.

'I remember being a star,' he whispered to the night air. 'A moving, burning ember going deathward to the womb.'

'Let's go away, Jack,' I said. 'Just me and you.'

'Yes,' he replied. 'Up into space.'

'I'm serious.'

'So am I, Mary-Lou. Or I once was. I once thought I would live to see the time when we make it up there.'

He pointed up at the cosmos.

'Maybe you will.'

'No,' he declared flatly. 'I won't live long enough.'

'Jack—'

'And in the meantime I'm supposed to be a normal honest citizen.'

'What do you mean?'

'Betty—'

'What about Betty?'

'She wants a baby,' he told me.

'And you?'

'Hell, no,' he muttered. 'I want to conjure a demon or create a homunculus. I don't want a real child. Maybe a moonchild.'

'A moonchild?'

Jack started to explain about how one could create a magical child, born on an astral plane, mightier than all the kings of the earth. He began to mutter oaths and curses. I knew that I should try to understand what he meant. That this might be a clue to possessing him. But it all seemed so absurd and as he rambled on I fell asleep.

The next morning there was still a furtive charge between us but I felt it wane as the hours passed. Whatever charm of the night I held, Jack was still in thrall to Betty by day. She seemed a little bored, though, and there was some spark of an idea in my head that I might use that somehow, that maybe I should not simply concentrate on getting Jack away from Betty. Perhaps I should find a way of drawing Betty away from him.

I started to practise with the Tarot deck. I learnt the Major Arcana. I asked Astrid about the Justice card, hoping it could mean redress, particularly for what I saw as the unfairness in my situation with Jack.

'The most misunderstood card in the whole pack. Justice does not belong to us. When I think of who was spared and who was lost,' she said, referring to her time under the Nazis. 'And these trials. So many will still get away with it. No, this card does not mean a human notion of justice. Oh no, this is the natural kind. Nature is a harsh judge but precise when she finds her balance. Exact, you might say. So you be careful when you go looking for justice.'

But I was impatient. I began to find ways of palming the deck to turn up the cards that I wanted. One evening I did a reading for Jack and I fixed the spread so I could offer him a provocative interpretation. It was a three-card divination (though in this case more of a three-card trick). The Two of Swords was the centre card between Strength and the Ten of Cups. The Two of Swords shows a blindfolded woman holding crossed swords, like Justice without her scales, indicating a difficult choice to be decided on instinct rather than logic. Strength, of course, referred to our lustful night, the Beast and his Scarlet Woman. The Ten of Cups depicts a couple embracing as their children dance – family life and faithfulness, that bliss of domesticity that I knew he dreaded.

This was a sort of spell aimed at Jack. I wondered what I might use against Betty. I had tried curses and blessings and all kinds of charms, but nothing had seemed to make any particular sense or had any effect. I decided to concentrate on willing a kind of animus that might work in my favour, a spirit that might tempt Betty away from Jack. One night I asked for a sign or a portent. The next day L. Ron Hubbard turned up.

He had just got out of the navy and he was looking for some-where to stay. Hubbard was a veteran pulp writer, well known in the fantasy and science fiction world. That's how he got to hear about our little commune in Pasadena. I never much liked him. We had met at Robert Heinlein's house before the war, the very same night I first saw Jack Parsons. Hubbard's presence was such a contrast to Jack's subtle charisma. I remembered then a domineering manner, an incessant craving for attention. A sly wariness in his eyes, a cunning twist about his mouth; he seemed alert to any opportunity. It was his gloating nature I found repulsive; there was something almost reptilian about him. With men he was merely arrogant, with women he was predatory.

His prose style was as brash and arrogant as he was but it was hard not to respect his sheer output and his power of invention. Ron was a verbal illusionist, a writer who had become convinced by his own fantasies and now seemed ready to try to fool others. He would constantly push the credulity of his audience as if searching for those who might believe in him unconditionally.

And it was clear that he was looking for something beyond the merely fictional for his powers of speculation. He boasted that he had written a manuscript that he could no longer submit to publishers as it had sent mad all those who had read it. In one of his better stories, a man finds himself a fictional character in a pirate romance and learns to anticipate action or danger when he hears the clatter of typewriter keys in the sky above him. Even back then the audacious storyteller dreamt of a higher calling.

For some of the household he provided much needed entertainment. He was a skilled raconteur, holding court around the big table in the kitchen at suppertime, telling tall tales that many fell for. He had learnt his trade on all types of pulp magazine and could rattle off stories of any genre, claiming them as his own experience. And he was full of bluster about his wartime exploits, though one could tell that duty had taken its toll in some way. There was a weariness in his pale eyes. They would gaze off in mid-sentence as if hunting for another racket.

I noticed them light up when they fell on Betty. It was easy to see he found her attractive and she clearly enjoyed the attention of this mysterious new member of the commune. They flirted openly. It was a performance, a game, but one that could easily turn serious. All at once it struck me that my prayer might have been answered.

I found Ron in the library one afternoon. He looked up furtively as I entered. He had been studying *The Book of Lies* by Aleister Crowley.

'Looking for ideas, Ron?'

'It's brilliant stuff,' he replied. 'A whole new religion. Needs to be more, well, scientific.'

He was fascinated by Jack's persona and curious about his ideas. Ron was a professional, always on the lookout for any material he could use.

'What do you think of Betty?' I asked him.

He shrugged, trying to look nonchalant, but his eyes flickered mischievously.

'She likes you,' I went on.

'She's Jack's girl.'

'The Order's in favour of free love, you know that. Betty wants you. And Jack wants what Betty wants.'

His lips pursed in a cruel smirk.

'She'll make her feelings known soon,' I told him. 'Make sure you act quickly before her passion cools.'

I was about to contrive a moment to talk to Betty on her own but it was she who instigated it. She actually confided in me.

'What do you think of Ron?' she asked me and I measured my response carefully.

'Oh, he's fascinating.'

'Yes,' sighed Betty. 'I think he's cute.'

I winced. Only Betty could think of L. Ron Hubbard as cute. But at least there was a kind of poetic justice in it. They deserved each other.

'What should I do?'

'Oh, you must act on your feelings,' I told her. 'Anything else would be dishonest. You must let him know how you feel.'

'What, tell him?'

'Oh no. Some sort of gesture would be better.'

Two days later in the garden Jack and Ron were fencing at sunset. The vigorous exchange of thrust and parry charged the air. There was a new intensity between the two men. I didn't realise it at the time but Jack was becoming just as obsessed with Ron as Ron was with Jack. But looking back now, I think Betty already knew it and was jealous of them both. The light was failing and as they were not wearing masks each new lunge became wilder and more provocative. Betty became agitated as she watched until she could bear it no longer. She grabbed the foil from Jack and launched a fierce attack on Hubbard, swiping at his unprotected face, forcing him to retreat. Stepping back, he regained his posture and with a sharp riposte knocked her sword to the ground. The sky had turned blood red. Betty and Ron glared at each other. It had begun.

We were all used to the wild affairs that would flare up at number 1003; they had become our sport. But this was different and the tension in the house became palpable. Ron and Betty made no attempt to conceal their lovemaking. It was a gruesome spectacle. But now everyone was watching Jack to see how he would respond to this direct challenge.

I felt sure that he would crack. He had been so devoted to Betty and now she had betrayed him openly. Hubbard had obscenely abused his hospitality. I thought that it was only a matter of time before he would throw them both out. But I underestimated his resilience.

'It is a test,' he insisted to me one night when we were alone together. 'I must suffer this ordeal of love and jealousy. I will find a way.'

'Yes,' I whispered urgently. 'Come to me.'

'I have to find my own way first. I have to find the darkness.'

'What?'

'Of myself. This is a sign, Mary-Lou. I must attend to magical ceremony. I have to go deeper within.'

So I left him to it, hoping that he merely needed time to get over Betty. But soon he became absorbed in new experiments of the spirit. He had been investigating Enochian rituals that had been

159

used by Doctor John Dee, Elizabeth I's court magician, who had used arcane language to communicate with the unseen. Jack now sought divine wisdom through angelic conversation.

Astrid knew all about Doctor Dee.

'He was the most brilliant man of his generation. A Renaissance magician with deep knowledge of astrology and mathematics. I suppose if he lived in these days he would have been a scientist. But he wanted to know too much. Like Faust he went too far. He fell under the influence of a charlatan named Kelley. Well, they practised magic together but in the end Kelley conned Dee out of everything – his wife, his fortune, even his knowledge.'

This should have been a warning for Jack but he embraced its dread premonition. He started to enact magic rituals with Hubbard. Ron had made many explorations into the unseen in his writing. He had known H.P. Lovecraft when they had both sold stories to *Weird Tales* magazine and had learnt that faked occult wisdom was far more plausible than any actual arcane knowledge that might exist. With a demon of an imagination, he was now ready to use his fictional prowess to influence reality. He had enchanted Jack and there was nothing I could do to break the spell. And Hubbard seemed all the more convincing now that he had so forcefully demonstrated his dominance over Jack by seducing Betty. They formed the passionate connection some men can achieve only when they have a woman in common to safely mediate it. Jack needed desperately to break through what he saw as his human weaknesses. And Hubbard preyed on him, willing to steal everything from the other man.

Jack had looked for the darkness and found it in L. Ron Hubbard, a man possessed with all the cunning and ruthlessness that he yearned for. They began to enact absurd rites, meaningless liturgies that seemed merely to solemnise Jack's degradation. The house became possessed with a grim and sickly atmosphere. Strange noises by day, hellish screams that pierced the night, the stench of incense and sulphur. They constantly played a record of Prokofiev's Second Violin Concerto at full volume as prelude to their ceremony. Ritualism became contagious, as members of the Order would themselves enact banishing ceremonies to ward off ugly spirits.

It became clear that most of the senior members of the OTO were appalled by Jack's sinister workings with Hubbard. Crowley himself wrote a letter denouncing them both. Astrid was quietly furious.

'When I think of how we have been persecuted down the ages,' she said, 'just so that these men can behave so foolishly.' She told me that she herself had been a victim of a Gestapo clampdown on astrologers and occultists in 1941 and had spent two months in a concentration camp.

After two weeks of tension and near madness at number 1003, Jack announced that he and Ron were heading off to the Mojave Desert together.

'We are going to attempt the Babalon Working,' he told me.

I nodded absently. I had long since lost touch with what any of this really meant. I just hoped that he would find some sort of catharsis.

'I love you,' I said.

'Love is the law,' he replied with a crazed smile. He hadn't slept properly for days. I kissed him gently on the lips and said:

'I hope you find what you're looking for.'

'I want to summon an elemental.'

I know now that I should have paid more attention at this point, but I was tired too. So I kissed him again and said:

'I'll be waiting for you.'

And so I waited. And like a fool I imagined that my patience would be rewarded. But somebody else got there before me.

No one seemed quite sure where Candy came from. She was an artist or something. So many people drifted in and out of number 1003, it was impossible to keep track of them all. Maybe Jack really did conjure her up through the spirit world as he would later claim. All that is really certain is that there she was, standing on the front porch when he got back from the desert. And she was perfect. His 'elemental', the Scarlet Woman par excellence. Candy had a shock of flame-red hair, bright-blue eyes and a broad-lipped snarl of a mouth. I didn't stand a chance. I watched as Jack slapped the dust from his jacket and walked right past me, transfixed by this vision of his delirium.

They fell in love with each other right there and then. Right in front of my eyes. I was devastated, of course, but I couldn't help thinking that I had only myself to blame. I had meddled too much and yet not enough. I had set things up so perfectly, but for somebody else. I thought about what Astrid had said. This was how natural justice felt.

And there was yet another adjustment we all had to make. It was 1946, the year when everything at number 1003 fell apart. Hubbard conned Jack into a business proposition and promptly ran off to Florida with Betty and twenty thousand dollars of Jack's money. There was a court case and Jack managed to get some of it back but he had to sell the lease on the house. I think he'd had enough of it by then. He left the Order and married Candy. By October, number 1003 was empty. The big old mansion was torn down to make way for modern apartments. I was ready to move on at that point but I couldn't help feeling some nostalgia for the place, for the fleeting sense of a community of misfits. All the writers, thinkers, out-of-work actors and aspiring magicians. It had been a flawed utopia for people who believed in free living and emotional honesty. A commune for lovers of science fiction and the occult. We had been too ahead of our time. But all the post-war hope was running out. Things were about to get bleaker.

I went back to live in LA. I was lucky in some ways. I still had my job at the studio, so I threw myself into work. I had started assisting the German émigré director Max Iann. He was adapting a hard-boiled novel titled *Hell is Empty*. A man comes back from the war and picks up a girl in a bar. At first neither of them remembers that they were once childhood sweethearts. He has been traumatised by combat; she has become a drunk and fallen in with an evil racketeer. Despite the brief glimpses of a sentimental past, they are unable to avoid destroying each other through confusion and betrayal. It was one of those *noir* movies that caught a dark mood lurking beneath the official optimism of victory.

'It's fear,' Max insisted. 'That's what's behind Technicolor. That's why people want happy films, because they're terrified. Of atom bombs and communism. But most of all of themselves. It's a neurosis of forced euphoria. But they're not smiling, they're gritting their teeth.'

I liked working with Max; he was a radical with bold artistic ideas who had worked in the Expressionist theatre in Berlin in the 1920s. A tall, broad-shouldered man in his forties, Max had impeccable manners, a quality rarely found in Hollywood. And I found comfort in the bleak melancholia of the script. In a strange way it meant that I didn't feel quite so alone.

LA seemed to have become a malevolent creature. It had grown crowded since the war, a ruthless boomtown teeming with strangers desperate for the main chance, full of failed dreams and broken promises, a bright and guilty place. The harsh noonday glare cast deep shadows, the light so fierce as to conjure a blinding darkness. A city of screens and blinds, of obfuscation, its watchful eyes hooded or concealed behind dark glasses, waiting patiently for you to grow old and die. Years would pass beneath the same sad blue sky. Then at sundown, beneath the hum of neon, the relentless drones of pleasure would seek out the night to settle the score.

We started filming *Hell is Empty* at the beginning of 1947, mostly on a studio lot, though Max liked to use LA locations for the outside scenes. By mischance or ill fate we found ourselves shooting in Leimart Park only two blocks down from the vacant lot where the mutilated corpse of Elizabeth Short was found. This became the infamous 'Black Dahlia' case, an unsolved murder that haunted the city that year.

I worked on the film right the way through from the script editing, continuity on set, to the final edit. Max had this deadpan humour and a sense of the absurd, but he was undeniably serious about the work and was always generous in the praise of others when things went right. For him cinema was an art form, even when it was just a low-budget thriller.

He was hoping that his next project would be another adaptation with a bit more money spent on it. He handed me this novel titled *Nightmare Alley* by William Lindsey Gresham, set in the carnival world of fairgrounds and freak-shows. The central character is a conman who works a mind-reading act and tries to make a fortune out of what he calls the 'spook-racket'.

'Tyrone Power has the rights,' Max told me. 'He's had enough of playing romantic, swashbuckling types. And you'll be interested in this book, my dear. You see, every chapter is named after one of those Tarot cards you're so fond of.'

Nightmare Alley was certainly an intriguing work, an American picaresque novel viewed through the lens of the darker side of spiritualism. The writing was hard-boiled and cynical but touched with the sophistication of one who must have known enough of this world to be disillusioned by it. Using the Major Arcana as a structure looks like a gimmick at first but in the end the Tarot bestows an ominous gravity on the narrative. The novel seems to suggest that human degradation is the ultimate spiritual journey. It made me think of Jack.

Near the end of the post-production for *Hell is Empty*, Max became withdrawn; he was brooding on something. At first I thought it was just the slight grief that comes at the end of a project. When I told him how much I had learnt from him and that I would like to work with him again, he smiled and said:

'You best stay away from me in future, my dear.'

I laughed, thinking that he was making a joke, but he added:

'I've been summoned as a witness before the House of Un-American Activities Committee.'

'What about *Nightmare Alley*?' I asked.

'They've given it to this Englishman, Edmund Goulding. Not his sort of thing at all but,' Max shrugged, 'I'm already *persona non grata.*'

I knew what this meant, of course. A Red Scare. I don't think that I really took it seriously at the time. There had been Red Scares in Hollywood before and they had never amounted to much. But Astrid warned me that this was something different. She was working in LA, too. Her fortune-telling business was doing well.

'People are very superstitious at the moment,' she told me. 'It's always like this at the time of a witch-hunt.'

'A witch-hunt?'

'Oh yes. You wait and see.'

And there was something strange in the atmosphere that summer. Nemo and Larry had been having this long-term argument over strange lights in the sky and mysterious objects seen in the heavens. The previous year there had been a whole spate of 'ghost rocket' sightings over Scandinavia. Larry took the line that it could be the Soviets testing reverse-engineered Nazi rocket technology. Nemo always liked to speculate about extraterrestrial activity.

Then in June a pilot in Washington State claimed to have spotted nine circular objects shooting past him in perfect formation. The newspapers picked up the story and some subeditor plucked a snappy headline out of the report of the weird craft. There was a word for them now – the 'flying saucers' had arrived. More sightings followed.

'Larry doesn't want to believe in them,' Nemo complained.

'Well, I'm yet to be convinced,' Larry retorted.

'What about those things you saw in the war?'

'Just because you see something doesn't make it real.'

'So what is this, mass hysteria?'

'A sign of the times,' Larry insisted. 'An adjustment between inner space and outer space.'

'What do you mean?'

'The flying saucers hover, don't they? They hover between disenchantment and re-enchantment.'

'Yeah.' Nemo nodded with a smile, obviously liking the idea.

'Remember what we said before the war?' Larry went on. ' "If you can't change the world, build a spaceship." Well, that's what's happening now. We're building spaceships in the air. Spaceships of the imagination.'

By that fall the whole nation was delirious with visions of flying saucers, with eyewitness accounts almost every week. Flying saucer clubs were set up across the country and regular articles in the press speculated about the phenomenon. They caused a split in the whole of the SF world, not just between Larry and Nemo. Most of the writers I knew didn't believe in them. I had this nagging feeling that they resented losing the monopoly of contact with other worlds. The craze certainly revitalised the genre, though. There was a demand for new stories and much reprinting of old ones. One of mine from 1941, 'Atom Priestess', was bought by a New York publishing house for a hardback anthology of short stories.

But elsewhere things were not looking so bright. In November, Max Iann was cited for contempt for refusing to give testimony to the House of Un-American Activities. He was blacklisted. I was known to have radical connections, I'd even been to a few Communist Party meetings before the war, but I wasn't important enough to warrant complete excommunication. Instead I joined that peculiar purgatory that came to be known as the 'greylist'. None of the big studios would hire me for the time being but I could get work on Poverty Row, that notorious collection of small-time production companies that churned out cheap B-movies.

Nemo lost his job at Lockheed. He'd been involved in the union and was still very politically active. Now he was certain that the FBI were keeping tabs on him. He and Larry were planning a road trip to Mexico.

Then in December, Aleister Crowley died. He had been in poor health for some time and addicted to heroin. He had worn himself out from his wild life, it seemed. I heard that Jack Parsons had wanted to be reconciled with his former master but had left it too late. I hadn't been to any Lodge meetings since leaving number 1003, nor had I kept in touch with any members of the Order. But it was the death of Crowley that finally marked the end of that part of my life, as it did, I think, for many others. I formally quit the Ordo Templi Orientis. And I kidded myself that I had finally got over Jack Parsons.

Larry came to see me the night before he and Nemo were to set off on their journey south.

'I just came to say goodbye,' he said.

'I hope you and Nemo have a good time.'

'He's driving me crazy with all this flying saucer stuff.'

'Maybe there is something in it.'

'Well, he says he saw something years ago. Remember that night at the Arroyo Seco?'

There was an awkward moment when I remembered what Larry had seen that night. That group of us, drugged and naked, making out in a glade.

'It certainly was a mystical night,' Larry continued, seemingly oblivious to my embarrassment, either arch or innocent: it was so hard to tell with him these days. 'That was the night we hexed the Deputy Führer into flying to Scotland, wasn't it?'

'Well.' I shrugged.

'Do you still believe in that stuff, Mary-Lou?'

He was staring at me intently. I felt sure that he meant whether or not I still believed in Jack Parsons.

'I don't know any more,' I told him.

'I remember you once said that you wanted to know everything.'

I laughed.

'I don't blame you,' he said. 'But, you know, in the 458th Bomber Squadron, when we were flying missions, we had this deal as aircrew that when we were talking informally and off the radio, there would be no real difference between fact and fiction. It made sense when you were up in the air, helped you through it.'

Larry hunched up a little as he said this and I could see the anxiety in his eyes.

'I'm having trouble on the ground, Mary-Lou. I'm writing this novel, you know, a proper novel.'

'That's good.'

'No it's not. It's not any good. I—' He sighed. 'I just need to get it out of my system. I'm still having trouble with reality, you know, this derealisation thing I told you about. How about you?'

'What?'

'Are you writing anything?'

'Just script notes.'

'You never did finish "The City of the Sun", did you?'

'No. Maybe you should have a go at it.'

'Yeah.' He grinned at me. 'Maybe I will.'

In the New Year I began work on *Zombie Lagoon*. The director was drunk for the entire four-week shoot, and with no first or second assistant I found myself having to take over at times. The producer was young and smart and sober. I always assumed that Dexter Roth had found himself on the greylist too. There seemed no other reason that someone as bright and ambitious would end up producing trash in Poverty Row. He would wear bright sports jackets with open-necked shirts and horn-rimmed glasses, looking every bit the hip intellectual. He liked to argue that mass culture could be experimental, and he was meticulous about the script, constantly tweaking lines of dialogue or even changing the emphasis of a line. He seemed to look for hidden meaning in the cheapest material.

And he had respect for my work as a writer. He read some of the stories I had written for the pulp magazines and he said that he loved science fiction and fantasy. He wanted to find a really good idea from that genre once we had finished the zombie movie.

Dexter was sensitive, with perfect manners and a fussiness about his appearance. I assumed he was a fruit until he made a pass at me on the night of the wrap party. I told him that I'd had my heart broken.

'What a dumb guy,' he said.

'No,' I replied. 'He's a genius.'

I thought that this would rile him but instead Dexter was intrigued. He seemed genuinely curious about everything and everybody, which made him easy to talk to. I told him all about Jack and my strange life at number 1003.

'So you, like, believe in magic?' he asked.

'I don't know what I believe in any more. What about you?'

'Me?' He smiled. 'I like to keep an open mind.'

By the time Larry and Nemo got back from Mexico, Dexter and I had started dating. It was a tentative kind of courtship, which suited me fine. I wasn't really ready to get too emotionally involved with anyone just then. And I wasn't sure what I felt about Dexter yet, except that I really enjoyed his company and I felt safe with him. And he had this ability to get on with almost anybody. He and Nemo hit it off the first time they met, engaging in a deep discussion about politics in Latin America. Even Larry, who was very wary of Dexter at first, soon warmed to him. I even felt a little disappointed that Larry didn't seem to be jealous.

We all ended up in a bar on South Broadway one night. It wasn't long before the conversation turned to science fiction and the flying saucer story Larry and Nemo had been working on together, which had come out of their long-running discussions on the subject. A spacecraft is spotted in the sky above Los Angeles. There is panic in the streets and an attempt by the authorities to explain the incident as natural phenomena. An exile from another planet seeks refuge on earth. As more spaceships arrive, looking for him, the alien goes into hiding.

Dexter got very excited and declared that this would make a great movie. The nation was still gripped in a flying saucer craze, after all. We talked into the night, soon convincing ourselves that this could be a vehicle for so many interesting ideas and a way of exploiting a popular market.

That week Nemo and Larry got a story treatment together and Dexter used it to raise some finance for them to write the script. We called it *Fugitive Alien*, and it all started to come together very quickly. I loved working with Dexter; he was so good at talking an idea into reality. I spent a lot of time with him at meetings, and it was fascinating watching him operate. And we went out to all kinds of places. He was into bebop and modern art, poetry and European cinema. He always seemed easy to be with. Cool but affable, sophisticated but relaxed with it.

There were constant notes and suggestions from him at script meetings. He had an original, playful mind and he was good at drawing out the thoughts of others, particularly Nemo. A theme emerged of a dissident from an advanced civilisation, exiled from a planet where once-utopian ideals had been corrupted by absolute power. Dexter declared that he was serious about using complex concepts in a popular genre.

Speculative fiction continued to be on the rise. There were reprints of our old stories in magazines and anthologies as well as a demand for new ones. And although Larry's 'proper' novel was roundly rejected, a New York publisher reissued *Lords of the Black Sun* as a paperback original that summer. Our once-beloved *Astounding* may have gone into decline (John W. Campbell had got taken in by a new therapy idea that L. Ron Hubbard was peddling, something called 'Dianetics', and was devoting the main pages to it) but we learnt that Tony Boucher was going to edit a new title: *The Magazine of Fantasy & Science Fiction*. And Boucher had just made the first English translation of Jorge Luis Borges, the Argentine writer that Nemo had told us about all those years ago at Robert Heinlein's house. 'The Garden of Forking Paths' made its first appearance in English in the *Ellery Queen's Mystery Magazine* in 1948.

We were about to go into pre-production with *Fugitive Alien*. I had taken what Larry and Nemo had done and edited it into a shooting script. We had cast the leads: Trey Anderson, an ageing juvenile with an other-wordly charm as the alien; Sharleen Stirling, a seventeen-year-old newcomer, as the earthly blonde ingénue who falls for him. A crew was being assembled and we were using the designer from *Zombie Lagoon*. All we really needed was a director. Dexter told me that he had somebody in mind but he wouldn't say who. Instead he suggested that we take the weekend off and go to Palm Springs together.

'But we really need to confirm who's directing,' I said.

'Well.' He gave me a sly smile. 'We can do that right now, can't we?'

'What do you mean?'

'I can't think of anyone who could do it better.'

'You mean . . .'

'You know this trade inside out. All good script girls do. And I saw you taking over on the zombie film, remember?'

'But I couldn't—'

'Why not? Because you're a woman?'

'No, it's just . . .'

'Don't worry, of course everyone is going to try to hold you back but just don't do their job for them. Okay?'

'Okay.'

'Right. You're hired. We've got a lot of prepping to do this week and I'll want your input. As a director.'

All at once I felt ridiculously happy. At last things were going right for me. I went over and kissed Dexter on the mouth. He pulled away from me and smiled.

'Hey,' he said, 'you better get to work. I'll pick you up on Friday afternoon.'

I was packing an overnight bag on Thursday evening when the phone rang. I assumed it would be Dexter. It was Jack. His voice was hoarse and slurred, tragic. Candy had left him. He needed to see me. He was staying in a motel out on 53rd and Western.

For an instant I was overwhelmed by a sense of relief. That finally I could say no to Jack Parsons, that everything in my life would be turned around by my saying no to him. This would be my way of getting over all the hurt I had been carrying around since he came back from the Mojave Desert that day. All I had to do was say a few words and put the phone down. But I couldn't speak and the receiver stayed in my hand as I heard Jack tell me his room number.

'Okay,' I mumbled and the line went dead.

I felt all the mad passion and desire come to claim me once more. And suddenly I knew that a luxurious weekend in Palm Springs with the kind and charming Dexter was nothing compared with a night in a seedy motel room with my fallen angel.

I called Dexter and told him that I had a family crisis. My mother was sick and I needed to go to the hospital. I was sorry but I couldn't go away with him that weekend. Then I finished packing and drove out to see Jack. He came to the door wearing a grubby singlet. Unshaven, wild-eyed and dishevelled, he'd put on a bit of weight but he was still beautiful. He was doomed, I saw that even then. Jack was a real romantic, full of danger and self-destructiveness. I knew that, like a drowning man, he would drag down those who came close to him. My love for him could ruin me but I didn't care.

As I moved into the room I saw an ashtray on the bedside table with reefer butts in it, and a bottle of tequila on the dresser. Jack went to the window, nervously fingering the slants on the blind.

'Did anyone see you come?' he asked. 'I've got to be careful. They're watching me.'

Jack explained that he had been investigated over his past activities. He'd managed to get security clearance for a job at Hughes Aircraft in Culver City, but he was sure that he was still under surveillance.

'It's only temporary. I'm just a pen-pusher in their rocket propulsion department. But I've got plans. I'm going to make a fresh start, Mary-Lou.'

He came over to me, his hands held out plaintively.

'What about Candy?' I asked.

'She's in San Miguel de Allende, south of the border. Some kind of artists' colony. She never really understood me, not the way you did.'

'I waited for you, Jack. All that time that you were with Betty. Then out in the desert with Ron. I waited for you and then you went off with her. It wasn't fair.'

'I know, Mary-Lou, I know. I've been bad. Everything's gone wrong.'

He poured us both a drink and told me how, left on his own, he had descended into madness and horror, conducting strange ceremonies on peyote and mescaline, hiring hookers to perform sex magic rituals with him. The Babalon Working had failed, he groaned; he had lost his Scarlet Woman and a chance to conjure a moonchild.

'Maybe it's all nonsense anyway,' I said.

He laughed. I wanted to free myself from all my beliefs and delusions. I wanted to obliterate my desire for Jack and break the spell that he still held over me. But the strangest mystery of all is how we can be utterly taken in by our own stupid emotions. Jack lit a reefer and sat on the bed.

'I've got a new quest,' he said. 'I'm getting out of this wretched place. I'm going to make the Black Pilgrimage.'

'What's the Black Pilgrimage?'

He started to explain about Chorazin, a cursed ancient city near the Sea of Galilee, with a black temple built of basalt. I tried to follow as he talked of a journey to a place where, it was said, the Antichrist would be born. But by then he had passed me the reefer and I was on my way to getting as drunk and as high as he was.

'Come with me,' he mumbled as he pulled off what remained of his clothes.

I undressed and got into bed with him.

I got back to my flat on Sunday afternoon. I had been there for only half an hour when my buzzer went. It was Dexter.

'How's Mother?' he asked breezily as I let him in. He had a briefcase with him.

'What?'

'Oh it doesn't matter. I know where you've been.'

His tone was at once flat and cold.

'Dexter, what's all this about?'

'I know you were with Jack Parsons.'

I felt a shiver in the pit of my stomach.

'But how did you know?'

'Maybe I have psychic powers, Mary-Lou. I certainly have access to hidden knowledge.'

Dexter's mouth twisted into a parody of a smile.

'Look,' I struggled to appear calm, 'this isn't funny. If you've been snooping around me—'

'Shh,' he shushed me, a finger to his mouth.

He patted the couch.

'Sit, Mary-Lou.' His voice was all soft authority. 'I need you to listen to me.'

He stared me down, his eyes hard and impassive.

'You want occult wisdom?' he went on, leaning over me and pulling something out of the briefcase. 'Take a look at this.'

He handed me a loosely bound sheaf of papers. New pages for the script, that was my first thought. Then I looked at it. *Bureau File* was the heading on the title page, then *Subject: Mary-Lou Gunderson; File No. 67-59674*. As I flicked through, strange details about my life leapt up at me: *Reported to have attended CP meetings and study groups in 1940 . . . Whilst residing at 1003 Orange Grove Avenue, Pasadena, California, she was a member of a religious cult believed to advocate sexual perversion . . . known associate of Nemesio ('Nemo') Carvajal, Cuban national, union organiser at Lockheed Corp., Burbank, California, and known communist agitator . . .*

It was as though I was in an awful waking dream. Dexter patted me gently on the shoulder in a delicate gesture of possession.

'You're a lucky girl,' he murmured. 'Not everyone gets to see their FBI file.'

'You work for the FBI?'

Dexter's laugh was dark and soft.

'God, no. My department is more, let's say, strategic. But we have a reciprocal relationship with the Bureau.'

'The film, that's just some sort of front?'

'Oh no. It's an important project. And I really do want you to direct it, despite your duplicitous behaviour. And this,' he tapped the file in my hands. 'Well, some things could be added, some things could be taken away. It all depends on what you tell me.'

'I don't understand.'

'No. But you will. What did Larry say about you? That you wanted to know everything, yes, that was it.'

'You talked to Larry about me?'

'I talk to everybody about everybody. It's my job. Now, I need some answers. About Jack Parsons.'

He went into a brisk interrogation routine. Demanding to know what had happened, what we had talked about. I found myself telling Dexter everything. I mentioned the Black Pilgrimage.

'What's the Black Pilgrimage?'

'I don't know. It's something about a city, I can't remember its name.'

'Try to remember.'

'It was somewhere in Galilee.'

'Galilee?'

'Yes, I think so.'

'Are you sure he said Galilee?'

'I don't know. Yes.'

'Did he mention Israel?'

'Israel?'

'Yes, Israel. Specifically the newly founded State of Israel, keen to develop its own rocket programme.'

'No.'

'I want you to ask him about Israel, Mary-Lou.'

'What do you mean?'

'I mean, the next time you see him. Soon, I hope.'

'And if I don't?'

'Oh, I think you will. Besides anything else, you're intrigued. The file, please.'

I handed it back to him.

'Don't worry,' he told me. 'Do this right and I'll explain everything.'

I went back to work on Monday but Dexter was nowhere to be seen. I tried working on the script but I couldn't think. I called the motel. Jack had checked out. I phoned some of the Lodge members that I still had numbers for but no one seemed to know where he was. In the end I thought of Astrid. She had a fortune-telling stall on Sunset and Vine so I went there.

'You're looking for Jack, aren't you?' she said.

'Well, you'd hardly need second sight to know that, Astrid.'

'He's in trouble, isn't he?'

'He's been in trouble all his life.'

'I know, dear.' She closed her eyes. 'I'm getting some sort of a fix on him. I see the sea. Don't worry, I'll find him for you.'

Astrid phoned me two days later to say that the rumour was that he was renting a place in Redondo Beach on the Esplanade, a strange Moorish-style villa with arches and crenellations all rendered in concrete. I found it but it was empty. I left a note and went down to the shore. There he was, staring out at the sea. I called out through the crash and hiss of surf. He smiled as he saw me. We walked along the beach together.

I wasn't sure what I was going to do. I thought that I could warn him, even save him in some way. I had this mad dream that we would run off to Israel together and live on a kibbutz. But first I had to know what he intended to do.

'You're planning to go away, aren't you?' I asked.

'Maybe.'

'To that place in Galilee?'

He laughed.

'Well,' I went on, 'you could visit there, couldn't you?'

He stopped. He turned and frowned at me.

'What do you mean?' he demanded.

'If you went to Israel.'

'Who says I'm going to Israel?'

'I worked it out. I'm a clever girl, you see. The Black Pilgrimage was a clue, wasn't it?'

He looked around anxiously.

'No one's supposed to know. Not even Candy. You see, I've been approached by the Israelis and they want a detailed breakdown of equipment costs for a rocket programme. So I've borrowed the proposal document I put together for Hughes Aircraft.'

'What do you mean Candy's not supposed to know?'

'The thing is, I've taken that and some details about rocket fuels and propellants. It's all my work, but it kind of belongs to the company.'

'Jack, why does it matter if Candy knows or not?'

'What? Well, it could get me into trouble over my security clearance.'

'But Candy's not even here, is she? Is she?'

'Well—'

'She's coming back. That's it, isn't it?'

'I don't know yet.'

'But that's what you want, isn't it?'

'Mary-Lou, wait—'

But I had already turned and walked away.

It was a small gallery on Wilshire Boulevard. A private viewing, the opening of a new exhibition, a sophisticated crowd. Dexter floating gently through space, one hand holding a wineglass, the other stroking his chin thoughtfully. I walked over and stood next to him.

'What do you think?' he said.

Large unframed canvases with abstract blocks of shimmering oil, jagged sprays of colour.

'I saw Jack.'

'Good, good,' he muttered absently, gesturing at the artwork. 'But what do you think of this? You wouldn't say this was un-American, would you?'

'I don't know.'

'It's democratic, that's what I'd say. And the good thing about abstract art is that it's empty. It's politically silent, you know? Though there are some people who actually believe that there are hidden messages in stuff like this, even maps of our secret defence complexes. That's wonderfully mad, isn't it?'

'Dexter, we need to talk.'

'I know, I know. Look, if you ask me, America really does have to establish its own modern movement. You can't be a great power without the great art to go with it. Right,' he declared, handing his wineglass to a passing waiter and clapping his hands together. 'Let's get out of here and get a proper drink.'

We went to a bar and Dexter ordered cocktails. I remember *him* getting drunk, *him* talking: not the way I imagined the evening would run. He was enjoying himself. This was his entertainment, his delight in invention.

'Here's to mass culture, Mary-Lou,' he announced, holding up his martini glass. 'So much more important than that long-hair stuff. And no one can deny that it's all-American. It's what we do best and I'm proud of it. Now, you have some information for me.'

I told him about Jack stealing documents from Hughes Aircraft to support his application to work for the Israelis.

'Good work, Mary-Lou. I'll pass it on.'

'But don't you want any more details?'

'Oh, don't worry. The Bureau will follow it up. And they'll be appreciative, too. We can get them to sheep-dip your file. What?'

I was transfixed, staring at him, not knowing quite what to say.

'Oh, yeah,' he continued. 'Of course, it's the moment, isn't it?'

'What?'

'The moment. You've just sold somebody out. No big deal, Mary-Lou. Everybody named names and snitched on their buddies. You loved the guy. I take it that you're through with that now, huh?'

'Yeah.'

'Good. Believe me, disillusionment is a marvellously liberating experience.'

'Is it?'

'Yes. You've done the right thing. You've proved that you can work for us.'

'Who are you?'

'We're the good guys. Psychological strategy, that's our remit.'

'What does that mean?'

'*Pax Americana*, Mary-Lou. This is our century now. So, we have to win the Cold War in terms of culture. The Soviets fund high art heavily. We need to try to match them, but through the private sector, with the fruits of capitalism. Then there's the obvious propaganda, the Technicolor stuff, our version of socialist realism, you know, the bright, cheerful, our-way-of-life-is-best attitude. Hollywood can deal with that; it polices itself, blacklists anyone out of line. With modernism, meanwhile, we've got to have

the appearance of a liberal agenda to win over the European intellectuals. Now look, what's down here at the bottom of the pile?
B-movies, horror and fantasy double features, all the stuff people
tend to think of as junk. But it's as important as any other part of
the culture. You know, I got sent to Poverty Row just to keep an eye
on the greylist. But I've been able to clear our little project with my
higher-ups. I told them that science fiction is the best propaganda
of all. Why? Because it's prophecy. Yes. It's about the future and if
you can imply that your future is better than your opponent's, what
could be better than that?'

'So you really do want the film to go ahead?'

'Of course! We've got a great team. Nemo's better at the anti-
Soviet stuff than any right-winger. He's got a more nuanced sense.
And the good thing about Trotskyists is they really know how to split
left-wing opinion. It's like nuclear fission with those guys. Larry,
well, he's disaffected, but it's the kind of disaffection that neutral-
ises itself. Deflects it somewhere else. He understands the popular
instinctively, how it tends towards conspiracy and suspicion.'

'And me?'

'You were always something of a wild card, Mary-Lou. But occult
knowledge is extremely useful, especially when it gives you an
understanding of your enemies' superstitions. When I was with the
OSS in London during the war I worked with British Intelligence.
We learnt so much from them about counter-intelligence and
disinformation. They were masters of the black arts. They knew
that so many of the top Nazis had mystical leanings. You know,
they forged this German astrological magazine and managed to
distribute it behind the lines. Some copies were antedated so they
appeared to include astonishingly accurate forecasts of events that
had already happened and from then on the magazine was used to
question everything from the choice of Hitler's doctor to the timing
of U-boat launches. They played around with the unknown, the
unseen.

'That's why this flying saucer storyline is such a good one. Larry's
right, it's shaping up to be a new cultural phenomenon. A new belief

system, even. Nemo's convinced that there's been some governmental cover-up about extraterrestrial activity. That's already part of the mythology of this thing. And we can use that too.'

'How?'

'By subtly encouraging the sense of a cover-up. Then if we want to keep new aircraft or rocket technology secret, put a tracking device in a weather balloon, if something goes wrong with a test flight or, God forbid, a controlled nuclear detonation, an incomplete report might lead people to believe that it was one of these strange spacecraft everyone keeps talking about. And it enhances the image of our power if it's perceived that we've got access to secret knowledge, especially if there's an official denial of it. The Russians have got the atom bomb by now, we're sure of that, and we know they're developing missile technology. We need to maintain complete air superiority. That includes extraterrestrial activity, even the way it's represented. Our flying saucers have to be better than their flying saucers.'

'You're crazy.'

'I know. But this is how we tell the truth, Mary-Lou. Isn't it wonderful? The rumour mill, that's what we have to grind. Start a conspiracy and watch how it gets passed on. We can see how information moves through the culture. Like a marked card in a shuffled deck.'

We started shooting *Fugitive Alien* a month later. Nemo became increasingly suspicious about changes in the script. Larry had an air of distraction on set. It was soon clear that he was falling for the female lead, Sharleen Stirling. With her milky-blue eyes full of fear and wonder, there was something damaged and ethereal about Sharleen. A natural blonde, almost albino, she had a light peach fuzz on her deathly-pale skin that carried a sheen of luminescence so that her face glowed under the lights. She had a real screen presence. But there was a sad hunger in her gaze, imploring and seductive, caught in a bad childhood she could never escape from.

I heard that Jack got fired from Hughes Aircraft and had lost his security clearance after an FBI investigation. This disqualified him from any job in serious rocket research in the US and, given the circumstances, the Israelis withdrew their offer of work. I felt a little bad about how things had turned out but it was all in the balance. For all those years that he had power over me, I was the one who finally controlled his destiny. Funnily enough, we ended up in the same business. He got a job with an explosives company that specialised in developing pyrotechnics for the film industry.

And now that I had caught a glimpse of the real secret world, I got over my fascination with the occult and a search for hidden meaning. Oh, I still believe in the supernatural, in something beyond. I just don't take it personally any more. After all, I managed to sell my soul. And I can't tell you how much of a relief that turned out to be. I could get what I wanted out of life. With a clean file I'd be off the greylist, and *Fugitive Alien* could be my calling card to getting work in the big studios. I knew that it was going to be difficult for a woman director to succeed, but I was determined to try.

There were arguments on the set over Dexter's suggestion that Zoltar, our 'dissident' alien, should discover the good things about the American way of life. This wasn't in the original script and Nemo wasn't happy. But when Dexter proposed that Sharleen's part be made bigger, that she should show Zoltar the benefits of our great nation, Larry was only too happy to write new scenes for her. I was worried that this might be too much for Sharleen to carry.

'Oh, she can't act, but then she doesn't have to,' Dexter reassured me. 'She believes in this stuff. It gives her this real intensity.'

'Really?'

'Oh yeah. She thinks she's seen one.'

'What?'

'A flying saucer. She has all these strange stories about her childhood too. She thinks Larry's a genius. I tell you, Sharleen's a whole project in herself.'

Soon after that Nemo stopped coming to the set, though Larry never missed a day's shooting. I wasn't happy about him and Sharleen falling in love but it was none of my business and I was far too busy to do anything about it. Dexter began to leave things to me with the filming but he would always come to watch the dailies. He was already planning his post-production strategy. He had decided that he would instigate rumours about the film: that the alien language used by Zoltar when he is aboard his ship is an occult incantation; that the mention of an air force report concerning flying saucer sightings refers to an existing top-secret memorandum (Dexter even suggested that a copy of this could be forged and used at a later date). His cleverest trick was to put about the story that we had used actual footage of a flying saucer landing as part of the movie. It meant that some of the special effects sequences were to be made deliberately blurred.

It was my idea to use Jack Parsons' pyrotechnics company for these scenes. I knew he'd understand what we were after and would get it right. He believed in these things, of course. He told me that it was no coincidence that the spate of flying saucer sightings began just after he had been performing magical workings in the Mojave Desert. 'We opened a portal,' he said, 'and something flew in.' Dexter, of course, loved this notion and did nothing to discourage it. It was odd for me, to be with Jack again after all that had happened. It was astonishing really, though I just felt a calm detachment. But he was bitter at the way things had turned out: other people who had worked on the Jet Propulsion Laboratory's early rocket tests had also lost jobs in the McCarthy clampdown, while captured Nazi scientists had had their war records laundered and were now in charge of research in the field.

'You know, when I was a kid I thought that science was going to save the world, that it would give us a universal language, progress, peace,' he lamented. 'The military men took it over. Science means one word now: security.'

When he was just a teenage rocket enthusiast in the early 1930s, Jack had written to the German aerospace engineer Wernher von Braun and had received a reply. An intermittent correspondence came to an abrupt end once Hitler had come to power. Von Braun was a science fiction fan too. It is said that even during the war he kept up his subscription to *Astounding* magazine, obtaining copies via a mail drop in neutral Sweden. And he had now become part of the fantasy. Countless space films used stock footage of the testing launches of captured Nazi rockets in White Sands, New Mexico. And the new annual prizes for best SF works and achievements, the Hugo Awards, were presented in the form of a statuette looking disturbingly like a V2.

But Jack Parsons became the forgotten story in the dream of space. It was sadly apt that he should play some part in our movie. I knew he would never suspect me for what had happened to him and I was glad that I could put some work his way. We lowered the plywood spacecraft, and Jack detonated its retro rockets. It looked fantastic. I caught sight of his face in the fierce firelight, alive once more in transcendent wonder.

The film came in on budget and it made a reasonable profit at the box office, going on to become something of a B-movie classic. A spate of flying saucer features followed.

Nemo went back to Cuba in 1951. He'd had enough of the USA. He felt harassed and constantly under surveillance (though he never guessed how close the watchers really were). There was real change happening in Latin America, he told me. That was where the future was.

Larry and Sharleen got married in the fall of that year. I don't know why I felt so resentful about it but I did. I'd taken him for granted for so long. And he'd stopped loving me just when I could have loved him back. Another adjustment. Who knows what could have been? So I concentrated on work. I had a career now.

Television, that was the new big thing for the 1950s. I got a job with an anthology series called *The Scanner*: half-hour dramas of fantasy and science fiction. *You are now tuned to* The Scanner. *Your television set is picking up signals from distant worlds, images from other dimensions* . . . I was hired to direct twelve of the episodes of the first season. We adapted existing stories by established writers including Isaac Asimov, Theodore Sturgeon and Robert Heinlein (as well as Larry Zagorski and Nemo Carvajal). I was even asked if I wanted to write something myself, or have one of my stories used, but I said no. I still loved the genre but now felt too detached about it. I didn't want to come up with any new ideas, or to end up in that world of fiction where reality and fantasy start to coincide.

Dexter came to see me at the television studio. He took me to lunch and told me that he had a new job as an art dealer, specialising in Abstract Expressionism. He hinted that he had moved on in his secret career as well. I had expected him to ask me to put little touches of his into some of my programmes but when I tentatively mentioned 'psychological strategy' he smiled and shook his head.

'There's no big conspiracy, Mary-Lou, really there isn't,' he insisted. 'We can let things run by themselves for a while. But you know what's really interesting? We all live in a science-fiction world now. It's become part of mass consciousness.'

It reminded me of what Larry had said about the great future being already behind us. Within our short lives so many fantasies had been made commonplace: atomic power, computers, rockets, automation, jet travel, television. With them came the horrors of nuclear weapons, biological warfare, radiation, eugenics and seemingly endless nightmares of power. Only space travel was as yet unrealised, and even that seemed already confirmed by countless flying saucer sightings. The biggest adjustment was in what and how people believed.

Soon after the best-selling success of *Dianetics*, his psychological therapy system, L. Ron Hubbard announced his new creation: the Church of Scientology. That someone from the field of speculative fiction was founding a religion was hardly a surprise to any of us. Every pulp writer I knew had at one time had that drunken conversation about setting up a cult; most of us had written stories based on the premise. But it took a truly brilliant charlatan to actually make it work.

Hubbard stole some basic elements from the Ordo Templi Orientis from his time at the Lodge at number 1003. And he looted all kinds of theosophical and esoteric traditions (some real, some taken from *Weird Tales* magazine). But his real genius was the instinct that pre-war mystical societies needed updating in order to succeed in the flying saucer age. So he added modern terminology and gadgetry: auditing techniques, engrams and e-meters; he used the very present fear of mind-control and brainwashing that had come out of horror stories of GIs captured by the communists in the Korean War. And he gave his faith a cosmic theology: a creation myth of aliens banished to earth by an intergalactic warlord. He took Jack Parsons' arcane utopia of rocketry and the occult, and transformed it into a grotesque space-opera. And he had a business plan: to charge high prices for his therapy system and cash in on tax concessions available to churches.

This was the belief system for our times: the flickering needle of an electronic device, the immortal soul measured by the galvanic response of human flesh. I wondered at first if Dexter might have had something to do with it. He denied it strenuously.

'Believe me, Mary-Lou, I'd love to have control over something like that. In actual fact my friends in the Bureau are quite worried about it.'

And I wondered, too, if anyone had been involved in the death of Jack Parsons. ROCKET SCIENTIST KILLED IN PASADENA EXPLOSION: the report said that he had died in a blast that had ripped apart his garage laboratory. That he had dropped a flask of fulminate of mercury, a highly volatile compound, which had ignited other chemicals in the room, causing an infernal holocaust.

If it was murder, it was cleverly done. More likely is was an accident, perhaps suicide. Maybe it was somewhere between the two. I imagine Jack a little high on something, halfway through some absurd ritual or obscure experiment, sad and weary, he who had seen too much, though never enough, just letting go, letting the explosive slip between his fingers.

I can mourn for him now as I do for that whole part of my life. A time of illusion and a hopeless search for enlightenment. I think of how he looked on the last occasion I ever saw him as we were setting up the special effects for *Fugitive Alien*. The expression of delight on his face as the flares ignited to fake the flying saucer landing. The young man who had tested rockets in the Arroyo Seco, the child who had played with fireworks and dreamt of space travel. It's how I'll always remember him.

9

the hermit

Cato found a room in a boarding house in Hastings Street. He'd decided that the best thing was to come to Detroit and start all over again. A new town, a new beginning. It was a good enough place to find work as a musician. Jimmy had said that the Flame Show Bar house band was looking for a new rhythm guitarist. And if he couldn't get a gig somewhere soon there was always the automobile factory. Jimmy was coming by that evening to take him to this meeting he'd talked about. Cato wasn't keen but Jimmy had insisted he come along. 'It's a good place to make contacts,' he had said.

The room was small, bare and gloomy. Cato heard a distant wailing. He went to the window. The view was the brick wall of the adjacent apartment block. He dropped his case by the bed and his whole body shook for a second in a sickening shudder of grief. There was something hard and heavy in the pit of his stomach, a solid lump of remorse that he could not shift. As he sat down on the edge of the bed the mattress let out a sorrowful creak.

Taking off his shoes, he stretched out, closed his eyes and tried to take a nap, but he felt restless. It was hard to sleep during the day with no radio to keep him company. His head just filled up with unwelcome thoughts. He felt so goddamn lonely, that was the worst of it. He sat up and hauled his suitcase onto the bed. Rummaging through his things, he found a handful of magazines: *Reader's Digest*, *Confidential*, a *Time* from last year with Martin Luther King on the cover, and an old copy of a garish pulp called *Incredible Stories*.

Something to read on the bus ride, he'd thought, though in the end he had simply stared out of the window at the passing world. He picked out *Incredible Stories*. It had a battered cover showing a blue-skinned humanoid flying through a red sky with a ringed planet on the horizon.

He stared at it, trying to work out why he had put this thing in his case. It belonged to Sharleen, of course. She loved this craziness. She had even been in one of those flying saucer B-movies back in the fifties. And she'd been married to a guy called Larry who wrote this kind of stuff. There were times when they got drunk or high that she would tell him weird stories of people from other planets and secret societies on earth who had made contact with them. Cato wondered if it hadn't been science fiction that had sent her a little mad. Or maybe all those bad things she said had happened to her when she was a kid were true.

He couldn't work out why she had kept this old pulp magazine. It was metaphysically out of date. With stories supposed to be set in a future that was already lost in the distant past. He read the date on the masthead. *June 1941.* Hell, that was three months before he was born. Over twenty-five years ago. He opened the book and one of the stories was called 'Armageddon 2243'. Numbers reeled in his head for a moment. Jimmy had told him that numbers were the key. According to him, the whole universe was some kind of numbers racket.

'God has three hundred and sixty degrees of knowledge,' he had told Cato. 'The devil has only thirty-three degrees. That's how the Masons calculate their learning. Masons are in the power of the devil, that's how they run things. They in charge of white folks.' And at another time: 'Eighty-five per cent of the people are the dumb masses control-led by the ten per cent who are the slave-makers. The other five per cent are the poor righteous teachers. Them that know the truth.'

Cato flipped through the magazine. There were advertisements for mouthwash and correspondence courses; line-drawing illustrations for far-out tales called 'Plague Planet' and 'Robot Mission to Alpha Centauri'. One story caught his eye, perhaps because it was shorter than the rest. He lay on the bed and began to read:

THE HERMIT
By Nemo Carvajal

A humble hobo hides a cosmic secret!

In saffron robes and with flowing white hair and beard, the Hermit was a familiar sight on Hollywood Boulevard. He patrolled that stretch of sidewalk between Orange Drive and

Highland Avenue in front of Grauman's Chinese Theater. He would never ask for money directly, though he would show passers-by his open palm and entreat them with a smile: 'Please, let me help you.' At other times he would offer this advice from Matthew 19: 21: 'If thou wilt be perfect, go, sell what thou hast and give it to the poor – and thou shalt have treasure in the heavens – and come, follow me.' But he knew it was hard for most people to understand his mission on earth. They judged him merely as one of the many eccentrics who furnished the streets of this absurd city. Progress was slow. Most days he simply noted observations and looked for possible new developments to transmit in his daily report.

Noticing a beat cop approach, he prodded Sirius, the spotted mongrel curled up at his feet. Sirius gave a plaintive whimper and looked up at him imploringly. The Hermit reached down and patted him gently. Dogs (he had noted long ago) were the only animals on this planet that had a clear understanding of injustice. They could hear a higher frequency and it gave them a more finely tuned moral instinct. Their howls were the lamentations of worldly iniquity and dispossession. It was a clear signal but one that only the Higher Ones seemed to understand. Most humans had no conception of injustice. They thought only of justice, never the lack of it. They failed to register the canine wail that could provide them with such precious information and guidance. They would insist upon some warped sense of entitlement, a self-righteousness that could lead to nothing but an escalation of suffering.

The Hermit started to walk towards the cop so that he would be on the move by the time the cop reached him. Sirius trotted along beside him. He found a gait that would match the confident stroll of the beat officer, so that when they met they were travelling at the same pace. A little dance to the jaunty swing of the cop's night-stick.

'Hi, Pete,' the officer called out with a smile.

'Blessed are the peacemakers,' the Hermit replied. 'For they shall be called the children of God.'

They passed each other to the count of three twirls of the baton. This was the rhythm of the upright and principled, thought the Hermit. This was the tick-tock in the minds of humans when they thought of the word justice. But he bowed graciously to the policeman. He did not despise the cops as some of the other Higher Ones did. At least they understood the burden of power that they carried. Sirius gave out a little yelp. She had spotted something.

'What is it, girl?' the Hermit asked.

Sirius yelped once more and the Hermit then understood what she was saying. She was calling the name 'Duke'. Sirius had the capacity to recognise his fellow Higher Ones – this was another canine virtue the Hermit had noted during his time on earth. He looked in the direction of his companion's call and there he was. The Duke of Sunset was on the other side of the boulevard. In his top hat and crimson-lined cape, he was the most famous bootblack in Hollywood. He spotted them both and crossed the road, shouldering his shoeshine box.

'Hey, Serious!' he said, crouching to stroke the dog. 'How's my best gal?'

The Hermit smiled. He tried to remain impartial but he couldn't help seeing the Duke as the favourite of all his fellow Higher Ones on the boulevard. The light poured out of him. His work was so diligent, his lesson to the humans so clear and simple.

'Gave Clark Gable a shine yesterday!' the Duke announced.

The Hermit frowned. By the look on the Duke's face he deduced that this 'Clark Gable' was one of the benighted wretches imprisoned in those high-walled mansions he often passed. Those who had had their spirits sucked out of them by the light machines and were turned into ghosts while they still lived. He patted the Duke on the shoulder, glad that he could have given this man some solace.

'You may have saved his soul,' said the Hermit softly.

'Aww,' the Duke replied, looking down at the Hermit's bare feet. 'I wish I could give you a shine, Pete.'

'One day I'll wear shoes just for you, Duke.'

The Duke laughed and began to move on.

'Yes, sir!' he called out to the Hermit. 'Patent leather!'

Cato sat up and put the magazine down. He fumbled in his pocket for a cigarette. He lit it and puffed away for a while, thinking. He blew a smoke ring and watched the pale blue vortex hover and disintegrate in the space above the bed. A strange story, he thought, as the ghostly O began to stretch out and distort. About the everyday but with a twist, like those TV shows *The Twilight Zone* or *The Scanner*, where something ordinary is revealed as belonging to another dimension. Cato thought that he had guessed the trick of the tale. It was that this hobo guy was really an alien. Then he made another guess. Maybe he just *thinks* he's an alien.

He thought about the black character in the story. At least there *was* a black character. It was just a shame that he had to be a shoeshine. Then Cato remembered a guy in LA just like that. A shoeshine who wore a cape and a top hat. Perhaps this Duke guy was an alien too. Maybe that was the point of the story. That all the street people were Higher Ones and had come from another planet.

Cato glanced at the blue-skinned man on the cover of *Incredible Stories*. He suddenly thought of a joke. Brother, he mused, nodding at the illustration, you aliens can come blue-skin or green-skin, just make sure you don't come black-skinned when you land on this here planet. He laughed and coughed. He stubbed out his cigarette in an ashtray on the bedside table.

Quit smoking, Jimmy had told him. Quit smoking and quit drinking. Quit eating pork. Lead a righteous life. Quit going with white women, Jimmy had said. Cato sighed. His mouth was dry and tasted bitter. Sharleen had just got more and more screwy. He didn't even know whether to believe her when she said she was pregnant. Only that there was trouble ahead and it was time to go. She told him the FBI were listening in to their phone conversations. She believed that the Nazis were controlling the space programme. She saw UFOs all the time. She could give details of many species of extraterrestrial, their particular worldly influence and their secret ambitions. The one thing she didn't understand, thought Cato as he cleared his throat, was that his people were the true aliens on this here earth.

He picked up the magazine once more and curled up on his side.

As he made his way through the day the Hermit met with some of the other Higher Ones of Hollywood. Doc Hegarty, who handed out pamphlets that warned against the eating of meat, fish and nuts, explaining that protein caused unnatural lusts; Preacher Bill, who could give clear advice on the coming apocalypse; and Madame Pompadour, an ancient ex-prostitute who walked the streets now out of habit and would often fetch coffee and doughnuts for the girls who still worked the boulevard. But mostly he tried to minister to the needs of the desperate souls who passed him by.

In all the time he had walked the earth, tramped its highways, hitched rides or jumped freight trains, he had never known such a forlorn place as Los Angeles. A city so ravaged by materialism and a people weighed down by so many possessions, deluded by ambition and the painful need for adulation. After his first report he was ordered to stay here. To continue to observe these extreme conditions. And maybe to help to bring some relief to this barbaric region.

It was not enough, his superiors had decided, simply to make contact with the most advanced and privileged classes of this strange planet. The Hermit had known the civilisation of the shanty towns, the refined society of mission halls and soup kitchens. And he had learnt much in the great university of Camarillo State Hospital, where white-gowned students came to learn wisdom from some of the greatest minds on the face of the globe. But he had to go beyond, to bear witness to the barren emptiness of this bright and gaudy wilderness.

There came a knock on the door. It was Jimmy.

'You ready?' he asked Cato.

'Sure,' he replied. 'But listen—'

'I know what you're thinking,' Jimmy broke in. 'Just give it a try, that's all I'm saying. Islam is the natural religion for black folks.'

They went together to a meeting hall that called itself a temple. Jimmy tried to hustle them both to the front but Cato shook his head and took a chair at the back. Jimmy shrugged and sat next to him. A light-skinned black man in a leopard-skin fez started talking. Cato had heard some of it before. That the African had been deceived by the slave-masters, cut off from their true knowledge and true religion. The Original Man was black and his was the root of all ancient civilisation. Cato yawned quietly. He felt all the weariness of his life flood through his body and pool onto the floor of the meeting hall. He was overcome by a blessed sense of calm. He closed his eyes. God is not a spook, came the voice of the preacher. God is a man. The devil is a man also.

Cato let go and felt himself falling. Then the physical weight of his body seemed to drop away and his spirit began to soar. The voice spoke of the civilisations that existed on other worlds, of how the moon and the earth were once one planet before they were split apart in a huge explosion. Then it was dark in his head. No sound, no light. No space, no time. A moment that lingered eternally. Then Cato's head nodded sharply and he woke up with a start. He kept his eyes closed and listened.

The preacher was talking of a great wheel in the sky. Like the vision Ezekiel had seen. The white man is planning for battle in the sky. Today he has left the surface for the air, to try to destroy his enemies by dropping and exploding bombs. But we too are ready for the battle in the sky. The great wheel is the Mother Plane and it can exist in outer space. Ezekiel saw it long ago; it was built for the purpose of destroying the present earth. It carries fifteen hundred bombing planes. The small circular planes called flying saucers that are talked of these days are surely from the Mother Plane, the preacher declared.

Cato opened his eyes and found that they were filmed with tears. A single drop warmly traced his cheek. Yes, he thought, of course. All this madness made some kind of sense. Everything flipped over with a complete change of polarity. The world turned upside down in a geomagnetic reversal. He closed his eyes once more and felt that calm shadow cool his mind. He thought of what it was like to see the darkness. He saw the darkness. And he saw that it was good. Yes. Black people belonged on the earth. It was the white folks who were the aliens. The meeting was coming to its end in a cacophony of scraping chairs. Cato wiped his face with his handkerchief and stood up.

Even Jimmy noticed a change in him as they walked back to the boarding house.

'You okay, man?' he asked as they reached the front door.

'Tired, is all,' replied Cato.

'Sure. Well, we'll talk soon, yeah?'

Cato nodded and shook Jimmy's hand.

Back in the room Cato switched on the light, stripped down to his underwear and got into bed. The bare bulb hurt his eyes but he wanted to finish the story.

Westward was the Hermit's journey along Hollywood Boulevard. By four in the afternoon he would reach St Thomas the Apostle Episcopal church. The Temple of Doubt. After Judas, the Traitor, the Hanged Man, Thomas was the greatest disciple. The patron saint of uncertainty, this great principle that now even the scientists know governs our puny universe. The humans think that they want belief; Thomas preaches that what they need is incredulity. Enlightenment on a need-to-know basis. Stick your finger in the wound. Then you might feel the pain of another. Compassion, the Hermit remembered: it means 'to suffer with'.

By sundown they had reached the far end of the boulevard, where it began to snake and twist its way up through Laurel Canyon. The city fell away as the Hermit and his dog Sirius climbed the Hollywood Hills. A grid of lights stretched out below, an illuminated cage. Above, the celestial mechanics were firing up. The constellations began to bloom as man and dog followed the winding path to their base camp in the foothills. Treasure in the heavens, thought the Hermit. The Dog-Star rose on the eastern horizon and he pointed it out to Sirius. She let out a howl of salutation.

'Yes,' agreed the Hermit. 'Home.'

They lived together in a wooden shack at the end of a footpath that cut through the brushwood. The Hermit lit an oil lamp and gathered together his equipment. From a Higher One who ran a junk shop in Santa Monica as cover, he had been issued with a Philco model 40-74T four-tube battery-powered radio set. He switched it on and as it warmed up he turned the dial until he found that particular band of pulsating static that he recognised as the native language of his home planet. He then began his nightly broadcast.

Cato got up and went to switch off the light. A trace of neon throbbed against the wall outside his window. He sat on the bed and smoked another cigarette. His last, he told himself. He might write to Sharleen, he thought. Maybe she would understand. Maybe she did already, in her own way. He could sleep now and not fear his dreaming. He silently thanked God or Allah or whoever for untying that knot of guilt in his gut. He stubbed out his cigarette and got back into bed.

10

the wheel of fortune

Avenida 9 # 1580 esq. Calle 19
Miramar, Habana
Cuba

15 October 1958

Dear Larry,

Well, I finally met my father. Two days ago, at a party in Vedado
for a man who had won the lottery. Such a frenzy of celebration
around us that we scarcely had to worry whether or not the two
of us had anything to congratulate each other about. This could
have been a chance meeting, like everything else in life. The
dancing and commotion granted us a sense of stillness, the loud
music a moment of silence. For which I was thankful because I
had no idea what to say to this man, nor him to me. He shook
my hand and named himself as a trumpet blared behind us.
People were spilling out onto the street, forming a procession
down towards the sea wall, and we were swept along with it all.

Two cops on patrol near by were nervously fingering their
holsters, ready to run if things got out of hand. One of the
women approached them, explaining that this was a party, not
a demonstration. Someone waved a 26 July Movement flag
anyhow. The people are becoming bolder now, ready to take to
the streets when the time comes. Civil unrest simmers beneath
the surface, bubbling up in all sorts of peculiar ways. Last
month there was an outcry when the fiesta for the Black Virgin
of Regla was banned (her statue was stolen, and a rumour
circulates that the authorities have substituted a fake one).

We found some space on the sidewalk, away from this
improvised carnival, and as we struggled to converse we soon
fell into a rhythm, with similar patterns of speech and diction.

And it was as if we were mimicking each other's gestures and affectations. We don't look very much alike, my father and me, but it's astonishing how much we share in mannerism. All the same tics and spasms of character: things one would think were socially learnt, habitual, are to be somehow found in the blood. And all at once I knew that it did not matter much what we really meant to each other. This simple familiarity suddenly made things easy between us.

It looked harder for the man who had won the lottery. He was greeting people with shouts of joy but I saw fear and panic in his eyes, an urgency in his loud insistence that he had known beforehand that his number was going to come up. This zealous belief in our own premonitions, as if we cannot bear for our will to be so diminished by such a random act. It is a disturbing notion that the most important moments of our lives, our greatest successes, are merely a matter of happenstance. As I turned to my newly found father I realised that I didn't even owe the fact of my birth to him, just to the luck of the draw. The turn of the wheel. The odds of any particular individual's existence are so narrow that it would be scarcely worth the gamble. It is enough merely to exist and to count our losses to the end. Perhaps that was what was troubling the man.

But I suspect he did not think like this at all. Nor did anyone else for that matter. Only myself, my head spinning like that helter-skelter helix of genetics. As we crossed the Malecón to the water's edge, I slapped my father on the back and said: 'Well, we won the lottery.' He turned and frowned at me. Then smiled. Alien features forming reflective expressions of a curious remembrance. We went to sit on the sea wall and he told me a story.

Larry, I'm afraid this is going to be a long letter but I have much to tell (who was it who said, 'I'm writing you a long letter because I don't have time to write you a short one'?). But first let me congratulate you on your incredible novel. I finally got hold of a copy of *American Gnostic* when I got back from the *sierra* this year (there's a bookstall just opened on the Plaza de

Armas that stocks a good selection of American science fiction and usually has the latest edition of *F&SF*). This is the best thing you've ever done. You've restored my faith in the genre. To be honest, I've become bored with so much SF lately, or disappointed (whatever happened to Heinlein? – all this quasi-fascist nonsense he's writing now; when we first met him he was a libertarian socialist). Maybe I don't need much speculative fiction at the moment when here everything and everyone is concerned with the future. But not in fantasy, rather in the real possibilities for radical change.

I've been all over the island in the last two years. In Guantánamo, helping to organise the railway workers, co-ordinating strike action in support of the Rebel Army in the hills. I was even in the Sierra Maestra, smuggling supplies from Santiago. I came back to Havana in late spring to rejoin the urban underground. The general strike of 9 April proved a complete fiasco with the loss of much of the leadership of all participating oppositional groups. Now we have to completely regroup the mass movements in the city, establish solidarity with the armed struggle and find a common strategy to defeat the dictatorship. At last the 26 July Movement is making constructive overtures to communists and the Marxist left. We're re-establishing the Revolutionary Workers Party as a challenge to the Stalinists, forming workers' committees and printing a newspaper once more.

There are many splits in the struggle: between *sierra* and *llano* (the Rebel Army in the hills; the working-class movements on the plains and in the towns); between nationalism and socialism; and, of course, among the left. But I fear the more profound schism, that universal dichotomy between the intimate vision and the shared ideal. Everybody has their own idea of what a perfect world is. For the moment we have a common enemy but that's never enough. We need to find a united front in our imaginations. We are too convivial in our nightmares. We must find a way of dreaming collectively.

I have a job as a waiter (can you imagine?). The Sindicato de Obreras Gastronomico is actually one of the few unions that retains a radical leadership. So much of the labour movement here is in the hands of *mujalista* gangsters. A week ago a customer called me to his table and asked if I was Angel Carvajal's son. I nodded, knowing not much more of my father than that he had been in jail when I was born. Then he told me about this party and said that my dad would be there, if I wanted to see him.

So that's how I ended up on the Malecón, at the age of thirty-six, face to face with paternity for the first time. I have little recollection as to what we talked about at the beginning. I was cautious in my speech, as if waiting for an explanation from him. Then he started to tell me of something that had happened to him.

'I hear that you're some kind of a writer,' he said. 'Here's a story for you.'

And this is what he told me:

'I was born out in Santiago de las Vegas. My father worked on a tobacco plantation. He was a real bastard. Sorry, I suppose he was your grandfather. Anyway, there wasn't much room, all five of us living in a shack, so I was hardly missed when I left. I was fifteen. I got a job in Marianao, working as a stable hand. I was shovelling horse-shit all day but it wasn't bad. Horse-shit is better than most kinds of shit, certainly better than human shit. It was a racing stables by the track at Oriental Park. I got there in November and there was plenty of work. American owners brought their horses over to race through the winter season. I earned a dollar a week and slept in the hayloft.

'There was a girl I worked with, Dominga. A light *mulatta* with a hard face but an elegant, long-limbed body. About my age but taller than me, more developed: you know how girls grow up quicker than boys. She was proud and haughty, and ordered me about with little mercy. Today I see her as a bossy girl; then she seemed a goddess to me. She showed me the duties of the stable and taught me how to roll a cigarette in one hand.

'One day I came across two strangers in a box stall. One had a vet's bag but he clearly wasn't a vet. They were sticking something into the backside of the horse. I went to tell the manager. I came across Dominga on the way and told her what I had seen. She nodded and asked me where I was going and when I told her she slapped me across the face. What was that for? I asked her. For you to remember, stupid. You see anything, come to me first.

'She told me all the tricks of the trade that we might witness. A horse might be doped to go fast, or to go slow. Or even be swapped with a ringer. In a race confined to three-year-olds, say, one of the horses entered might be substituted with an older, stronger horse that looked the same. She explained that there was always the possibility of making a dollar here or there. Errands to be run, lookouts to be posted, leaving a bucket of water in a certain stall before a race to load a horse down. When I looked, astonished, at the lengths people would go to to cheat the odds, she pinched my cheek and called me Angelito, the little innocent.

'One afternoon in the hayloft she showed me another kind of trick. The oldest. She rode me hard and when I begged to have a turn at jockey she shook her head and pushed me down into the straw. Man, whenever I smell horse-shit I think of Dominga. Later I plucked up the courage to tell her I loved her and she slapped my face again. Don't be stupid, Angelito, she told me. You're just a stable hand. That's not going to work, is it? So that was that.

'Then came the night we helped a gang bring in a ringer for a race the following day. This time it was a substitute for the favourite; this ringer was meant to lose. It was the same size and shape but there was one problem. It was the wrong colour; the tone of its coat was too light. The favourite was a deep chestnut, the ringer was bay. I stood to one side and watched how everybody argued over what was to be done. Dominga suggested that we paint the thing. The men laughed but she assured them she had seen it done. With something called henna. You mix this red pigment in water and it works as a dye. In the end they agreed. We would do it at first light, and then they would come and see the result. They offered five dollars, but Dominga haggled up to seven. She had to go into Havana to get this stuff and at dawn we mixed it in a bucket and started to brush it on. We managed to get some sort of a match, a little blotchy in places maybe, but the gang seemed happy and paid us our money.

'It was only after they had left that we noticed how frisky the ringer was getting. This could be trouble, Angelito, she told me. Perhaps there was something in this henna that was irritating the horse. By the time it was in the paddock it was fairly jumping around. I asked Dominga for my split of the money and she suddenly gave me this look. No, she said. Get all the money you've got and bring it to me. Hurry. I had five dollars and two bits saved that I had stashed by my bedroll. I ran to get it and brought it back to her. What are you going to do? I asked her. She shook her head and told me to meet her later behind the grandstand.

'You can judge a race easily enough simply by the sound of it. I heard the commentary on the tannoy, the roar building up. I knew that somehow our ringer was coming in as favourite and that we were in a whole pile of shit. The gang would be after our blood, and so would most of the bookies on the track when they learnt what had happened. I nearly jumped out of my skin when I felt a tap on my shoulder. But it was Dominga, and she told me that we had to get going. What are we going to do? I asked her. She said that we'd think of something. But, look. She showed me the money she had got. With a sudden thought that, in its henna-induced delirium, the ringer might go like the wind, Dominga had staked everything she could scrape together on it at two to one. We had nearly fifty dollars. Time to go, Angelito, she said. Enough of horse-shit for us.'

He smiled and gave a plaintive gesture to indicate that his story was done. 'And then?' I asked him.

'Then we hitched a ride to Havana and found a place to flop in the Barrio Chino. Dominga got a job in a nightclub. And I started getting into real trouble.'

We both gave out the same long sigh. Then I was puzzled and wondered about him meeting my mother and how he ended up in jail. I'd expected somehow that his story would lead to that. We walked back to be part of the crowd once more. I took hold of his hand. It was hard and calloused. For some reason I told him about Juanita, a girl I've been seeing for the past few weeks. She's a waitress at the restaurant and a comrade.

Larry, I'm truly sorry that things did not work out between you and Sharleen. It's an easy thing to say now but I really never thought that you were right for each other. Of course, I always thought that it would happen between you and Mary-Lou. I remember you telling me about that night you tried to explain quantum mechanics to her. Maybe there's always been an Uncertainty Principle between you. But even Einstein had problems with quantum theory (and a fear of blind chance, perhaps) – 'God does not play dice with the universe,' he says. No, not dice but roulette (and none of us likes the house odds). The Wheel of Fortune is one big particle accelerator.

And gambling is certainly a huge problem here. American gangsters use our country as a playground with all their casinos in Havana. Come the day, we will kick every one of them out. But Cubans are not immune to gaming tables themselves. We'll probably keep the lottery after the revolution (one of the few nationalised industries, after all, though terribly corrupt). And there are so many people involved in the business that there'll have to be a transitional period. We discussed it in a meeting last week and called for the appointment of a Commissar for Games and Chance (I'm already thinking of applying).

Seriously, though, Cuba's curse is that it has become a boun-tiful source of pleasure for others. We are so good at indulging vice in what we produce: sugar, rum, tobacco, prostitution and, of course, betting. This place is a Garden of Earthly Delights for foreign tourists, while so many of our own people live in poverty. But now we have a chance to change everything and create our own utopia. Nowhere has there been a greater opportunity for a genuine revolution, a permanent revolution. I feel such optimism that it almost scares me, Larry. Remember how I said when we first met that I had always been too late, historically speaking. Too late to join the militias in Spain; too late to meet Trotsky in Mexico. Well, now my time is here, I'm sure of it. I'm in absolutely the right place at the right moment. A real jonbar point, if you like. I wish you could be here to see it, my friend. Come, if you can.

Because the struggle has to be international, universal. I truly believe that change here can change everything. The whole world is watching, and maybe beyond too. Remember I told you and Mary-Lou about Tommaso Campanella and his uprising in Calabria. In the dialect there they had this word for it: *mutazione* (like mutation, remember those 'mutant' stories in *Astounding*?). Anyway, *mutazione* means not only a worldly revolution but also an astronomical shift, a time of cosmic change. And there are signs of it in the sky.

Yeah, I know you think I'm crazy but I've seen them again. There is definitely extraterrestrial activity close by, observing. I've seen UFOs over the Florida Straits on a couple of occasions. And I think I know now why they didn't make contact before, in America. They simply weren't interested. If they detect a real civilisation that they can communicate directly with, or at least the possibility of one, then we might see something spectacular. Now, with the launch of the Sputniks, and the demonstration that socialism can beat capitalism into orbit, we are surely ready for extraordinary advancements in science and society. Maybe we are not alone (and I'm not alone with my mad interstellar ideas – there has been much discussion of these concepts among the Latin American Bureau of the Fourth International).

Perhaps we can solve that old conundrum of ours: we can change the world *and* build spaceships.

Back on earth the struggle continues. Batista's regime is collapsing. Castro now controls almost all the countryside in Oriente. Cienfuegos and Guevara are advancing rapidly westwards through Las Villas. The people of Havana are ready to rise up and take control of the city. The future holds many risks and uncertainties in this glorious venture. This has always been the biggest gamble in history. That great spin of the wheel that we call the Revolution.

Hasta la victoria, siempre (a Rebel Army slogan),

And affectionate regards,
Nemo

II

lust

He closes his eyes on a true darkness, submits his will to nothingness. The void. The empty, parallel world where he is zero. Everything descending into blackness: matter, energy, information.

Now.

He is on his knees, face at her feet in calm supplication. Nose up against toes that flex and creak in polished hide. He tries to kiss the glossy leather but she shifts her weight to stoop down over him. With gloved hands she loops the collar around his neck, buckles it, clips the dog leash on. She straightens up.

'Hup!' she commands with a swift tug of the lead.

His head jerks back. He feels a jolt of power run through him. That almost forgotten impulse of desire. Good Lord, he thinks with a wistful smile, there's life in the old dog yet.

'Open your eyes,' she tells him.

He looks up. Booted and stockinged legs bestride his face. He sets his gaze on her pelvis thrusting forward, girdled in black lace. She grabs a meagre fistful of his wispy grey hair. Pins and needles tingle his scalp.

'Naughty boy.' She holds his head an inch or two from her crotch. 'You want this, don't you?'

'Please,' he whimpers.

'But do you know what I've got for you there?'

He thinks for a moment. She glares down at his wrinkled, frowning face.

'Whatever you care to give me, Mistress.'

'Yes,' she whispers. 'Good boy.'

Marius Trevelyan had first spotted her on his way to Curzon Street on the morning he was recalled by the Service. She was tip-toeing up Shepherd Market on high heels. A short black bob, a fur-trimmed jacket, buttocks twitching in a tight skirt with that absurd erotic waddle. It was just before 9 a.m. but she wasn't on her way to work, he decided. Oh no, on her way back, more like. He picked up his stride and followed at a discreet distance. All his years in retirement hadn't blunted his appetite to pursue and observe. He felt a twinge of lust and an odd sense of recognition. She had finished for the night. She was coming off the game.

Coming off the game. Just as he had so many times. Only to be pulled back by the Service to consult on some little project or other. They never quite let you go, just kept you dangling. Trevelyan noted the hint of a swagger in this tart's gait. A little too much emphasis in the upper body, he thought. Yes, that was interesting. Maybe this one really was in the same trade as he was.

The Curzon Street offices were not as changed as he had feared. He had imagined banks of computers replacing the musty confusion of Archive and Registry, the gloom of partitioned offices torn down and replaced in a bright and unforgiving open-plan. But as he made his way along the corridor, it seemed still the same dank labyrinth he had known from his days at Information Research.

The director of his old department was a woman. That was the shock he could not quite adjust to. Oh, he knew he had to. After all, there had been eight years of a female prime minister. They were everywhere in power these days. He remembered this one from when she was an assistant desk officer fresh from the Colonial Service. She'd had long hair then, and a habit of wearing exotic Indian silks. Now she had a cropped fringe and a skirt suit with shoulder pads. He noted the flat shoes when she stood up to greet him. Sensible shoes, isn't that what they called them? She had beady, intelligent eyes.

'Thank you so much for coming in, Sir Marius,' she said, shaking his hand.

'Not much choice,' he retorted a little too sharply, baring his teeth in a grin. 'You know, one is never completely retired. Just in suspended animation.'

She offered him a drink. Not a real one of course. That was another thing of the past.

'There's not a problem with this recall, is there?' she asked him.

'No, no.' He shrugged.

'You'll be reporting directly to me, but if there is any, well, difficulty, we now have a staff counsellor.'

'A what?'

'It's a new post. An independent officer that any member of the Service can consult with, concerning any problem that they might not feel able to discuss with their line management.'

'Good Lord.'

'We set it up after that officer from Counter-Subversion went to the press about being asked to carry out inappropriate investigations.'

'I hope you don't think that I'm going to go public about anything.'

'Not at all, Sir Marius. I just feel obliged to let you know about new conditions of work within the Service.'

'Since this *Spycatcher* business, Head Office really is worried about people blabbing, isn't it?'

'I'm afraid so.'

'Even got an injunction on Joan Miller's memoirs. Ridiculous.'

'Joan Miller?'

'Worked for Maxwell Knight during the war in Counter-Espionage. All the stuff in her book is about that time. Nothing that could threaten national security. Though some of her work was tangential to Operation Mistletoe and the Service is still very cagey about that. Especially now, I suppose. I mean, that's why I've been called back, isn't it?'

'I'm sorry?'

'Prisoner Number Seven. Hess.'

'Oh. Yes.'

'Hanged himself in the summerhouse in the Spandau garden. Not easy if you're over ninety.'

'Quite. We've always known his death would be a political event so we've had a procedure laid down and ready for this, agreed to by all the Four Powers. The autopsy and investigation have been our responsibility.'

'He was always our prisoner. First and foremost.'

'Yes. And that is why we've called you in, Sir Marius. You're the only one left who has known the case from the beginning.'

'So the Service wants my post-mortem?'

'Yes. And your take in terms of information strategy, naturally.'

'Don't expect much clarity.'

'Nuance, that's what we're after.'

'Because this one was dark right from the start. A perfect example of the craft. Nobody knew the whole story and nobody ever will. So it can be told again and again. Controlled confusion, that's the key to negritude.'

'Negritude?'

'Sorry, an old section nickname. You know, the Black Game. Black propaganda. What the Americans insist on calling psychological warfare. As if there was anything scientific about it. The Yanks, well, they were always a bit heavy-handed. Never learnt how to play it as a game.'

'And the Soviets?'

'Brutal but playful. Like a cat with a mouse. Old liars, like us. And, like us, probably better at import than export. What are they up to with this one?'

'It's rather strange. They appear to have shifted their attitude just months before Hess hanged himself. In April, *Der Spiegel* ran a story that Gorbachev was considering agreeing to Hess being released. In June, a similar statement was issued to the German-language service of Radio Moscow.'

'That's odd.'

'Yes.'

'They've always exercised their veto before. If it hadn't been for the Russians the old Nazi would have been out years ago.'

'The obvious analysis is that this is all part of the *glasnost* policy.'

'*Glasnost*,' he sneered. 'If you ask me *glasnost* is the slyest form of disinformation we've ever seen. Oh yes. What we said in the past is a lie but this, *this* is the truth. It has this confessional, redemptive trick to it. What about our side? What have we been up to?'

'There we might have a little problem.'

'Really?'

'Just a matter of detail.'

'The autopsy?'

'No, not that. The son has commissioned another post-mortem but I don't think that should cause us any problems. No, there was a note.'

'He left a note?'

'Yes.'

'A nearly blind ninety-three-year-old left a suicide note?'

'Yes.'

'Christ.'

'We're sure it can be verified.'

'Sounds as if someone's been a little over-zealous. What does it look like?'

'It's with our senior document examiner. We'll get it to you as soon as possible.'

'Good. And I'd like to run it past one of my old team, if that's permitted.'

'Eric Judd?'

Sir Marius Trevelyan nodded.

'Yes. He should give it the old once-over.'

He spent the afternoon back in Archive, once more trying to make some sense out of the affair. Over the years it had continued to confuse him, even as he had been part of the confusion himself. Now the old bugger was dead. Prisoner Number Seven had a long history of attempted suicide. In June 1941, soon after his capture, he had thrown himself down the stairs of the country house where he was being held for interrogation. The banisters had broken his fall and he had merely fractured a femur. In February 1945, he had stabbed himself in the chest with a stolen bread-knife and later gone on hunger strike. In 1959, in Spandau prison, he had used the jagged edge of the broken lens of his spectacles to open a vein in his wrist; in 1977, he had severed an artery with a knife. But on none of these occasions had he ever left any sort of note.

And the contents of the missive were perplexing. Addressed to 'all my loved ones', most of the thing was taken up with an apology to his former secretary for having to act as if he didn't know her. During his examination by psychiatrists at Nuremberg, he had been confronted with Hildegard Fath, who had worked for many years as his personal assistant, and he had claimed that he had never seen her before. She had been reduced to tears, but this was back in 1945, over forty years ago.

The note brought everything back to the question of the man's sanity. Marius Trevelyan once more attempted to thread his way through the maze of delirium and forgetfulness. The Soviet doctors had always maintained that Hess had been faking his loss of memory. The British had been more ambivalent, concluding that he had 'suggested an amnesia for so long he partly believes in it'. Hess protested that he had been subjected to hypnosis and psychoactive drugs. American Intelligence had been intrigued by the possibilities in the case for advancements in mind-control. A psychiatrist on their panel later developed brainwashing techniques for the CIA.

Trevelyan began to make notes on a series of index cards, a one-line subject heading on one side, details on the other. After some time he shuffled through this small pack of cards and turned up a blank one marked 'American'. He buzzed for a desk officer and called up all the files pertaining to US Intelligence regarding Prisoner Number Seven. He had remembered that there had been an American commandant at Spandau in the 1970s who had got into trouble when it was discovered that he had been working on a book with Hess. He made a request for this file also, along with any relevant documentation.

By the end of the day they had got the suicide note to him. It had been written on the reverse side of a letter Hess had received from his daughter-in-law, dated a month before his death. A nice touch, thought Trevelyan, if it indeed was what Eric Judd would call a 'moody one'. Yes, Eric might be able to spot something, he concluded, as he carefully replaced it in the evidence bag.

'But what do you think is in there?' she asks, a gloved hand still holding him by the hair.

'Mistress?'

He feels the pressure sores as his bony knees dig into the floor and a tremor of arthritis in his right hip. His old and withered flesh is cramped and weary, trembling. She places her other hand between her thighs, lets out a little burlesque purr.

'People often wonder what I've got down here,' she says. 'There's uncertainty. You like that, don't you?'

'Oh yes, Mistress.'

She was right. That was what he liked. Subterfuge.

'Yes. Well, it doesn't have to be one thing or the other, does it?'

'No, no it doesn't, Mistress.'

'It could be both.'

'Yes.'

'In fact it is both, isn't it?'

'What?'

'Until you look at it, it's both, isn't it?'

'I don't, um. I don't understand.'

She lets go of his hair and slaps him across the face, sending him sprawling onto the floor.

'Concentrate!'

She pulls on the leash and he is up on his knees once more.

'You have to concentrate. This is a thought experiment.'

'Mistress?'

'Until you look at it,' she goes on, adjusting the straps on her satin cache-sex, 'it really does exist in two different states at once. It's Schrödinger's pussy. Now close your eyes and see what's real.'

Eric Judd ran an antiquarian bookshop in Coptic Street. He had worked for Trevelyan in the Service as a senior art-worker in Technical Operations, and was an expert in handwriting and typography. Judd had been recruited in 1966, from Wormwood Scrubs, when he still had six months of an eighteen-month sentence to serve. For forgery. He had quite the genius for it.

He had worked in Trevelyan's section, creating fake political pamphlets that could be used to discredit left-wing groups, forging letters from Eastern Bloc organisations to militant trade unionists and other documents essential for state security. When Trevelyan was posted to Ulster in the 1970s, Judd went with him.

Together they disseminated black propaganda, mostly aimed at undermining Republicans. One of their more obscure operations had been in disseminating disinformation that the IRA and other paramilitary groups had become involved in witchcraft and demonology. They circulated counterfeit literature on the occult throughout the province; black magic ritual sites were fabricated in derelict houses and on waste ground near army observation posts; animal blood and ceremonial objects were left on altars decorated with arcane symbols; and rumours were generated that some sectarian killings had actually been instances of human sacrifice. Judd became obsessed with the project, meticulously researching every detail of liturgy and sacrament, reading widely on the occult and the unseen. In the end, much to Trevelyan's bemusement, he started to believe in it himself, which culminated in some sort of mental breakdown. He was given early retirement from the Service in 1979.

Eric Judd was now a book dealer specialising in the esoteric. As Trevelyan entered his shop, Judd was at the counter with white gloves on, carefully examining a battered incunable.

'So.' Trevelyan leaned over Judd's shoulder. 'What do we have here?'

'Careful.'

'A book of spells. Some ancient *grimoire*, is that it?'

'Nothing of the sort. An early bound version of Otto von Friesing's *Gesta Friderici I Imperatoris.*'

'Oh.'

'It's extremely rare, so keep your grubby mitts to yourself.' Judd began to wrap the book in cloth. 'So, shall we get down to business?'

'It's good to see you too, Eric.'

'The pleasure's all mine, I'm sure.'

'Now, don't get tetchy.'

'I'm not. Just want to get on with it. Besides, you were never one to stand on ceremony. I'd better close the shop.'

Judd put down his shutters and locked up, then they both went out the back to a small workshop. With a magnifier he showed

Trevelyan how he had compared the suicide note with other samples of Prisoner Number Seven's handwriting.

'It's considerably distorted, of course. That's to be expected. The bastard's old, ill, about to kill himself. But see? The shape, the integrity of the signature, it's still there. Now, any old fucker can copy shape. Getting the dynamics right, that's the difficult thing, the movement of a line, acceleration, deceleration. If you're copying something, the chances are you're going to lose speed and make a coastline.'

'A coastline?'

'Even with the smallest loss of flow, you can end up with tell-tale little crenellations. That's a coastline and you know it's a copy. Look, the hand may be unsteady here and there, and there's a natural jerkiness to it. There are vibrations that tell us all kinds of things. But no coastline. I mean, we could enlarge it even further and do an analysis in terms of fractal dimension.'

'Do you think we should?'

'I think I've seen enough, Marius.'

'Your eye's still good enough, is that it?'

'Well—'

'All those years of kiting cheques. So, what does Eric's clever little eye tell us?'

'It's a bloody good job, or . . .' Judd shrugged.

'It's genuine?'

'Could be. Or a very good copy of an earlier suicide note.'

'I told you, he never left any notes on other attempts.'

'Well, I've got a feeling that he did with this one.'

'Why?'

'I don't know. It's just that—' Judd sighed. 'There's another way of looking at whether or not this thing is true.'

'How?'

'The emotions.'

'The emotions?'

'Yeah. I can read the emotions from this.'

'Oh for goodness' sake.'

'I knew you'd be like this.'

'What, your extrasensory intuition or something?'

'Do you want to know what I think or not?'

'Go on, then.'

'Because whether you like it or not, handwriting can tell you most of what you need to know about the writer's personality. Their state of mind. And as I said, I got a feeling from this one.'

'What kind of feeling?'

'That whoever wrote this was sure that they were going to die.'

'Eric—'

'It's all there in the hand. I can feel a vibration there, a shake to it that isn't just illness and old age. A strange tremor of intent.'

'Right.'

'Look, you wanted my analysis.'

'Yes, I did. Thank you.'

'Still the unfeeling old bastard, aren't you?'

'Now, Eric, you're not being very fair.'

'Cold, that's what you are, Marius. I might have been the one that went a bit doolally, but you—' Judd stood up and opened a cabinet. 'We'll have a drink, that might warm you up.'

He produced a bottle of scotch and two glasses and poured them both a measure.

'Cheerio.' Judd toasted his old boss and nodded at the papers scattered on the work surface. 'Curious business, the Hanged Man.'

'What?'

'Hess. That's what we should call him. You know, the Hanged Man hangs upside down. An invert. Is it true that the KGB file of Hess is code-named Black Bertha?'

'I wouldn't be at all surprised. The Russians were always a bit petulant over Prisoner Number Seven.'

'They thought the Service lured him over, didn't they?'

'Eric, there's been so much nonsense over this affair. Negritude of the highest order.'

'Is it true that astrologers were used to convince him to make the flight?'

'Rumour and disinformation.'

'So why did the Gestapo round up all those astrologers afterwards?'

'Because they fell for all that mumbo-jumbo. All those Nazis, many of them fell for that New Age stuff, just like you.'

'I'm not into New Age stuff.'

'No?'

'No. Nothing new about it. I'm into the Western Mysteries. Traditions that we're all part of, whether we like it or not. I've tried explaining it to you, Marius, but you never listened.'

'Well, try me now.'

'Influence can be brought to bear on events. Especially in moments when probabilities are so finely balanced. It's known as sympathetic magic.'

Trevelyan laughed.

'So, we put a spell on him, is that it?'

'That's not what I'm saying. You know that all sorts of things were played with. And they have an effect: we saw that in Ulster.'

'A psychological effect, yes.'

'That's all magic has to be, Marius. A psychological effect. If you believe in something, it has power over you.'

'It's true some people on our side believed in some pretty strange things. Even Fleming was convinced that the whole episode had been predicted in a novel.'

'Precognition: there's proof of it everywhere.'

'Proof, that's a good one. You know, you can be very limited in your ability to spot fakery.'

'You think so?' Judd glared at Trevelyan and refilled their glasses. 'Well, maybe I can spot one now.'

'What's that supposed to mean?'

'We always wondered about you, Marius. In the Service.'

'Not this again, Eric.'

'It was never much a question of political loyalties but, you know.' Judd gave a shrug. 'We often wondered which side you batted for.'

Trevelyan swallowed a gulp of whisky. He sighed sharply.

'Shit-house gossip.'

'Gibbs had the best theory,' Judd went on. 'Remember Gibbs from field projects? Well, he always said: "Trevelyan? Likes a bit of both but doesn't get much of either".'

'I'd forgotten just how full of shit and shit-house gossip you were, Eric.'

'Old times, eh, Marius?' He raised his glass once more. 'Old times.'

'Should have left you to rot in the Scrubs.'

'One of the best, you were. No one could ever work you out.'

No, thought Trevelyan, and no one ever will. There had always been two sides, two possibilities. The self and the other self. A double agent. Something Fleming had once let slip. The man inside. The unknowable one.

Back at his flat he found it hard to settle. He paced around, trying to align his thoughts. The Hess affair had come at the very beginning of his career in deception. Now it still haunted him at his retirement. Like his own life, the case was shrouded in rumour and now it conjured other remnants of intelligence. Things that he couldn't possibly include in his report. Perhaps he should book an appointment with the staff counsellor, he mused. The modern confessional: therapy, analysis. All this fear in the Service of officers going public. They didn't have to worry about him.

But he did have the sudden urge to write something, not for anybody else but for his own record. A memory system in which he might encode something of himself. A narrative, something more like a short story than a file or a dossier. He found a pad of paper and a pen and poured himself a brandy. The warm fuzz from the scotch he had shared with Judd was dying out. He rekindled the glow. All that shit-house gossip, yes, that was part of it too. He remembered an anecdote, something that he could hang a few ideas on. Yes. And the title came to him at once. That image Eric had used, a great symbol of ambiguity. He quickly wrote the heading: *The Hanged Man*.

'Suck my pussy,' she commands and pushes her penis into his mouth.

Sweet dissembler, mistress of disinformation, of transubstantia-
tion. His mind is a labyrinth of corridors, a *bal masqué*, a school of
night. Her flesh unhoods itself against his tongue, a worm uncoil-
ing, growing inside him. Oh yes, she's in the same trade as him. The
art of deception.

She looks down as he groans ungrudgingly. An easy mark, a
grateful punter. She won't have to give him much. She'll be quick.

A fluid pulse on his palate. Too soon, he thinks, surely. But no,
another swift surprise, a secret blessing. She is pissing in his mouth.

On his last day at Curzon Street, Trevelyan carefully initialled off
all the files he had drawn and arranged for a desk officer to take
them back to Archive and Registry. A secretary came to shred all
his handwritten notes and memoranda into a burn bag. He walked
down the corridor to the Establishments office and signed off all his
current secret indoctrinations with the duty officer. Then he went
to see the director.

His report was on her desk.

'It's fairly routine stuff,' he assured her. 'Only one area of concern
really.'

'The note?'

'Yes. I've come up with a theory about its source. Completely
deniable, thank God, but it might be an idea to follow it up. Make
sure it's watertight.'

In the American files in Archive he had come across a file dated
November 1969, a report that Hess had been transferred to the
British Military Hospital in Berlin, suffering from stomach disor-
ders and a perforated ulcer after a prolonged hunger strike. On the
night of 29 November, the American commandant noted that Hess
had declared on more than one occasion that he was sure he was
going to die. Prisoner Number Seven had claimed that there had
been instances when his heart had stopped beating and his pulse
had disappeared. He had written a letter that night.

It was shortly after this incident that he agreed to receive visits
from his wife and son, and on the first of these he mentioned his

former secretary and his desire to explain his failure to recognise her at Nuremberg.

Trevelyan concluded that the 'suicide note' found in the summerhouse was actually a copy of the letter written when he was dangerously ill in 1969. Eric Judd was right: he *had* thought that he was going to die, only nearly twenty years earlier.

Had Hess been murdered? It seemed unlikely. More probable was that somebody had made a clumsy attempt to force a verdict of suicide on the inquest. Somebody with no sense of negritude. It would have to be dealt with. But not by him. It wasn't his case any more.

He remembered what they used to say in the Political Warfare Executive: 'There's no such thing as intelligence, only counter-intelligence.' In the last few days he had spent more time on his private narrative than with the official report. A personal account on how the case had marked his career, betraying a few secrets, offering a few conclusions. And something of a memoir of his own life. A chapter in his autobiography. Who had hanged the Hanged Man? He doubted if they would ever know for sure.

The story was in his briefcase. He was taking it with him. Completely against the rules, of course. He should have either submitted it or had it destroyed. But they didn't have to worry about him going public. It was for his own amusement as much as anything. A souvenir for his own archive. A fragment of memory saved for posterity.

He said goodbye to the director and went out into the street. He hailed a cab and went to dine at his club. There was nobody there he knew. Such a lonely business, eating by oneself. For a moment he was overwhelmed with melancholy. He thought of Clarissa, his wife, who had died nearly twenty years before. The marriage had been a bit of a mistake really, but in the end they had learnt to bear each other's company. He regretted that he had never found the time to thank her for putting up with his life of duplicity.

It was getting dark when he got home. As he was paying off the cab he saw the tart he had spotted that morning in Shepherd

Market. Sturdy-looking and big-boned. A bit top-heavy. Oh yes. There is no excellent beauty that hath not some strangeness in its proportion. He went up to her.

'Would you care to join me for a drink?'

She smiled.

'You're a naughty boy, aren't you?'

'Oh yes. Come back to my place.'

She didn't waste much time once they were in his flat. She carried the collar and leash in her handbag. It often came in handy on occasions like these. Playing away from home.

To finish she allows him to masturbate on her boots then lick them clean. He begs her to stay just for a little while longer. He wants to talk.

He has been so lonely for so long. He needs to share something of his own secret life. He feels that she knows the code somehow, that she understands the double world.

'What's your name?' he asks her.

'Vita. Vita Lampada.'

'Oh yes.' He laughs gently at her cover name. 'Like the Newbolt poem. "Play up! Play up!"'

'I'm on the game!'

They laugh together now. She indulges him. A real gentleman, she decides. Only public-school boys ever get the joke of her name.

'I'm on the game, too,' he tells her.

'Why, you naughty boy,' she purrs. 'Well, don't expect me to pay you.'

'Of course not. It's another game I play. The Black Game.'

'The Black Game?'

'Telling lies and making up stories.'

'What sort of stories?'

'I can't tell you. It's a secret.'

'Naughty boy. Are you some sort of spy?'

'I'm retired. Well, they never quite let you go. I've been pulled back for this wretched business at Spandau.'

'Spandau?'

'Look, I really shouldn't be telling you anything.'

'Like the Spandau Ballet?'

'Yes, it was rather like a dance. A sort of quadrille between the Four Powers. You know, it was the last thing the wartime allies continued to do together. To guard an old man.'

'I knew them, you know?'

'What?'

'Spandau Ballet. They used to come to Billy's and the Blitz. I preferred Danny Osiris and Black Freighter.'

He frowns at her. He has no idea what she is talking about.

'I used to be a bit of a New Romantic,' she tells him.

He smiles. And he feels compelled to answer:

'I used to be a bit of an old romantic.'

But he knows it's a lie.

He falls back into his armchair. Exhausted. Sated. He lets out a satisfied sigh. Now he feels he has finished his job, though little flashes of Hess run through his mind. The Spandau Ballet: what made her say that?

'I'd better get going,' she is saying.

'Yes. I hope you don't mind me not seeing you out. I'm rather tired.'

He has already paid her. No need for that awkward ritual at the door.

'See you again, perhaps.' She grins and her eyes flash for a moment.

And she is gone.

She sees the briefcase in the hallway and says to herself, no, it'll only get you into trouble. Her hand is already on the latch; she is ready to let herself out without looking back. But at the last moment she turns and grabs it, swinging it out of the door with her.

Back in her little studio flat she lights the gas and turns the case out onto the hearthrug. A copy of *The Times* and an A4 manila envelope. She opens it and pulls out a sheaf of papers. A manuscript. She sits down and begins to read.

12

the hanged man

My first job in the Service and my last. There's always a danger of giving random events undue significance but it was hard not to see a pattern in the Hess case. His flight marked a curious apex in the rise and fall of the Third Reich; his death now becomes part of the Cold War endgame. But years of study have rendered little of substance or meaning. Perhaps he merely represents something of my generation of intelligence. A Secret Service tradition that went from fighting a war we had to win to facing off a war that we could never allow to happen. Now it appears that the latter game is over too. By all accounts the Soviets were finally ready to let him go. Then suddenly his suicide. Eric Judd calls Hess the Hanged Man, which seems an appropriately mysterious symbol. Because whatever you believe, there was an occult aspect to this case. After all, what 'occult' means is to be hidden or obscured.

What you have to remember is that none of us involved in the affair ever knew the whole story. I for one was only ever told about a plan to reactivate our tame Nazis in the Link, that pitiful bunch of Fifth Columnists run by the Political Warfare Executive, and even that was quickly aborted when Joan Miller's cover was blown. Everyone close to it picked up strange clues and hints that something very odd might have transpired but nothing could be proved or verified.

It's true that after the capture of Hess in Scotland, Commander Fleming did issue a memorandum recommending Aleister Crowley as an advisor in his interrogation. But there is certainly no record that the Great Beast played any part in a scheme by elements within the Service to lure Hess over. And if any of the files of Operation Mistletoe ever see the light of day, they will probably merely hint at a vague disinformation campaign that used faked paranormal material to provoke the superstitious elements within the enemy. It was certainly part of our broader strategy. The Political Warfare Executive eventually employed its own astrologer, the rather absurd Louis de Wohl, who was given a captain's rank on the understanding that this was a mere payroll technicality. He caused great embarrassment to our department when he was spotted in Piccadilly, sporting a very shabby uniform that he had acquired for himself. The colonel in charge of our section said he looked 'just like an unmade bed'.

In the spring of '42, Fleming came to Political for a liaison meeting. He was putting together a special commando unit for intelligence gathering. It was then that he told me about the queer book titled *Swastika Night* that he was certain had in some strange way predicted Hess's flight to Scotland. He had even interviewed the author, who turned out to be a woman writing under a male pseudonym.

In 1985, an American publisher, the Feminist Press, reissued *Swastika Night* and revealed its author as Katharine Burdekin. I got hold of a copy and found that there was indeed a reference (on page 87) to a character called Hess leaving the Nazi inner circle and travelling to Scotland. It seemed an odd coincidence.

The next time I saw Fleming was in Normandy in '44, just after the D-Day landings. I was with a reporting unit at Carteret where the Allied armies were regrouping before advancing to the north-east. He was with this commando squad he had formed, the 30 Assault Unit. He called them his 'Red Indians'. I remember that bloodhound expression on his face. Handsome, dashing, keen for the fray. His battledress just a bit too clean and well tailored.

We got a chance to inspect the huge rocket installations the Germans had left behind: vast concrete bunkers, launch pads and gantries. We walked around dismantled missile parts, nose-cones and finned engine assemblies. In retrospect it was like the setting of one of his books. As we picnicked on K-rations amid futurist ruins, I asked him what he intended doing after the war. I nearly choked on my Spam when he replied: 'Why, write the spy story to end all spy stories.'

For a moment I had a vision of him telling some imaginative account of Operation Mistletoe. I was professionally appalled but personally intrigued by the possibility of someone making sense of one of the greatest mysteries of the war. Perhaps it would make sense only as fiction. Maybe Fleming had worked out some sort of key to it.

It was a full ten years before his first book came out. I scanned it for any obvious clues but soon realised what a futile task it was to chase after hidden meanings in novels. Granted, the figure of 'M' in *Casino Royale* is clearly Maxwell Knight: everyone in the Service knew him as such (Fleming even gives him a Chief of Staff named Bill, just as Knight had). This was telling since really Fleming had dealings just with Knight over Mistletoe. And Joan Miller is certainly the template for the attractive assistant that Bond flirts with. Most playful of all was the obvious use of Crowley as inspiration for the villain Le Chiffre (French for cypher). But then this would hardly be the first time the Great Beast had been turned into a fictional character. And there was nothing else in the book that even hinted at any solution to the puzzle of Operation Mistletoe. I have to say that I was more than a little disappointed.

I was by then married to Clarissa Devereux, the third daughter of the Lord Marshalsea. It had been a brief engagement, just after the war when everything seemed hopeful. It's shocking to think now how innocent we were, especially of sexual matters. Soon after our honeymoon I was posted to Kuala Lumpur as Security Liaison Officer to the Colonial Special Branch. It was the time of the Malayan Emergency and I was co-ordinating psychological warfare and propaganda strategies in the counter-insurgency against communist terrorists.

Clarissa took to the tropics at first. It was a big adventure for both of us and for a while it seemed like paradise. She spent a good deal of time and energy making our house beautiful. Most expat residences tended to be a little dreary, filled with gimcrack furniture, gaudy ornaments, tiger skins and the like. She supervised the decoration herself and made our bungalow bright and spare with clear lines. We had a long spacious veranda and a well-tended garden. Beyond it wild and lush foliage thickened along the bank of a broad and gently flowing river. Clarissa loved the astonishing natural world that surrounded us. When we could she liked to trek through the pathways in the jungle, to bathe in a nearby river pool so clear that one could see the golden sand of its bed.

But security was very tight for most of the time we were there. The communists were targeting rubber planters. Barbed wire went up around our little compound. She began to feel trapped. Clarissa had a charming obsession with Eastern mysticism but she soon found that colonial society was actually quite dull and suburban. Once the novelty wears off one can feel trapped in a sort of exotic boredom. I had my work, of course; I was absorbed by it. But Clarissa grew tired of the languid routine, the dreary cocktail parties.

It was all very disappointing for her and I couldn't help much. There had been a spark to our marriage at first, but that's all it was, a flicker that could so easily go out. I tried everything I could but I don't suppose anyone would find my company particularly exciting. Intelligence work does tend to make men dull and introspective.

She began a prolonged flirtation with a handsome veterinary surgeon attached to the Commissioner-General's office. Alan Munro was charming, sensitive and, above all, interesting. He knew most of the native fauna and could describe it exquisitely; he played the piano and read poetry. After six months of this I finally challenged her. I couldn't blame her for having an affair but in my professional pride I could not bear being deceived.

'But, darling,' Clarissa assured me, 'Alan's queer. I thought you knew that.'

I did not but the thought of it suddenly unsettled me. Clarissa noticed it almost at once.

'This business about Alan has really upset you, hasn't it?' she asked me later. 'I didn't think that you were particularly anti.'

'No, I'm not.'

'What then?'

I couldn't say. It was a sense of uncertainty, something disjointed and fugitive. Like a fragment of encrypted intelligence. An awkwardness developed in our relationship. We bluffed our way through our time in Malaya, keeping up appearances and following the pattern of a well-bred marriage. There were other postings: to Beirut, Cairo, Berlin. But each move in the Service seemed to consolidate the distance between us. Clarissa spent more and more time back home. When I finally returned to London, what was left of our shared life had all but reduced to the politeness of strangers.

Quite by chance Clarissa had seen something of Fleming in town. She was an old friend of his wife; Ann Fleming, *née* Charteris, granddaughter of the 11th Earl of Wemyss, once widowed, once divorced, now on her third marriage, a formidable creature of London society and its most impressive hostess. Her parties brought together the elite of cultural and political life. She was elegant and imperious, with a sharp and outrageous tongue. Clarissa confided to me that she found Ann more than a touch frightening.

The Flemings had set up house in Victoria Square and on the night we were invited there the guests included Cyril Connolly, Lucian Freud, Hugh Gaitskell and Teddy Thursby. But no sign of Fleming. As it got late the drawing room became packed with people. I found myself standing out in the hallway. Clarissa was in the heart of the throng, looking on as Ann Fleming told a joke to James Pope-Hennessy. I heard the front door slam and someone brushed past me, calling a terse greeting to the hostess, then turning to mount the staircase.

'Come and join us, Commander!' a voice shouted above the drone.

The man sighed and shook his head. As he looked up I saw it was Fleming.

'Good Lord, Trevelyan,' he said. 'What on earth are you doing here?'

'I was rather hoping to see you.'

'Sorry. I can't abide these gab-fests. No place for our sort of talk. Come to lunch at Boodle's.'

We made a date and he thundered upstairs. I wandered back to the doorway. Ann Fleming was telling everybody about the routine at their house in Jamaica.

'Well, darling, I'm in one room, daubing away with a paintbrush, and he's in the other, hammering out the pornography.'

Over lunch Fleming confided to me that it stung a little that Ann and her literary friends rather looked down on his novels. And despite achieving some commercial success, he felt trapped by his own creation.

'He began as a sort of empty alter ego,' he said of his central character. 'I mean, I even gave him a slave name. But now he's becoming the master.'

He shrugged and made a small wave of the hand, indicating that we should change the subject. He lit another cigarette. I noticed then how much he was smoking. He seemed constantly wreathed in fumes, smouldering away.

He wanted to talk about the *Rote Kapelle* or Red Orchestra, a series of anti-Nazi espionage rings that had operated in Germany in the early years of the war. He was working out the background for a Russian character in his new book, a spymaster who would have had dealings with the Red Orchestra. We discussed the theory that one of the networks was a Service operation to get Ultra decrypted information about Operation Barbarossa to the Soviets in a way untraceable to our code-breaking system and in a form that might not be dismissed by Stalin as British disinformation.

'This would have been just before the Hess flight,' I said.

'So?'

'Perhaps the Service was also using the Red Orchestra to send messages to the Deputy Führer.'

Fleming smiled.

'That's an amusing idea,' he said, as if it were an idea for one of his plots. 'A faked astrological chart giving him the most auspicious time for his mad mission. A soothsayer insisting that he must go now, before it was too late!'

We laughed.

'Of course,' Fleming went on, in a lowered tone, 'there was a Gestapo round-up of all the astrologers a month after he landed in Scotland. It was called *Aktion Hess*.'

'Really?'

'Yes. So if you were to find somebody who had been picked up in that *and* had a connection to the Red Orchestra, then you might be on to something.'

He gave me that bloodhound look of his. One was never really sure how serious he was. After lunch we wandered out on to Pall Mall: a bright boozy day, a truant afternoon. Fleming broke into a wheezing cough. All at once he looked haggard, his noble face drawn and blotched, his blue eyes dulled to grey. I stupidly asked if he was all right.

'Yes, yes,' he snapped, lighting up another of his hand-made cigarettes. 'He's killing me, that's all.'

I didn't know what he meant but laughed almost out of politeness. As we parted, he told me that he was off to his place in Jamaica the following week.

'You must come and visit some time,' he called out as a parting shot.

At this point my career in the Service was on the rise. I'd just been promoted to section chief of a new department at Head Office. A more permanent job in London meant that Clarissa and I had to decide what we were going to do about our fragile marriage. I begged her to let us give it another try. We got a charming flat in Cheyne Walk with a view of the river. Clarissa once said that she liked to watch the tide go out, because it gave her the promise of escape if things went wrong.

Then she got pregnant. It was like a miracle. It seemed as if everything now would be all right. She had desperately wanted a child and this finally seemed to prove my worth as a husband.

When she miscarried I couldn't help feeling that this was some dreadful judgement on us both. She had an awful time of it and for a while she was quite ill. I felt helpless, overwhelmed by grief and guilt. In a pitiful way it brought us closer than we had ever been. But only for a while. Once she had recuperated Clarissa grew cold and distant to me. And I became anxious in her presence, wary of any kind of intimacy.

I threw myself into work. There was plenty to do. A comprehensive restructuring of a Service that had been riddled with defections, double agents, security leaks. In an atmosphere of rivalry and suspicion all the best intelligence officers were keeping their heads down. And when there wasn't quite enough to keep me occupied at Head Office, I pursued my amateur obsession with the Hess case and Operation Mistletoe. My senior position gave me access to all manner of files and documents.

In the meantime Clarissa got used to my coming home late. She knew that the Service insisted I be on call at all hours. I'm sure she suspected I occasionally played away, just as I presumed she had an opportune affair now and then. Discretion was our unspoken rule. I tried not to even think about what my wife might be up to. And what I did hardly counted as infidelity. I hadn't even planned it.

I'd often go for an evening drink with some of my staff but one night, after working into the early hours of the morning with an officer on secondment from Counter-Subversion, I ended up in a seedy after-hours club in Paddington. There was a cabaret of sorts: girls took turns to dance on stage or mime to gramophone records. They then sat out in the audience at the end of their 'act'. It was obviously a knocking shop, but there was something more than usually exaggerated in the make-up and demeanour of the tarts as they plied their trade.

It was just when my colleague gave me a nudge and a knowing smile that I realised what was going on. The illusion was suddenly revealed, yet still intriguing. They were all female impersonators, and very good ones too. This was a silly entertainment for my fellow officer, at most a voyeuristic pleasure. I laughed along with him heartily as we got mildly drunk together. But a fortnight later I went back there on my own.

I found that I liked the uncertainty, the ambiguity. It made sense of that unsettling feeling I'd had in Malaya all those years ago. It was the pretence as much as anything, the act of disguise. I didn't feel I was being unfaithful because what I was doing wasn't entirely real. I certainly didn't consider myself homosexual. I think you'll find that most men who occasionally have sex with male transvestites feel the same way. It was a game: colluding in someone else's deception, escaping from one's own self. There's an unbreakable code within, like that curious line that Iago utters at the beginning of *Othello*: *I am not what I am*. I've long since given up trying to decipher myself. Curiosity becomes its own definition.

This activity was a high-level security risk, of course, and at a time of the greatest paranoia in the Service. And I enjoyed the danger and the sense of transgression. But I wasn't stupid; I didn't do it too often. That made the whole thing more rare, more interesting. I took few risks and was diligent in covering my tracks. My sense of duty made me careful. And my marriage kept me stable. I was determined to save it and I endeavoured to spoil my wife whenever I could. I suggested a proper holiday, which we hadn't had in years: three weeks in Jamaica with a visit to the Flemings while we were there.

In February 1963 we flew to Montego Bay Airport. We felt the heat as soon as we stepped off the aeroplane. That thick, slightly sweet smell of the tropics hit us, that familiar scent from when we had first disembarked at Singapore, which brought back memories of when we were young and in love. Our plan was to spend a week at the Flemings' and then explore the island a bit. We picked up a hire car and set off for their villa at Oracabessa. Once we had left behind the hotels and cement villas of Montego, we were on a winding road through tumbling countryside, jungle interspersed with cane fields and mangrove swamps. Green hills that sloped gently into coves and headlands, a bright-blue sea diffusing into the horizon. We passed porched wooden houses and one-roomed shacks, whitewashed Baptist chapels with signs exhorting each passer-by to repent for the end is at hand. We smiled at each other, knowing that we'd made the right choice going there.

It was over fifty miles to the Flemings' house. An idyllic place, built on a cliff overlooking the sea with a sunken garden and steps leading down to a beach of pure white sand and deep clear water.

After we had showered and unpacked we joined Ann and Ian for cocktails and they showed us around their little estate. That evening Violet, their black cook and housekeeper, served us lobster and curried goat and rice. We retired early, just after sunset. As we said goodnight Ian was leaning against the railing at the bottom of the garden, looking out to sea and smoking incessantly, his aquiline profile patrician and melancholic, vigilant as darkness fell.

The night pulsed with tree frogs and cicadas as we made love. It was as tentative and romantic as it had been in the early days of my first colonial posting. A moment saved from time.

But though we felt briefly blessed in coming to Jamaica, it was soon clear that staying with the Flemings was a terrible mistake. There was a palpable tension between them and we were drawn into the conflict, as guests so often are, used as witnesses or referees in an endless round of accusations and point scoring. It made us realise that perhaps things weren't so bad between us but it was awkward and embarrassing.

His body battered by serious heart disease, his ego bruised by continued criticism of his writing, Ian felt that Ann was cold and lacking in affection towards him. Ann in turn thought that Ian had become spoilt and insufferable with the success of his novels. She felt that he was now overly content with the adulation he received and no longer appreciated the challenge of their relationship. Both suffered deeply from the other's infidelities and took little account of all the sacrifices they had made for one another.

One day we drove out to Port Maria with Ann. Ian stayed behind to write. On our way back we went by a large white bungalow on a headland overlooking the harbour. Ann gestured vaguely at it, deliberately averting her eyes.

'That is the house of Ian's Jamaican mistress,' she declared. 'You may look, but I cannot.'

Another morning when we found Ian breakfasting alone in the garden, he confided to us: 'I'm utterly exhausted by Ann's ceaseless complaints and wounding attacks on me. I'm ill and I'm desperate. I need a little compassion.'

Finding ourselves constantly in the crossfire grew tiresome but that night in our room my wife seemed in a mischievous mood.

'It's said that they used to like whipping each other.'

'Clarissa, really.'

'Oh, come on. Everybody knows. I heard that when they stayed at Willie Maugham's at Cap Ferrat they used up all the towels, running them under the tap and taking turns to flog one another with them. You think I'm shocked by such things, don't you, darling?'

'Well—'

'Nobody's completely normal, I know that, Marius,' she said pointedly. 'And I think I know what their problem is now. You see, before, they were acting it out. Playing out all that anger and resentment. Now it's become real. They should play things out more.'

She turned and gave me a knowing smile.

'Everybody should play things out more, shouldn't they, darling?' she demanded in a tone that offered hope for us yet. 'Otherwise they end up killing each other.'

As the week wore on Ann tended to confide her feelings to Clarissa just as Ian vented his to me. He liked to drink and smoke late into the night.

'I tried to kill him off, you know,' he told me as we drank bourbon together. 'I'm even writing his bloody obituary this time but it won't do any good. I even had him in a health farm in one book, just so I could go and relax. But he won't lie down. He'll kill me first.'

And I remembered the strange remark he had made that afternoon on Pall Mall. He was talking about his hero, his fictional creation. His other self.

'I punish him with pain. He punishes me with pleasure,' he went on. 'You see, like him I drink too much, smoke too much. Rush around in a constant state of nerves. Wear myself out. Except here. Here I write him and count the cost of the damage he has done me. Maybe it's just guilt.'

He poured another drink, lit another cigarette.

'You're like me, Trevelyan. A staff officer. Sticking pins into maps and sending men into danger. From a desk. A handler: yes, that's what I thought I was doing, handling another agent. But he's ended up running me. He's the revenge for all the men I've sent into danger.'

I wanted to ask him about this but he changed the subject. He was keen to talk about current intelligence concerns and Service gossip. The conversation quickly turned to Cuba. It was Jamaica's nearest neighbour, after all, and it had only been three months since the Missile Crisis had nearly blown us all to kingdom come.

We agreed that American policy towards Castro had been a disaster. All the CIA's interventions and black ops had only forced Cuba closer to the Soviets.

'They should have set about deflating Fidel, rather than building him up as a threat to world peace,' Fleming suggested.

'I've always found that the Americans lack a little finesse in negritude. They're not very good at lying. Too bloody sincere.'

'They should have found a way of ridiculing Castro. I said as much to Kennedy.'

He explained rather sheepishly that the president of the United States was something of a fan of his novels and that they had met when he was still a senator.

'I told him that they should generate black propaganda, purportedly from the Russians, informing them that atomic testing in the region had caused beards to become radioactive and advising them to shave them off, thus undermining the whole revolution. One of their security advisors actually thanked me for my idea with a completely straight face. They don't seem to realise that you need a sense of humour. And a sense of luck.'

'Luck?'

'Good fortune, yes. That's what it mostly relies on, isn't it? You have to find a way of using it. Take Cuba. You know what happened when Castro marched into Havana and gave his first televised speech in front of the cheering crowds? Two doves appeared. One perched itself on his shoulder. Now, in Santería, the Cuban version of voodoo or whatever, that meant he had the protection of the gods and was all-powerful. I mean, imagine being able to engineer something like that?' He smiled. 'Political power is largely a matter of superstition. Intelligence too. Magic, some of it.'

'Like Operation Mistletoe?'

He let out a wheezing laugh and stood up, swaying a little.

'Too late for that now. We'll talk more tomorrow.'

The following night Fleming gave me his final word on the Hess affair.

'You remember what Winston said? "In wartime, truth is so precious that she should always be attended by a bodyguard of lies." That's what worked so well for us. Perfidious Albion, yes, we've always been good at that. Our lies were better than theirs. Some of it was Maxwell Knight's fantasy. M believed in some of that mumbo-jumbo so it appeared convincing.'

'Stalin was sure that the Service had a part in the Hess flight.'

'Yes, and we know now how well informed he was about British Intelligence. But I'm not so sure, you know. Crowley had some occult contacts in Germany that we used but nobody was sure if they actually had an effect. What did you find out?'

'Not much.'

I told him that I'd managed to track down an astrologer and psychic who had been some kind of voice teacher. Astrid Nagengast had been arrested during *Aktion Hess* and also had a record of being connected to a Munich section of the Red Orchestra. Along with some occultists she had been interrogated and detained in Sachsenhausen concentration camp for two months.

'What happened to her?'

'She survived the war and went to live in California.'

'You could go out there and see her.'

'Perhaps. But, you know, once you start investigating that part of the world it becomes more and more absurd. Crowley had something of a cult out there for a while, of course, but it's easy to get carried away with conspiracies and all kinds of nonsense.'

Fleming poured us both another drink.

'I circulated a paper for Naval Intelligence in 1940 titled *Rumour as a Weapon*,' he said. 'I wrote that we had the ammunition; we just needed the device to direct it. In Political you called it the Black Game or negritude. Later I found my own name for it. For where it all belonged. The House of Rumour.'

'The House of Rumour?'

'At the centre of the world where everything can be seen is a tower of sounding bronze that hums and echoes, repeating all it hears, mixing truth with fiction. It's from Ovid's *Metamorphoses*. A lovely image, don't you think?'

'It is, rather.'

'And that's what every intelligence service is, at its heart. It's been the same since classical times. It was from the House of Rumour that the Trojans learnt that the Greeks were coming. An advance warning system. And we knew that Germany was planning to invade Russia and that's what would save us. But we had to make sure. So there were all manner of phony peace feelers to help convince the enemy that they might not have to fight a war on two fronts.'

'Like Operation Mistletoe?'

'Perhaps. Though we'll never be sure if it really had any effect. I think it was mostly good fortune. And bad luck on their side. You have to remember that in the end the Trojan War was won by deception and counter-intelligence.'

'Oh yes, the wooden horse. Particularly nasty piece of negritude.'

'Another phony peace offering. Well,' he sighed, 'we still need the House of Rumour. To make sure our own Trojan War never takes place. I mean, we had a bloody close shave last October.'

And that was the last time I spoke to Fleming about the case. He died the following year of a massive heart attack. Looking back, I think it was from that night on that I began to stop chasing after the affair. The myths and conspiracies continued to circulate but I chose to conclude that it was more likely that the Deputy Führer was deranged and had acted on his own.

The most ludicrous theory that I came across about Hess was that a doppelgänger had flown in his place. An absurd hypothesis with scant evidence or explanation, yet one that presented a compelling image: the double, that great theme of fiction and intelligence. And of two worlds, too – a splitting of possible outcomes. Fleming told me that there were only two crucial moments in any life (and he used this conceit in the title of the novel he was working on): that of birth and death. But by then he was facing the end. Now, it's nearly all over for me too. I'm left with the final mystery of the Hanged Man. Just why was a 'suicide note' planted on him?

In the last two days of our stay the bad feeling between the Flemings became almost unbearable. Ian became tetchy even with me. I had been told that if I went for a morning swim, I was to make a detour around the front of the house because he didn't like anything passing in front of his view out to sea at that time. It was then that he gazed out at the ocean and thought about what he was going to write that day. Well, I forgot and he bawled me out for it.

Later he was in a more sombre mood. He said that the greatest sadness in life was the failure to make the one you loved happy. He told me of his quantum theory of affection: that if not a single particle of comfort existed between two people, then they might as well both be dead.

And Clarissa was shocked when Ann confessed to her that being with Ian was like living with a wounded animal and at times she simply wanted to put him out of his misery.

'Of course,' she added with a cold smile, 'I still love him, you see.'

So it was with great relief that we left the following morning. There were breezy farewells and promises to meet up back in London. Behind the clenched smiles and alert eyes, one felt the murderous intensity between them. It made one almost fearful to leave them on their own together.

We had gone only two or three miles when Clarissa realised that she had left a bracelet behind.

'Can't we get them to send it on?' I reasoned.

'For goodness' sake, Marius, it belonged to the duchess.' She meant her grandmother. 'It's a priceless heirloom.'

I turned the car around and drove back to the entrance to their driveway.

'Please,' pleaded Clarissa, 'will you go? I don't think I can bear going back there. It's on the table in the garden.'

As I approached the house my first thought was to walk around the side but that would mean passing Ian's window and interfering with his precious morning view. So I went up to the front door and knocked. It was off the latch so I let myself in. There was no sign of Violet the housekeeper. As I passed through the living room I heard a fearful row. The sound of violence, of blows, of cries of pain and harsh oaths. It was coming from the Flemings' bedroom.

The door was ajar. I readied myself for the ghastly task of coming between them, of breaking up some pitiful domestic fight. But as I gently pushed at the door I saw the two of them standing naked, Ann armed with a riding crop, Ian with a thin bamboo cane, gleefully taking turns at one another. They were utterly oblivious to my presence in the doorway. The air sang with the swoosh of their thrashing, with loud yelps, exquisite insults and obscenities.

I turned on my heel and swiftly made for the garden to retrieve Clarissa's bauble. Then around and back out to the driveway. I felt a spring in my step as I made my way back to the car. My mind still vivid with the image of them, the look of sheer joy beaming from their faces. The pure, bright energy of it. I remembered what Clarissa had said those few nights before and I found myself laughing out loud. Who knows what true happiness is? It's the greatest mystery of all.

13

the devil

Haven't you noticed how aliens always seem to look like pre-pubescent girls? Their heads too big for their skinny little bodies. You see them naked with no hair, no external genitalia. These are the ones called the Greys. I was ten years old when I became one. For them. They took off all my clothes and put a nylon stocking over my head, covering my hair, making my head bulge a little. My ears were flattened, my nose became two nostrils, my mouth a slit. Then they put dark goggles over my eyes and dusted me all over with talcum powder. Becoming a Grey was just one of the many rituals I performed for the cult that ran Operation Paperclip.

This was just after the war in Manhattan Beach in Los Angeles County. Mother drove me out to a big house there one evening. She had spent years pimping me out as a child actress. I figured that this was just another job.

Larry always thought I was making this stuff up. He never called me a liar to my face. He couldn't. Lying and stealing, that was *his* job. He stole all my life experiences for his stories and novels. Fantasy, that was his racket. He admitted it. He told me once that he had developed this problem with reality. And he said himself that science fiction was a ridiculous conjunction, a contradiction in terms. I mean, how can fiction be scientific or vice versa? No, I know the truth. He took it from me. And he used it to give his stuff credibility.

I know now what happened in that mansion in Manhattan Beach. At the time I was a confused child, made to think of it all as a game. They took pictures of me. Some as a Grey alien, some of me naked. I was made to pose with other kids, with adults. Then there were parties where me and other children were made to work the room. The cult used blackmail as control. Operation Paperclip was a secret mission to recruit Nazi scientists after the war. Their files would be sheep-dipped. That meant they would falsify their employment records, clear them of war crimes, cover up the fact that they had been Nazi Party members.

Most important of all were the rocket scientists and the ones who had been experimenting with anti-gravity technology. That's why they needed pictures of aliens: to spread rumours about the Greys, to hide the fact that the Nazis were in possession of advanced interplanetary knowledge and had now established themselves in America. That was the cult that used me and countless other children. And every new religion needs a new devil to blame the bad things in creation on. Something to frighten people. The Grey alien became a sort of scientific Satan.

And when they had finished posing me and the other children as Greys, they would take pornographic photographs and get us ready for the evening parties. It has taken me a long time to recover the awful memories from that time. For many years I suffered from traumatic amnesia. Now I can recall everything, just as I can recall many of my past lives.

I was abused not merely for pleasure but as a form of control for the people who attended the parties. Influential figures that the cult could use: the rich, the powerful. I remember how I watched them and felt their desires, their ambition. Their fear. They weren't necessarily paedophiles; often our job was to trick them. Drunk or drugged, the guests could be fooled into incriminating positions. I remember Walt Disney and Wernher von Braun. I remember Ronald Reagan and Howard Hughes.

And I remember the devil. I mean, the real devil. He ran the show and sometimes he would appear in person. In disguise. He wore a lounge suit and dark glasses. He had a little goatee beard. He smiled and spoke softly but when he took his sunglasses off you could see the infinite cruelty in his eyes. Red-lined, the whites yellow as brimstone, jet-black irises like scorch marks burning into you, making you do whatever he pleased. He cast a spell with a simple gesture, a sign of abominable power.

The devil's device is a five-pointed star, inverted so that the two points stick up like horns. Like legs in the air. You see, the pentagram is a benign symbol when it is the right way up. It represents humanity. A human figure, star-shaped, with the head on top, two arms, two legs. But when it gets turned upside down, it loses all reason. Its genitalia are exposed and above all the other organs of the body. Then the head is at the lowest point, where the private parts should be, the mind hanging down, all dizzy and shameless. Every man and every woman is a star but when they get turned over they become a fallen star, a fallen angel, a demon. A slave to desire and debasement. This is how the devil exerts his power. The devil knows all about sex, you see.

The devil taught me. Just as my mother and my stepfather did. And all the casting directors that Mother told me to be nice to. Dexter Roth was the first person I met in show business who didn't want to demean me. He cast me in *Fugitive Alien* because he said I had a luminous kind of innocence. He saw that I could have been the right kind of star. By that time I had forgotten all about the cult in Manhattan Beach, but when we started rehearsing all these strange flashbacks came to me. I got to know Larry Zagorski when he was doing the rewrites. He seemed to understand me. Dexter encouraged me to go deep into my character, to imagine what it would actually be like to meet someone from another world. I know now that this was a message because one night after filming I saw my first flying saucer hovering over the Hollywood Hills.

The film itself used actual footage of a UFO. It's become quite well known; people still remember me from it. A 'cult' movie, they call it: now, doesn't that tell you something? Mary-Lou Gunderson who directed it was a bit cold towards me. Maybe she knew that I had been involved with the house at Manhattan Beach and Operation Paperclip. It was those people who killed her ex-lover, the rocket scientist Jack Parsons, by blowing up his laboratory. He knew too many of their secrets and had planned to use his technical skills in Israel. The Nazis certainly didn't want the Jews to have their own missile programme.

But wait a minute, no. This was after we'd finished filming. No, I think Mary-Lou was hostile because she and Larry had had something in the past. Larry always claimed that they'd never slept together but he was certainly still in love with her when we started dating. It didn't bother me to begin with but I didn't realise then what a mess Larry was in.

At first, you see, he'd listen to what I had to say. He'd let me talk without interrupting. And I thought he understood. I read everything that he wrote when we first started seeing each other and it all made sense to me. The problem was that *he* didn't understand his own writing. He didn't understand how he was being used. They had got to him and were using him to send messages. He didn't even know it.

I saw all the good things in Larry then. We fell in love and got married. But it was me that supported us both, before he'd had any real success with his books. I'd imagined that writers could make good money just by getting their stuff into print, but this wasn't the case. Larry worked like a demon: he sold stories to magazines and wrote the occasional script for the *Dimension X* radio programme. But they didn't pay that well. Then he had a couple of short novels published. Larry complained that they paid only a five-hundred-dollar advance with little chance of royalties. He hardly made enough money to keep going without me.

I was struggling to make some sort of career for myself. I was the female lead in a couple of B-movies: *Dead Men's Tales* and *Dangerous Juvenile*; I got a small part in *The Blue Gardenia*. All the time I was preyed upon by directors, producers, studio men. I even tried to get Larry more screenwriting work but he wasn't interested. Oh no, he always had a story to finish or a great novel to start.

I'd come home from work to find him unshaven and barely dressed, hammering away on his typewriter in a sort of trance. He hardly noticed me when he was inspired. I often wondered where all this writing came from. It's all out there somewhere, isn't it? You have to tune in and it all gets typed out. But I learnt this only later when I met the Watchers.

I know that people now think of me as the crazy one in that marriage but both me and Larry had psychological problems. And it was Larry who was taking all those drugs, drinking all the time. Gin or vodka or both, with lime juice and lots of sugar. He'd picked up a reefer habit, too, from Nemo, his Cuban friend he wrote the film with. Then there was all his prescribed medication. Semoxydrine for his anxiety, Nembutal to help him sleep, and any number of other drugs he tried along the way. He became quite the pharmacist, knowing all these pills with names as curious as the alien life in his fiction. It became a running joke that he would be 'on planet Dexedrine' or 'in the fabled city of Pentobarbital'.

Larry tried to blame his mental instabilities on his wartime experiences but I knew that his problems were deeper than that. Neurotic conditions, labyrinthitis, vertigo, agoraphobia. He'd been seeing a psychiatrist before the war. He had all these confused feelings of guilt and anxiety, mostly about his mother who, of course, never approved of me. And I had my own troubled childhood to deal with. An irresponsible mother, who taught me to always act seductively towards men. A stepfather, transformed from a kind and gentle man into a monster after a few drinks. When Larry was in liquor it would sometimes bring back awful memories.

'There ain't no devil, Sharleen,' Stepfather would slur with bleary and lustful eyes. 'It's just God when he's drunk.'

I went to a Dianetics therapist once. They did something called 'auditing' with this funny little machine like a lie detector called an 'e-meter'. They said they could clear me of all the bad stuff in my head from the past. Larry didn't approve. He said it was all baloney. He made me promise not to go again but he also asked me all these questions about it, like he was really curious. It was from the auditing that I first learnt about my past lives and started to have a clear idea of what had really happened in my childhood.

Nineteen-fifty-six was a really big year. I got a small part in the television soap opera *A Family Practice*. I played Nancy, a new character to the series, a secretary in the Henderson law firm. It was hard to know whether Nancy would become a regular or not: there were hints of a romantic storyline between her and Adam Henderson, the son of Buck Henderson, the gruff patriarch of the show. But Buck didn't approve of his son's interest in Nancy, the flirtatious blonde, so it could go either way. There was a chance of some stability in our lives for a while. Back then I was happy to work so that Larry could write at home and not worry about the bills. That was before I found out what was really going on.

Nineteen-fifty-six was a big year all right. It was the year of the flood.

It was in November that me and Larry went along to a meeting of a local flying saucer club. This was unusual: Larry had cut himself off from all sorts of social groups that might have interested him in the past. He had long since stopped attending the Los Angeles Science Fiction Society that met at Clifton's Cafeteria. He said that he didn't want to get stuck in what he called the 'SF ghetto'. But a member of this club had written a charming letter, inviting Larry to talk about his work. I think it gave him some encouragement. Anyway, we were treated like celebrities. Larry pretended that he didn't care for all the attention but you could tell that secretly he loved it. Actually, I think that he was even slightly resentful of the fact that more people knew who I was that night. Some of them had seen me in *Fugitive Alien*; a few recognised me from *A Family Practice*. And after Larry had talked, as many of them wanted to ask me questions as they did him. I saw him frowning when I told everybody that I had seen a flying saucer. So I got him to talk about the strange 'foo fighters' that he had witnessed during the war when he was in the air force.

At the end of the meeting a woman called Martha came up to me and Larry. She said that she was part of a group called the Watchers who met in a community church near by. It was a kind of study group for people who wanted to know more about the visitors from other worlds. Martha said that they had already made contact and there were warning signs of some great disaster ahead. She invited us along. Larry was very polite but I caught this kind of mocking half-smile on his lips.

It was like he always thought that he knew more about these things than anybody else. But he was curious enough to come with me when I went to the next Watchers meeting. It was here that Martha first explained the different beings located in 'the astral'. She said that there were good and bad forces out in space. Knowing that she had the power to make contact with them, she had prayed very diligently that she might not fall into the wrong hands. I understood this at once, especially when she mentioned that Lucifer was actually a star being who, under his guise as the 'bright one', was intent on bringing chaos into the astral as well as here on earth. Lucifer is abroad in the world, leading our scientists to build ever greater weapons of destruction. In the past, Martha explained, there had been a great apocalypse when the two great lost civilisations – Atlantis in the West and its sister continent Mu in the Pacific – were destroyed with ancient atomic weapons.

Martha stated that two kinds of alien have been visiting earth: the 'Space Brothers', who seek to help us, are from Sirius and from the constellation of Pleiades; the bad aliens (who I know now are the Greys) are from the fourth planet of the star system Zeta Reticulum. She told us that she had been in contact with the Space Brothers and that they had some important information for us. When I asked her how she communicated with them, she told me that it was done psychically. This made sense to me as I remember clearly, when I saw the flying saucer over the Hollywood Hills, a distinct feeling of an unintelligible message being transmitted directly to my mind. Martha demonstrated that she could decipher these signals with automatic writing. She went into a sort of trance. Then, with a simple pencil and paper, she wrote down what the Space Brothers wanted to tell us. That night their announcement was: 'We are coming soon to gather up the Chosen Ones. But take heed: those who instruct the people of earth in slaughter will soon meet a dark and awful justice.'

On the way home Larry didn't say much. When I asked him what he thought about the Watchers, he said: 'Well, they're pretty good material for a story.' He was working late that night. He often wrote through the hours of darkness and slept during the day. I had this strange dream that the whole city was in a panic about a great catastrophe that would occur any day now. I woke up and went to get a glass of water. The study door was open and I caught sight of Larry at his desk, pecking away at the typewriter. I crept up and stood in the doorway to watch him. He didn't notice me there and in that moment I felt a grim knowledge creep over me. Larry's face was blank, an empty mask of strange intent. I realised that what Larry did was automatic writing also. He claimed his work as his own but I knew then that he was being used to send messages just as Martha was. And I feared that it might not be the Space Brothers who had made contact with him. Maybe he was possessed by the star being Lucifer, or the Greys, or even the devil himself.

I went to the next meeting of the Watchers on my own. It was there that I met Dr Headley, another leading member of the group. He was a retired physician who had served as a medical missionary in Africa. He had studied theosophy and told us that all the world religions revealed sacred evidence of extraterrestrial life forms that had visited earth in ancient times. He led the meeting in a group meditation, imploring us to 'tune in with each other's frequencies of spirit'. Afterwards he passed around a letter that he had composed, addressed to President Eisenhower, calling upon him to make public the secret information that the air force had accumulated on flying saucers. We all signed it.

Then Martha announced that a special message was coming in from the Space Brothers. We all sat around her as she started writing. It took her over half an hour to finish the communication. She then handed it to Dr Headley and he read it out loud. The news was shocking. Los Angeles and the whole of the Western seaboard were going to be destroyed in a great flood and the lost continent of Mu would emerge from the Pacific once more. The Space Brothers were to send spaceships to save the 'Chosen Ones'. I remembered the dream I had had about the commotion in LA and of a great disaster coming, and it all suddenly made sense. Martha told us that the Space Brothers would give us more information next week. The meeting broke up with everyone feeling shocked and a bit elated.

When I got home Larry asked me about my evening with the Watchers. At first I didn't want to tell him about the prophecy. I was worried that he would think it was all nonsense. I also had this feeling that it was dangerous knowledge. I remembered the panic in my dream. But Larry was gently insistent and in the end I told him everything.

But I was right to be cautious. Soon there were complaints to the community church about the Watchers and it was decided that from then on we would meet at Martha's house. All the group's energy now went into preparing for our evacuation from the city in the flying saucers sent by the Space Brothers. At first there was a message that they would come on Christmas Day, but later Dr Headley amended that to 21 December. This was the date of the winter solstice, when the earth's axis is tilted on its furthest point from the sun, creating the best conditions for spaceships to land. He also added that this was the day on which 'the Essenes left their house and went looking for a new master and teacher. It was on the twenty-first, you know, not the twenty-fifth, that Jesus was born.'

This was only two weeks away! I didn't know what to say to the studio. My shooting schedule had started to get hectic; there were big scenes coming up between Nancy and Adam Henderson. And Larry started to pester me about when we would visit his mother over Christmas. I told him: 'How could any of this matter now?' We had a row but after he had calmed down I told him that he could be one of the chosen ones too. You see, I really wanted to save him.

But he just got more and more angry with me. In the last few days I did everything I could to prepare us both for the coming of the Space Brothers, even though I was very busy recording *A Family Practice*. Dr Headley had told us to remove any metal from our clothing because he said that, while we were travelling in a flying saucer, contact with metal could produce severe burns. When Larry came home one night to find me cutting the zip fasteners out of all of his trousers, he went crazy. I tried to explain to him but this just made him worse. In the end I decided that I would stay at Martha's until the solstice.

We all gathered together on the evening of that day. The final message had been sent through Martha, telling us that the flood would come on the twenty-second, and that we would all be picked up at the hour of midnight on its eve. There was a small crowd outside the house, some of them press reporters as there had been some reports of the Watchers' prophecy in the newspapers and on the local radio stations. The phone kept ringing and Martha or Dr Headley had to answer all these questions from people about the coming flood.

Midnight came and nothing happened. We waited in silence for nearly an hour and then Martha stood up and said that another message was coming through. There had been a delay, it read. We must wait for a sign. As the hours passed some of the group got up and questioned Martha and Dr Headley. There were arguments and a few people left the house. Then, at six-thirty in the morning, Martha announced that something wonderful had happened.

She wrote out a communication from a supreme being called the Creator, of a higher power over the Space Brothers. He told us that the great cataclysm had been averted and earth had been spared by his intervention. The Creator and the Space Brothers thanked the Watchers for holding vigil and keeping faith. More information would follow but in the meantime the Creator and his astral brotherhood were sending a message of peace for all on planet earth. Martha went out to the few reporters that were left outside to give them this as a sort of press release. Everybody else started to get ready to go home. Some people were taking pictures. I didn't want to be recognised so I put on a headscarf and dark glasses. Dr Headley gave me a ride back to my house.

Larry was in a silent rage when I got in. The studio and my agent had been on the phone all morning, wanting to know where I was. It was the day of the big scene between Nancy and Adam. I tried to explain to him the good news, that the whole city had been saved from disaster, but he just stared at me, dumbfounded. When I told him that this miracle proved the power of the Space Brothers and that the Watchers had been right, he lost his temper.

'No, Sharleen, no!' he shouted. 'It proves the opposite, doesn't it? It proves that the prophecy was wrong. And now you've lost your job with the studio and your agent says he never wants to see you again!'

Larry loved to think that he had been proved right about Martha's prophecy. This sense of righteous anger was far more important to him than the possibility that the world had been saved from an apocalypse. But I had lost my job. So I promised Larry that I would find a new agent and not get too involved in anything like the Watchers for a while.

In the New Year we had some good news. A novelette of Larry's that had run as a magazine series was reprinted in an Ace Double, a cheap paperback format where two stories are bound together. And, more encouragingly for him, a publishing house offered him a hardback deal for a novel he had submitted, with an option on a second. *The Translucent Man* got him a thousand-dollar advance and came out in June 1957. We still had to struggle that year but it wasn't nearly as bad Larry made out. He was half in love with the idea of being the starving artist.

And I soon found myself another agent. For glamour photography at first, then later for these odd 8mm films. It would be me and another girl, both in corsets and suspenders. She would tie me up and gag me, then make out that she was spanking me hard with a hairbrush or a riding crop. In another one she was dressed in a nurse's uniform and I was on an examination table. She would put on rubber gloves and do all kinds of physical tests on me. I found that I could act in these scenes really easily, as if I was meant to do it. I secretly felt that the devil was punishing me, laughing at me for being a bad actress. I kept the truth about this work from Larry. I told him that I had been making 'training films'.

I didn't want to disturb him. He was working so hard trying to finish his next novel, *American Gnostic*. He would shut himself away for long writing sessions, fuelled up on amphetamines. He could go three, even four days without sleep. Then he would collapse into bed for forty-eight hours or so, occasionally waking to eat something or scribble notes, then he would be up and at it again. I worried about his health but Larry kept going, writing obsessively, convinced that this thing was to be a major work for him. It was as if there was some evil force driving him on. I suspected even then that there was something bad about this book.

And I felt lonely. I even considered making contact with some of the Watchers again, just on a social basis. But the group had completely split up. Martha had gone to join a Scientology centre in Arizona. Dr Headley had sold his house and was travelling the country, spreading the word of the Space Brothers. He had joined something called the College of Universal Wisdom and had spoken at a flying saucer convention at Giant Rock, California.

There was a kind of panic that October, when the Russians launched Sputnik. Fear that the Reds had beaten us into space. Along with many others, we went out to watch the night sky and try to catch a glimpse of this artificial satellite. Larry seemed pleased that the Soviets had been the first to put a spacecraft in orbit. He told me that it felt good to see the masses shocked out of complacency. And as he gazed up into the heavens I saw something of the Larry I had known when we had first met: a childlike wonder at the universe. He had just finished the novel and was happy and calm for once.

I remember being more affected by the second launch a month later. Sputnik 2 was sent up with a dog inside. Laika was a stray mongrel bitch that had been found wandering the streets of Moscow. She was chosen for the space mission because of her resilience. The American press called her 'Muttnik', but I didn't see the joke. I felt a strange kinship with this poor creature. When I thought of her trapped in that metal capsule, hurtling through the cosmos, I was overwhelmed by despair and emptiness. When Larry asked why I was crying I told him: 'Laika. I'm like her. I'm a bitch in space.'

Larry decided that we should go away that Christmas. I think it was because he felt that the previous December had been so traumatic and he was determined to avoid any memory of it. He also had delivered his novel and had received part of the advance. So we spent two weeks in Honolulu. The time passed like a dream: warm sea and cold cocktails, the palm trees fracturing the sunlight. But I felt a static charge, a fuzzing in the head; the distant surf was like TV interference in the next room. Anxiety in paradise. A growing fear of going home.

I don't know quite what made me so dread the publication of Larry's next novel. Maybe it was because he didn't talk to me about it while he was working on it. Larry would usually show me something of what he was writing or read out sections to me. But not this one. Oh no, this one was a big secret that he wanted to keep from me. And when it came out in the spring of 1958 I could see why.

American Gnostic is as confused and rambling as any other of Larry Zagorski's works but there were whole chunks of it I got straightaway. The mystery of Seth Archer, the rocket scientist with occult knowledge assassinated in a laboratory explosion; Lucas D. Hinkel, science-fiction writer and founder of the now-established state religion, the Cult of Futurology; obvious 'borrowings' from his past. As usual it was hard to understand what Larry really believed in. He portrays John Six, a humanoid visitor from another planet, arriving at the Sunday Mass of a 'flying saucer chapel', using language and information similar to that of the Watcher meetings. It was as if all along he had known that the Space Brothers existed, but he could deal with it only on his own terms. Worst of all for me was the character of Bella Berkeley, a naive and credulous actress in a 'holovision blip-opera' who falls in love with Six. It seemed a malevolent transformation of my personality. Bella is a constant victim of cruel comedy, of morbid sexual fantasy. And I realised with horror that this was what Larry really thought of me.

Of course he insisted that it was fiction, that he had merely used some aspects of my life, that Bella wasn't me at all. Writers think that they can write what they like and just by changing the names they can get away with it. And they actually think that they can control it all. Whatever you might think of Martha and her automatic writing, at least she was honest, admitting that she just wrote what came to her. As I said before, Larry stole. He took all these ideas and experiences and claimed it as his own work. His own fiction. His own great novel.

And we had terrible arguments. He shouted at me that he had to be free to write what he wanted. So I told him what this freedom had cost. I told him what I had done to pay the rent and the bills. I saw the look of disgust on his face.

I couldn't bear to be with him any more after that. I told him I was leaving him but he said that I should stay. He would go and live with his mother until he found a new place. It was pathetic.

So he left. He took a few things, put them in his car and drove away. I was alone.

I started to feel scared. Someone was watching the house.

Someone was listening in.

I took some of Larry's pills that he had left behind. Nembutals. They helped me sleep but when I woke up it took me a long time to work out where I was. What time was it? The sun was going down. I had the vision of an inhuman horizon. A star descending on a distant planet. A dead planet.

I went for a drive downtown. Bright lights. Messages. A movie-house marquee spelling out: *I Married a Monster from Outer Space.* I had to get out of the city. I kept driving. I didn't know where I was. There was a bright light in the sky. Following me. I had that same feeling that I'd had when I saw the saucer over the Hollywood Hills. A message beamed into my brain from the spaceship. Except that it wasn't the Space Brothers. Oh no.

Oh no.

It was the Greys.

They had come for me. I drove faster but the light kept up with me. Hovering. Waiting. I knew then that I had to get out of the car. I swerved off the road and got out. I was in the desert, running, running. Then I fell. I blacked out.

I woke up three days later in Camarillo State Hospital. I was told that I had been found wandering by the side of the highway by a state trooper. I had been examined by a doctor and was diagnosed as suffering from 'involuntary psychosis and paranoid-type schizophrenia'. I had been sedated and brought to Camarillo as a mentally ill person.

It was awful there. I was kept in a locked ward. They fed me with liquid medicine that made me feel like a zombie. They gave me electric shock treatment. They were trying to make me forget what had happened to me. I found out later that one of the doctors there was a memory expert and had been a chief psychiatrist at the Nuremberg trials where he tested these top Nazis who claimed to have clinical amnesia. He was part of MK ULTRA, a secret CIA research project into mind-control techniques. It all came out a couple of years ago, in 1975. A congressional committee revealed that the CIA had experimented on ordinary citizens in state institutions without their knowledge or consent. They used truth drugs and brainwashing techniques on them. I was one of these guinea pigs, I'm sure of it.

But they didn't stop me from remembering what had happened to me before I had been found by the side of the road. You see, there was all this time unaccounted for, twenty-four hours or so. It came back to me slowly, like all these memories do. There was a beam of light. Then I was inside the alien ship. I was naked and on this sort of platform. All around me was a group of Greys. God, I was scared. The chief Grey came forward and spoke to me telepathically. He told me that they were going to do some tests. They put tubes in my mouth and in my ears. They put these suction cups over my breasts. They stuck probes in my vagina and in my anus. Then the chief Grey picked up a long needle and pierced me right through my navel. I screamed with pain, then he put his hand in front of my eyes. The pain went. I blacked out.

I was in Camarillo for three months until Larry came to take me home. I was released on 'extended home convalescence', given some drugs and a prescription to take to a doctor. When he drove me back Larry said: 'I can't go on, Sharleen. It's all too much. I'm the one who should have been committed, not you.' He was a weak and useless man in so many ways, but at least he was honest about it.

We finally divorced in 1960. By then Larry was a big success. The paperback edition of *American Gnostic* was a best-seller. I saw the cover everywhere. A mock-up of that famous painting of the farmer with a pitchfork, standing next to his spinster daughter, their heads replaced with those of aliens. So Larry could afford alimony. It took a while, though, before I got regular payments, so I had to find work to make ends meet.

I was in my late twenties and already getting a bit too old for the glamour game but I decided to use it while I still could. Besides, I knew little else.

I met Cato Johnson when I was working as a go-go dancer in a seedy club on Sunset Strip. He was a guitarist in the house band. Cato acted cool and confident when he was with the other guys but he was shy and nervous really. Sensitive. Beautiful. Such smooth skin that seemed to be pulled tight over his forehead and cheekbones. Bright, sad eyes and a thick pouting mouth that was always slightly open. I'll admit that I was attracted to his blackness, but he was drawn to me in the same way. I'm so white, after all. It was an electrical charge, you know, magnetic. We were like opposite polarities. And it was a natural thing. I think nature wants us to mix, I really do.

But society always wants to keep us apart. And the atmosphere in LA at that time was pretty bad. So much race hatred below the surface. I hardly noticed this before I went with Cato. Things were supposed to be getting better but they weren't. There was just more hypocrisy. That's the problem with Los Angeles: the people there pretend to be sophisticated but they can be just as prejudiced as in the South. Especially the LAPD.

When Watts went up in flames in the riots of 1965, I feared for his life. And though Cato acted like he was some kind of soft-spoken tough guy, I knew that he was scared too. Scared of me. It's a deep-down thing. Going with a white woman can give a black man a little bit of power but a hell of a lot of danger. And besides all that, he thought I was a touch crazy.

Getting pregnant by Cato was a big mistake. But it was the best mistake of my life. I never resented Cato going away, because he left behind such a wonderful gift. Martin Stirling Johnson was born on

13 June 1966. For the first time I had a real purpose to my life. A gorgeous baby boy to bring up. And having Martin to take care of took care of me too; it gave me a centre to my existence.

And I just about managed to make ends meet. The alimony cheques now came in regularly from Larry; he even offered to pay me a little extra. We got back in touch with each other and found that we could actually get on quite well as friends. He was living in this sort of commune in Venice Beach. Larry's books had become a big hit with the hippies and he became one of them. He was well into his forties but the look kind of suited him, an ambling figure in beads and baggy clothes, long hair and a beard. He was with this young woman called Wanda. Half his age, yet he seemed the child of that relationship. Happy though. He wasn't taking speed or downers any more; he was a lot calmer. He still smoked dope, though, and had been experimenting with LSD.

Larry loved Martin and he was very good with him. He confided in me that he was sure he couldn't have kids of his own (something about side-effects from the mumps he'd had as a child). He asked me if I wanted to move into the house in Venice, saying it would be easier than bringing up a child on my own. But I couldn't do that hippie thing. I mean, it works for guys because that style can suit any old slob but it's not a very flattering look for women. It's fine for the young chicks but I didn't want to look like an old witch just yet.

You see, I never got back my figure after Martin was born and I put on a bit of weight. It was a relief, to tell you the truth. People didn't look at me in *that* way any more. It made me feel much more relaxed about myself. So, no more glamour work. I certainly didn't miss it much. When Martin was old enough for school I got a job cleaning houses and apartments. It was simple, easy work that I did part time.

Now I just had to get used to the looks I would get when I was out with my son. The cold stares that fall upon a white woman with a black child. I started to worry about the world he was growing up in. Poor Martin was only eight when we heard that his father had been shot dead by the police in Detroit. They said that Cato was part of a bank hold-up but I wasn't sure about that. I think he was involved in something political. Muthaplane, the funk band he was in, recorded songs with secret messages in their lyrics, signals to a mothership from some distant planet.

I started to get scared again. I didn't want the fear to get the better of me. I felt that if I didn't find the right path, the devil might come for me once more. I had managed to keep one step ahead of him for a few years but now he was catching up with me again. Martin would soon be a teenager and I dreaded him getting into trouble and ending up like his father.

I was on medication for my nerves. I had tried all kinds of therapy to make sense of what had happened to me but nothing seemed to work. I was looking for something to believe in, a simple life, somewhere to settle down, to raise Martin and grow old in peace. I asked the heavens for guidance and I was shown the way.

A friend took me along to a Peoples Temple service at a big old church in Alvarado Street. I was never much one for church but there was so much joy and hope in that place, I was overwhelmed. And Martin loved it. He was singing along with the choir before long, being very musical just like his father. What really impressed me was the mix of peoples. The congregation was mostly black and coloured so they could never feel that they were a minority at the Peoples Temple. But there were plenty of white folks too. This was the sort of integration white liberals had been going on about for years but had never made happen. And Jim Jones, the leader, had this incredible aura, full of righteous energy. A handsome man with Native Indian features: high cheekbones, jet-black hair. All the young members of the Peoples Temple called him Dad. He wore electric-blue robes and sunglasses.

He and his wife Marceline had experiences I could share. They have what they call their 'rainbow family' with Korean and coloured children. They were the first white couple in the state of Indiana to adopt a black child. Marceline told me that she had been spat on in the street when she had carried him as a baby.

266

So after a while we got on a Peoples Temple bus and came to San Francisco. I'm glad to have left LA behind. I really do believe it's where the devil lives. It's certainly a city that promises heaven and gives you hell. Me and Martin are having a much better time up here. We spent a summer in the commune in Redwood Valley. It was pure joy to see my son run free in the countryside.

It's 1977 now and I feel that we're at the start of a new beginning. Martin has been listening to a lot of reggae recently and he tells me that there is a Rastafarian prophecy that great changes will come the year that the two sevens clash.

A spacecraft called Voyager has just been launched. It will visit the planets and eventually leave the solar system and in thousands and thousands of years' time it may reach another star. On it is a long-playing record of pure gold that has music from earth: Beethoven, Mozart, Chuck Berry. It also has recorded voices in different languages sending greetings to whoever might be out there.

I like to think that my voice will float up through space into the heavens. That one day, a million years from now, somebody might hear this story and remember me.

But that is for the future. Right now we have great plans. A new community has been set up in Guyana, the Peoples Temple Agricultural Project. We're calling it Jonestown and it will be a chance to make a utopia, to go back to Eden. Me and Martin are going to live there real soon.

Jim Jones is already there. I remember the last time I saw him preach, talking about the Cause and how we have to free ourselves from bondage. The choir was singing: *Soon, yes, very soon, we are going to the Promised Land.* Jim Jones was burning with a fierce light and calling out: 'We can't wait for it to come out of the sky! We've got to make heaven down here!' He has this maniacal charisma. And I had a strange vision of his impish face transformed. The dark lenses of his shades like empty eye sockets, rounded by high Cherokee cheekbones and the bright white teeth in his wide mouth smiling like the skull. I saw the death's head grinning at me, at the whole congregation. It should have been frightening but it wasn't.

I know now. And I fear no evil. Even if I cannot escape the devil, he cannot escape either. Angels bright or angels dark, all are messengers of God and the great astral purpose. Though the devil may will forever evil, he does forever good. I don't have to fear him any more.

14

art

Although I should feel honoured to find myself described in a recent essay as the first and foremost of the post-utopian Cuban artists, I am duty bound to defer to the greater accomplishments of my contemporaries. Of the many exponents of this beleagued aesthetic that emerged from the Special Period, I could point to the work of Carlos Garaicoa, particularly in his use of architectural models; Kcho's installation *Regatta* that caused so much controversy at the Fifth Havana Biennial; and the video performances of Alejandro López. All these artists (and many more) have engaged with themes and forms attributed to me with more intelligence and wit than I could ever muster.

It is not false modesty that seeks to assert a diminution of my talents or reputation but a desire for clarity. My ambitions have always been, quite deliberately, on a smaller scale. My only real desire in artifice was to make models of things. And though critics have insisted that my sculptures reflect a millennial anxiety, the impulse behind them was a futile attempt to achieve a sense of calm. As a child with his toys, I wished to impose an infantile theology on my surroundings and, in imagining absolute control over a miniature world, avoid engagement in the real one. What has been called art was merely my wish to exert this sense of moderation on my surroundings.

But even before my work gained recognition, my friend Nemo Carvajal insisted that I was part of a tradition; that Havana has always nurtured elements of a temperate culture amid its tropical climate. He also suggested that my calling as a miniaturist had a political context. That our little island was like one of the dots in the yin-yang sign surrounded by the capitalist empire, just as the other dot, West Berlin, was engulfed by the communist bloc. This was one of his favourite analogies back when the Cold War was still coldly raging: of a Taoism that determined that neither system was entirely separate from the other, each containing its opposite in diminished form. These dots are jonbar points, he explained to me. When I asked him what he meant, he told me this was a science-fiction term, that a jonbar point is where history is finely balanced and can go in many directions. Apocalyptic, he said with a wistful smile, remembering the Missile Crisis he had lived through in the early 1960s. I remember nodding with anxiety at this, hoping then and always for a focal point that would reduce rather than escalate.

As a child I had been making models out of wood and Styrofoam for as long as I could remember, my most treasured possession being a Chinese plastic kit of a MiG 19 fighter plane (a present for my ninth birthday), but my epiphany came on a school trip to the Havana Marqueta in Miramar. I remember gazing in calm awe at the 1:1,000 scale replica of our native city spread out over 144 square metres, my known universe reduced to dimensions that allowed me a childish omniscience. I mistook a gasp of delight for my own, and turned only when I heard the word that followed. Incredible. It was softly muttered on the lips of Lydia Flores, a tall and intimidating girl with cropped hair and thick eyebrows, standing transfixed beside me. Had I not been in a partial trance myself, I probably would have kept quiet. Lydia scared me (and most of our class for that matter). But her wide-eyed stare seemed benign and beatific. I imagined, quite wrongly, that we were sharing a moment and I whispered some inane praise of the diorama before us.

No, no, she murmured absently. Not down there. Up here. It was then I realised that she was far above it all. Some of our party marvelled at the baroque wedding cake that was the old city; some followed the broad swoop of the Malecón or picked out the prosaic honeycomb of blocks that marked out our own neighbourhood of Playa. Meanwhile, I tracked down a network of streets to find the effigy of the very building we were in, a tiny box in which, I mused, another even more microscopic simulacrum of the city might reside. But, with outstretched arms, Lydia looked beyond, to the painted horizon behind the panorama.

You're flying? I asked her and her absent smile gave me the courage to carry on asking stupid questions. You want to fly? To be a pilot?

Well, she replied nonchalantly, I'll have to do that first.

First? I retorted.

If I want to become a cosmonaut of course, she declared, turning to me with those magnificently frightening eyebrows. I'm going to be the first Latin-American woman in space.

It had been the year before, in 1980, that Arnaldo Tamayo Méndez, our first cosmonaut, had blasted off from Baikonur Cosmodrome and spent eight days orbiting the earth. Not only the first Cuban in space but the first from any country in the Western Hemisphere other than the United States, and the first cosmonaut of African descent. A street kid orphaned at thirteen, who had worked as a shoeshine before the Triumph of the Revolution had given him an education and trained him as a pilot, Arnaldo Tamayo Méndez was living proof that almost anything was possible under socialism. We have gone from fiction, announced Fidel Castro, our Maximum Leader, in his celebratory address, because space flights were fiction when many of us who are not so old now were still children.

It was a brave kid who openly challenged Lydia's ambition, but, even so, she had learnt to detect doubt on the faces in the school-yard. I decided that it was my mission to have absolute belief in her aspirations, to be ground control to her soaring dreams. And with my encouragement she confided in me. Her plan was to be a straight-A student in science and sport. She would take a degree in physics at the University of Havana, train as a pilot with the Cuban Air Force Academy, then apply to join the Intercosmos Programme at Star City in the Soviet Union. She would have to be a good communist too, of course. My first gesture was to make her a model of the Soyuz 38 that had taken Méndez up beyond the stratosphere. It looked like a huge insect: a spheroid module head with a docking proboscis, cylindrical body and filmy solar panel wings. She took me under her wing, me, the geekiest kid in the class. We constructed balsa-wood gliders and launched home-made rockets. I was entranced by her adventurous obsession with flight and followed doggedly when she suggested that we go investigate the Space-Man.

The Space-Man was one of those legends that gets passed around by kids in any neighbourhood. There were many stories about the eccentric Nemo Carvajal who lived in a run-down Art-Deco house on the corner of Ninth Avenue and Calle 19, the most absurd and intriguing being that he had come from another planet. Lydia and I dared each other to take a closer look at this alien's habitat, a decrepit shell with its strange curves and ziggurats styled in the 1920s version of the future, a relic of ancient modernism that indeed had the air of a fossilised spacecraft. Through a partly taped-up window we spied his study by the dim glow of bare neon strip lights. Posters of American science-fiction films and lithographs of mystical symbols lined the walls. There was a desk cluttered with papers and arcane electrical equipment, a bookshelf crammed with gaudy paperbacks and, hanging from the ceiling, a silver model of a flying saucer.

Where's the Space-Man? whispered Lydia.

Here's the Space-Man, came a soft voice behind us.

We turned and there he was. Tall and thin in a Hawaiian shirt, long grey hair swept back in a ponytail, a gaunt face framed by a goatee beard and green bug-eyed sunglasses. I shrieked the loudest and moved the slowest, and the Space-Man grabbed me by the arm.

What do you want? he demanded, his voice still soft, calm.

With my free arm I pointed at Lydia. She, I began, implicating my companion with a combination of cowardice and ingenuity, she wants to be a cosmonaut.

The Space-Man's laugh was a deep rumble. So, he went on, so you want to find out how it's done? He let go of me and started up the front steps. He turned and gave us a casual cock of the head. Come on then.

Nemo Carvajal was a writer of speculative fiction whose work had mostly been banned since the mid-sixties. He had finally been expelled from the Cuban Fantasy and Science-Fiction Union after he distributed a story titled 'The Hive' in 1971. Featuring ant-like visitors from another planet addicted to sugar for which they trade for an energy source, it was seen as a vulgar satire both on our Soviet allies and on our economic dependence on them. In his defence Nemo Cavajal insisted that earth had been visited by aliens and claimed to have seen evidence of it himself. He told us that he had often spotted UFOs hovering over the Florida Straits.

It could be the launches from Cape Canaveral, Lydia suggested, re-entry flare from discarded rocket stages. Nemo Carvajal smiled and nodded, obviously happy to have a guest so knowledgeable on space exploration. But he urged us to consider the importance of finding out about extraterrestrial activity, and would do so again during the further visits we made to his house. We soon learnt that he had once been a member of the Revolutionary Workers Party, a Trotskyist group that followed the teachings of the charismatic Argentinean, Juan Posadas. Central to the doctrine of Posadas was the necessity of making contact with UFOs. If such things exist, it was argued, they must be piloted by socialists since only the most advanced form of society would be capable of interstellar flight. These beings should be called upon to intervene and assist in building a world revolution, Nemo Carvajal declared. I was captivated by such cosmic imaginings but Lydia grew cautious. The Posadists were a prohibited organisation, denounced by the Maximum Leader at the Tricontinental Congress of 1966 as a pestilential influence. Lydia had joined the Union of Communist Youth and hoped to be accepted by the Young Pioneers Air Cadet Force. She didn't want any association with subversive elements to get in the way of her application. Eventually I went to see Nemo Carvajal on my own.

Counter-revolutionary? he retorted indignantly when I ex-plained the reason for my solitary presence. They tell her that I'm a counter-revolutionary? The Revolutionary Workers Party called for an attack on Guantánamo, to get rid of the Yankees for good! He shrugged and bemoaned how the Stalinists had betrayed the Revolution. I don't think he ever felt betrayed by Lydia, though. He continued to enquire after her, curious about her ambitions for space travel. And she would ask after the Space-Man too, on the now much less regular occasions that I would see her.

So it was Nemo Carvajal who inspired in me the determination to become an artist. Without him I might still have come across this perfect alibi for my unsociable obsession, but he certainly gave it form. Artists and cosmonauts, he insisted, both seek to conquer deep space. He sought to tutor me, finding Spanish translations of the classic science fiction of H.G. Wells and Arthur C. Clarke, and citing the work of Alejo Carpentier and Jorge Luis Borges as proof that fantasy was at the heart of the Latin-American literary tradition. But the imagination is the biggest threat to the state, he told me. The state wants a monopoly on utopia; it cannot accept any competition in creating new worlds. And it demands an earthbound idealism. He quoted Carpentier at me: by creating the marvellous at all costs, the thaumaturgists become bureaucrats.

Thaumaturgists? I asked, not knowing the word.

Magicians, he replied.

You believe in magic? I demanded incredulously.

No more than I believe in realism, he declared with a sigh.

But it was clear that it would be the plastic arts, not literature, that would be the discipline I would follow. I had already shown great interest in the silver model that hung from his ceiling, a trophy of a flying saucer film he had worked on when he had lived in California in the forties and fifties. And when I told him about the moment I had looked at the Havana Marqueta and imagined a model within the model, he nodded sagely and went to his bookshelf. The abyss, he muttered, yes, yes, the abyss. He found a passage in an essay by Borges titled *Partial Magic in the Quixote* that made reference to the mapmaker Josiah Royce, and he read it out to me. I remember the vertiginous sense of recursion, of continuous regression, of echoes as he spoke, quoting a writer quoting another writer, and so on. Let us imagine that a portion of England has been levelled off perfectly, he droned. And on it a cartographer traces a map of England. The job is perfect: there is no detail of the soil of England, no matter how minute, that is not registered on the map; everything has there its correspondence. This map, in such a case, should contain a map of the map, which should contain the map of the map, and so on to infinity.

By the late 1980s there seemed a world of possibilities for Lydia and me. I had started studying sculpture at the Juan Pablo Duarte Elementary College of Art. Lydia was taking her degree in physics at Havana University and had been accepted by the School of Military Aviation at San Julián. The Mir space station became operational, the first consistently inhabited, long-term research base in orbit, offering even wider opportunities for the participation of guest cosmonauts from countries friendly to the Soviet Union. But everything was about to change.

The crisis in Russia and the collapse of the Eastern Bloc at the end of the decade was greeted first with indignation, then with bafflement by most of us in Cuba. Nemo Carvajal was at first enthusiastic, declaring that Stalinism was being overturned and a true revolution was taking place. He got particularly excited when, in an apparently overzealous moment of *glasnost*, the Soviet news agency TASS authorised a report of an alien spacecraft landing in the town of Voronezh in October 1989. However, his great Posadist expectations were never substantiated. Then the Soviet Union cancelled its economic obligations to Cuba, the Maximum Leader announced the Special Period in a Time of Peace, the shortages and power cuts began, and before long Nemo Carvajal became as gloomy as the rest of us.

It was hardest for Lydia; just at the moment that she was due to take her first pilot exams, all flight training was suspended owing to fuel scarcity. But my world of symbols, of shadows and representation, was strangely enriched by our new circumstances. Perhaps there was a desire to find hidden meanings in an age of uncertainty, a desire for some kind of divination. Maybe the sense of artistic freedom was merely a mirage allowed by the authorities in a time of drought. There was certainly a surge of interest in Cuban art from the outside world during this period but we did not know the reason for this curiosity. More than anyone, I was utterly unconscious of what can now be seen as trends or greater influences, but that is what made my work possible.

I had my first major show in the winter of 1991, as part of the Fourth Havana Biennial: a series of sculptures, assemblages made from found objects glued or welded together to form model spacecraft, prototypes of a deranged imagination, effigies of a lost futurism. They were constructed in a bricolage of Soviet memorabilia, revolutionary propaganda, Catholic iconography and Santería fetishes. A tail fin of a 1950s Chevrolet jutted out from one like the sleek wing of a jet fighter. It is entirely possible that the phrase 'post-utopian' was first used to describe this exhibition, a term that later came to describe a whole movement of Cuban art, but I had then no awareness of such a concept. I merely carved out these clumsily graven images from the transcendent hope of Lydia Flores and the mad dreams of Nemo Carvajal.

The exhibitions of the Biennial were taken down just as the great edifice of the USSR was finally being dismantled. For Lydia, bemused by the meagre scale of my vision, a more pertinent symbol was the fate of Sergei Krikalev, the remaining member of the last Soviet mission to Mir, marooned in orbit as the last citizen of the communist motherland. He would re-enter the atmosphere to a newly fractured earth, to a federation of independent states. He was the first interplanetary traveller, insisted Nemo Carvajal; he has voyaged through space from one absurd world to another.

Yet as so many fortunes seemed in decline, mine was in the ascendant. I had my first success. The renowned Catalan art dealer Gonçal Figueras bought my entire show and invited me to exhibit it in Barcelona the following spring. And so it was I, not Lydia, who ended up taking their first flight. I arrived in Barcelona to find the city in a great burst of renewal; so much was being built and renovated for the Olympics they were hosting that summer. Perhaps it is a city under constant construction, the great unfinished Cathedral of the Sacred Family its symbol, with ballistic spires poking up through scaffolding like stone rockets pointing at heaven.

On Nemo Carvajal's instructions I visited the replica of Narcís Monturiol's nineteenth-century submarine on display in Barcelona harbour. He was the first post-utopian, Nemo assured me. Having given up on experiments in communal living, Monturiol had turned to technological dreams and built strange prototypes for underwater travel. The model looked like some artefact of early science fiction. Nemo Carvajal said that Monturiol had inspired a motto that he and an American writer had once used: 'If you can't change the world, build a spaceship.'

I loved walking around the city. I felt sophisticated, cosmopolitan. But for all its triumphs of architecture, nothing in Barcelona inspired me as much as what I found in the concourse of the Estació de França.

Within the vaulted vestibule of that railway terminus, enshrined in a perspex box, a delicately crafted model of the station was on display like a holy relic. This, in itself, would have delighted me, but imagine my strange joy when I spied a model of the model encased within it. Here was a demonstration of infinite recursion as foretold by Borges, himself the consummate miniaturist. Thousands of miles from home, feeling lost and weightless, I suddenly found a sense of gravity and depth that offered refuge. A moment of calm in a turbulent world, the eye of the storm, the dot in the yin-yang sign. I knew now why I found such solace in models: though our experience of time and space is terrifyingly finite, that which we inhabit can yet be divided and subdivided continually into eternity. Whatever strange meanings might be rendered to others, my work could hold this simple purpose. It could be a place I could control.

My show in Barcelona was heralded a success and seen as an important international debut. Gonçal Figueras told me that if I wanted to stay he could sponsor my application for residence in Spain. Some even suggested that I seek political asylum, though as I had no convictions of that sort, this suggestion seemed ridiculous to me. Besides, I was keen to get back to Havana. I missed my family. I missed Lydia and Nemo Carvajal. But my time away ill prepared me for how hard things had become at home.

Living on short rations, everyone had learnt to hustle in some way. Even artists. I was approached by fellow practitioners to lobby the Cultural Property Fund, the centralised body that controlled the international sales of our work. They sold us for dollars and paid us in pesos (now virtually worthless) and some people hoped to get a better cut of the hard currency. The blackouts over Havana rendered the firmament above ripe with starlight and one could even make out the odd blink of a satellite passing overhead, which gave no comfort to Lydia Flores. Even Nemo Carvajal seemed to have given up hope in watching the skies. Perhaps they will never come, he murmured darkly, perhaps we are all alone in the galaxy.

I cultivated an air of indifference to the changing circumstances by withdrawing into my work but I feared for Lydia. Now that she had been betrayed by the optimism of the past, I felt that all her hopes and expectations were turning to bitterness. She had given up her studies and had left or been expelled from the Air Force Academy. I assumed that she would be greatly disappointed when, in April 1993, Ellen Ochoa became the first Hispanic woman in space on the NASA space shuttle Discovery. But my unworldly obliviousness made me inattentive to other changes that were happening in her life.

She had left home and was living with another girl in a run-down apartment overlooking Beach 16 in Miramar. Her hair had grown and a hydra of light-brown ringlets sprouted from her crown. Lydia was no longer the surly tomboy I once knew. Now she was a provocatively attractive young woman who wore expensive American street-wear. Make-up, even. The flat she shared was used for illegal parties and I dreaded that she, like so many others in those desperate times, had turned to prostitution. But when I reluctantly went along one night I found that, though almost all the guests were men, they were really interested only in each other. I saw as well, for the first time, open displays of close affection between Lydia and her flatmate Eva. The revelation that she was homosexual came like a distant memory: I must have suspected it somehow. But I felt a jealousy that was almost metaphysical: unconfined by any person or persons but rather directed at destiny. I hadn't realised until then just how much in love with her I really was.

We are the antisocial elements seeking our own Earthly Paradise, she announced, quoting a comment made by the Maximum Leader. I tried my best to be nonchalant, to assume the air of the bohemian artist. But I was short of breath; the party was crowded and hot. I found myself amid a group of men doing synchronised dance moves, a sign language incomprehensible to me. The atmosphere was intimate and suffocating. I left early and wandered down to the shore to feel the sea crash against the concrete and coral of Beach 16.

Lydia began hanging out with Nemo Carvajal once more. They listened to Sun Ra records together and composed *samizdat* leaflets for an anarchist organisation. Calling itself the Association of Autonomous Astronauts, it declared its intent of establishing a planetary network to end the monopoly of corporations, governments and the military over travel in space. They entered into a playful conspiracy that somewhat excluded me. I have always found it hard to understand humour, though people constantly seem to see elements of it in my work. I couldn't help feeling that the laughter they shared so easily mocked me in some way. And I was so absorbed with my sculpture at this time, creating a number of intricately nested wooden cabinets sometimes referred to (incorrectly) as my Chinese Box series, that I didn't see much of either of them for a while. I concluded that Lydia, like me, was finding consolation in the imagination and that this led her to engage with the insane fantasies of Nemo Carvajal. But any thoughts I might have had that she had lost her spirit for real adventure were to be proved quite wrong.

It was clear by the middle of 1994 that the Special Period had reached crisis point. As our economy collapsed in on itself and the US blockade was tightened, ordinary people in Cuba were driven to desperation. It was the summer of the *balseros*, the rafters who used makeshift vessels in an attempt to cross the perilous straits to Key West or Florida to claim asylum. It was hardly a new phenomenon, but the number of those willing to take the risk to get to America that year swelled to tens of thousands. Even I could not distance myself from a growing sense of panic and confusion in the air. Ferries and tugboats were regularly hijacked from Havana harbour, only to be recaptured or sunk by our National Coast Guard. In August there were riots on the streets; the Maximum Leader himself appeared at a disturbance on the Malecón to try to restore order. It was here that Fidel made his announcement, clearly to force the Americans to change their policy, which restricted official immigration while welcoming illegal refugees. He declared that those who wanted to leave could do so and commanded the Coast Guard to stand down. In these circumstances, he said with a brilliant and ruthless rhetoric, we can no longer continue to guard the borders of the United States.

The fact that rafts were now allowed to be launched openly, and the sure knowledge that this permission would not last forever, generated a clamour of activity. Crowds gathered to cheer on the *balseros* in an absurd carnival. Few could hope to survive a voyage across perilous and shark-infested waters and I was determined not to be witness to this cruel spectacle. Until I learnt that Lydia was one of the participants. I found her on Beach 16, already assembling her craft on one of the concrete walkways. I did all I could to try to persuade her not to go but Lydia was, as always, absolutely determined in her mission. She wavered for only a moment, when I asked her about Eva. She's left me, she said, turning from her task to look at me with a terrible sadness in her eyes. I knew then that her heart had been broken too many times and that there was nothing I could do. She then quickly and very deliberately brightened her mood. Listen, she told me, when Valentina Tereshkova, the first woman cosmonaut, went up in Vostok 6, she travelled thousands of miles into space, orbiting the earth forty-eight times. Key West is only ninety miles away.

She had built a wooden frame with stabilisers made from plastic containers lashed around a huge Russian tractor inner tube and had improvised an outboard motor from a Ukrainian lawnmower engine. Good old Soviet technology, she commented wryly. I thought of what Nemo had said about Narcís Monturiol. Lydia certainly planned her journey carefully. She had rations of water, bread and salted coffee to restore lost sodium. Her vessel carried an extra tyre and a pump, a flashlight and a compass; there was a canopy to shield her from the sun and to collect rainwater. I couldn't bring myself to help her but I found it intolerable simply to stand there and watch. Before I knew what I was doing, I had started to fashion something from odd bits of junk that were strewn everywhere from the preparations of the *balseros*. I think Lydia noticed before I did that I was making a model of her raft. She smiled and shook her head slowly.

When other rafters and their onlookers noticed what I was doing, several of them asked me if I could do the same for them. I obliged, knowing instinctively that these miniatures could somehow be endowed with the power of a fetish, to give a necessary sense of luck to their originals. Where I didn't have time to create objects, I hastily drew sketches or made notes, with the urgency that there might be some spiritual record of this hapless armada. I was astonished by the creative ingenuity of the *balseros* with their constructions of rubber, plywood, plastic and aluminium. Many of the rafts had been given names: *Yemayá, La Esperanza, Tio B, Santa Maria*, and so on. Lydia named hers *Vostok 94* in honour of Valentina Tereshkova, with the bitter irony that acknowledged this would be her own first journey into outer space. Nemesio Carvajal and I watched her launch on the following dawn, her little spacecraft cresting the waves as it headed towards another world.

The Maximum Leader's gamble worked: the Yankees could not cope with an increasing flood of refugees. In a matter of weeks the American president ended the automatic right of entry for Cubans picked up at sea (they were taken instead to the US Navy base in Guantánamo) and an annual quota of twenty thousand visas was agreed for those who wished to apply for legal migration. Since a criterion for applications was unlikely ever to be agreed between the two countries, this was to be done by lottery. The Cuban Coast Guard went back on duty and the sad and euphoric farewell parties on the beaches came to an end. To this day no one knows how many thousands died that summer. And we had no idea whether Lydia had made it or not.

I gave away some of my models of the rafts, but more often than not people wanted me to keep them with the others I had made, as part of a collection. Everyone staggered back to some kind of stability with a sense that there had been a ritual release of discontent, and that maybe we had gone through the worst of the Special Period. But it was a topsy-turvy world compared to the one I had grown up in. People now relied on the black market, hard currency sent by families abroad and the now growing tourist industry. Those who had once held important jobs found that they could make more money doing the most menial tasks in hotels and restaurants where they might get dollar tips.

Nemo Carvajal told me a joke that autumn that I did understand. Two Cuban men are sitting on a porch. I hear your daughter is seeing a waiter, says one. I'm afraid he's only a doctor, the other replies.

Even the Maximum Leader seemed cast adrift, lost in space. Before, we were described as a satellite of the Soviet Union, he declared at a press conference. Today we could be described as a solitary star, like the star of our own flag with its own light, but nobody could say we were a satellite. Now we could be told that we are nostalgic.

And my own situation seemed ridiculous. I was hardly known in my own country, yet I was an artist with an international reputation. My work sold abroad for high prices, converted into a meagre peso allowance by the Cultural Property Fund. But I was happy enough with the moderate living I could make, hoping that my vocation as a sculptor could render some stability to my life. Then I won the lottery.

Nemo Carvajal laughed out loud when I told him the news. It had been he who had persuaded me to put my name forward in the raffle for American visas. The Lottery in Babylon! he exclaimed, naming the Borges story where all state activities, punishments as well as rewards, are dictated by a game of chance. I wasn't sure whether or not to accept this peculiar act of fortune but he urged me to do so. A marvellous fantasy, he said; it proves that all is speculation. Then he caught my eye and in a more sombre tone whispered: you must go, you must find Lydia. And I knew he was right. It would mean saying goodbye to my family, but it also meant that I would be able to support them properly. When Nemo came to say goodbye he had a package with him. It was a manuscript that he wanted me to take to the United States. On the wrapping was the name Larry Zagorski and a Los Angeles address. I asked him about America and the time he had spent there but he did not have much to tell me. It's a failed state, he sighed, like all states. Go. I will stay here. My friends, he murmured, his eyes rolling skyward, they know where to find me.

I arrived in Miami an alien – a frightening identity but a liberating one. It forced me out of introspection. I now had a sense of purpose and I needed to connect. I got in touch with the Transit Center for Cuban Refugees and other exile organisations. None had any record of Lydia Flores. I consoled myself that the documentation of those who had survived or had been lost was as yet incomplete and that, after all, she could be in Guantánamo. Hope and fear are very close companions. My new circumstances filled me with a tremendous energy and with that I went to work.

Using the many contacts I had accumulated in the art world, I found a studio and a gallery space more than willing to present my planned exhibition. I duplicated from memory all the models of the rafts I had made, adding sketches, notes, fragments of testimony. I put it all together quickly; my own urgency and an acceleration of outside interest in what I was doing gave the work momentum. The central piece was a reconstruction of Lydia's *Vostok 94*. But this was not to scale. For once I wanted to recreate the exact dimensions of my subject. Life-size, I found myself muttering, as if in prayer.

The show generated an immense amount of publicity, featuring in current affairs and opinion columns as well as in reviews and articles on cultural criticism. It became a talking point for debates on the function of art and on the discourse in international relations in a new world order. More importantly it became a place of contact and an information exchange for the recent Cuban exiles. But I was quietly determined not to become any kind of spokesperson. I relied on Tommy Bernstein, the affable, red-haired gallerist who so diligently curated my installation, to deal with the media coverage and requests for interviews. His Spanish was as rudimentary as my English but I found him easy to get along with and was relieved to have him as my protector.

I started to float in a kind of euphoric exhaustion. I found it hard to sleep. In the early hours, ghosts of the lost *balseros* would visit me, chanting their names, their stories, their innumerable tragedies. By day all the fresh opportunities that were now open to me as a successful artist, of course, offered no solace or peace of mind. The one personal outcome that I had sought from my exhibition remained elusive.

Then late one evening I received a frantic phone call from Tommy Bernstein. I was to meet him the next day at an address north of Miami Beach. His voice was agitated and I found it hard to follow all that he was saying, but he mentioned Lydia and *Vostok 94*. Just one phrase stuck in my mind and reverberated with the shock of hope. I've found her, he told me.

That night Lydia Flores came to me in a dream. It was just her voice coming through the airwaves, crackling with deep-space static carrying a simple message: I've made it, don't worry, I've made it.

Tommy Bernstein was waiting for me as I arrived at a gas station at Biscayne Point, our designated rendezvous. He smiled at me as I walked across the oil-stained forecourt, and I wondered what strange miracle of survival had brought me here. But when I asked him where Lydia was, his expression slackened and I realised there had been a terrible misunderstanding. I had learnt that English does not usually use gender in the naming of inanimate objects, but I was hopelessly ignorant of some notable exceptions: that ships and seagoing vessels are always given the feminine article. When he had said: I've found her, he didn't mean Lydia but her raft, easily identifiable from the duplicate of it I had made. And there she was, the real *Vostok 94*, lying outside the gas station restroom, having been found washed up on the shore earlier that week.

After months of waiting with no word, the discovery of Lydia's craft was the closest I'd get to confirmation that she had been lost. I knew from conversations I'd had with members of the US Coast Guard that, after any rescue at sea, rafts would be burnt or sunk to avoid them becoming navigation hazards or false targets for other ships or helicopters. And in my delirious grief I felt that the meaning of my dream of Lydia that night was that she had made it in some other way. Into the outer space she had always longed for. I cannot think of her anywhere else but up there, somewhere in orbit above me.

I had to leave Miami and decided to give up my US citizenship. But I could not face going back to Havana. Besides the desperate sadness I felt, I found myself constantly being used in an argument I had no part of. Some claimed me in their attack on the iniquities of the Cuban Revolution, others to blame American imperialism and its economic blockade. I grew tired of insisting that I was a moderate. But I could no longer diminish the world with my art. My work had become a memorial and the number of those it commemorated continued to increase. I felt a growing sense of responsibility that I could not bear. I sought asylum from myself.

So I accepted the long-standing invitation of Gonçal Figueras and went to stay in Barcelona. And this is where I live now. I've managed to find some comfort in my work here, though nowadays it tends towards the abstract, despite the conceptual analysis that critics persist in applying to it. I try not to give in to disillusionment but to find the logical beauty of simple objects. But there are times when I feel completely alienated from the world and can no longer find any refuge in it.

Only last week I found myself in the Estació de França, on my way to Paris by train (I rarely fly now if I can help it). Passing through the ticket hall, I noticed that the model of the station was missing. I'd scarcely thought about the thing over the years. The glimmer of inspiration I had once felt before it had left little mark on my conscious memory, though it must have been deeply ingrained on my instincts. A brief regret for its absence gave way to something like relief: that I would be spared the inevitable disappointment when revisiting a moment of illumination. But then as I made my way to the train, I realised with dread that the maquette had been moved. It now stood near the entrance to the platforms and I could not stop myself looking once more into this miniscule abyss, though I knew that everything would be out of joint. The model of the model within the model was now in the wrong place. It is the carelessness of dislocation that so disturbs me and I am overcome by an incomprehensible weariness. No one knows (no one can know) the endless regression of loss and displacement.

15

death

Then Dad's voice comes over the tannoy, calling us all to a meeting at the Pavilion, and we know that we are in for another long White Night. And back to hard work with rice and gravy tomorrow. Just when we thought that the party for the Congressman and the Concerned Relatives had gone so well. What with all the singing and dancing and everything, and all that good food that we hadn't seen in such a long time. The Congressman even said so. He told us he could see that there are people here who believe this is the best thing that has happened in their whole lives. Then we were betrayed again by the enemies that Dad says are always in our midst. Somebody passed a note to one of the reporters, telling them that a group of them wanted to leave with the Congressman and the Concerned Relatives, to go back to America and capitalism. Some of us said let them go: they are only fifteen, we are over a thousand. But Dad said that they will spread more lies and that will mean even more trouble.

So I find Mom and we make our way to the Pavilion. I hold her hand and sort of guide her. I'm supposed to be raised communally since we've been here but I've been allowed to spend more time with my mom lately. She has been sick from the sun. She is sensitive to the heat and she burns so easily because she is so white. She don't have to work in the fields no more and instead she cleans rice with the seniors in the senior tent. I know tonight we will have a catharsis session and that will be hard for her so I have to make sure that I'll be near by. White Nights can be pretty tough even on the young folks.

It's been hard for Mom down here. Sometimes she says that she wants to go back but I tell her to keep faith. We can't expect paradise overnight. To build a garden in the jungle takes time. A promised land is a promise that works both ways, that's what Dad says. It's not easy to build a world free from injustice, inequality and racism. I try to remind her how proud we can be as socialists, not victims of capitalism where money and greed mean everything. Even if this means making personal sacrifices. But Mom gets sick, not just physically. She has problems with her mental state and I have to watch out for her sometimes, make sure she takes her medication.

I've had a good time here. I've done well in class at the school tent, never once sent out on the Learning Crew like some of the bad kids. I have a good understanding of social consciousness, that's what one of the teachers said. We learn all kinds of things in the school tent. We even had a Russian visitor come and teach us some Russian. *Kak vashi dela?* (How are you?) Then there's volleyball and basketball. There are film shows in the Pavilion some nights, or we listen to broadcasts on the BBC or Radio Moscow. Every so often Dad will let us have a dance night with live music or a disco. I had a party for my twelfth birthday in the summer. *Harosho, a kak ty?* (Fine, and how are you?)

Me and Mom first found the Peoples Temple back when we lived in Los Angeles. I remember the first time I saw Dad in his robes and sunglasses, calling out to the congregation like an old-time-religion preacher. Except he was talking about struggling for justice, for equality and righteousness. He said that Jesus Christ was a revolutionary, that Christianity had never really been tried out properly. And when he spoke about creating a world where there was no racism, it was the first time I ever felt that was a possibility.

You see, growing up, I never felt I fitted in anywhere. At school the white kids called me nigger and the black kids called me an oreo (meaning I was black on the outside, white on the inside, just like an Oreo cookie). But I couldn't help that, I never knew my black father. Just Mom, who is blonde white. The black kids might call me brother, but every time one of them said they hated whitey it was like they were saying that they hated my mom. Life was always like I was looking over my shoulder. When we walked into that big old church on Alvarado Street, that was the first time I really belonged.

There were black kids, white kids, all colours of the rainbow. The choir was interracial, and the whole congregation mixed with each other, not sitting in groups of their own kind. It was like I had come home.

Dad looked interracial himself. Jet-black hair and high cheek-bones. He's got Cherokee blood, they say. He's kind of white but he talks like a black man. Calling out the sermon like a revival meeting.

Soon after that we got on the Peoples Temple bus and left Los Angeles for good. It was a bad place, Mom said, full of evil. We went up to live in San Francisco and then spent a summer at the commune in Redwood Valley. It was beautiful up there. That's where I first learnt what socialism was. We were one big happy family and nobody called my mom crazy any more.

She told me that I had a new dad now. A real dad who could take care of me. My own father had been shot dead by the Detroit Police Department in 1974 during a bank hold-up. I'd never really known him anyhow. His name was Cato Johnson and he was a guitarist with a band called Muthaplane. I have a cassette tape of their album *Afrostronomy*.

When we get to the Pavilion, Dad has already started speaking, standing on the platform with the sign above his head. The one that reads THOSE WHO DO NOT REMEMBER HISTORY ARE CONDEMNED TO REPEAT IT. He talks of a catastrophe. A bad thing that is about to happen. A catastrophe is going to happen to the plane taking the Congressman back to America. And we can't just wait for it. We have to do something. Someone is going to shoot down the pilot and the plane will crash into the jungle. And Dad tells us that we better not have any of our children left when that happens because they will come and butcher them. Dad sighs. We have been so betrayed, we have been so terribly betrayed. He looks tired and sick. If we can't live in peace, he says, let's die in peace. Let's be kind to children and to the seniors and take a potion like they used to in Ancient Greece. Step over quietly. Because we are not committing suicide. It's a revolutionary act.

We've heard this before on White Nights. Revolutionary suicide. Dad gets this barrel of punch and says its poison but it's not. It's just a loyalty test to see that we're ready to die for the Cause. On

White Nights we're on alert, ready for when they come for us. You can't have a revolution without discipline. Sinners have to go to the front for a lecture, maybe a beating. Traitors and class enemies get revolutionary justice. Time in the box, or out with the Learning Crew, cleaning the latrines or digging ditches. If you're really bad you get taken to see the tiger. I'm not even sure what that means but I know it must be bad.

It has been harder down here than in San Francisco. There it was more like a party, a carnival. Every week the Peoples Temple would join in on a demonstration or a political rally. Civil rights and workers' rights, women's rights. Gay rights too. Dad told us that gay people should be equal just like women and black people. That we're all field hands on the plantation called America. We have to build our own garden, our own agricultural project. But it's been hard work making our dream come true.

It's been hardest on Dad. He looks tired nearly all the time now. He has told us before of his illness. High blood pressure, low blood sugar. He suffers with us, for us. And the American government has tried to destroy us. With its infiltrating and wire-tapping and plots to assassinate Dad.

The Red Brigade security have now started to line up around the Pavilion, some with rifles, others with crossbows. Eyes hard, looking to Dad, then out to the crowd. And I start to feel real scared for the first time. Some of the Red Brigade are not here. There is a rumour running round that some of them went to the airstrip, after the Congressman. Dad looks so weary. He asks if there is any dissenting opinion.

Is it too late for Russia? A woman's voice comes on the tannoy as she takes the microphone from Dad. It's Christine, a black senior that we knew from the Los Angeles Temple. She's never been afraid of speaking her mind. Russia, she says.

No, no, Dad replies. It's too late for Russia. These people have killed. I can't control them. I can't separate myself from them. I've lived for all. I'll die for all.

Well, I say let's make an airlift to Russia, says Christine. That's what I say. I don't think nothing is impossible if you believe it.

I suddenly felt something rise up inside me. Yes. Russia. We'll go and live there. *Harosho, a kak ty?*

Dad asks Christine, How are we going to do that? How are you going to airlift to Russia?

And Christine says, Well, I thought you said if we got in an emergency, that they gave you a code to let them know.

I grab Mom's hand tightly. I want to join in the discussion. But I'm too young. So I speak to Mom and tell her we could go to Cuba. It's nearer. We could go by boat if we couldn't get a plane. I learnt in the school tent that in Havana they have the best ice-cream parlour in the world and it's cheap enough for everybody.

Then Dad says that the Russians only gave us a code that they would let us know on that issue, not us create an issue. They said if they saw the country coming down they agreed they'd give us a code. You can check on that and see if it's on the code. We can check with Russia to see if they'll take us immediately. Otherwise we die. I don't know what else to say to these people. But to me death is not a fearful thing. It's living that's treachery.

The crowd breaks out in loud applause and Mom starts talking about an airlift. Except for her it's the Space Brothers from Sirius or Pleiades that will land and take us to another planet. Only if we have the right code. I'm trying to concentrate on the argument up front on the stage while she babbles in my ear about a spaceship coming to save us.

Dad is up there saying that Russia isn't going to want us now. He says that he is standing with the people. That he could never detach himself from our troubles. He is speaking as a prophet today; he has taken all our troubles right on his shoulders. And Christine is saying that where there's life there's hope. That the children have a right to live. That we all have a right to our own destiny.

And the crowd is getting upset by what Christine is saying. As if Dad could be wrong. And I realise that is the most frightening thing for us. And people are shouting Christine down. It's over, sister, it's over! You'll regret it if you don't die! Let's make it a beautiful day! And Dad says, I've been born out of due season, just like we all have, and the best testimony we can make is to leave this goddamn world!

There is more cheering and I hold Mom's hand tight. Christine tries to talk some more and there is more shouting. You just scared to die! What fucking good would you do in Russia! How can you tell the leader what to do! Dad talks once more about revolutionary suicide. That we lay down our lives in protest against what's being done. Death, Death, Death. It's like we've talked of Death so much we've actually summoned him up. And the voice of Death is speaking in tongues. Like when you stand at the edge of a cliff and look down and you hear a voice say, go on, go ahead and jump. Except now it's out loud. Communal. And a senior wails, we're all ready to go, if you tell us we have to give our lives now, we're ready. At least the rest of the brothers and sisters are with me.

There is the sound of a truck coming into the compound.

What comes now, folks? Dad calls. What comes now?

A commotion outside the Pavilion. The rest of the Red Brigade is back from the airstrip. Everybody hold it. Everybody be quiet, please. Sit down, sit down, sit down. Gather in, folks, Dad says softly on the microphone. It's easy, it's easy. One of the Red Brigade is taking to Dad. He nods. It's all over, he says. The Congressman has been murdered. It's all over.

And everybody knows now that this is it. Please get us some medication, says Dad. It's simple. It's simple. Just please get it. Before it's too late. They'll be here, I tell you. Get moving, get moving, get moving.

Time for medication, says Mom. She squeezes my hand and I turn to look at her. She shakes her head. Medication is for sick people, Martin, she tells me.

A table is being set up at the front. A big tub with the punch is being brought out. Mothers and babies go first. They are lining up on the wooden walkway. They have syringes without needles to squirt the poison into the children's mouths. Everyone get behind the table and back this way, okay? Everyone keep calm and try to keep your children calm. They're not crying from pain. It's just a little bitter tasting.

Everyone can see that this is for real now. Not just another White Night loyalty test. Death is coming for us.

Mom whispers in my ear. You've got to get out of here, Martin.

Somebody has the microphone and is talking about how they used to be a therapist, and the kind of therapy they did had to do with reincarnation and past life situations. Whenever people had an experience of past life all the way through death, everybody was so happy when they made that step to the other side.

Mom shakes her head again. No, no, no, she mutters.

The Red Brigade have taken up positions around the Pavilion. I look around to see if there's a way out. How are we gonna escape, Momma? I whisper.

Not we, she says. You, Martin. I'm ready to go.

And I squeeze her hand tighter.

Listen, she says. I see her try to concentrate. It's like she is trying to make sense of things.

More and more people are going up and taking the potion. There is crying and screaming but also people testifying. This is nothing to cry about. This is something we could all rejoice about. They always told us that we can cry when we're coming into this world. So when we're leaving, we're going to leave it peaceful.

I'm sorry, Martin, Mom is saying. I've always had trouble in my head. I know that hasn't been easy for you.

Mom, I say. Please.

But I know now, she tells me. You see, I know what madness is. I always have done.

Die with a degree of dignity, lay down your life with dignity, Dad is calling out. There's nothing to death. It's just stepping over into another plane. Stop these hysterics. This is not the way for people who are socialists or communists to die. We must die with some dignity.

You see, says Mom. Dad is God.

She points up at him.

God is Dad.

Yes.

She nods.

But, Martin, you see, Dad is mad.

God is mad.

Death, death, Dad is saying, death is common to people. Let's be dignified. If you adults would stop some of this nonsense. I call on you to quit exciting your children when all they're doing is going to a quiet rest. Hurry, hurry, hurry, my children. Hurry. There are seniors out here that I'm concerned about. Quickly, quickly, quickly, quickly. No more pain now.

Come on, Martin, Mom tells me. I'm ready. You pretend.

What? I ask her.

You got to play dead. You can do that, can't you? Play dead.

And Dad is calling for another vat to be brought out. The vat with a green C marked on it. Bring it here so the adults can begin.

We're in the queue and they're moving us quickly now. Mom finds it hard to keep up so I put my arm around her waist and let her rest an arm on my shoulder. Take care of her, someone says. Yes. That's a good boy. They are giving paper cups to the adults now. Someone hands one to me. I've only got one arm free so I take one cup and Mom reaches out to it.

Help me, Martin, she says. It's at that moment that I realise that if I help to kill my mom, I might just get out of this alive. And that makes me feel bad. Like I'm a traitor. But I want to live. We're walking away from the vat and I'm holding up Mom as she takes a drink of the potion. She coughs and drops the cup on the floor. She's going to die. Part of me wants to get another cup for myself and go with her. Everyone is going together. Most people die on their own but now they are all going together. Mom is choking and shuddering but all the time leading me away from where people are taking the poison. And nobody has noticed that I haven't taken mine. Mom starts to stumble and I stumble with her. All around us people are dropping to the ground, holding on to each other. Choking and coughing, crying and wailing. Calling out for the last time. Calling out to each other. Calling out to a God that has gone mad. I help Mom down gently and lie next to her. The sun is sinking. The sky is red like blood. Mom tries to say something to me but a froth comes out of her mouth. I hold on to her as she shakes and shakes. Then I feel the life go from her. And I'm on my own now. All around me people are dying and I'm lying among them, pretending to be dead, like Mom told me to. I'm on my own now.

It's getting dark and there is some shouting up at the Pavilion. Gunshots. One. One, two, three. Somebody calling out. One more shot then silence. Just the sounds of night. The chirp of insects and the sad calling of the birds. I raise my head to look around. I can't see anybody left standing. No Red Brigade standing guard no more. I look down and see Mom dead next to me. I look across all the bodies lying all over the ground as far as I can see through the gloom. I feel like I'm the last person left alive on the whole earth. I get up and start to run. Run towards the bush.

In the bush it's dark. Pitch black. It's hard to make my way through the tangle of branches but I just want to find a place to hide. I find a place where I can curl up. I just want to sleep. For my mind to go black like the jungle. I feel so sad and alone and my mind is racing, racing. I close my eyes and try to think of sleep. All I can think of is Death.

Then I hear something rustling in the bush. At first I think that it's somebody come after me. I curl myself up even tighter. Try not to move, not even breathe. Then I realise that it's not a person. It's an animal of some sort. It comes closer and I feel the presence of it, like it can feel me too. I don't know what it is. I think maybe I've taken myself to see the tiger and I'll finally know what that means. I think that now I'll die in the bush anyway. All on my own. The animal is sniffing, like it's sniffing me. Then I think this is Death itself come to get me. And I shout out and the thing rushes off. And I start to sob all alone in the jungle, crying for Mom and everybody else.

And that's when I get to sleep.

I wake up and see the sun burning green and yellow through the bush. I make my way back, not really believing what has happened the night before. Somehow thinking that it was just another White

Night and everybody will be back to life in the morning. Then I see all the bodies in the daylight. And I know that it's true even though I still don't believe it. Mom was right. God must have gone mad for this to happen. Everybody is gone. Passed. There's an awful stink in the air and the low buzz of flies. Like Death is a crazy child humming to himself.

Then I see a lone woman walking with a cane. A black senior limping and trying to make her way through all of the dead bodies. I hid under the bed, she tells me. I never, I never thought, she starts to say then stops. Looking all around then back to me. Mercy. Are we all there is?

16

the tower

The metaphysicians of Tlön do not seek for the truth or even for verisimilitude, but rather for the astounding. They judge that metaphysics is a branch of the literature of fantasy.

Jorge Luis Borges, *Tlön, Uqbar, Orbis Tertius*

Larry Zagorski is a prolific author who has enjoyed intermittent commercial success and some critical acclaim (mostly in Europe and Japan) but owing to his chosen field remains largely unrecognised by the American literary establishment. 'I always looked for the obscure, for something hidden from view,' he said in 1989. 'It's little wonder that I was claimed by what I sought.'[1]

Born in Los Angeles in 1922 to estranged parents of Polish descent (Zagorski is a topographic name meaning 'one who lives on the other side of the hill'), he found refuge in fantasy and speculative writing from early childhood. When at the age of seven he was isolated and bedridden for three weeks with a severe case of mumps, his constant companion was a copy of Joseph Jacobs' *English Fairy Tales* with full plate illustrations. Later influences were the Martian novels of Edgar Rice Burroughs and the pulp magazines *Weird Tales* and *Wonder Stories*.

By his own account he was a sickly child who lived mostly in his own imagination. The young Zagorski's search for the unknown was also a quest for an absent father. Zagorski senior left the family home when Larry was barely three years old with a chaotic trail of rumour and hearsay in his wake. 'I was told variously by my mother that he was a private detective, a gold prospector, a circus horseman, and God knows what else. I eventually learnt that he was none of these things, merely a cheap conman, but as a child to me he was some kind of totem, a mysterious monolith. I looked for him in comic books and adventure stories.'[2]

His first published story, 'The Tower' (printed in *Amazing Stories* in 1939 when he was seventeen), is a reworking of 'Childe Rowland' from the Jacobs stories of his childhood. A fatherless group of children find themselves trapped in a dark tower, the enchanted domain of the elfish ones. The interior is described (as in the original) as a wondrous fretwork of precious stones, magical lamps and illuminated crystals. It becomes clear (in Zagorski's version) that this is the control panel of a spacecraft and the elfish inhabitants are visiting aliens, physically weak but able to bewitch with drugs and hypnotism. The children overcome the elfish extraterrestrials and escape as the tower blasts off into the firmament.

'Childe Larry to a dark tower came,' Zagorski writes in a later author's note on this story, linking it to his fruitless attempts at understanding his relationship with a lost parent. It was a process that transformed Larry's attitude so that from then on, rather than identifying his missing father as the hero of pulp stories, he instead becomes the strange creature, the alien. This liberated his creative sense, launching it into outer space. He joined the Los Angeles Science Fiction Society and began to sell stories regularly to *Amazing Stories* and *Fabulous Tales*, replete with ray guns and bug-eyed monsters. But science fiction was itself undergoing a transformation, and was about to enter what some were to call its 'Golden Age'.

Generally agreed to have commenced when MIT physics major John W. Campbell Jr assumed editorship of *Astounding* magazine in the late 1930s, the Golden Age[3] brought about what came to be known as the 'hard science' school of speculative fiction. While recognising the need for some background logic in SF, Zagorski was never entirely at ease with the tendency towards pseudo-rationality and technology fetishism, or a new orthodoxy with strict rules for robots and regulations on how to solve faster-than-light travel. To focus on scientific feasibility rather than the potential of the imagination went against his instincts as a writer. As Jorge Luis Borges observes, the fiction of Jules Verne speculates only on future probability (the submarine, the trip to the moon, the talking picture), while the work of H.G. Wells surpasses it by conceiving 'mere possibility, if not impossibility (the invisible man, a crystal egg that reflects the events on Mars, a man who returns from the future with a flower from the future, a man who returns from the other life with his heart on the right side, because he has been completely inverted, as in a mirror)'.[4]

Zagorski, however, was intrigued by the opportunities that quantum mechanics offered SF at this time. The first of two great inspirations for him in this period was Jack Williamson's *The Legion of Time*, serialised in *Astounding* in 1938. Though heavily freighted with all the clichés of the pulp era, *The Legion of Time* breaks new ground in SF in its treatment of the Uncertainty Principle, alternate futures and parallel worlds. Other authors have cited its importance (Brian Aldiss declared that 'its influence of later time stories has been strong'[5]) and it created a new term in the SF world, the 'jonbar point' – a point of divergence where history can go either way, in this case towards utopia or dystopia.

The possibility of a dystopic future was, of course, a very real danger at this time and Zagorski's second big influence in the late 1930s was the novel *Swastika Night*, first published in 1937 under the pseudonym Murray Constantine. Reclaimed as a lost feminist classic in 1985 when it was revealed that it had been written by Katharine Burdekin, *Swastika Night* is probably the first and certainly the most frightening of the many novels based on the premise of a Nazi victory. Zagorski acknowledges that it inspired him to write his first successful full-length work, *Lords of the Black Sun* (serialised in *Fabulous Tales* in 1940, first reprinted as a novel in 1948). 'It might seem a fairly crass attempt at this now familiar conceit,' he wrote in the introduction to the 1978 reissue, 'but bear in mind that at the time of writing this was neither an alternate history nor a counter-factual exercise; this was the possible future.'

It was probably the recognition he received for *Lords of the Black Sun* that gained him entry to Robert Heinlein's celebrated

SF salon in Los Angeles – the Mañana Literary Society. In Anthony Boucher's *roman-à-clef Rocket to the Morgue* (1943), based on the Mañana group, Zagorski is clearly identifiable as Matt Duncan, the 'up-and-coming young science-fictioneer', alongside fictional versions of Heinlein, L. Ron Hubbard, Williamson and the rocket scientist Jack Parsons. There was much interest in alternate realities among this circle, as well as in the exploration of propagations of influence and even complex quantum notions like backward causation. In Boucher's novel, Austin Carter, Heinlein's alter ego, writes a story that proposes a world where far-left democrat Upton Sinclair wins in California while Roosevelt loses in 1936, causing a schism in the nation, civil war and the eventual 'establishment on the West Coast of the first English-speaking socialist republic'. It was to be called 'EPIC' (with a nod to the End Poverty in California campaign that Heinlein had been part of).

'Heinlein was something of a radical back then,' Zagorski was to recollect in the 1960s. 'I don't know what happened to him later.' It was at Heinlein's salon that he first met friend and erstwhile collaborator, the Cuban SF writer Nemo Carvajal. 'Interesting times for American science fiction,' notes Carvajal. 'The future was bound up in ideology, so even the space-opera writers could scarcely avoid a political critique in their work.'[6] Indeed, the genre itself was ideal for geopolitical speculation and there emerged a collective and progressive approach to a world-view made possible by projections in time and space.

Larry was in love with Mary-Lou Gunderson, a fellow writer (later director, producer and television executive), but it remained unrequited. The year 1941 saw the emergence of jonbar points, in Zagorski's life as well as that of the planet. 'He was a shy and sensitive kid,' remarked Gunderson, 'the last person you would imagine going to war.'[7] Yet the day after Pearl Harbor, that great point of divergence in American history, he signed up with the USAAF for combat duty.

Zagorski served as a radio operator in a B-24, flying bombing missions over Germany and occupied Europe. It was a harrowing experience as the conditions under which the air war was fought were extremely harsh. The long-range sorties were exhausting, some lasting over eight hours and in sub-zero temperatures with the crews wearing electrically heated suits and oxygen masks. Larry was to describe the experience as a 'lethal parody of all my childhood dreams of flight and space travel'. Any simple technical malfunction could prove fatal and frozen oxygen lines could cause death from hypoxia. Then there were the swarms of enemy fighters and the flak from 88mm anti-aircraft batteries or the 108mm radar-controlled guns. The chances of surviving the thirty-mission requirement were very slim indeed.

'Along the azimuth arc, from zenith to horizon flew death, and down below we saw planetary destruction, cities turned to moonscape, and we smiled.' So begins 'Fee, Fi, Foo, Fum', one of the few stories he wrote that directly recall his experience of the war. The crew of a B-24 witness strange craft in the stratosphere:

> 'Foo! Foo!' went the call on the intercom. That nonsense word from some alien dialect. But the radioman knew what it meant. He had tuned himself in to them, ignoring all the arguments about whether such things were hallucinations, Nazi prototypes, or from another world. He knew what *foo* meant: it meant the future. Something had broken through the space–time continuum; that's what they were seeing. A vision of what was to come, of the even greater terrors that awaited them in the heavens.

Returning home, Larry took his share of a collective post-war trauma. For a year or so he lived with his mother, supporting them both on his GI Bill allowance. And for some time he turned away from SF. All its predictive powers seemed used up, its dread fantasies of power made real. The future seemed a bleak choice between unremitting banality and inconceivable terror.

Between 1946 and 1947 he attempted a mainstream novel. *The Attendant* is set in an unspecified institution where the protagonist Tommy Buhl works, having been invalided out of the military following a nervous breakdown. He tries to make sense of what has happened to him as he plods through a dreary daily schedule. In a series of recollections, he is constantly in search of the point in his life where it all went wrong. *The Attendant* meanders aimlessly in its surviving 436-page draft, though it features several strong supporting characters, most notably the Mexican fortune-teller Angel Fernandez and the army air force chaplain Ignatius Creed. Zagorski failed to find a publisher for it.

It was during a trip to Mexico in 1948 that Nemo Carvajal and Larry came up with the story that was to become the script idea for the film *Fugitive Alien*. Directed by Mary-Lou Gunderson, starring Trey Anderson and Sharleen Stirling, *Fugitive Alien* (1950) is one of the many B-movies that cashed in on the flying saucer craze. It was cheaply made and rich in the Cold War atmospherics of paranoia and suspicion. Unlikely stories about its production persist to this day, most notably the rumour that there are references in the dialogue to an actual secret air force memorandum on UFOs.[8]

What is certain is that Nemo and Larry argued quite vehemently over proposed script changes during the shooting. Larry fell in love with the leading lady. He married Sharleen Stirling on 4 October 1951. Nemo Carvajal went back to Cuba that same year.

The 1950s were an extremely productive time for Larry, though not all of his work saw the light of day. In a decade he wrote nineteen novels (five of which were published), fifty-seven stories (twenty-eight of which he managed to sell), and eleven scripts for the *Dimension X* radio programme (two of which were made).

Larry found something of a champion for his work in Anthony Boucher, whom he had known from the Mañana days and who had begun editing *The Magazine of Fantasy & Science Fiction (F&SF)* in 1949. Urbane and generous of spirit, Boucher was to nurture many of the more left-field SF writers, most notably the young Philip K. Dick. Boucher favoured intelligent fantasy over the 'hard-science' school and was keen to promote a more literary style within the genre. He had, after all, produced the first English translation of

Borges and sold it to what was more or less a pulp magazine (his rendering of 'The Garden of Forking Paths' appeared in *Ellery Queen's Mystery Magazine* in 1948).

F&SF was an ideal home for Larry's work at this time. His stories had become increasingly fractured and recursive. Zagorski insisted to Boucher that he was no longer interested in prophecy, but rather 'prodrome, that is, the early symptoms of an oncoming disease, an aura of disquiet'. He never liked to distinguish between what was 'fantasy' and what was 'science fiction'. He confided to *F&SF*'s editor that the stories he placed with them were 'inner projections of character, memoirs of the imagination'. In 'Dummy' (1954), a prisoner convicted of an unnamed crime and convinced of his innocence digs a tunnel via the ventilation grille in his cell. He makes a dummy to leave as a decoy for when he escapes. The construction of the mannequin starts to obsess him, particularly the sculpting of the face, which takes on a 'lurid grimace that seemed to mock his protestations of guiltlessness'. One morning the guards search his cell. The tunnel is revealed but the dummy is missing. It has escaped, and in the months that follow the prisoner begins to hear of ghastly misdeeds committed by his puppet doppelgänger.

The other main market for Larry's work in the 1950s was Ace Books, where they were a good deal less sensitive with his material. One of the editors there, Donald A. Woolheim, a science fiction fan and veteran of the pulp years, would publish SF in 'Ace Doubles', a cheap format that bound two novels together, head to toe, with lurid covers on both sides. Titles were regularly changed to match the glib and sensationalist cover art, so that Zagorski's *Parker Klebb's Purgatorio* became *A King of Infinite Space* (1955) and his *With Splendour of His Precious Eye* was transformed into *The Prophet from Proxima 6* (1956). One of Woolheim's fellow editors at Ace, Terry Carr, is reported to have remarked: 'If the Holy Bible was printed as an Ace Double, it would be cut down to two twenty-thousand-word halves with the Old Testament retitled as "Master of Chaos" and the New Testament as "The Thing with Three Souls".' By the end of the decade, professionally at least, things were looking up. In 1957, Larry secured a two-book deal with the prestigious hardcover publisher Doubleday, the second of which was to prove his breakthrough novel. But in the meantime his private life was falling apart.

All through the 1950s his prolific output was fuelled by a considerable intake of amphetamines. This was augmented by a heavy barbiturate habit that Larry relied on to bring him down from all the uppers he was taking, and a steady recreational use of marijuana and alcohol. Consistently existing in an altered mental state often inspired astonishing bursts of creativity, but it proved profoundly destructive in his emotional relationships.

He had married Sharleen Stirling in haste, after a brief but intense infatuation. 'She had an unearthly, ethereal beauty,' he recalled. 'If I'm honest she reminded me of those beautiful alien girls I'd gawped at as a teenager on the cover of *Wonder* or *Planet Stories*. I loved her but I was still emotionally immature and weighed down with psychological problems I hadn't dealt with.' Sharleen herself had long-term mental health issues and her once promising acting career was falling apart. 'She believed what I wrote was real and I fed off her psychosis as inspiration for my characters. It was parasitical.'

The Translucent Man (1957), the first of his books for Doubleday, was indifferently received but *American Gnostic* (1958) achieved considerable critical acclaim and went on to become a paperback best-seller. This success, however, coincided with Sharleen's mental breakdown and their subsequent divorce in 1960.

A harsh satire on the nation's perverse relationship with both materialism and spirituality combined with a dystopian vision of the near-future, *American Gnostic* is an exemplar of what Kingsley Amis described, in his 1962 critique of SF, *New Maps of Hell*, as a 'comic inferno'. Set in a twenty-first century where religion and culture are based on a 'pulp mythology' (fictional entities like Doc Savage and Batman are accepted as historical figures, while real people such as John Wayne and Greta Garbo have been transformed into deities), the established church is the Cult of Futurology founded by SF writer Lucas D. Hinkel. The economy is centred on sacramental consumerism and an overambitious space programme that is not only draining industrial and natural resources but is in stasis due to technological shortcomings (spacecraft landings on other planets are faked in 'holovision' studios). There is a growing faith in the coming of a being from outer space to save a polluted and overpopulated world, and fraudulent appearances are reported every week. John Six, a real extraterrestrial, finally does appear and, after a brief spell as the 'Space Messiah', elects to become the host of the holovision game-show *All-American Alien*.

The success of the novel crossed over into mass consciousness, particularly among younger readers, and it became a cult book of the 1960s. Overnight Larry Zagorski was hip, and *American Gnostic*, like *Stranger in a Strange Land* and *Naked Lunch*, became one of the iconic SF titles talked about in coffee bars and passed around college campuses.

Three novels with Doubleday followed: *Stupor Mundi* (1960), *Psychopomp* (1961) and *Laugh at This Hereafter* (1962). Zagorski was adopted by the nascent hippie movement and he rapidly adopted their style. Despite having just turned forty, he moved into a shared house in Venice Beach and began what was to be an eight-year stint of communal living. He weaned himself off the uppers and downers; he began experimenting with mescaline, LSD, counter-cultural pursuits and radical politics.

Soon after the terrifying jonbar moment of the Cuban Missile Crisis in October 1962, he attempted to set up the Non-Aligned Science Fiction Writers Association with his old friend Nemo Carvajal. The Polish writer Stanislaw Lem rejected an invitation to join because of his extremely low opinion of American SF. The proposed NASFWA did not last very long in any case. Zagorski quickly fell out with Carvajal who, in accordance with the principles of the Posadist Fourth International of which he was a member, believed that nuclear war could be a good thing in that it might 'finish off capitalism for good'. Larry was horrified by

Nemo's insistence that the NASFWA should issue a statement, declaring that 'Atomic War is inevitable, humanity will quickly pass through this necessary stage into a new society – socialism.' He swiftly disbanded the association and responded with the story 'Sycorax Island', which appeared in *Galaxy* magazine in 1963.

Set in a parallel world where the Missile Crisis has escalated into all-out nuclear war, a disparate bunch of survivors find themselves stranded on an idyllic island in the Caribbean. American embassy staff and their families, a detachment of Cuban women's militia and a group of Russian technical advisors overcome their initial hostilities and attempt to build a new world together. They find traces of a long-dead culture on the island: the circular ruins of some kind of temple that becomes the focus of the emerging community. At the end, just after one of the militia women has given birth to a mutant baby of uncertain paternity, a unit of US Marines arrives and promptly kills all the Cubans and Soviets. 'Hey!' their captain calls out to reassure his now hysterical fellow Americans. 'It's all right! You're safe! Didn't you hear the news? We won! Yeah, we really clobbered the bastards!'

In September 1964, Larry attended the Twenty-Second World Science Fiction Convention in Oakland and met Philip K. Dick for the first time. They indulged in a long and drug-addled conversation concerning Dick's most recent book *Man in a High Castle*, a counter-factual novel where the Nazis and the Japanese have won the Second World War. Zagorski had assumed that this had been influenced (as his own first novel had been) by *Swastika Night*. Dick assured him that he had in fact been guided by the ancient Chinese book of divination, the *I Ching*.

It seems clear that this is what inspired Larry to start work on what was to become *The Quantum Arcana of Arnold Jakubowski* (1966), a cycle of twenty-two interconnecting stories structured around the trump cards in the Tarot deck. Zagorski spent longer on this novel than any other and he was never happy with it.

It started with such promise, I mean it just seemed to write itself until I got up to the sixteenth card, and then – wham! It was the Tower! I was back at my first story, back trying to find my lost father. I felt that I was being led into a hall of mirrors, stuck in some awful time warp. I'd been doing primal therapy, rebirthing, stuff like that, and, of course, ingesting huge quantities of LSD. I used Crowley's Thoth pack, which is pretty psychedelic anyway – and there it was: the ego, the phallus, that vision of authority I could never overcome, plus I'd just learnt that I was infertile so I felt emasculated and cut off from fatherhood at both ends of the continuum. I found myself wandering up and down Venice Boardwalk, muttering, 'The tower must fall, the tower must fall.' I had an overpowering sense of doom – after all, the Tower represents ruin and catastrophe. I got through it but after that it was a hard book to finish.[9]

Now the Tower had perhaps become a symbol of an existential despair in the midst of apparent success. As Blaise Pascal had written: 'We burn with a desire to find a secure abode, an ultimate firm base on which to build a tower which might rise to infinity; but our very foundation crumbles completely, and the earth opens before us unto the very abyss.'

The critical reception of *The Quantum Arcana of Arnold Jakubowski* was mixed. *Village Voice* declared it a 'meta-fictional masterpiece'; *The New York Times* called it 'a confused and self-indulgent mess'. It was joint winner of the Hugo Award for best novel awarded at the SF Worldcon in Cleveland, Ohio in 1966.

Much of Zagorski's work was now being hailed as part of the 'New Wave' of SF writing. Larry certainly liked to be seen as radical and he pushed the idea of an 'alchemical reaction between pop culture and the avant-garde'. His stories found their way into Michael Moorcock's militantly *nouvelle vague* journal *New Worlds* and he was asked to contribute to Harlan Ellison's seminal anthology *Dangerous Visions* (1967). But already one can detect an uneasiness concerning the permissive age in Zagorski's writing. His *Dangerous Visions* story, 'The Crazy Years, Mass Psychosis in the

Sixth Decade' (named after Robert Heinlein's uncanny prediction for the 1960s in his 1941 'Time-Line of Future History'), depicts an increasingly barbaric youth cult called the Subheads, whose idea of liberation is to progressively burn out their brains with highly potent hallucinogens. It was also a desperate reflection of his fears concerning his own drug addiction.

In 1968, Larry married Wanda Ferris, a sculptor aged twenty-eight who had been a long-time resident of the commune in Venice. They moved into a beach house in Malibu together. Wanda recalls:

> We'd had this freewheeling kind of affair for years. Larry was great company, so full of ideas, funny and charming. To be honest I was happy with an open relationship. But he was never any good with the free-love ethic. Oh, he wanted to be but he just couldn't do it. Basically he craved emotional security. He kept on at me about living as a couple, just the two of us. He made it sound like a wonderful dream and I knew that the idea of it would make him happy so in the end I agreed. But it was a big mistake.[10]

As the sixties drew to a close Larry became more and more paranoid. He was convinced that he was being watched by the FBI and the Church of Scientology. He had a high-security fence rigged up around the beach house and began to amass a small arsenal of firearms. Wanda remembers asking him: ' "What's all this really about, Larry?" and he replied: "Guilt". "Guilt, what about?" "I don't know, everything".' In 1969, during the Tate/LaBianca murder investigation, it was revealed that the Manson Family used names and rituals from *Stranger in a Strange Land* as part of their cult, and a heavily annotated copy of *American Gnostic* was also found in their Spahn Ranch headquarters.

The Peregrinations of Percival Pluto (1970) was completed during a sustained LSD binge that was excessive even by Zagorski's standards of the time. Despite the gruelling complexities of his last novel, Larry was determined to continue to stretch the boundaries of the SF form by attempting what he explained as 'a science fiction version of Wolfram von Eschenbach's *Parzival*'.

> I'd thought long and hard about the term 'space-opera' and how it's a pejorative term, but I thought what if you wrote something truly operatic? So *Peregrinations* became this Wagnerian project. It was insane! It was this interplanetary quest and I really did want to explore spirituality and symbolism on some deep level but it ended up in a whole series of psychological dead ends. And yes, Childe Larry to a dark tower came once more. This time it was the Grail Castle with its castrated king. I didn't have any answers. I'd forgotten what the question was.[11]

Despite being scarcely readable, the novel sold steadily throughout the 1970s. It was thought to contain many hidden messages and references to self-awareness and spiritual growth. 'It was a mess,' was Larry's later verdict on it, 'but its success had a woeful effect upon me. For a while I was convinced that I had this visionary gift so the writing really suffered.'

From Here to Alternity (1972) features a time-travel organisation called the Office of Counter-factual Affairs, which intervenes at volatile moments in history such as the Battle of Hastings or the Third Crusade of 1198. The novel's protagonist, Baxter Brahma, jumps from one unstable jonbar point to another, occasionally falling into an alternate universe that he has to escape from. Brahma holds the key to *scientia media*, or middle knowledge, a concept devised by the sixteenth-century Jesuit, Luis Molina, to reconcile divine providence and free will: that God has prevolitional knowledge of all conditional contingents and possible counter-factual worlds.

'I spent most of the 1970s doing a lot of coke and developing a warped understanding of Renaissance philosophy and particle physics.' Larry became convinced that alchemy and astrology had a deep connection with quantum mechanics and believed that occult and hidden traditions could provide some unifying theory. In 1973 he experienced a series of hallucinations that elemental forces were attempting to contact him with the information that God existed on a subatomic level. In *The Hieroglyphic Monad* (1974), Zagorski uses Elizabethan magician John Dee's universal symbol of the cosmos, a unifying motif that attempts to connect a series of discursive stories set in a twenty-second-century Europe where the Enlightenment never happened.

Wanda Ferris left Larry Zagorski in 1976. 'He was a pharmaceutical mess, yes, that was for sure; he was slowly but surely killing himself. But the worst thing was that he'd lost all his charm. He'd become grandiose and insufferable.' By the end of the decade he had descended into near madness and degradation. His old friend Mary-Lou Gunderson was shocked when they met in April 1978.

> I'd just got a new job as a television producer at one of the main studios and suddenly science fiction was on the rise again after the massive success of *Star Wars* – there was big money ready to finance TV franchises like *Battlestar Galactica* and *Buck Rogers in the 25th Century*. So I took a meeting with Larry, which I thought would be fun, imagining that we'd catch up on the past and talk about rehashing all the pulp and space-opera ideas from when we'd started out. But it was awful. Larry was this jibbering wreck, constantly wandering off to the restroom, obviously to take drugs. He kept muttering that this heretic monk had been in touch and had a message for me.[12]

In June, Zagorski was admitted to Los Robles Hospital with diluted cardiomyopathy. He was told that if he did not change his lifestyle he would be dead within six months. 'I've not much to live for,' he wrote in a letter to a friend, 'so I guess I should prepare myself for death.'

Then in November came the appalling news of the Jonestown Massacre in Guyana. Larry's first wife Sharleen had been a resident of the Peoples Temple community and was one of the 918 victims. 'Utopia turned into a death-camp,' Larry later commented. 'Jim Jones twisted idealism, calling mass-murder "revolutionary suicide". But out of the darkness came one small spark of hope.'

Martin Stirling Johnson, Sharleen's son by Cato Johnson, was among the few survivors. Earlier in the year Larry had joined the Concerned Relatives group that had voiced fears about the welfare of family members in Jonestown and he now involved himself directly in the care of the twelve-year-old orphan.

> It took a lot of work convincing the social workers that I was up to it but, after an initial period of fostering under supervision, the California Department of Social Services authorised my legal guardianship of Martin. Of course I had to turn my life completely around and the irony is that it was my own life I was saving. At last I had a purpose. All those years of feeling sorry for myself and thinking that the universe was out to get me had been a complete waste of time.[13]

Zagorski got a part-time job lecturing on science fiction at UCLA as part of their creative writing programme and devoted the rest of his time to the challenging task of raising a deeply traumatised adolescent. Beyond the obvious psychological problems Martin had to contend with, Larry noted that the young man had 'lost a normal capacity for imagination; in warding off nightmares he cannot permit himself dreams'. In trying out many types of play and art therapy, Larry noticed that his own faculties had somewhat diminished. 'I realised that since the mid-sixties my work had become increasingly pompous. I'd lost so much of the capricious energy that had drawn me to SF in the first place. Luckily I wasn't too old to learn from the young.'

And it was not only watching Martin grow up that gave him inspiration. He was picking up new ideas from his students at UCLA and other young Turks on the SF scene. He appeared on the now notorious Cyberpunk Panel at the 1985 North American Science Fiction Convention in Austin, Texas, sporting a shaved head and mirror shades, declaring: 'I'm a punk. I'm an old punk but a punk nonetheless.' It's fair to say that his two subsequent attempts at the form, *The Cut-Throat Laser* (1987) and *Zap-Gun Boogie-Woogie* (1990), rather fall short of cyberpunk. They do, however, conjure a sharp and highly entertaining pastiche of mid-twentieth-century futurism.

In 1996, Zagorski provided an introduction to *Beach 16* by Nemo Carvajal, a SF novel set in Cuba during the 'Special Period' of post-Soviet austerity. In his preface to Carvajal's book, Zagorski uses the term 'post-utopian' (first coined by art critic Gerardo Mosquera) as a way of describing the theme of the novel and also as a possible new point of departure for SF: 'What then is the future of the future? If, as Fukuyama insists, we are at the end of history, how can we think about tomorrow? What is the point of any fiction, let alone speculative fiction, unless we can find new ways of dreaming, new ways of imagining the universe?'[14] In 1998, Zagorski co-edited with Carvajal an anthology of new short stories by writers from North and South America, titled *Post-Utopian SF*. A second collection was planned but abandoned after Carvajal's death in 1999.

In 2000, *Fugitive Alien* was remade by Multiversal Studios with British singer Danny Osiris in the role of Zoltar the extraterrestrial.

The House of God was published in September 2001 and caused a certain amount of controversy at the time. Its cover depicted an image of a falling tower from the Tarot, and a central event in the book is the destruction of a skyscraper by a fanatical religious sect. It was inevitable that people would draw parallels with the events of September 11. But, as Larry would later explain, that wasn't what got him into trouble.

I was very clear in interviews that it certainly wasn't meant as any kind of prediction. The House of God is an alternative name for the Tower in the Tarot but the cover image was unfortunate. I'd actually intended that an image from the Minchiate deck be used, which depicts Adam and Eve's expulsion from Eden, as the book had a strong post-utopian theme. But instead we had the falling tower and, yes, there is a nod in the novel to the Tower of Babel story where a monolithic culture collapses into chaos. But there it was, that ill-omened card turning up once more. I pointed out that in Thomas Pynchon's *Gravity's Rainbow* the Tower becomes the rocket, the V2, the avenging missile. It represents catastrophe, and I've had my share of that. Susan Sontag said that science fiction stories are 'not about science. They are about disaster which is one of the oldest subjects of art.'[15] Interestingly the word disaster comes from the Italian *disastro*, meaning the unfavourable aspect of a star or planet. And I would have been fine continuing to intellectualise about the 'aesthetics of destruction' like this but instead I went on to make an unintentionally provocative comment. All I'd meant to say was that the attack on the World Trade Center was a 'science fiction moment' but then I added that 'some disaffected people would see it as Luke Skywalker blowing up the Death Star'. And a great many took offence at that, mostly *Star Wars* fans.[16]

A volume of autobiography, *Leaving the Twentieth Century*, was published in 2002. Zagorski has sometimes insisted that *The House of God* is to be his last work of fiction, though he has also given enigmatic hints of a novel in progress. 'A great unfinished work,' he told a journalist in 2006, 'that will remain unfinished.' Pressed as to whether this was a comment on his life, he said: 'Oh no, I'm still writing, still speculating. But I'm just a contributor, you know, just one of the voices.'

The span of his career has seen SF go from being about the probable, the possible, the impossible, the metaphysical to the ordinary, the everyday. It seems the one form that can truly grasp the essential strangeness of modern living, the cognitive dissonance that seems all-pervasive. 'Perhaps one can use the narrative projections of SF to reverse-engineer a sense of reality into contemporary culture,' says Zagorski. 'I think it was William Gibson who said that SF is set now to become an essential component of naturalism in fiction.' Now more than ever, Zagorski's writing deserves to be rediscovered and re-evaluated, though he remains phlegmatic about his position in American literature. 'Almost all my work is now out of print. I'm unlikely ever to be taught in schools or studied in universities. But I'm out there where I belong. In thrift stores and yard sales, in battered paperback editions with lurid covers and yellowing pages. Part of that story told by the lost and forgotten, the cheap pulps, the junk masterpieces.'

NOTES

1. Larry Zagorski, *Leaving the Twentieth Century* (2002), p. 4.
2. Ibid., p. 9.
3. The end of the 'Golden Age' of SF is usually seen as the mid to late 1950s when there was a rapid contraction of the inflated pulp market. Various critics have commented that the 'Golden Age of SF is twelve' in the harsh judgement that the genre forever belongs to early adolescence.
4. Jorge Luis Borges, *Other Inquisitions 1937–1952* (1964), p. 86.
5. Brian Aldiss, 'Judgement at Jonbar', *SF Horizons* magazine (1964).
6. Nemo Carvajal, introduction to *Post-Utopian SF* (1998).
7. Mary-Lou Gunderson, *Small Screen Memories* (2000), p. 34.
8. In the film, an air force officer of unspecified rank mentions 'the Magenta Memorandum', explaining it as a 'top-secret document on these flying saucers'. This is thought by some to be a reference to a highly confidential briefing in 1948 by CIA director Rear Admiral Roscoe Hillenkoetter to President Harry S. Truman, concerning 'Operation Magenta' – a top-level investigation into UFO activity that is said to have uncovered evidence of actual human contact with extraterrestrials. An FBI investigation of copies of this alleged document concluded that they were forgeries, pointing out formatting errors and false chronologies.
9. *Leaving the Twentieth Century*, p. 114.
10. Wanda Ferris, interview with the author, June 2010.
11. *Leaving the Twentieth Century*, p. 196.
12. *Small Screen Memories*, p. 301.
13. *Leaving the Twentieth Century*, p. 234.
14. Larry Zagorski, introduction to *Beach 16* by Nemo Carvajal (1996).
15. Susan Sontag, 'The Imagination of Disaster', in *Against Interpretation* (1966), p. 216.
16. *Leaving the Twentieth Century*, p. 301.

17

the star

Danny Osiris was finding it hard to sleep. It was the Adderall, of course. He had upped the dose just when he was supposed to be cutting down. He went up on the terrace and watched the dawn break over the valley. Venus burnt low in the sky to the east. Danny's mind buzzed with flashes of pure knowledge, epiphanies. He was thinking so clearly now but in ways that he could scarcely articulate or express to others. His speech slurred in demented aphasia. Even the voice in his head seemed disconnected, sampled song lyrics re-edited in his mind. *There's a starman, over the rainbow.* The sun just below the horizon, tinting the edge of the sky. Red diffused into turquoise like blood in a swimming pool. The bright planet began to fade. *How art thou fallen from heaven, O Lucifer son of the morning.*

He shook out a couple of blue and white capsules into his palm, with ADDERALL XR 15mg engraved on each. Thirty milligrams in an extended-release delivery system. He swallowed them. Chased them with the bottle of Evian he had brought out with him. *Somewhere, waiting in the sky.* He lit a Marlboro Light and looked across the canyons at the city beneath him. The reward system in his brain was firing up, a dopamine release in his mesolimbic pathway. As above, so below. Something hovered over Westwood, a red light pulsing. A helicopter, probably. *There's a starman. Somewhere.*

Danny was scared. He was convinced that the Church was out to get him. They didn't like it when somebody tried to leave. And an old friend had warned him that there was a journalist out there snooping around the Vita Lampada case. Johnny had phoned him. Johnny who used to be Jenny. Lucky creature, thought Danny, to be able to escape the self like that. Danny felt trapped. A man trapped in a man's body.

He still had the manuscript Vita had given Jenny just before she was found dead in her flat. Danny didn't understand all of it but he knew it contained official secrets about Rudolf Hess. He had known Vita from the New Romantic scene; she was a hustler and something of a con artist but very entertaining. It was Vita who had turned Danny on to science fiction. He remembered her talking about alien abduction, saying: 'Doesn't everybody just want to be taken away to another planet?' Danny had agreed. We all want to escape. Maybe Vita was a little crazy. She had been seeing a shrink as part of her gender-reassignment process and said the psychiatrist's definition of transsexuality was 'gender dysphoria'. Funny word, dysphoria, thought Danny: the opposite of euphoria, he supposed. Just like dystopia is the opposite of utopia.

Well, Vita had finally escaped the self all right. Most people now thought that it was suicide, that she just made her death look mysterious. The last great trick she played on everyone. But Danny couldn't be sure. He had to hide the manuscript properly this time, without it being traced to him. He would find a place for it so that even Johnny wouldn't know where it was.

Arthur arrived at eight. He wore a Blonde Ambition black satin tour jacket, white T-shirt, black 501s, black Nike Air trainers. Stocky build, jet-black hair close cropped, Navajo features. Arthur was his bodyguard, his chauffeur, his personal trainer.

'Morning, boss,' he greeted Danny. 'You wanna work out?'

'Uhn . . . hi . . . is, er, Lorry? Is Lorry with you?'

'Lorraine's coming at nine, boss. So we've got time. What do you say?'

'What?'

'A quick workout. We could do the White Crane Chi Gong. Get you centred.'

'Uhn . . . no. I . . .'

Danny shrugged. He saw the concern on Arthur's face and he wanted to explain that everything was all right but he could not form any kind of coherent sentence. He tried a smile but suspected that just made him look more wasted.

'At least have some breakfast, boss.'

'Uhn . . . sure.'

In the kitchen Juanita had laid out an array of fresh fruit. Danny picked out a mango, two bananas, a pear and three oranges. He gestured to Juanita.

'En la licuadora . . . por . . .'

Juanita smiled and nodded. She peeled the bananas and put them in the liquidiser.

He took the glass of juice and wandered out into the front garden. He looked up and saw a figure standing in his driveway. A man in a grey suit. He turned back to the house.

'Arthur,' he tried to shout but his voice was a feeble croak.

He looked back at the driveway. The man in the grey suit had disappeared.

Lorraine arrived at nine. His manager wore a Helmut Lang suit in light gunmetal, a Bikini Kill T-shirt, black slip-on loafers. Her hair teased out in a shock, her face more made-up than usual. Danny noticed dark rings under her eyes.

'Uhn . . . are you . . . okay?'

'I'm fine, Danny. Just, you know—'

'Working too hard?'

'No, no, I'm loving the job, I really am. Playtime's been a little crazy, that's all. But good news. I think I've found the lawyer that can get you out of your recording deal. Name's Paul Moss. He's going to argue that you didn't have full and proper legal advice when you renegotiated back in 'ninety-one, that you didn't enter into the contract knowingly.'

'That's . . . good.'

'And that they were negligent in promoting your last album. They just don't understand the new direction.'

'Uhn . . .'

'So, shall I set up a meeting?'

'Yeah.'

'Right. Item two: the film project. Are you sure this is the right part for you?'

'Uhn . . . yeah.'

'But you'd be playing a fucking alien, for Christ's sake. Won't that mean make-up and latex shit all over your face?'

'Uhn . . . no . . . it's not going to be like that.'

'Okay. I'll have another look at the script. You've got that writer coming over at four, right?'

'Yeah.'

'Now, Danny, I don't understand. I checked with the production company and this guy isn't even attached to the project.'

'He wrote the . . . uhn . . .'

'He wrote the screenplay for the original. That was back in the 1950s. He's not doing the remake.'

'I like his work.'

'Okay. But, look, Danny, if they do offer you the part, the insurers will want you to have a medical.'

'Uhn . . .'

'You sure you're up to that right now? I mean, you're coming through a difficult period, making a break with the past. Maybe now's not the time to have too much stress in your life.'

'I'm okay.'

'Sure. But, you know, you're worried about old friends giving you a hard time about moving on.'

'Uhn . . .'

'Arthur can look after you, you know. And we can always get more security if you want it.'

'Thanks.'

'And I'm always just down the road. Don't let those freaks get to you. We'll get through this. Then you can get back in the studio and do what you do best. Anything else?'

'No, no, I don't think so.'

'Well, if there is I'm in the office all day.'

As Lorraine got up to leave Danny stood also. He reached out his arms clumsily to touch her, as if he was still learning how to make some gesture of friendship. Something between a hug and a hand-shake. Lorraine smiled.

'It's going to be fine. It really is. Just try to relax. We can take our time over all of this.'

'Uhn . . . thanks, Lorry.'

She ruffled his hair then turned and left the room. Danny collapsed back onto the couch. He fished the pill bottle out of his pocket, clicked off the lid and carefully poured out the capsules onto the glass surface of the coffee table. He counted them out. He had twelve left. He looked at the label on the bottle.

06/27/97

OSIRIS, D.

TAKE 1 CAPSULE 3 TIMES A DAY

NO REFILLS.

He was nearly through this month's prescription. Dr Nielson had told him that he wasn't going to write him another before the due date. They were for his anxiety and his attention deficit hyperactivity disorder, he had said, and it was important that he stick to the recommended dosage. He would have to find another doctor. He picked out two capsules and then put all the other drugs back into the bottle. He went to the kitchen and got a Diet Dr Pepper from the fridge.

Arthur was practising a series of Muay Thai boxing moves on the kickbag when Danny went down to the gym.

'Hey, boss!' Arthur called out when he saw him, and gave the bag one last kick.

He was wearing shorts and a singlet, his loosely muscled body slick with sweat. He moved across the floor towards Danny with a little disco hustle punctuated by Sui Nim Tao postures as he launched into the second verse of 'Kung Fu Fighting' by Carl Douglas.

Danny broke into a nervous spasm of laughter as Arthur reached for a towel.

'Whaddaya say?' he panted, rubbing the back of his neck. 'Wanna boogie?'

Danny shook his head.

'Come on. Just a little exercise, boss.'

'Yeah. I want to . . . uhn . . . go out.'

Arthur wiped his face.

'Where d'you wanna go?'

'Walk.'

'Right. So, Griffith Park?'

'Uhn . . . no.'

'Elysian Park? Sycamore Grove?'

Danny shook his head, dismayed that after less than one month in his employment Arthur already knew all his favourite cruising haunts. But there was another place he thought of. A tranquil little Garden of Earthly Delights.

'Cowboy Park.'

Arthur smiled.

'Cowboy Park?'

'Uhn . . .'

'You mean that little place by the Beverly Hills Hotel?'

'Yeah.'

'Kippy yi yay, boss. I'll get changed and have a car out front in ten minutes. Which one do you want?'

'Uhn?'

'Which car, boss?'

Danny thought about it. He had a 1950s electric-blue Cadillac convertible, a 1974 bright-red Pontiac GTO, a silver Mercedes E-Class, a black BMW Z3 and a tan Jeep Cherokee. He could drive none of these vehicles.

'The Merc.'

They wound down through Laurel Canyon Boulevard onto Sunset with the radio on. As they drove through the Strip, 'Set Adrift on Memory Bliss' by P.M. Dawn was playing. Danny felt his heart flutter. He wondered if it was a side-effect of the Adderall or just a scattering of the emotions. He had a fleeting vision of another version of himself, in another universe, crying uncontrollably. He nodded his head gently to the break-beat, sighing to the sighs of the Spandau sample. *Reality used to be a friend of mine . . .*

They passed through West Hollywood.

'Nearly there, boss.'

'Uhn . . . tell me about . . .'

'What?'

'The cowboy.'

'Will Rogers? He was a cowboy actor. Did a vaudeville rope act.'

'Uhn . . .'

'Kind of philosopher too. Homespun stuff, but kinda funny.'

Arthur pulled up at the Will Rogers Memorial Park.

'Affable.'

'Affable?'

'Yeah, affable. He had lots of sayings: if you find yourself in a hole, stop digging, things like that. But you know his most famous saying?'

'Uhn?'

Arthur gave a deep laugh and put on an Okie drawl.

'I never met a man I didn't like.'

The park was a tree-lined enclosure, gently landscaped with mani-cured lawns and planted borders. Shallow steps led up to a central promenade with raised beds along its centre. Danny walked down to the fountain. He was wearing purple Versace jeans, a Ramones T-shirt, wraparound Ray-Bans, black suede New Balance trainers. When he got to the fishpond he crouched down and looked into the murky water. Koi carp swam in aimless circles. A fat goldfish looked up at him, mouthing mournfully. The creature looked trapped in its dismal element, staring out from another dimension.

Danny put his hand in his pocket. Last time he was here he had thought of bringing breadcrumbs or something, but he hadn't remembered. All he had was the pill bottle. He took out one of the Adderall capsules and carefully took it apart. It was full of tiny extended-release beads, which he spilt out on to the palm of his hand. As he sprinkled some on the surface of the water the fish came up and swallowed one. Other koi were alerted and joined in the feed, thrashing about, struggling with each other to take some of the bait. Danny wondered what visions the fish might have. Perhaps they would see him as an alien god, feeding them gnosis. He watched until every fragment of the drug was gone then stood up and continued past the fountain.

The restroom was a vine-covered building in a secluded corner of the park. Another man in a hooded top was slowly approaching it from the perimeter path. Danny checked the man was looking his way, as he adjusted the crotch of his jeans, feeling the hard-ness of hopeful anticipation. The man glanced back at him then entered the restroom. As Danny made to follow him he felt a rush of energy course through his body. But as he reached the doorway he stopped. All at once excitement turned to fear. Panic.

He turned and strode back to the promenade. He felt his heart shudder again and he was sure that he was about to have a heart attack. He would die here, in this little park. He was hyperventilating. He had to calm down. He found a bench and sat down. He tried to exhale slowly, remembering the breathing exercises he had learnt. Out breath, count one, in then and out breath, count two and so on up to ten. It was all right, he told himself. It was going to be all right.

'Danny?'

He looked up and saw a man with grey hair in a lightweight grey suit looking down at him. It was the man he had seen on his driveway that morning, he was sure of it.

'Here.' He offered Danny a small bottle of Evian.

Danny took a sip, wiped his mouth and handed it back.

'Thanks.'

The man sat down next to him. He let out a sigh.

'Danny, Danny, Danny,' he said, shaking his head. 'You really are a lost soul, aren't you?'

'Uhn . . .'

'Just be glad it's us watching and not the press. Or the Beverly Hills Police Department.'

'Uhn . . . I . . .'

'Come back. We can protect you. No one else can.'

Danny shook his head. He must be from the Church, he thought.

'Those pills, they're killing you, you know? What you need is niacin, vitamin B3, purification therapy. We can get you clean again.'

The man in the grey suit made a vague sweeping gesture with his left hand.

'And all this. Danny, I mean, really. These rumours we've been hearing. But we understand, we really do. I've been looking through your audit records. It's all there. We know all about you. And you were making such good progress. You were operating level. Now you want to blow that? Disconnect yourself? Become a suppressive person again?'

'Uhn . . .'

'You've not been sleeping, have you? I think I know what's really keeping you awake. It's not just the drugs. You came on too quickly, you weren't ready. You can't deal with the secret knowledge of the Church. You've been trying to work things out on your own. Wanting to find out all about UFOs and extraterrestrials, hiring that investigator.'

'Uhn?'

'Oh, we know all about that, Danny. You paid that guy twenty thousand dollars to gather information on UFO sightings and government cover-ups about contact with aliens. What did you get for that? We've got what you need. You need to let us take care of you.'

'Uhn.'

'You need to rid your body of those space-alien parasites.'

'I don't want . . .'

'You'll go insane unless you let us help you. I can clear you, Danny. I can clear you today. Come to the Celebrity Center, we can book a VIP room.'

'No . . .'

'Remember, Danny, it isn't just this life you're messing up. You're risking all your future lives! Your spiritual immortality is at stake.'

Danny looked up at the blue sky and thought of the fish thrashing about in the fishpond. His eyes began to water. He turned to look at the man sitting next to him but he had vanished. He looked around the park but the man in the grey suit was nowhere to be seen. Maybe he had imagined him. Maybe he wasn't from the Church at all. Maybe he was one of them.

Danny stood up and started to walk. Grey suit, grey alien, he thought. It could have been them all along. But what could it mean? Perhaps they were after the manuscript that Jenny had given him. He let out a sob. He was tired of all his secret knowledge. And frightened. When he got into the car Arthur noticed that he was shaking.

'Are you all right, boss?'

'Uhn . . . yeah. Home.'

Back at his house in Laurel Canyon, Danny Osiris went to his bedroom and collapsed onto his bed. He tried to sleep but when he shut his eyes his visual cortex was flooded with vivid Technicolor images. It seemed less bright when he opened his eyes. He got up and watched his favourite porn video. It was a man fucking another man who was wearing a black rubber hood with a gag in it. He imagined himself as the man doing the fucking, then as the one being fucked, yin-yang, yang-yin, an alternating current in his consciousness as he masturbated. He got hard but he couldn't come.

He went downstairs and got Juanita to make him an egg-white omelette. He ate it on wholemeal toast with a glass of orange juice. He went to see Lorraine in the office.

'When uhn . . . Mr Zagorski . . .'

'The writer guy?'

'Yeah . . . show him . . .'

Danny pointed at the vast open space of his house.

'Where do you want me to show him?'

'Library . . . uhn . . . I'll be there.'

Danny's bookshelves were filled with books about the occult, the paranormal and UFOs. He had a considerable selection of counterfactual and alternate histories, and a whole section devoted to works that speculated on the nature of ancient civilisations. He found the box file that contained most of the papers he had acquired from the professional investigator the grey-suited man had mentioned. He removed a dossier and put it on the table in the middle of the room next to a pile of notes.

Larry Zagorski arrived just before four. He wore an aloha shirt, cargo pants, black Birkenstocks. Cropped grey hair. Lorraine introduced them. As they shook hands Danny felt a surge of power pulse into his limp palm.

'Wow, this is quite some library,' Larry said, looking around at the shelves.

Danny gestured at his science fiction section.

'Do you want me in this meeting?' Lorraine asked.

'Uhn . . . no.'

'Are you sure?'

'It's fine.'

Lorraine shrugged and walked away. Danny saw that Larry was stooping over a bookshelf.

'Can I . . . uhn . . . help?'

'You'll have to forgive me. I always start at Z. Writers, you know, can't help checking if we're on the shelf. Good God. They're all here!'

'I'm a fan.'

'I'll say. Even I haven't got some of these. You want me to sign them?'

'Please.'

Larry stood up holding a battered paperback of *Lords of the Black Sun*, a garish illustration of a spaceship with swastika markings on its cover. He opened it.

'This one already has a dedication. "To the gorgeous Danny, my favourite space cadet, love, Vita." A girlfriend?'

'Uhn . . . no.'

Danny made a sign for them to sit down at the table.

'You know,' Larry said, 'all the big West Coast SF writers used to meet up around here. At Heinlein's house. Just up the road, Lookout Mountain Avenue.'

'Heinlein? Robert Heinlein?'

'Yeah. He had this salon. The Mañana Literary Society, he called it. I met them all there. Jack Williamson, Leigh Brackett, L. Ron Hubbard . . .'

'Uhn . . . Hubbard?'

'Yeah. Jack Parsons, too. You know, the rocket scientist.'

'Uhn . . .'

'So, Lorraine tells me that you're up for a part in this remake of *Fugitive Alien*.'

'Yeah.'

'Well, you know, I'm not involved in it. They've offered me this one-off payment, but I don't think I even own any residual rights. I should really ask Mary-Lou about it.'

'Uhn?'

'She was the director and, well, we were friends.' Larry sighed. 'You know, the older I get the more I think of her. Back then. Sorry, what were we saying?'

'I . . . uhn . . . just want to . . .'

Larry looked at Danny with sudden concern in his face. For a moment he seemed about to have a seizure or something.

'Uhn . . . talk.'

Larry smiled, relieved.

'Yeah, sure.'

'Uhn . . . I find it hard to talk . . . but . . .'

'It's okay. Take your time.'

'Thanks.'

'So, you want to talk about the film?'

'Yeah, and . . . uhn, ideas . . . you see things . . .'

'See things?'

'Visions . . . imagination . . .'

'Well.' Larry shrugged. 'Not so much any more.'

'Uhn . . . here . . .'

Danny picked up the dossier on the table and handed it to Larry who opened the folder and looked at the first page.

'Read . . . uhn . . . please.'

'"Dated 19 September 1947. Memorandum for the military assessment of the Joint Intelligence Committee. Subject: examination of unidentified disc-like aircraft near military installations in the state of New Mexico: a preliminary report. 1. Pursuant to the recent world events and domestic problems within the Atomic Energy Commission, the intelligence reports of so-called flying saucers and the intrusion of unidentified aircraft over the most secret defence installations, a classified intelligence project is warranted . . ." Wow, is this supposed to be the Magenta Memorandum?'

'Uhn . . . yeah.'

'Well, I've heard all the rumours about it, of course.'

'In the film . . .'

'In the film it's just a bit of dialogue. I don't think it was even in the original script. Just something Dexter added.'

Danny jabbed a finger at the dossier.

'What do you . . . uhn . . . think?'

Larry shuffled through the file.

'About this? Well, it's a great plot idea.'

'It's an . . . uhn . . . fake?'

'Who knows any more? Look, you know there's all this stuff about the government covering up UFOs and things like that? The TV's full of it at the moment.'

Danny nodded.

'But what if there was some other kind of cover-up going on? Take Roswell. No one made much fuss about it at the time. Back then there were flying saucer stories in the papers every week. Believe me, it was a craze. No, Roswell became big only when a book was written about it in 1980. *Close Encounters of the Third Kind* had just made UFOs big again. And at a second glance, the Roswell incident did look a little strange. The air force issued a statement that a flying disc had been recovered and then later denied it. Then they say it's a weather balloon.'

'Uhn . . . yeah.'

'It's all a bit suspicious and confusing. Because maybe there was a cover-up at Roswell.'

'Yeah?'

'Yeah. But not in the way all these conspiracy theories play it. Okay, it's 1947. The Soviets have just started running atomic bomb tests, ballistic missile launches. Everybody's paranoid as hell. We're sending up radar-tracking balloons over enemy airspace. If the Russians find out, there could be an international incident. Flying saucers, they're perfect disinformation. You can use them to confuse a situation, then you can deny them. You can blame it all on the aliens. They become a convenient myth for all kinds of security issues. Maybe the Magenta Memorandum is just part of that.'

'But, I see . . . uhn . . . things.'

'Sure. We all see things. We wouldn't have much of an imagination if we didn't.'

'There might be . . . uhn . . . something.'

'Yeah, maybe. Maybe we see some things that we don't understand. That's why they are called *unidentified* flying objects. Because
we just don't know. Sometimes we don't know what we see.'

'Uhn . . . yes . . . I always . . . uhn . . . the stars.'

Danny gestured at the space above his head. He wished that he
could explain to Larry Zagorski all the thoughts that he had been
having. He grabbed at the pile of notes on the table and sorted
through them. He found a page and put it in front of them. Larry
looked down at the sheet of foolscap.

John Six explained the secret of the universe to Bella Berkeley telepathically, using an analogy that he knew she would understand.
It came to her like a memory. She had grown up watching holovision, the three-dimensional images that were beamed into every
household by the Corporation. As a child Bella had thought of this
seemingly solid phantasmagoria as an independent entity, but now
she knew them to be projected from another source. John's wisdom
came into her mind as a simple revelation: that the whole of the
cosmos was one vast projection, a vision expanding from a surface
of pure information.

Larry Zagorski, *American Gnostic* (1958)

Appollonius of Tyana, writing as Hermes Trismegistos, said, 'That
which is above is that which is below.' By this he meant to tell us that
our universe is a hologram, but he lacked the term.

Philip K. Dick, *Valis* (1981)

According to t'Hooft the combination of quantum mechanics and
gravity require the three-dimensional world to be an image of data
that can be stored on a two-dimensional projection much like a
holographic image. The two-dimensional description requires only
one discrete degree of freedom per Plank area and yet it is rich
enough to describe all three-dimensional phenomena.

Professor Leonard Susskind, *The World as a Hologram* (1994)

'Wow,' Larry murmured. 'Yeah, I saw something about this
hologram theory. I thought it was some kind of gimmick.'

'Uhn . . . volume of space encoded on its boundary . . . on an event horizon . . .'

'Complex stuff. But, you know, a physicist once told me that you can't really use these theories as a description of the world we live in.'

'Uhn . . . or appear to . . .'

'Sure, but—'

'The entire universe . . . uhn . . . an information structure.'

'Well, I never had enough of the maths to get to grips with this. I once tried to explain quantum theory on a date. I really blew it there.'

'But you saw . . .'

Danny pointed at Larry's quote on the page.

'I was mostly stoned when I wrote that book. And I can't remember coming up with that bit. Sometimes you get lucky with ideas. Phil Dick certainly did. He had a thing about precognition, of course.'

'And . . . uhn . . . you?'

Larry sighed.

'When you get to my age precognition isn't so much of an issue.'

'Uhn.' Danny smiled and suddenly had a thought.

He went over to one of the bookshelves and crouched down in front of it. One section was a false front that clicked open as he pushed at it to reveal a small wall safe concealed behind it. He dialled the combination lock, opened the door and took out a padded envelope. He stood up and shook its contents out onto the table. There was a sheaf of yellowing sheets of A4 paper. A manuscript with a heading on the first page: *The Hanged Man*. With it were newspaper clippings, articles about Vita Lampada and Marius Trevelyan.

'What's all this?' asked Larry.

'I want you to have . . .'

'Is this a story you've written?'

'Uhn, no . . . Secrets, official secrets.'

'Listen, I'm really not looking for material, you know.'

'Please.'

Danny knew now that he had found a safe place. Where better to hide a pebble than on a beach? Larry would have stacks of papers and manuscripts. And he was a writer, so he might be able to do something with the story.

'You, uhn.' He looked imploringly at Larry. 'You understand.'

'Well, you know how to flatter a guy.'

'Take it . . . uhn . . . please.'

Larry looked at Danny and then down at what was scattered across the table. Words, words, words, he thought. As if I need any more of them. Then he shrugged and scooped them all up. Danny smiled.

'Uhn . . . thanks.'

Larry left at six. Danny then went to see Lorraine. He asked her to find him a new doctor and to order him some sushi, four types of nigiri and miso soup. At eight he watched an episode of *The X-Files*. In the show the FBI agents Mulder and Scully investigated a series of assaults in a community of carnival sideshow performers. The attacker turned out to be one of a pair of co-joined twins who had found a way of detaching himself from his brother but was then compelled to find another body to connect with.

After sundown Danny went up onto the terrace. He lit a Marlboro Light and looked out over the constellation of lights in the valley. A matrix: each bright dot a soul. An airliner crept across the horizon, a signal pulsing against the night. *Somewhere, waiting in the sky.* Danny felt that he had let go of some of the dangerous knowledge of the world. Maybe now he would get his voice back and he could take some studio time, sing again. Part of him wished that he could go to the Celebrity Center and get clear. If only he could really be brainwashed, his mind wiped clean of it all. But it hadn't worked. He was still lost in space, in the free-fall of a slow decaying orbit. *There's a starman, over the rainbow.* But he had never landed. Danny had watched the skies for years but they had never come. Alone. Set adrift on memory bliss. Sampled sighs and feedback distortion, his mind a tape-loop. He felt a great weariness, all his experience repeats and reruns. Perhaps this whole universe was just a remake, a cover version.

18

the moon

Hitler had always despised the moon.

'You know, Rudi,' he had told him when they had been in Landsberg prison, 'it's only the moon I hate. For it is something dead, and terrible, and inhuman. And human beings are afraid of it . . . It is as if in the moon a part of the terror still lives which the moon once sent down over the earth . . . I hate it! That pale and ghostly creature.'

Yet Hess had allowed himself to be beguiled by it. Inconstant, deceptive, a reflected light illuminating a hidden imagination. A journey into the unknown, a dream or a nightmare. The astrologers had delivered an auspicious reading for the night of his flight. The horoscope had indicated six planets in the constellation of Taurus, enough bias to cause the earth to tilt. But it was the conjuction of a full moon that had spurred him on.

In Spandau he followed the Apollo landings. He obtained minute-by-minute timetables from NASA giving details of space activity. That they might get to the moon first: this was his adamant wish as he followed the flight of Armstrong, Aldrin and Collins. With, of course, the legacy that Germany had bequeathed them. Then they might defeat the Russians in space, as the Reich had failed to defeat them on land.

On the eve of the launch Wernher von Braun eulogised his adopted nation at a press conference. 'Tonight I want to offer my gratitude to you and all Americans who have created the most fantastically progressive nation yet conceived and developed,' declared the former *SS Sturmbannführer* and chief architect of the Saturn V rocket that would propel the Apollo spacecraft into orbit.

Hess listened to the launch on the radio in his cell:

Guidance system goes internal at seventeen seconds leading up to the ignition sequence at 8.9 seconds. We're approaching the sixty-second mark on the Apollo 11 mission. T-60 seconds and counting. We have passed T-60. Fifty-five seconds and counting. Neil Armstrong has just reported back: 'It's been a real smooth countdown.' We have passed the fifty-second mark. Forty seconds away from the Apollo 11 lift-off. All the second-stage tanks are now pressurised. Thirty-five seconds and counting. We are still GO with Apollo 11. Thirty seconds and counting.

On 10 May 1941, he had his own countdown. Alfred Rosenberg, head of the party Foreign Affairs Department, had arrived at noon. Hess had given him lunch, his mind distracted with thoughts of instruments, jettison fuel tanks, auxiliary oil pumps, radio-direction finders, Scottish mountain altitudes. A light meal of cold meats and salad had been laid out in the dining room. They ate alone – Hess had given instructions to the household staff that they were not to be disturbed, and his wife Ilse was in bed with a cold.

Hess did not speak of his secret mission but merely listened while Rosenberg told him of his own preparations for the planned offensive against Russia. 'The solution of the Jewish question will presently enter its decisive phase,' Rosenberg assured him. Himmler was busy preparing his *Einsatzgruppen* who would follow in the wake of the offensive to eradicate communism and its carriers. Special instructions had already been issued concerning the army's operational area that 'commissioned the *Reichsführer-SS* with special tasks resulting from the final settlement of the struggle between the two opposed political systems'. Directive 21, the order to invade the Soviet Union, had been given the code name Barbarossa.

This made his own operation all the more crucial. He had seen Professor Haushofer only days before and they had talked once more of the geopolitical situation, and his former mentor's theories on the subject. Peace in the West was essential so that all the Reich's resources could be concentrated against Russia. Finally the source of Jewish Bolshevism could be burnt out and purified. This was the very presage of their *Weltanschauung*.

In his final conversation with the professor they had talked of the struggle for survival. A war on two fronts must be avoided at all costs. The continuing war in the West was suicidal for the white race. He did not tell the professor of his planned flight. Haushofer had described a dream in which he had seen Hess striding through the tapestried walls of an English castle, bringing peace to the two great Nordic nations. Did he suspect something?

Rosenberg left at one o'clock and Hess went to take tea with his wife. She had been reading *The Pilot's Book of Everest*, an account of the first flight over the Himalayas by the Duke of Hamilton. Albrecht Haushofer, the professor's son, had been a close friend of Hamilton before the war. Albrecht was a passionate advocate of peace between Britain and Germany and had tried to contact the duke via a dead-letter drop in Lisbon.

Hess and the Haushofers had been exploring all possible channels for negotiation with the British. Peace feelers reached out all over neutral Europe: Switzerland, Portugal, Spain. There was talk of arrangements for a secret meeting between Hess and the British ambassador to Spain on an abandoned tennis court outside Madrid. There were intelligence reports of a power-ful underground in England, virulently opposed to Churchill and ready to make terms. And all this time his astrologers had marked out the auguries for his own personal intervention. For now all boded well in his stars, but this could not last. At times his mood rose in exultation, then descended to deep melan-choly. He was impatient, overcome with a growing sense of romantic destiny.

As he set down the teacup on his wife's bedside table he had picked up the book and opened it. In the front there was a full-plate photograph of the duke.

'He's very good-looking,' he said.

She had frowned, unsure as she so often was of her husband's true sentiments and unaware that Hamilton had become the key to his quest. Hess had an intuitive understanding of the man: an aviator, just as he was. Hamilton had been selected as chief pilot for the Mount Everest expedition on account of his flying skills and his exceptional physical fitness.

'He is very brave,' he added, as if to reassure her. 'Had his mission failed there would have been no hope of rescue.'

Hamilton had flown over the world's highest mountain in 1933 when such an endeavour was only just technically possible, pushing the limits of the high-altitude flight, into the stratosphere and the edges of space.

The book had astonishing aerial photographs of the Himalayas that reminded Hess of Arnold Fanck's mountain films with the young Leni Riefenstahl, when she was still just an actress. The stark sunlight on monumental rock and ice; the purity of a cold and frozen landscape.

Yes, flying had given Hamilton a greater understanding. Like Lindbergh, he must have a broad, clear vision of the world. Above all, he would comprehend the symbolism of Hess's mission. The sporting gesture of it, replete with chivalry and mysticism. The aeroplane a deus ex machina in a flight of peace to bring to an end the war between brother nations.

Albrecht Haushofer had told him of his close personal relationship with Hamilton before the war. Hess had seen the man once, at a banquet in Berlin in 1936 during the Olympic Games. He was indeed handsome, with a strong and noble bearing. Hess had checked and found that a duke was the highest rank in British aristocracy below the monarch. Hamilton was an officer in the RAF, commanding the air defence of an important sector in Scotland. Albrecht had stayed at his country estate, Dungavel House, and had observed that it had its own airstrip.

This would be the chance for Hess to re-establish his authority in the Reich and in the eyes of his leader – his Tribune. In the last few years his star had been eclipsed but his mission would be spectacular. Yes, he would outshine them all.

He said goodbye to his wife. He kissed her hand.

He put on his trench coat and took a valise containing his charts, a wallet of family photographs, Albrecht Haushofer's calling card and a flat box of homeopathic medicines. He walked out to his waiting Mercedes. They started out towards the Messerschmitt works at Augsburg, but they were ahead of schedule so Hess bade them stop by a wooded glade by the road and in the fading sunlight he walked among the spring flowers.

On the runway at the Augsburg works it was waiting for him: the Messerschmitt Bf110D, radio code VJ+OQ, fitted with heavy drop-fuel tanks for long-distance flight. His chariot. He was ready for take-off. Ready as he waited in the summerhouse. Ready as he sat in his cell listening to the broadcast of the Apollo mission:

Thirty seconds and counting. Astronauts reported, 'Feels good'. T-25 seconds. Twenty seconds and counting. T-15 seconds, guidance is internal, twelve, eleven, ten, nine, ignition sequence start, six, five, four, three, two, one, zero, all engines running. LIFT-OFF. We have a lift-off, thirty-two minutes past the hour. Lift-off on Apollo 11.

He flew north over Hanover and Hamburg, over the North Sea coast, tuning his radio compass to the Kalundborg radio station in Denmark that was on the same latitude as his intended landfall in England. Kalundborg transmitted directional beams, interspersed with classical music. That night Wagner's *Parsifal* was being broadcast. Or had he imagined that? Albrecht Haushofer had called him a Parsifal. The innocent seeker.

He was approaching the point at which he would have to turn due west, out of friendly airspace, towards the unknown. Like the Apollo astronauts he would have to leave orbit and head into deep space.

CAPCOM: Apollo 11, this is Houston at one minute. Trajectory and guidance look good and the stage is good. Over.
ARMSTRONG: Apollo 11. Roger.
CAPCOM: Apollo 11, this is Houston. Thrust is good. Everything is still looking good.
ARMSTRONG: Roger.

The signals kept coming in from Kalundborg. In Act One of *Parsifal*, the old knight Gurnemanz rebukes the young Parsifal for shooting down a flying swan but when he learns that the boy has been raised in ignorance of courtly manners, he suspects that he might be the prophesied 'pure fool'. He tells him of the Grail.

PARSIFAL
Who is the Grail?

GURNEMANZ
There's no saying; but
If you are the chosen one,
The knowledge shall not escape you.

Yes, thought Hess. He had been chosen. This had been his quest, his Everest, his moon-shot. He was reaching the point of alignment with the radio transmitter.

CAPCOM: Apollo 11, this is Houston. Around three and a half minutes. You're still looking good. Your predicted cut-off is right on the nominal.
ARMSTRONG: Roger. Apollo 11's GO.

They completed their final manoeuvre around the earth and prepared for translunar injection. Hess turned due west, the Jutland coastline falling away below him. It was nearing twilight.

PARSIFAL
I hardly move,
Yet far I seem to come.

GURNEMANZ
You see, my son, time
Changes here to space.

Time and space and a holy mission. Six planets in the constellation of Taurus. Full moon in the Second House.

CAPCOM: Apollo 11, this is Houston. We show cut-off and we copy the numbers in noun sixty-two . . .

ARMSTRONG: Roger, Houston. Apollo 11. We're reading the VIL 35 579 and the EMS was plus 3.3. Over.

CAPCOM: Roger. Plus 3.3 on the EMS. And we copy the VI.

ARMSTRONG: Hey, Houston. Apollo 11. This Saturn gave us a magnificent ride.

CAPCOM: Roger, 11, we'll pass that on, and it looks like you are well on your way now.

They jettisoned the final stage of von Braun's Saturn V. Soon Hess would jettison the drop tanks from his Messerschmitt.

The astronauts blasted out of orbit and fired up towards the moon.

Hess was out of German radar range now, out over the cold, deep North Sea. He had never flown above open water before.

GURNEMANZ
Now take heed and let me see,
If you be a fool and pure,
What knowledge may be granted you.

What knowledge! To find the Grail Castle at Dungavel House. He was the bringer of peace.

The evening light over the ocean was magically beautiful; small clusters of red-tinged clouds bejewelled the shimmering sea. He found himself profoundly affected by the northern latitudes, feeling a surge of magnetism. What was this? he wondered. Then at once he remembered his childhood fancy. Thule! Yes, the mythic island of the black sun. This was the journey he had foreseen amid the hot and dusty afternoons of Alexandria. The Hyperborean Atlantis spoken of at the Four Seasons Hotel in Munich as they valiantly resisted the Bavarian Soviet.

It was not yet fully dark, the time of civil twilight when the sun descends to six degrees below the horizon. He could just make out land, the knoll of Holy Island marking out the far edge of the Northumbrian coastline. A veil of mist hung over England. The full moon had risen above the thin cloud, shrouding it in phosphorescence. Hess gasped at the brightness of the heavenly body. For a moment it shone, the blazing beacon of his great purpose. Then he had a moment of doubt.

Hitler had always despised the moon.

His Tribune might think that this flight was out of fear, not love of hazard. Hess had left him a letter that alluded to Schopenhauer's notion of a heroic passage through life encountering great difficulties that receives a poor reward or no reward at all. He had assured his leader that should the project fail, it need not have any evil consequence for Germany. They need only declare him mad.

Moonstruck. In a second he saw the clear and stark lunacy of it. If you be a fool and pure, what knowledge might you be granted. He could see the sharp details in the pock-marked face. Mountains and craters, sublime desolation.

ARMSTRONG: We're about 95 degrees east, coming up on Smyth's Sea . . . Sort of hilly-looking area . . . looking back at Marginus . . . Crater Schubert and Gilbert the centre right now . . . a triple crater with a small crater between the first and the second, and the one at the bottom of the screen is Schubert Y . . . zooming in now on a crater called Schubert N . . . very conical inside wall . . . coming up on the Bombing Sea . . . Alpha 1 . . . a great bright crater. It is not a large one but an extremely bright one. It looks like a very recent and, I would guess, impact crater with rays streaming out in all directions . . . The crater in the centre of the screen now is Webb . . . coming back toward the bottom of the screen into the left, you can see a series of depressions. It is this type of connective craters that give us most interest . . .

CAPCOM: We are getting a beautiful picture of Langrenus now with its really conspicuous central peak.

COLLINS: The Sea of Fertility doesn't look very fertile to me. I don't know who named it.

ARMSTRONG: Well, it may have been the gentleman who this crater was named after, Langrenus. Langrenus was a cartographer to the King of Spain and made one of the early reasonably accurate maps of the moon.

CAPCOM: Roger, that is very interesting.

ARMSTRONG: At least it sounds better for our purposes than the Sea of Crises.

Enemy radar would have detected him by now, and the moon had become a celestial searchlight. He had to get below what cloud cover there was. He put the Messerschmitt into a dive and flew at full throttle, greeting England with the wild scream of his engines. The aeroplane burrowed through the light haze. At low altitude and high velocity he turned to starboard, then to port, heading almost due west to Dungavel House. He was enjoying himself, hedge-hopping mere metres above trees and rooftops. He reached the Cheviot Hills and climbed the slope with both throttles open, dropping down the other side, across the border. He was in Scotland.

He had the chart of his route strapped to his right thigh but he had memorised every landscape that marked his way to Dungavel House. He passed through the peaks of Broad Law and Pikestone, banking right and descending towards his destination. He flew over Hamilton's country seat, trying to discern the runway. He could barely make out a blacked-out house below. Had he expected the landing strip to be marked somehow?

He flew further west to check his position on the coastline. He turned around over the Firth, its waters as flat and silvered as a looking-glass. Turning southwards he followed a spur of land curling out to the sea at Ardrossan, then inland he spotted the glint of the railway line that led north-easterly to Glasgow. The track made a bow at Dungavel; a small lake shimmered at the south of the estate. Illuminated by the moon, the Grail Castle now appeared to him and for an instant he felt triumphant. Then he saw that the duke's airstrip was nothing more than a landing field for sports biplanes.

There was no flare path or marking of any kind. It would be suicide to attempt a landing here in the heavy two-engined Messerschmitt.

All at once the whole enterprise seemed transformed into some awful trick. So close to triumph, he was now facing utter defeat. And an interceptor was closing in on him, a Hurricane perhaps, flying low. He climbed to two thousand metres and shut off the engine ignition. The propellers feathered as he set the pitch of the airscrews to zero. He would make a parachute jump, something he had never attempted before. He opened the cockpit canopy and tried to bail out. But as the plane was still at cruising speed, the pressure of the airstream pushed him back into his seat. Then he remembered something a fighter commander had once told him: that the best way to get out of a moving plane was to turn it over and simply fall out. He pulled up and went into a sharp loop. He blacked out.

Radio silence from the lunar module. Programme alarms and low-fuel warnings.

CAPCOM: Eagle, Houston. If you read, you're GO for powered descent. Over.

COLLINS: Eagle, this is Columbia. They just gave you GO for powered descent.

CAPCOM: Columbia, Houston. We've lost them on the high gain again. Would you please . . . We're recommending yaw right 10 degrees and reacquire.

When he came to he was in a complete stall. The speed gauge was at zero, his aeroplane on its tail, hanging upright in space. He kicked with his legs and pushed himself out into the night air.

He pulled the ripcord and his parachute blossomed abruptly above him. He felt the sudden lift of its soaring drag. His machine crashed into the moorland beyond.

CAPCOM: You are GO to continue powered descent.

ALDRIN: Roger.

CAPCOM: And Eagle, Houston. We've got data dropout. You're still looking good.

ALDRIN: Okay. We got good lock on. Altitude light is out. Delta H is minus 2900.

CAPCOM: Roger, we copy.

ALDRIN: Got the earth straight out our front window.

He floated down over the moonlit meadow. Suspended between heaven and earth. Exposed and triumphantly alone. You see, my son, time changes here to space.

As above, so below. He was ready once more. Ready as he listened in his cell. Ready as he waited in the summerhouse. He reached for the cable.

ALDRIN: Drifting forward just a little bit; that's good. Contact light. Okay. Engine stop. ACA out of detent.

ARMSTRONG: Out of detent. Auto.

ALDRIN: Mode control, both auto. Descent engine command override, off. Engine arm, off. 413 is in.

CAPCOM: We copy you down, Eagle.

Space changes to time.

He hit the ground hard and blacked out once more.

19

the sun

She thought she spotted him standing in a corner, staring absently at a gently oscillating light projection. It was the after party for the première of the *Fugitive Alien* remake, a nightclub in West Hollywood transformed into a spaceship interior. Supporting pillars of the open space encased in airbrushed fibreglass, dressed with glowing tubes and pulsing hieroglyphs; waiting staff in lycra costumes, extraterrestrial hair and make-up; a bar at one end decked out as a huge control panel.

She weaved through the crowd, still not quite sure if it was him. Stiffened into a rented tuxedo, white hair ponytailed, he held a frosted green highball in one hand. Something about the angle of his head, the goofy half-grin, the curious-child eyes that stared out of the collapsed mask of his face. Recognition. Memory. Loss.

'Larry,' she said, trying to catch his gaze.

He frowned and dropped his line of sight. Could he see her properly? she wondered. He seemed to be gaping into the middle distance. Maybe his vision was shot, though he wasn't wearing glasses. Maybe his hearing was shot.

'Zagorski!' she called out.

His face opened up into a smile and slowly she saw the Larry she had known all those years ago. Her perception shifting, making that illusory adjustment whereby all the traces of age fade in one who is familiar and an expression long remembered pulls into focus. He reached out and grabbed her elbow, as if steadying them both from a sudden earth tremor. His hand was gnarled and spattered with liver spots. Blue veins stood out like wiring.

'Wow,' he said. 'Mary-Lou. Look at you.'

Her hair was up in a loose chignon and she was wearing the fuchsia Issey Miyake Pleats Please dress she had bought back in 1993. She had thought it would be just right for this event, a clever choice. Maybe it was just too bold for a seventy-nine-year-old.

'Well, look at yourself, Zagorski.' She bristled in his grip. 'All got up in a monkey suit.'

'No, I mean . . .' He let go of her and made a vague gesture with his hand. 'I mean, you look fantastic.'

A sparkle in his rheumy eyes. She smiled then looked away. A waitress sidled by in pale-blue face-paint offering a tray of tiny dishes. Larry looked over at an arrangement of delicately tentacled canapés.

'So,' he asked the waitress. 'What do we have here?'

'Seared baby squid with truffle oil on a mango–lime pipette skewer,' she replied.

'Mmm, yeah.' Larry picked one out and popped it into his mouth whole.

'Well,' said Mary-Lou. 'We've sure come a long way from Clifton's Cafeteria.'

'Uh-uh.' Larry swallowed and wiped his lips with a napkin. 'Some of us are still here for the free limeade.'

He held up his glass to her then took a sip.

'What is that?'

'Mojito. Thought I'd have a drink for Nemo. You know, it was his idea in the first place.'

'What was?'

'The story that became *Fugitive Alien*. He just had the sense to take his name off the credits of the original.'

'Sure,' said Mary-Lou drily.

'Sorry, I didn't mean . . .' Larry gestured vaguely at something. 'I meant the script. Your film, you know, it was a cult classic.'

'Oh, come on, Larry, let's not be precious.'

'It's true. This remake, I suppose it's meant to be clever, post-modern or whatever. But it's not. It's just dumb.'

'So why did you come?'

'Well, I sort of know Danny Osiris, but the real reason I'm here,' he shrugged, 'is I thought I might just bump into you.'

'That's sweet.'

An alien waiter passed with a tray of champagne flutes. Mary-Lou took one and clinked it against Larry's glass.

'It's really good to see you, Mary-Lou,' he said.

'You too, Larry. Here's to Nemo. Have you heard from him lately?'

'Aw, Jesus, you don't know, do you?'

'What?'

'He died last year.'

As she let out a groan of exasperated resignation, an eerie wail pierced the air. On a stage at the far end of the club a girl in a silver dress was playing the theremin, furiously sculpting the air with her hands.

'Let's find somewhere to sit down,' Mary-Lou suggested.

Larry got another drink and they grabbed a booth in a quiet lounge area.

'I guess you're used to these things,' he said.

'What do you mean?'

'Film premières, smart parties, you know. You were a studio executive.'

'Yeah, in television. And nearly twenty years ago. What happened to Nemo?'

'Massive stroke.'

'Oh, Christ.'

'You know we fell out in the sixties. Then five years ago I got this manuscript from him through a Cuban guy living in Florida. We started working together again, on this post-utopian thing. We kept talking about meeting up. In Mexico. Well, we left it too late.'

Larry took a long swig from his glass.

'Hey,' said Mary-Lou. 'Go easy on the limeade.'

'Don't worry. It's not a problem for me any more. I hardly drink at all these days.'

'All the more reason to go steady.'

'Sure.' He rattled the ice in his mojito and settled it on the table. 'All those people we knew from the film. Gone. Sharleen, Nemo.'

'Come on, Larry, let's not get maudlin.'

'Jack.'

'What?' Mary-Lou frowned.

'Jack Parsons. Well, he did the special effects, remember?'

'Oh. Yeah.' She stared off into the distance.

'You never got over him, did you?'

She looked back at Larry.

'Let's not talk about Jack.'

'Okay, okay.'

Larry drained his glass and handed it to a passing waiter.

'Can I have another of these?' he asked. 'Mary-Lou?'

'Sure. A glass of champagne, please. How's Martin?'

'He's good. He's living up in Seattle. Working as a sound technician. I don't see so much of him these days.'

'And you? Still writing?'

'Yeah. Another novel. Not sure where it's going. I'm calling it *The House of God*.'

'Good title.'

'Yeah. Could be the best thing about it. But, you know, there is something I want you to see. Something I wrote a while back.'

'Oh?'

'Yeah. Something I wrote for you.'

Their drinks arrived and Larry chinked his glass against hers once more.

'This *is* like being back at Clifton's,' he said. 'Me trying to impress you. You know, that's what my writing career was really based on.'

'Zagorski, the limeade is making you sentimental.'

'In mojito veritas. You were my inspiration.'

'Okay, okay. Let's change the subject.'

'Okay. Well, you know, this film is really dumb, but Danny's quite an interesting guy.'

'Who?'

'Danny Osiris. Yeah, quite an interesting guy. He believes in all this UFO nonsense, just like Sharleen used to. But he gave me this strange manuscript. Sort of a story but it refers to some crazy stuff that happened in the war.'

Larry was trying to focus but the rum was fuzzing his mind.

'Mary-Lou, wasn't there a woman called Astrid at your commune in Pasadena?'

'Now you're losing me, Zagorski. You're talking about Astrid?'

'Yeah. German woman. Fortune-teller.'

'Astrid, yeah. What about her?'

At that moment a production assistant from Multiversal Pictures came up to the table and told Mary-Lou that the director would really like to meet her.

'Sure,' she replied. 'I'll come over. But look, the writer of the original is here too. Why don't I bring him with me?'

'Er, yeah,' the assistant replied with a doubtful shrug. 'Sure.'

The director of the *Fugitive Alien* remake was earnest and full of respect for Mary-Lou. He was barely in his thirties yet astonishingly cognisant of 1950s pop culture. And he knew all about her television work on shows like *The Scanner*. Mary-Lou struggled to include Larry in the conversation, but she knew that people rarely want to talk to the writer.

Larry hovered and continued drinking. At one o'clock Mary-Lou said she wanted to go.

'Are you staying, Larry?'

'No, no.'

'Then, come on. I'll get them to order us cars.'

They went down to the foyer, arm in arm, for support as much as anything else.

'So good to see you,' Larry said once more.

'Yeah.'

'Come and have lunch with me.'

'Sure.'

'You promise?'

'Larry, of course I'll have lunch with you.'

'Soon then.'

His car arrived first and she walked out to it with him. He put his arm around her. At first she thought he'd lost his balance as she felt his hand catch hold of her shoulder and pull her closer. Then he kissed her. At first he simply meant to brush his lips against her cheek but instead his mouth found hers. It was clumsy but passionate. She tasted rum and mint and lime juice.

'Hey.' She gave a little laugh as she pulled away from him.

'Oh.' The shocked look on his face, just like the teenager she had known. 'Hey, I'm sorry, Mary-Lou.'

'Get outta here, Zagorski,' she said and pushed him into his car.

A week later they met at a restaurant by the boardwalk in Venice Beach. Larry chose the spaghetti alle vongole; Mary-Lou ordered a cheese omelette and a salad with no tomatoes.

'No tomatoes?' Larry asked. 'You allergic?'

'No, well, it's this diet I'm trying. The blood-type diet.'

'Blood type?'

'Sure. It's based on the theory that blood types evolved at different eras of human development. Type O is the earliest, hunter-gatherers, so if you're that blood group you get the proteins: meat, nuts. A comes next, which is the type that evolved when humans started cultivating so As should eat vegetables and cereals. I'm a B and us Bs were nomads, pastoral people who lived with their herds. We're pretty omnivorous and we get to eat dairy.'

'Nice. But no tomatoes.'

'No. No shellfish neither, so I won't be picking at yours.'

'A diet based on blood type. That's insane. You believe in it?'

'I don't know, Larry. It seems to work for me, that's all.'

'It's just some mad idea.'

'So?'

She gave him a cold stare. He ducked his head a little.

'Okay,' he said. 'I'm sorry. I shouldn't be so dismissive. What do I know? And look, I'm sorry about the other night. My behaviour. Too much free limeade.'

'I hope you didn't kiss me like that just because you were drunk.'

Her mouth widened a little into an arch smile. Larry grinned and shook his head.

'No. But I shouldn't have been drunk. I've put all that behind me. That time we met in the late seventies, God knows what I must have been like. I was clean for fifteen years. I did the meetings and everything.'

'AA?'

'AA, NA, the lot.'

'And they got you through it, right? The Higher Power stuff?'

'Yeah. I know what you're thinking. I didn't really believe in it.'

'But it worked for you. For a while.'

'Yeah. Point taken.'

Their food arrived. Larry looked over at Mary-Lou's plate as it was set down in front of her.

'Wow,' he said. 'That is a lot of dairy.'

'The thing is,' he went on after a few mouthfuls of pasta, 'what we believe in just seems to get smaller and smaller. Diets, therapy, exercise regimes, support groups. Little superstitions. We worship household gods.'

'Nothing wrong with that.'

'But there used to be so much more. You know what really bugs me? People going on about "the planet".'

'You're not saying global warming's unimportant?'

'No, no, just that phrase. When did it become *the* planet? Singular. Definite. Like there aren't any other planets or something. It's like an admission of defeat. We used to dream of going to other planets. Now?'

'Jack used to dream of going to the stars,' Mary-Lou murmured.

'Yeah. And you know the last time people went out into space? I mean, going properly out of orbit. Apollo 17, 1972. We've got all these satellites whizzing about up there but most of them are just looking back down on us. It isn't space exploration, it's a sophisticated surveillance system. *The* planet. It's positively pre-Copernican.'

'Does it really matter any more?'

'I don't know, Mary-Lou. Nemo used to have this theory of interstellar socialism.'

'Now, that is insane.'

'Official policy of the Posadist Fourth International. At least it was bold. Utopian.'

'We all had crazy ideas at one time or another, didn't we?'

'And that's what this story I wrote is all about.'

'What?'

'The one I told you about. The one I wanted you to see. Can I send it to you?'

'Yeah,' she replied with a hint of dread in her voice. 'Sure.'

After lunch they took a stroll along the boardwalk and looked out at the ocean.

'I must have walked this path a million times,' said Larry.

'It's a beautiful day.'

'Do you have any regrets, Mary-Lou?'

She laughed.

'Very few. I don't even regret marrying Walter.'

Walter Nugent was an advertising executive she had wed in 1961. The marriage had lasted three years.

'I often wonder how things might have been different,' said Larry. 'A change in direction here or there. Those little jonbar points of life.'

'Yeah, but regrets?'

'I guess not. I wish I could have saved Sharleen somehow.'

'Yeah.'

'And I wish I could have explained quantum mechanics to you that night.'

'What?'

'Remember? That night we got drunk on slivovitz.'

'Oh yeah.'

'Hell, I really wanted to impress you. But listen, here's this great new theory. Danny Osiris told me about it, you know, the English guy in the remake. Guess what? Turns out the universe is a hologram.'

'A hologram?'

'A complete memory system encoded onto a flat plain. All of reality is projected from a distant event horizon.'

Mary-Lou stopped and turned to him.

'Larry, do me a favour.'

'What?'

'Just shut up and walk for a while.'

*   *   *

Three days after that a large envelope came in the post for Mary-Lou. Inside was a brief note from Larry and a manuscript. She made herself a cup of coffee and sat down to read it.

THE CITY OF THE SUN
by Larry Zagorski

None of us in Heliopolis knew quite when it was that the nightmares began. A sense of unease and disquiet had descended over every district of the city. Perhaps we had all nursed dreadful visions in secret for some time, unwilling to admit to the terrors that haunted our sleep. For months, maybe longer, we suffered a double burden: the horror of these unconscious phantasma; the guilt at their concealment. For here everything is held in common.

The knowledge of these dreadful spectres of the mind finally became public at the fourth Council of the New Moon when a woman called out to the whole assembly that she could bear it no longer. She spoke of an incessant dream of confinement, of being shackled and lying on a damp and befouled mattress. The walls of a dungeon that ran with slime, with an evil, all-pervading stench. Worst was the consuming darkness, a sense of years spent seeing neither light nor sky. A mere tremor of fear ran through the Council Hall at first, that instinct of revulsion in the face of madness, a condition that can seem as contagious as any other disease. But it was not long before we were in doubt as to the soundness of our own minds.

At night I dwell in the depths of a ruined world! cried one, a living death, damned between perdition and oblivion. Another accused our unnamed creator of being oblivious to our pleas. Then at last came a shocking outcry against the sun itself. I address my prayers to you, it began, to see you risen in glory, but if I honour you, great sun, more than any other thing, why should I be condemned to cold and darkness? You give life and movement to the meanest worms; the pale snakes turn to life at the touch of your rays. I, in my misery, envy their wanton play.

Though nothing is considered blasphemy in Heliopolis, this final statement had the ring of it. For ours is the City of the Sun, and the sun forms the centre and very meaning of our existence. As it provides all energy in nature, so we harness it as our chief source of power. We worship it through reason rather than superstition, as the bright countenance of our unnameable creator. It has never forsaken us and yet now in the few hours when our world turns from its face we are plunged into hopeless fright. In days given to freedom and enlightenment, thoughts of darkness and imprisonment made no sense and curses against our beloved sun seemed plainly absurd. Yet all the peculiar words and utterances used in these lamentations were dismally familiar.

At once our Council resolved to pursue the meaning and, indeed, the very cause of these nightmares. The authority of our great city is divided equally between Power, Wisdom, and Love. Power sees to the security and defence of Heliopolis, Love to its care and nurture. So it was left to those of us in Wisdom, which concerns itself with the liberal arts, sciences, mechanics and our education, to institute an investigation.

In the beginning we tried to define the substance of these dreams. In Heliopolis we consider the knowledge of the senses to be above the knowledge of reason, so we looked within ourselves. We called witnesses and analysed the description and the strange choice of language used in recollection. It all sounded utterly alien yet disturbingly memorable and we feared some terrible prophecy. Something existed beyond yet we could not apprehend it.

In the City of the Sun we have lived in a state of permanent happiness, health and virtue, and we had considered ourselves resolved to a calm understanding of life. We count the world to be a living thing. As is said in the old song of childhood:

The world's a book where the eternal Sense
Wrote his own thoughts; the living temple where,
Painting his very self, with figures fair
He filled the whole immense circumference.

And in this way we have built our city: divided into seven circles, each arrondissement named for the planets as they orbit the great central temple of the sun. Everywhere there are walkways and galleries adorned with mathematical figures, definitions, propositions, equations. There are botanical gardens and illustrations of every known creature. Samples of common and precious stones, minerals and metals are displayed. There are projections on every wall. The temple of the sun is domed; above the altar hangs a globe of earthly representation; in the vaulted ceiling stars are depicted in their different magnitude, with the powers and motions of each expressed separately in three little verses. Heliopolis is a wondrous machine dedicated to the art of memory and simply by walking through it all the arts and sciences may be learnt. Indeed, this is how we educate our people and sustain our culture. Now for the first time we felt lost as we promenaded its pavements and avenues, finding no answer there to our maddening dilemma.

We had hoped that by openly expressing our nightly derangements we might banish them, or at least that the sharing of discomfort might bring its moderation. Instead there came a despairing magnification of our collective woe. The nightmares became ever more brutal and intense. Our imaginations now conjured tortures of the body, torments hitherto unspeakable with curious names: *corda, coccodrillo, polledro*. The agonising suspension by rope, the hideous spectacle of being stretched to breaking over a wooden horse. The worst of all was called by some cruel muse *la veglia* or 'awakener'. Here we are tied above a bed of wooden spikes in such a manner that only the strength of our arms prevents our lower parts coming to rest on them. The harrowing memory of forty hours of this grim punishment was imprinted on our minds.

And as we continued to investigate these torments we were possessed with a feeling that it was we who were being questioned. But if some entity had become our inquisitor, we could not comprehend the nature of this vile interrogation. A few of us demanded that a confession might be offered so that the agony might end. Elsewhere a rumour spread of a man among us who had endured the forty hours of *la veglia* without ever having revealed his secret. When challenged no one actually knew this person by name, only at some second or third remove as is common in the reporting of gossip. It made no sense in any case as it would not be possible to endure such hideous treatment at the hands of anyone in the City of the Sun.

Indeed, it was decided that the source of the nightmares was another realm entirely since their barbarity was inconceivable to our dominion. They must be a communication from another world, a distant star or planet. We do not doubt that there are worlds beyond our own and account it foolish to believe otherwise. So while our astrologers scanned the heavens for any new disturbance in the cosmos, others of us in Wisdom proceeded to our Great Library.

This treasure house often appears neglected amid all the palaces in Heliopolis and it is true that so much of our experience is read through life that we have scant need of it. The world is our book and our city a sublime school whose very walls form pages of knowledge (as children we learnt the alphabet from its walls as we walked around it). There may be endless volumes, copied with countless errors, but we can read from the one true original. The guardians of the Library have been working for many years on the Great Encyclopedia, and even they confine their individual study to a mere handful of books in a whole lifetime. It is said that it is not the reading that matters so much as the rereading. Nevertheless we cherish all books, especially the unread ones, for who knows what secrets they might yield one day? And as we count the world our book, might not other worlds be other books, strange and unprecedented?

So it was in the unfamiliar sections of the Great Library that we decided to search for evidence of life beyond our own reality. Guided by its guardians, we began an examination of works of speculation. The countless books consulted on this matter included: Lucian of Samosata's *True History*, which describes journeys to the moon, the sun and the morning star; *Of the Wonderful Things Beyond Thule* by Antonius Diogenes, which contains similar references; Al-Farabi's *Al-Madina, al-Fadila* featuring an ideal state; the Arabic *grimoire* the *Picatrix*, which contains an account of the miraculous City of Adocentyn with a central sun temple that projects planetary colours from its lighthouse; the *Letter of Prester John*, which reports an Earthly Paradise and various *mirabilia:* endless possibilities of other worlds and also the disturbing prospect of non-existence. We were particularly perplexed by Thomas More's *Utopia* whose very title means 'no such place'.

But while we in Wisdom seemed lost in futile scholarship, a vernacular narrative was emerging outside the confines of the Library. The whispered story of the man who had endured the worst of all tortures and kept silent had continued to circulate. Though we are loath to give credit to any rumour or heresy, in desperation we picked at any meagre fruits of the grapevine. And though no one had yet named or given any description of this supposed man, the nomenclature of his persecutors had been sporadically voiced as the 'Congregation of the Holy Office of the Inquisition'.

It did not take us long to establish the nature of this body. Though we found many references to various holy inquisitions, this one was said to have been founded by the great hierophant of a city called Rome, a place distant in time and space. Many great philosophers were punished by this organisation. One who claimed rightly that the earth goes around the sun was shown their instruments of torture and forced to recant; another who wrote of a plurality of worlds in an infinite universe, of every star being a sun with its own planets, was burnt alive.

In time our attention was drawn to the life of the rebellious monk Tommaso Campanella who as a novice had been briefly imprisoned and tortured by the Inquisition for offences ranging from composing a blasphemous sonnet to harbouring a familiar demon under the nail of his little finger. He went on to engage in practices forbidden in that land: natural magic, astrology and the belief in heliocentrism. He led a revolt in the South that was both a revolution against worldly authority and an evocation of a great cosmological shift in the heavens, a *mutazione* in the local dialect of the rebels, that would bring about a paradise on earth. Guided more by the inspiration of portents and prophecies than practical strategy, the uprising was quickly suppressed.

Campanella was imprisoned once more and tortured more severely. His one defence against the penalty of death was to assert that he was insane, but in order to prove this he would have to face a dreadful ordeal. The test that the Inquisition used on one claiming madness was forty hours of *la veglia*. His torturers would watch all the while for signs that he was feigning his lunacy and wait for him to call out in confession. Tommaso Campanella survived. It seemed we had found our rumoured man.

If we felt something of a respite in locating the cause of our mental anguish, this relief did not last long. Soon came a foreboding of a deeper disquiet. Campanella was imprisoned for twenty-six years or more in appalling conditions of deprivation, yet his literary output during this time is remarkable. In the darkness of his cell he wrote or dictated in secret, risking further punishment by smuggling manuscripts out into the world. Many of his works were confiscated and destroyed; we examined what remained in the Great Library with awe and astonishment.

We know not whether the world was made from nothing or from the ruins of other worlds, but we certainly think that it was made and did not exist from eternity. We worship the sun and our unnamed creator and we do not question our origins. So it seemed a superstitious conjecture that many of Campanella's sonnets appeared to be reworkings of our ancient folk-songs and that his philosophy of a sentient world was identical to ours. In his book on metaphysics he writes that man lives in a double world: according to his body, he exists in only so much space as is least required, held fast in prison and in chains; according to the mind, he is contained by no physical space and no walls; he is in heaven or earth, in Italy, in France, in America, wherever the mind's thrust penetrates and extends by understanding, seeking, mastering. We found a description of hermetic magic that he practised to ward off the ill effects of the sun's eclipse: in a sealed room two lamps and five torches were lit and hung to represent the planets and the signs of the zodiac – just as they are in our own solar temple.

A seditious memory threatened our right of permanence. Our provenance at once became momentary, fleeting, obscure. When we finally unearthed Campanella's greatest work, *The City of the Sun*, it was with recognition rather than enlightenment that we discovered its pages to be blank. We knew at once what we had always known: that we are his book, his great vision of an ideal world.

The nightmares come no longer; the reality that conjured us has passed, as will all things. Tommaso Campanella composed our happy city from the depths of his suffering; our bright existence was conceived from hellish darkness. We cannot exist but as shadows of an imagined sun, letters that crawl like insects across this page. But we console ourselves that for our creator, words are not merely cyphers for the thoughts they represent; they have a power of their own; they are analogues of a divinised cosmos, evocative, charmed, incantational.

Larry came to visit in the afternoon. Mary-Lou didn't know what to say when he asked her what she thought of the story. He had been so keen for her to read it that she had imagined it might reveal something urgent and emotional, some deep truth about himself. Instead it was some sort of conceptual parable. Clever and well crafted, maybe, but dry as dust. She couldn't help feeling a little disappointed.

'It's wonderful,' she told him, hoping that he would not detect the hesitancy in her voice. 'It's a great conceit.'

'Well, Campanella's notion of the world as a book, it's something like the hologram theory.'

Mary-Lou recognised a nervous crease of a smile. Larry had always looked like this when he thought he had come up with a good idea.

'But I don't understand,' she went on, annoyed at him now. 'You said you wrote it for me.'

'Don't you remember? That series you did for *Superlative Stories.* You never finished it.'

'Christ. "Zodiac Empire". I'd forgotten all about that.'

'And remember Nemo was obsessed with Campanella? I suppose they both had this idea of cosmic heretical socialism.'

'Maybe you should have dedicated it to him.'

'I wanted you to have it.'

'Thanks, but—'

'It's about all those ideals we used to have.'

'So you finish a series I wrote for a pulp magazine that paid a cent a word.'

'Yeah, it's dumb, I know.'

'What is it, some sort of closure?'

'Oh, please, Mary-Lou. Don't you hate that word? No, I just wanted to revisit the sort of stories we used to believe in. As I get older I think about those times a lot.'

'When we were young and had all those dreams.'

'Yeah, and, like I said, ideals. And, you know, you were my ideal, Mary-Lou.'

'Oh Christ, Larry. I really wish I wasn't.'

'Well, it's the truth.'

'Right.'

'And we still need ideals, don't we?'

'Oh, I don't know, do we?'

Larry felt frustrated by the way the conversation was going. Couldn't they just talk about the story he had given her? He had thought there was some point to it. What he had learnt from their strange century: that utopia can come from suffering; that suffering can come from utopia.

'You used to believe in so much, Mary-Lou,' he said.

'Yes, and then I became a cynic. A hard-nosed television producer.'

'I don't believe that.'

'Good, because, like I said, I don't regret my life.'

'Not even Jack?'

'Oh, please, Larry.'

She glared at him with a sudden feeling of resentment. Why had he brought this up again? That far-off world of the past. It was a distant planet yet it still held an influence, a faint gravity of sadness.

'I'm sorry,' he said. 'It's just—'

'Do we really have to go through all of this?'

'You still find it hard to even talk about him.'

'Maybe I just don't want to. All this stuff about ideals.'

'What's wrong with that?'

'Yeah, okay.' Mary-Lou got angry. 'Okay, let's talk about all the dreams that never came true.'

'Yeah,' he retorted. 'Why not?'

'All the idealistic communes that never worked, the revolutions that failed. Let's talk about how you still feel guilty because Sharleen went and drank the fucking Kool-Aid.'

'Hey!' Larry called out and held up a hand.

He glared back at her. Mary-Lou closed her eyes and shook her head slowly.

'Jesus, Larry,' she said. 'I'm sorry.'

'Really, it's—'

'I don't know where that came from.'

'It's okay.'

'No.' She opened her eyes. 'That was a horrible thing to say.'

'Maybe it needed to be said.'

'No, it didn't.'

'Well.' He shrugged.

'Look, maybe you are right about Jack. Maybe I never did get over it.'

'I shouldn't have brought it up.'

'But I got through it. That's what I did. That's what we all did. Those of us left.'

'Yeah.'

'And maybe you want to live in the past. I don't blame you. We had better dreams back then. Some grand cosmic vision of the City of the Sun, or whatever. You want to go back to those times when we used to sit in Clifton's and talk about that future. Well, here we are in the year 2000 and we're old and worn out. And all we talk about is the past. Even all that space stuff, it's in the past, Larry. I want to talk about the real future, not some hypothetical idea of it.'

'What do you mean?'

'I mean me and you.'

'What?'

'Yeah. We've got precious little time left, Larry. And I'm tired of that boy from the Los Angeles Science Fiction Society, still desperate for my approval.'

'Christ.' Larry winced. 'I'm sorry, Mary-Lou.'

'Look, don't act all hurt. I mean it about me and you.'

'I don't understand.'

'We know each other so well. Too well, maybe. But we still get on in our own particular way. And I've really liked spending time with you.'

'That's good.'

'But I want to keep going, not look back at things too much. And I really don't want to be the person you want to impress with your writing. I was never meant to be your muse, for Christ's sake.'

'Yeah, but you were.'

'Not any more, okay?'

'Okay.'

'And I don't want any closure either. Maybe we could try something new.'

'What?'

'Well.' She smiled at him. 'You know what really impresses me?'

'What?'

'That you still might find me attractive after all these years.'

'Huh?'

'Yeah. Well, you do, don't you?'

'Yes. Yes, I do.'

'Good. So, what are you going to do about it?'

Larry stared at her.

'Don't look so scared, Zagorski.'

'I'm not, well, I guess I am, but—'

'Come here.'

She got up slowly and beckoned to him. He went and stood before her. They reached out and held each other in a tentative embrace.

'Well, I'm nobody's ideal any more, Larry. Maybe you don't fancy the reality.'

'Hey,' he whispered, moving in closer, sliding his arms around her. 'You're in pretty good shape.'

'Yoga.' She shrugged. 'A bit of power-walking.'

'The blood-type diet.'

'The blood-type diet. Hell, Larry, I'll try anything.'

'Well, you're looking better than I am. I don't see how you could find me attractive.'

'Don't worry. I don't have any illusions. I just want a bit of companionship. Some comfort, maybe.'

'That's probably all I'm good for.'

'Listen.' She stroked his face. 'You've still got a bit of passion left in you, that's the main thing. That night at the party, when you kissed me—'

'Like this?'

He pressed his mouth against hers and they held on to each other. For dear life. Against decrepitude and mortality. Closing their eyes and travelling in the time machine of the imagination. Pressing their old bodies together, seeking sanctuary from the shadow, feeling for remnants of desire. Mary-Lou drew her hands up to his chest and pushed him away from her.

'Wait,' she said. 'If this is going to work we're going to have to take it slowly.'

A low sun strafed the city as they drove east on Santa Monica Boulevard.

'A date,' he said, repeating what she had requested. 'What kind of date were you thinking of?'

'Oh, I don't know. A movie and then dinner?'

'Okay. You know *Battlefield Earth* has just opened.'

'Christ, that Hubbard thing?'

'Yeah. We could go see Travolta as a giant humanoid alien.'

'I don't think so.'

'No, me neither. What then? A romantic comedy?'

'Yeah. Something like that,' she said and shielded her eyes from a sudden blast of pale light.

Larry glanced across at Mary-Lou, her profile mottled, reptilian. Ancient beauty mutated with age. Yes, he thought, time makes strange aliens of us all. Rare creatures facing extinction. She was right: not much future left. Precious little, she had said. And the thought of that made him happy. So close to the end, there still seemed some absurd sense of hope. All the years lost in a flicker of expectation.

Beyond, Los Angeles was drowning in fire, a gilded sprawl burning with memories. A lifetime flashed on steel and glass, on the hot asphalt of the freeways. The sun itself seemed exhausted, a weary god descending. But this was all his. Matter, energy, information, it all belonged to him in that moment. The past was getting closer with time. Home, a humming chant, an incantation. LA, that dystopian utopia: heaven in the hills, hell in the valley. A simple illusion, fleeting and terminal, but he had found it after all. This, yes this. This was his City of the Sun.

20

judgement

'In order that I may be allowed to continue to attend my trial and to hear its judgement alongside the others, and in order not to be declared unfit to plead, I submit the following declaration to the court.'

He stared directly at the judges and prosecutors as he spoke, carefully unfolding the scrap of notepaper he had taken from his pocket. Then he looked up to the press box beyond, pausing to allow for the delay as the translation was relayed through their headphones.

'My memory has returned,' he went on, 'and is once more at the disposal of the outside world. The reasons for simulating loss of memory were of a tactical nature.'

He continued with his prepared statement but already the courtroom was stirred into commotion, the time-lapse of comprehension adding to the drama. Gasps of shock and anger from the court officials, a wave of laughter breaking out along the gallery. He declared his willingness to accept responsibility for his actions while insisting on the incompetence of the tribunal. He referred to the good faith of his defence counsel who had been taken in by his antic disposition, but already the chamber was in uproar. He smiled, savouring this moment, this great *coup de théâtre*. As the president of the court rapped his gavel for silence and called for an adjournment, there was yet another clamour as the reporters rushed to their telephones.

Oh yes, there is an art to forgetting.

The day before, the defendants had been shown a documentary film of concentration camps made by US troops in the final stages of the war. Darkness in the court but for the fluorescent strip lights built into the edges of the dock that underlit the faces of the accused. The flicker of the projector pulsing out its ghostly parade. Hess's attention was caught at once, rapt with wonder, his sunken features hollowed in white-face, a gaunt pierrot caught in the footlights. On the screen the grounds of a slave labour camp: a harvest of corpses, the bodies starkly exposed as if broken out of the earth like the dead on Judgement Day.

'I don't believe it!' he called out.

Earthbound oblivion, then a rush of wind, a blast of moon, a violent spasm wrenching his shoulders. He was dragged out of his blackout by the parachute that pulled him across the field in spastic convulsions of flight. Like a trapped bird. He rolled onto his back and tried to unbuckle his harness. There was somebody there, calling out, grabbing at the cords, taking the strain so that he could free himself. Hess crawled a few paces, tried to stand. His right foot gave way. The other man reached out and held him.

'Are you German?'

A civilian. A farmer or farmworker. Hess tried to catch his breath.

'Yes,' he panted, his English halting but precise. 'Please. Take me to Dungavel House. It must be close by. It is most important I speak with the Duke of Hamilton. I have an important message for him.'

But he never reached his intended destination. The man fetched the Home Guard. Hess was taken into custody, handed over to the regular army. By the next morning he was in a barracks hospital in Glasgow. Hamilton finally arrived but did not acknowledge all the intricate overtures for peace that had been set in motion. He claimed to know nothing of the contacts in Lisbon, the letters from Albrecht Haushofer. When Hess asked the duke to assemble members of his party to discuss peace proposals, Hamilton replied that there was only one party in the country now. Hess continued to outline what German terms might be but Hamilton told him that any kind of agreement was unlikely.

He wondered, was this some kind of ploy in the negotiations? He asked the duke to request parole for him from the King. He had come unarmed and in good faith yet they treated him as their prisoner.

They took him to London. To the Tower. This gave him some hope. He was under the protection of the King. The guards that paraded outside his window were merely ceremonial. The peace talks might soon begin.

But already the airwaves buzzed with announcements, communiqués. He was running out of time. His mission relied on discretion. All could be lost to rumour, disinformation, propaganda.

The Reich issued a statement. He had suggested in the letter that he left behind that if his quest seemed doomed to failure, they might declare him insane and they took him at his word. The report spoke of his mental disturbance, declaring that he was the victim of hallucinations, under the influence of mesmerists and astrologers. In this deranged condition, it went on, he may have been lured into a trap. Of course this would have to be the official line. To be branded a fool. Yes, but a pure fool. The Parsifal.

His horoscope had been clear enough: it had given him the precise moment to make his flight. But other readings had indicated a dangerous change in the fortunes of Germany. They had to strike the East but secure the West also. Perhaps for now he would be a trump card ready to be played at a later stage. Once the Russians had been defeated, Britain would be forced to make terms.

But soon the fear of real madness began to stalk him. All this talk of being duped, of being hypnotised. Now his mission would have to change its nature. The Chariot card he had been given signified an inner journey as much as an outer one.

He was taken to a stately home in the country. It was designated Camp Z; he was designated Prisoner Z. It was run by the Secret Service. Churchill's clique of warmongers were hiding him away and trying to get information from him. He thought that they might try to poison him, or fake his suicide. He asked one of the officers guarding him to get in touch with the Duke of Hamilton and request that the duke arrange an audience for him with the King. If he would do it, Hess assured the man, he would receive the thanks of the monarch for a great service to humanity. He was told this was impossible.

At times he felt quite strange. A warmth rising over the nape of the neck into the head; feelings of extraordinary contentment, energy and optimism followed by awful despair and a harrowing fatigue of the brain. He was being drugged, he was sure of it; he was being deliberately disturbed at night by noises and lights that flashed into his room. Some of his guardians would suddenly adopt peculiar facial expressions and glassy-eyed stares. Were they trying to hypnotise him? Were they hypnotised themselves? Had he been surrounded by mesmerised lunatics who would drive him insane?

He could not bear the thought of going mad. Early one morning he dressed in his Luftwaffe uniform and charged out of his room. He threw himself down the stairs but the banisters broke his fall. A week later Germany invaded the Soviet Union. 'So, they have started after all,' he said to the officer who told him the news. History had already left him behind.

So his inner journey began. In the words of Goethe that he cherished: according to eternal, iron, great laws must we all complete the cycles of our being. They tried to undermine his self-esteem, question his long-held beliefs. And strange drugs they used. Brain poison, he called it. He'd heard of a Mexican herbal extract that induced hallucinations and delirium.

They were intent on sending him insane but he was determined to control his own madness, to keep them guessing. This would be his interior campaign of psychological warfare. He soon found that the wilful loss of memory was the most perplexing stratagem he could use against his captors. It would undermine them on a subliminal level – no one likes to be forgotten, after all, while he could assume an air of indifference, a charmed cocoon of unconsciousness, free of history or future. Free of time itself. Then he would stage miraculous recoveries to perturb them further. It started as a game. Once he had taken a glass of wine and claimed to an astonished British officer that it had completely restored his faculty of recollection. He watched the horrified and confused face that witnessed this eucharistic act of anamnesis. The sacred loss of forgetfulness in a sacrifice recalled. Do this in memory of me, the redeemer implored. An ancient idea: that all knowledge is remembrance.

The war was being fought in his head. There could be times of lucidity: the great triumphs of Operation Barbarossa. Then anxiety and depression: a winter that froze out the advance on Moscow, the shocking Russian counter-attack. The Japanese dragged the Americans into the fray and all that his mission had been intended to prevent came to pass. This was now a global war with Germany caught in the maw of its two hemispheres: an immense economic and industrial power to the west; a barbaric vastness of space, people and resources to the east. This ran contrary to the great *Weltanschauung* he had learnt from Professor Haushofer. And now a world-view was compressed into confinement, occupying the prison of his consciousness, the soul of his tortured body. The great destructive forces that were ranged across oceans and continents battled in his brain for meaning.

It was the Jews who were behind it all, of course. He knew that clearly, though he had to be careful what he said. They would be listening, after all. When the question came up he would refer to the Madagascar Plan. All the Jews in Europe could be settled on that large island to the east of Africa. It was under French colonial control; all it needed was for the British fleet to collaborate in the massive immigration to this *Gross-Getto*. There was documentation of this proposal in the Foreign Ministry and the German Admiralty, though he knew from his conversations with Rosenberg on the day of his flight that the Reich had abandoned the idea. The war in the East was now a matter of extermination. But he could always hide behind the fanciful notion that if his peace plan had worked, Madagascar could have been an option.

Manic episodes punctuated his growing depression. The success of the Afrika Korps in the Western Desert; the Sixth Army sweeping through the Caucasus; fanfares on the radio as Berlin announced another U-boat victory. But all the time he was struggling to outwit those around him.

When all the good news from the outside world began to peter out he retreated into a mental oblivion. He told the doctors who examined him that a fog had descended, obliterating past events, people, ideas. He claimed to have forgotten his childhood in Egypt, his schooldays in Germany, his service in the Great War, the leading role he had played in the early years of the party. He could no longer recall the names of visitors or sometimes even the orderlies and officers who guarded him.

He reluctantly agreed to drug therapy, feeling that this might prepare him for greater tests that lay ahead. They were desperate to prove whether or not his amnesia was real. They injected him with a truth serum and conducted an interrogation. It took all his will to remain conscious while miming unconsciousness, to maintain his antic disposition. But as he passed this stage of inquisition he knew that one day a greater trial would come. There was already much talk about war crimes and tribunals. In the meantime he prepared his own judgement on a mad world.

One morning in February 1945 he woke early and called for a doctor, announcing to him that his memory had been restored and that he had something important to tell the world. He had composed a list of all the people who had been hypnotised by the Jews and he wanted it forwarded to Churchill. Churchill, of course, was named: hypnotism had changed him from anti-Bolshevik to pro-Soviet. The Jews, Hess explained, had a secret drug that could put people in a trance during which they would act in an abnormal way. The king of Italy, von Stauffenberg and the others who had plotted to kill the Führer, General von Paulus, Anthony Eden, the Bulgarian government – the catalogue went on. The doctor remarked that even the name Rudolf Hess appeared on the list. Oh yes, Hess replied; once at a state banquet in Italy he had been very rude to his hosts and the only explanation he had for his behaviour was that he must have been under the influence of this Jewish drug.

That night he took a bread-knife from the kitchen. He dressed in his Luftwaffe uniform, leaving the tunic open. He stabbed himself in the chest. He thought that he had aimed for the heart but when they came for him they found the wound to be quite shallow and wide of the mark.

The Russians had swept through Poland and were now inside

Germany. The British and the Americans were ready to cross the Rhine. And the bombing of the cities became ever more intense: now Dresden had been incinerated in a firestorm. The air war he had dreaded. He had flown for peace, to end this battle in the heavens.

Newspapers carried haunting photographs, terrible accounts of atrocities as the advancing Allies entered the concentration camps. Fearful apparitions of a horror he refused to face. This was the dementia of history, he decided. He would wilfully forget such things. So instead he concentrated on composing an account of his own captivity, noting that for four years he had been guarded by people with a mental condition caused by a secret chemical hitherto unknown to the world.

When out walking in the grounds he found a small key, for a desk drawer or a cabinet perhaps. He kept it as a talisman. Berlin was besieged; he was surrounded on all sides now. He retreated further within.

He developed a ritual: dropping the key on a book or his pile of papers and watching where it landed. Divination of some obscure miracle that might save him. He had to divert his mind from the constant reports of an impending German surrender. He must not give in. He continued to write his statement.

He was adamant that he must not allow them to see his true grief and despair. He said nothing when he heard that Hitler had killed himself. The man he had loved with such mystical fervour. He dropped the little key and watched where it landed.

He was flown back to Germany to stand trial. His plane circled the ruins of Nuremberg; parts of the city were a flattened moonscape but the Palace of Justice was still standing. They took him there and put him in a small stone cell. The Americans had their own ideas about how to provoke his memory. They showed him ancient newsreels and documentaries of all the old party rallies. Of course he didn't recognise himself. He had been a different man then. Then they brought in people he had known. Goering hated being forgotten: such an affront to his monstrous ego.

'Listen, Hess,' he boomed indignantly. 'I was the Supreme

Commander of the Luftwaffe and you flew to England in one of my planes! Don't you remember? First I was a field marshal and later a Reichsmarchall, don't you remember?'

Hess looked at him blankly.

'No.'

The old bully looked so crestfallen, it was hard not to laugh. But when they confronted him with Professor Haushofer he had to restrain all his emotions.

'Rudolf, don't you recognise me any more?' his old teacher pleaded.

Hess maintained his performance of incomprehension with a cold precision even as his friend and mentor gave Hess news of his wife and son.

'I can only assure you that the doctors tell me my memory will come back and then I will recognise you again. I am terribly sorry.'

'Your son is very well,' Haushofer whispered. 'I saw him. He is a fine boy, and I said goodbye to him under the oak, the one that bears your name, the one you chose at Hartschimmelhof, where you were so many times.'

Hess shook his head. The professor's eyes brimmed with tears.

'Don't you remember Albrecht, who served you so faithfully? My eldest son. He is dead now.'

'It doesn't mean anything to me.'

It was even harder with Hildegard Fath, his former secretary. She was so loyal, so innocent. She had a photograph of his son. She burst into tears when he turned his face away.

An American psychologist tried the Rorschach Technique, a projective test using ten inkblot cards where the subject is encouraged to interpret a series of ambiguous designs and then assessed in terms of personality and emotional functioning.

'This one.' Hess pointed at the second card. 'I see a monster, yes, a human monster. There's its mouth and this is its eyes, these red parts. It could be a negro with a big mouth, red lips and red eyes.'

'Two men are talking about a crime,' he deduced from another image. 'Blood is on their minds.'

The Nuremberg Trials had already begun and there was still argument among the prosecutors as to whether Hess was fit to stand. Four commissions of international experts had submitted reports: psychology professors from Moscow, neurologists from London, psychoanalysts from Paris, neuro-psychiatrists from Chicago. Evidence was given of hysterical amnesia, paranoid delusions, schizoid personality with obsessive components, culturally conditioned paranoia, auto-suggestion, pseudo-dementia, neurotic manifestations, habitual behaviour patterns, psychopathic tendencies, psychotic episodes. There was no agreement over the status of his sanity but a consensus was forming, despite strong Soviet objections, that his competence was impaired, his amnesia manifest enough that he would neither be able to follow proceedings nor challenge witnesses. The court was on the verge of deciding that he would be tried *in absentia*.

It was then that he made his spectacular announcement. Once more conjuring a miraculous anamnesis, this time on a very public stage. To the astonished court he ceremonially relinquished his forgetfulness and admitted his deception. His performance was a triumph of absurdity. And it presented a baffling paradox: if he was indeed sound of mind why had he insisted that he remain on trial at the very point that he might have been acquitted? This declaration of sanity was clearly the action of a madman. A wilful lunatic. But the pure fool had fooled the world.

Throughout the rest of the hearings he refused to concentrate. He would read a novel or stare off into space, rock backwards and forwards, double up in feigned stomach cramps. He deliberately ignored the entire tribunal, denied it his consciousness or memory. He was aloof, indifferent, utterly detached from reality. This was his own judgement on the court.

He did not testify in his own defence. Instead he prepared his final statement. He assured his fellow defendants that there was to be a great revelation, that what lay before them was an illusion, an apparition that might at any moment disappear. But when the time came for him to speak he found it hard to explain to the court the nature of the sinister forces that had caused so much blood-shed. He tried to make them see that these were show trials, just like political trials in other countries. The accused here had made false statements and incriminated themselves in astonishing ways because they had been put into an abnormal state of mind. This could explain the atrocities in the camps and elsewhere, and the actions of those who gave the orders. The whole world had been put into an abnormal state of mind. He did not name the culprits because he knew that they were in control here.

He concluded by saying that he was happy to have done his duty, to his people and as a loyal follower of the Führer. He regretted nothing.

'No matter what other human beings do, some day I shall stand before the judgement of the Eternal. I shall answer to Him, and I know He will judge me innocent.'

He was found guilty of conspiracy and crimes against peace; not guilty of war crimes and crimes against humanity. He dwelt within his theatre of oblivion to the last, neglecting to put his headphones on as they passed sentence, looking away as they passed their verdict. He expected Death.

They gave him Life.

What could that mean?

They hanged Frank, Frick, Jodl, Kaltenbrunner, Keitel, von Ribbentrop, Rosenberg, Sauckel, Seyss-Inquart and Streicher. Goering took poison on the eve of his execution. Hess learnt that Professor Haushofer and his wife had committed suicide. 'No form of state or church funeral, no obituary, epitaph or identification on my grave,' his note demanded, 'I want to be forgotten and forgot-ten.' His son Albrecht had been shot by the SS for his involvement with the German resistance. A collection of poems were found on his body. One called 'The Father' ended with the lines:

> My father broke the seal
> He did not see the rising breath of evil
> He let the demon escape into the world.

What Hess thought of this no one knows. He kept himself busy. As he sat in his cell awaiting transfer to Spandau prison, he composed a lengthy document outlining his plans for the time he would be released and appointed as a new leader for Germany. He mourned the loss of his fellow prisoners, adding that their appalling treatment was made all the worse since he was not able to convince them that their captors were insane. He issued bulletins to be published in the press under his direction: specific directives concerning labour, food distribution and liaison with Germany's occupying powers. If the Jews request to save themselves from the rage of the German people and ask to go into protective camps, he said, their wish should be fulfilled. His tailor was to make a new uniform with flared breeches and adjustable seams since he would probably have put on weight by the time he was released.

He concluded by warning the West that World War III was already being prepared:

The real instrument of power is in the hands of the Jew and the Bolshevist. It is proved by the fact that for years a Jew has been at the head of the research department of the United States Atomic Power Organisation. Is anyone going to believe that this Jew, hitherto completely unknown among scientists, has suddenly been put in this high position where all the secrets relating to the future war must be available? The atom bomb will be the main weapon of the Jewish-Bolshevist war leadership in spite of the fact that it is also in British and American hands.

The Soviet Union will probably use it first and be able to destroy everything in the West. They have the best possible excuse for doing so because they can say that the West used it first. The Anglo-Saxon countries will be the first to go under – I, Rudolf Hess, have warned you!

Forty years later, it is a summer afternoon in the ruins of Speer's garden. Ready to fly once more. The black American warder circled as he approached the summerhouse. Hess turned and smiled, trying to hide his disdain. He had explained many times to superior officers that he found it demeaning to be guarded by negroes. Another example of how the United States had failed. A precocious child of a nation, spoilt and degenerate, riddled with racial integration, drugs and sexual licence. The space programme had once seemed their only hope of aspiring to higher things. Hess had written to his son about this, quoting Kant's reply when asked what he considered the greatest miracle: 'the starry heavens above us, the prickling conscience within us'. But here too the Americans were found wanting. They had got as far as they had only because of German technology. Von Braun had wanted to go further, to Mars. Instead they stayed safely in orbit, firing off unmanned probes into the void.

The atomic war he had predicted never came. They had been spared the great Day of Judgement, but only just. He remembered, during the Missile Crisis, Speer talking up some idea of West Berlin being swapped for Cuba to balance things out. Spandau was in the British sector, a tiny polarity surrounded by opposing forces. The Four Powers divided up their time. After 1966, Hess was their only prisoner.

A hostage of the Cold War, he still indulged in the art of forgetting from time to time. It had become something of a habit, to keep them guessing. And forgetting had become something of a protocol.

Only the previous year, in 1986, it had been revealed that the new President of Austria, Kurt Waldheim, had lied about his war record. Whilst serving with the Wehrmacht, Waldheim had witnessed, and perhaps been complicit in, many more war crimes than Hess ever had. The Deputy pondered on this more with relish than indignation.

He had taught the world its gentle amnesia.

But he let no one judge him. He was still the pure fool.

He looked back again at the black guard. The man kept his distance. Perhaps there was a mutual sense of contempt. Hess entered the summerhouse unescorted.

He had heard strange rumours that the Cold War was coming to an end. A new Russian leader with a policy of openness. The Soviets had always refused to let him go. Until now.

He had regretted nothing, remained loyal until the very end. He closed the door of the summerhouse and went to sit by the window.

That spring there had been an article in a German newspaper claiming that the Russian premier was considering his release. The thought of it filled him with terror.

He looked out of the summerhouse. The Soviet warders would usually watch him through the window. He could see no one. An electrical extension lead for the reading lamp was tied to the latch.

He had always denied their right to try him. Ignored their verdicts and sentences. They had no power to grant him freedom now.

He carefully wound the cord around his neck, judging the distance he would have to fall. It was simple enough, to slip sideways off his chair. Yes. He was ready. Ready to pass the final judgement on himself. Ready to fly once more.

21

the world

If you can't change the world, build a spaceship.

Ever since we started dreaming, we dreamt of flight, of escape.

And as I write, the Voyager 1 space probe is 10,843,294,886 miles from the sun, about 0.00183 of a light year away. It's been travelling for thirty-four years and will soon cross the Heliopause, a terminal boundary where the solar wind's strength is no longer sufficient to repel those of other systems. Then it will enter the Interstellar Medium, the space between the stars of our galaxy.

It will be the first human artefact to leave our solar system and it might well be what we are judged by one day. About the size and weight of a Volkswagen, it's moving at 38,185 miles per hour with no particular place to go, though in forty thousand years it will come within 1.6 light years of a star known as AC+793888 in the constellation of Ophiuchus. On the probe is a gold-plated phono-graphic record encoded with music, sounds and images from earth, intended for any extraterrestrials that might one day encounter it. On the disc are greetings, the breath of fifty-five languages and a message from the Secretary-General of the United Nations, the offi-cial spokesman of our world.

Forgive me if I wander – now that I am so close to the end, my mind is firing off in all directions. I can offer few conclusions, no great revelation at the Last Trump. It's merely been a fool's journey through an arcana of knowledge. I feel like the solitary space probe, hurtling towards the furthest reaches of deep space, yet still emit-ting faint signals of particle data. I have no belief in an afterlife, only the unmanned hope that information survives and can continue to be understood. Maybe Voyager will outlast us all and tell our story to the rest of the universe.

As above, so below.

Built by the Jet Propulsion Laboratory, Voyager 1 is still respond-ing to messages and commands sent from its mission control in Pasadena, now an industrial complex built on the scrubland of the Arroyo Seco where Jack Parsons and his group tested rocket engine prototypes over seventy years ago. I remember the night of the party there back in '41 and what might have been a special Mass to lure Rudolf Hess to Britain. I see Mary-Lou's face haloed by firelight, naked figures flickered in shadow, and I think of it more as the site of my own foolish emotional trajectory. The brief euphoria; the abrupt falling to earth.

But it was there Jack Parsons dreamt of his own cosmic journey. He has since become a cult figure with a counter-culture mythology so rare and glamorous that it's sometimes hard to believe he actually existed. Always on the edge of fantasy and reality, he embodies that wondrous time when magic and technology merged, and science fiction became fact. And the conventional world eventually recognised his contribution to space exploration. In 1972 the International Astronomical Union named a crater on the moon after him (on the dark side, naturally).

Mary-Lou once said that it was I who never got over him and she was right. I couldn't help feeling eclipsed by him when I was with her. Ours was a tentative relationship, to say the least. The uncertainty that comes when two people know each other so well. I knew that it was never going to be a grand passion and for a while I was happy enough to hold on to what we always had. There was this warm charge of potential, as if it might be the beginning of something. I just wish it could have been more than that.

I wasted far too much time trying to make sense of things. Asking her stupid questions, brooding on all the strange connections in our past. I'm still doing it now. It's clear that Astrid, the German fortune-teller who lived at the commune in Pasadena, was the same woman mentioned in Trevelyan's manuscript, and though Mary-Lou didn't know about her having any direct involvement with the Hess case, she was sure that Astrid had been arrested as part of a Gestapo crackdown on astrologers. So I did my own reading on the subject and found out that on 9 June 1941, the Reich Main Security Office ordered *Aktion Hess*, a widespread arrest of astrologers and occultists. Books and papers were confiscated; hundreds of men and women were questioned and many were detained in concentration camps.

Trevelyan mentions this but he overlooks the possibility that this action might have been an aspect of German disinformation – that they too could have used the Hess affair to confuse their enemies. It certainly caused the Soviets to distrust British Intelligence at a time when it was warning them of an impending invasion. The Nazis' response to the Deputy's flight stressed an occult symbolism right from the start and their own House of Rumour became a vortex for conspiracy theories. Aktion Hess could well have been an exercise in counter-intelligence since some of its guidelines are patently absurd. A questionnaire drawn up by an SS 'ideological research' unit, to be used during interrogations, lists as question 11: *Should members of different races (Aryans, Jews, Chinese and Negroes) born at the same place under identical constellations expect the same astrological interpretations? If yes, then do you not admit the racial requirements of fate?* But then such is the logic of National Socialism. Perhaps Hitler was determined to prove to the world that he no longer feared any superstition. He ordered the surprise attack on Russia thirteen days later on 22 June, the precise anniversary of Napoleon's ill-fated campaign against Imperial Russia, and he gave it the code name Barbarossa, after the doomed emperor who drowned in the River Saleph during the disastrous Third Crusade.

'When Barbarossa begins,' Hitler declared, 'the world will hold its breath.'

The largest military operation in human history and the most devastating in loss and suffering: this was the destiny of the Nazi *Weltanschauung*. Along a frontier eighteen hundred miles long, Germany and her allies massed 4.5 million troops with 600,000 motor vehicles, 7,000 field guns, 3,580 tanks, 1,830 aircraft and 750,000 horses. The Soviets were utterly unprepared for the attack. Stalin deliberately ignored clear warnings, even from his own Red Orchestra intelligence network, denouncing them as disinformation. When the mobilisation against the invasion did come, however, the struggle became ruthless and apocalyptic. 'If the Germans want a war of extermination,' Stalin announced in a speech marking the anniversary of their great utopian revolution, 'they shall have it.'

The world held its breath.

Millions perished in a conflict of unimaginable cruelty while at the same time the Third Reich began to fully implement its genocidal Final Solution. Yet Barbarossa failed. Overstretched and frozen into paralysis by an early winter, the Nazis were pushed back from Moscow. Despite enormous losses in territory, people and resources, the Soviets fought on and survived. This was the turning point of the war; from then on the Nazis began losing. And finding itself at a logistical disadvantage with depleted resources, the Reich began investing in research and development to create *Wunderwaffen*: super-weapons that they imagined would give them a strategic advantage. Science fiction prototypes and the rocket technology that would become an essential component of the American space programme.

I'm tempted to read the Hess affair as a jonbar moment – that crude device of SF's Golden Age. In a time of uncertainty when we clumsily applied quantum ideas to pulp narratives with multiple worlds and parallel universes, 1941 seems the point when fiction was at its most speculative. It was the heyday of the Mañana Literary Society and the year that Borges' 'The Garden of Forking Paths' was first published. And the flight to Scotland was like the double-slit experiment, where any event can have more than one outcome. If Hess had made peace in the West, could the Nazis have won in the East? In a labyrinth of dangerous possibilities, any number of brutal alternate histories or guilty fantasies of power proliferate. Hess himself was drawn by his paranormal sense of destiny – to make his leap in space to try to disrupt the order of time. And, in turn, I start to retrace my own steps. All memoir can become an exercise in counter-faction in the end. What might or might not have been. I might have been spared combat duty and never have flown those thirty missions, nor seen those strange lights in the sky over the Rhineland. I would not have had to come home from a European war to find Mary-Lou still in love with Jack Parsons and, out of some misplaced shell-shocked bravado, pretend that I didn't care any more. I could have acted even then but I left it too late. And the scarce time we had together was spent at the wrong end of our lives. Mary-Lou died five years ago, but it hardly seems like anything at all. Everything speeds up so much when you get this old.

A half-life of memories in decay: my twilight affair with Mary-Lou short-term and fading fast; the image of her and Jack burning brighter than ever. Mary-Lou once showed me a poem of his:

> I remember
> When I was a star
> In the night
> A moving, burning ember
> Amid the bright
> Clouds of star fire
> Going deathward
> To the womb.

This now seems such a prescient image of the Voyager probe, that tiny starship forever linked to him, sent out on a grand tour of the solar system, taking advantage of an auspicious alignment of the planets that allowed for gravitational slingshots to extend its trajectory so that it could visit Jupiter, Saturn, Uranus and Neptune before being catapulted into deep space. A flight augured by an astrological conjunction, as if guided by that synthesis of science and the occult that Parsons tried to conjure. It even calls to mind 'Zodiac Empire', Mary-Lou's space-opera that I tried to finish.

But the universe has a nasty sense of humour. When you try to force these sorts of connections on it, it's liable to respond with irony rather than revelation.

Trace another particle, tease one more individual out of the cloud mass of history. Take Kurt Waldheim, a cavalry lieutenant in the Wehrmacht in 1941. His true path is uncertain: wounded during the Russian counter-attack to Barbarossa, he later lied about his war record, claiming that he was discharged from further service at this point. We know that he became an intelligence officer in Bosnia and Greece, that circumstantial evidence links him with atrocities committed there, but we may never discover the truth of his actual involvement in them. This has been lost in the art of forgetting. There have even been allegations that his subsequent diplomatic career was part of a Cold War game, that both the CIA and the KGB knew of his dishonourable past and blackmailed him for their own purposes. Echoes in the House of Rumour. What is certain is his soaring trajectory in international politics. In 1965 he represented Austria at the UN; in 1968 he was president of the First Conference on the Exploration and Peaceful Uses of Outer Space. He achieved the highest office as de facto spokesman and leader of the United Nations when he was elected Secretary-General in 1971. In 1977, in his second term as the official spokesman of the world, he was invited by the Jet Propulsion Laboratory to make a recording.

Yes, it is Waldheim's breath etched into the golden disc aboard Voyager 1, sending greetings of peace and friendship to the occupants of outer space. W.G. Sebald, in his book *The Rings of Saturn*, has pointed out this rather bleak joke: that our diplomatic representative to the galaxy is a suspected war criminal. Perhaps we deserve nothing better. But I feel sorry for Nemo; he put so much faith in the Posadist vision that interstellar craft would necessarily be piloted by progressive socialists.

We looked to the stars for utopian ideas; like Campanella and his cosmic *mutazione*, we drew down dreams from above of other worlds and other possibilities. I still believe in the essential idealism of science fiction. But it's best when it doesn't struggle too hard for meaning. Fantasy can be the most honest of literary genres when it doesn't pretend to realism. Absurd speculation is a simple necessity and warnings from the future can be useful, but we should be wary of prophecy and cautious of that yearning desire for connectedness. Fleming saw the House of Rumour as the image of an intelligence service; we can know it now as an ancient vision of the internet. The haunt of credulity, rash error, empty joy and unreasoning fear. The world whispers stories to itself. This is what conspire means: to breathe with.

'Let us inhale!' declared Tommaso Campanella as he walked the French countryside in his last years. Despite decades of suffering and confinement, he was finally able to enjoy his liberty. An admirer from Dauphiné, Nicolas Chorier, records a joyful and light-hearted man strolling in happy recreation, calling out: 'Let us inhale life from the life of the world!' He thought of air as the spirit of the earth, the soul of nature.

Campanella was finally released from imprisonment in 1629. He never gave up his ideal of the City of the Sun, that great utopia and memory system conceived amid terrible agony and privation. At Louis XIII's court he dedicated new writings to Cardinal Richelieu and implored him to build Héliaca, a French form of Heliopolis. His final work was to chart the horoscope and compose a sonnet commemorating the birth of the future Louis XIV: the Sun King.

Campanella saw the world as a book from which we learn; the world as a great animal, within which we are mere parasites. That the world is a living thing was, says Campanella, 'first taught by Hermes Trismegistos'. Philip K. Dick claimed that this same Trismegistos tells us our universe is a hologram, the world a book in which we are read. Our dimensions are projected from a distant event horizon somewhere at the far reaches of the universe.

Weltanschauung. A world-view. In 1990, Voyager 1 took a photograph of the earth from a record distance. Taking up less than a pixel, our planet showed up as a pale-blue dot in a grainy band of light. Up close, our world is overwhelming; at a distance, utterly negligible. A mote of dust in a sunbeam, a lonely speck in the enveloping darkness.

I still look up at its sky, its thin veil of atmosphere a delicate breath. I wait for darkness, a night full of stars, the pattern of our past. It's 2011, and I realise this was the date for a story I set on

Mars, which I tried to sell to *Amazing Stories* in 1939. I always wanted to live in the future. Well, here I am. Just. I remember Robert Heinlein saying, if you keep going for long enough they'll find a cure for death. I'm very glad they haven't. Of course I'd like to hang around a little longer just to see how things turn out. After all, that's what I spent my working life trying to do. Some say that 2012 will bring a profound spiritual transition, a transformation of the consciousness, a *mutazione* or something like the 'Age of Aquarius' that was all the rage when I lived in that commune in Venice Beach in the 1960s. I'm not so sure of such grandiose notions any more. But then I've already had my future, in my work and in my imagination.

My son Martin has moved back to LA. He says he wants to be nearby now that I can't get about so easily. We were talking about paradise the other day and he told me that the word comes from the Old Persian *pairidaeza*, meaning 'walled garden'. 'So,' he said, 'do you think the wall is there to keep people in or out?' He still has nightmares about Jonestown, that Garden of Earthly Delights that went so horribly wrong. If the world is a book, we should be careful how we read it. Maybe we should stay out of paradise and be wary of what we dream of when we look up at the stars, hoping for something better.

As above, so below.

On the particular level, all is uncertain. Everything has the power to be in two places at once, but as soon as we observe it it stops happening. And we experience only a fraction of reality. We pick a card from a shuffled deck and make that one choice out of an infinite number of possibilities. Yet all the possibilities that can occur, do occur.

And we never face the direction of travel; like Voyager 1 we turn and send our tremulous signals back home. So with the past in front of us we can go backwards into the future. History is unpredictable. Any number of things might have happened. On parallel worlds or in counter-factual realities, at forking paths and at jonbar points, the world is a speculative fiction. A breath of conspiracy.

Whisperings of Doubtful Origin in the House of Rumour. Utopia or dystopia are a moment away, just waiting for creation. At every point.

The world holds its breath.

Acknowledgements

Thanks and praise to Stephanie Theobald, Jonny Geller, Carole Welch, Jasper Stocker, Hamish Arnott, Michael Arnott, (all the Arnotts and those that dwell among them), Tanya de Villiers, Pablo Robledo, Melissa Pimental, Patricia Duncker, Michelle Graham, Mandy Colleran, Jeremy Reed, Ib Melchior, Cleo Baldon, Rodrigo Fresán, Stephen and Anastasia Webster, Geraldine Beskin, Mark Simpson, Lucy Foster, Celia Levett, Amber Burlinson, Alasdair Oliver, Simon Blow, Ben McManus, Barnaby Rogerson and the two lesbians who ran the illegal club by Beach 16 in Miramar, Havana in 1994.

In *The House of Rumour*, fiction is mixed with the truth. Some readers will note the similarities between Vita Lampada and real-life transvestite con artist Vikki de Lambray (*né* David Lloyd Gibbon), who died in suspicious circumstances after being involved in a sex scandal with a retired senior intelligence officer. 'The Watchers' flying saucer cult is partly based on *When Prophecy Fails*, the 1956 classic sociological study of a UFO religion by Festinger, Riecken and Schachter. Larry Zagorski and Danny Osiris share my wonder and confusion at Professor Leonard Susskind's sublime and actual theory of the World as a Hologram. The poem in Larry's story is an extract from John Addington Symonds' translation of Tommaso Campanella's sonnet 'The Book of Nature'.

Rudolf Hess's flight remains the most puzzling event of the Second World War, and was a contentious issue throughout the Cold War and beyond. At a banquet at the Kremlin in October 1941 attended by Stalin and Churchill, the Soviet leader proposed a toast to the British secret services for their skill in luring the Deputy Führer to Britain. When Churchill protested that his government knew nothing of the flight beforehand, Stalin replied archly: 'well, there are many things my intelligence service does not tell me about'.

For further sources, bibliographies and other 'whisperings of doubtful origin' visit: www.houseofrumour.com.

Join a literary community of
like-minded readers who seek out
the best in contemporary writing.

From the thousands of submissions Sceptre
receives each year, our editors select the books
we consider to be outstanding.

We look for distinctive voices, thought-provoking
themes, original ideas, absorbing narratives and
writing of prize-winning quality.

If you want to be the first to hear about our
new discoveries, and would like the chance to
receive advance reading copies of our books
before they are published, visit

www.sceptrebooks.co.uk

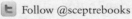 Follow @sceptrebooks

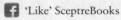 'Like' SceptreBooks

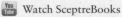 Watch SceptreBooks

JAKE ARNOTT

The Devil's Paintbrush

'A great read full of compassion, humour
and riveting detail'
Sunday Express

Witness the scene. In a Parisian restaurant Aleister
Crowley, the notorious occultist, chances on
Major-General Sir Hector McDonald: once one of the
greatest heroes of the British Empire, now facing ruin
in a shocking scandal – and vulnerable to Crowley's
curious offer of help.

Follow this unlikely pair on an extraordinary night of
revelation and transgression. Be transported to the
battlefields of Sudan, the backstreets of Edinburgh
and the sultry tropics of Ceylon. And discover Sir
Hector's tragic secret . . .

In this enthralling tale of imperialism, sexuality and
the nature of belief, Jake Arnott probes beneath the
surface of Victorian conformity and captures a world
trembling on the brink of a brutal new era.

'Brilliantly expansive and original' *Daily Mirror*

'A virtuoso work of near history . . . immensely
enjoyable' *Guardian*

SCEPTRE

JAKE ARNOTT

truecrime

'Sparklingly witty, immensely profound . . . his fictional (or, more accurately, factional) characters bristle with authenticity, ensuring that the reader is drawn willingly alongside them into the mire . . . The acid-house scene, the rave scene, new lads meeting old lags, Brit gangster films made by mockney directors, ecstasy, the teenage girl whose death after taking it filled the tabloids: Arnott marshals these seedier elements of the last decade in superb style . . . It should be read as a matter of urgency' *Guardian*

'Fast, funny, witty and brutal . . . Whenever he's got a new book out I drop everything, knowing that the next couple of hours are going to be pure gangland bliss' David Bowie

'Arnott pinpoints with devastating accuracy how today's world leads to the survival of the shallowest. His ear for low-life patois is as sharp as ever and the narrative proceeds at a cracking pace.' *The Times*

'*truecrime* brings [Arnott's] trilogy into the 1990s, and it blows the gaff sky high . . . the most expansive, ironical and funny novel of the series' *Daily Telegraph*

'Arnott earned his spurs in [his] first two novels, both pin-sharp and tough as hide. In the conclusion there's a little less action and a little more conversation, but that only furthers Arnott's credentials, allowing his ear for dialogue to cut through . . . The prose is as hard, stylish and memorable as our antihero himself.' *Arena*

'*truecrime* [is] the last in his gangland trilogy and the funniest; probably the most astringent satire yet on what was probably the slimiest of decades, the Nineties.' *Independent on Sunday*

'Chilling, funny and caustic . . . he manages to pull off the difficult trick of satirising a decade while maintaining realism through careful and sometimes brilliant detailing' *Time Out*

SCEPTRE

JAKE ARNOTT

He Kills Coppers

'Brilliant . . . you won't be able to put it down.'
Mark Sanderson, *Sunday Telegraph*

'Easily as good as, if not better than, the superb *Long Firm*.
Arnott returns to the world of 1960s gangsters, except this
time it's the cops as well as the robbers who take centre stage.
The novel is a stylish tour-de-force, Arnott's taut lucid prose
moving the reader effortlessly from the 1966 World Cup to
the 1980s and the age of Thatcher's Boot Boys and the
Battle of the Beanfield. Smashing.'
Julia Bell, *Big Issue*

'A wonderful mix of period detail and atmosphere, this is a fine,
evocative novel'   Stuart Price, *Independent*

'Many thought that Jake Arnott's debut, *The Long Firm*, was
good but not quite as good as the hype tried to convince us it
was. Frankly, Hemingway, Hammett and Greene together would
have been hard pressed to come up with anything that good.
His eagerly awaited follow-up, *He Kills Coppers*, has arrived –
and it's better . . . a fine piece of work that can only increase
Arnott's reputation further.'
Jim Driver, *Time Out*

'Arnott's tough and streetwise novel packs a powerful punch'
Simon Shaw, *Mail on Sunday*

'Incendiary stuff.'   Neil O'Sullivan, *GQ*

'The story and its characters ride perfectly within the setting,
to the benefit of both . . . It propels Arnott even further into a
league of his own. You don't have to be a crime fan to enjoy
Arnott's books, you just have to be interested in the lives of
ordinary, fallible people.'
Christopher Fowler, *Independent on Sunday*

'Told from the point of view of each of the three
central characters . . . they embody a dark and unhappy
Englishness. Although we know these lives will all intersect
at some point, it's a tribute to Arnott's mastery of plot
that the twist is wholly unexpected.'
Sukhdev Sandhu, *Daily Telegraph*

∫ SCEPTRE